Praise for Ken McClure

'McClure's forte is to take an outside-chance medical
possibility, decide on the worst possible outcome
. . . and write a book'
THE SCOTSMAN

'McClure's intelligence and familiarity with
microbiology enables him to make accurate
predictions. It's [his] creative interpretation of the
material that makes his books interesting'
GUARDIAN

'Scotland's very own Michael Crichton'
ABERDEEN EVENING EXPRESS

'Well-wrought, plausible and unnerving'
THE TIMES

'Real page-turning stuff . . . thoroughly believable
and entertaining'
EDINBURGH EVENING NEWS

'The whole thing grabs the attention as it hurtles
to its terrifying climax'
INDEPENDENT NEWSPAPERS (IRELAND)

'A gripping and thought provoking thriller'
BOLTON EVENING NEWS

# Also by Ken McClure

*Pestilence*
*Requiem*
*Crisis*
*Chameleon*
*Trauma*
*Fenton's Winter*
*The Scorpion's Advance*
*Pandora's Helix*
*Donor*
*Resurrection*
*Tangled Web*
*Wildcard*

# DECEPTION

## KEN McCLURE

*Best wishes*
*Ken McClure*

POCKET
BOOKS

LONDON • SYDNEY • NEW YORK • TOKYO • SINGAPORE • TORONTO

First published in Great Britain by Simon & Schuster UK Ltd, 2001
This edition first published by Pocket Books, 2002
An imprint of Simon & Schuster UK Ltd
A Viacom Company

1 3 5 7 9 10 8 6 4 2

Simon & Schuster UK Ltd
Africa House
64–78 Kingsway
London WC2B 6AH

Simon & Schuster Australia
Sydney

www.simonsays.co.uk

A CIP catalogue record for this book is available from the
British Library

ISBN 0-7434-1574-4

Typeset by SX Composing DTP, Rayleigh, Essex
Printed and bound in Great Britain by
Bookmarque Ltd, Croydon, Surrey

'If a man deceives me once, shame on him;
if he deceive me twice, shame on me.'

J. Kelly, *Complete Collection of
Scottish Proverbs* 1721

# Prologue

**Blackbridge**
**West Lothian**
**Scotland**
**Summer 1999**

Unusually for Scotland, it hadn't rained for the past two weeks so, when Alex Johnston put his BMX bike into a rear wheel skid and brought it to a halt on the canal towpath, it threw up a satisfying cloud of dust. He completed a 180-degree turn and rested his elbows on the wide handlebars to grin and dare a second boy to emulate this feat. The second boy, Ian Ferguson, started his run down the embankment, looking distinctly nervous but still determined to take up the challenge. All went well until the turn was almost complete but suddenly, at the last moment, his rear wheel lost all grip and bike and rider came down in an ungainly, whirling heap in the dust.

'Bloody useless!' cackled Alex.

'Hit a bloody stone, didn't I?' retorted Ian, known to his pals as Fergie.

A third boy came cycling towards them along the towpath and stopped with an amused look on his face to watch Fergie get to his feet. 'Shit, Fergie,' he said with a shake of the head, 'you're going to be looking out your arse for the rest of the holidays when your old lady sees the state of your keks.'

Fergie examined the damage to the back of his jeans. The right hand pocket had been ripped clean away, leaving a gaping hole in the remaining denim. He swore and turned his attention to the state of his bike, putting the front wheel between his knees to straighten up the handlebars. 'I know what,' he said with a sly grin, 'I'll tell her Rafferty's dog got hold of my arse.'

Alex and the newcomer, Malcolm Watson, aka Wattie, both roared their approval. 'That's one mean fucker,' agreed Alex. 'You won't catch me going within a mile of Rafferty's place if there's any chance Khan's on the loose.'

'Between Khan on Crawhill and Laney bringing in security guards to look after his GM shit on Peat Ridge there aren't going to be many places left where we can hang out round here,' complained Wattie.

'My dad says that bonfire night might be coming a bit soon this year at Laney's place,' said Alex.

'Serves him right too; planted all that GM shit without saying anything to anyone, my old man says,' said Fergie.

'And they reckon that shit's dangerous,' said Wattie.

'My old man says it's gonna fuck up Rafferty's organic farm scheme if Laney isn't stopped,' said Alex.

Wattie snorted and said, 'My old man works for Rafferty

but he says Rafferty knows as much about organic farming as he does about "gynaecology".'

'What's "gynaecology"?'

'Fuck knows.'

'My old man says that organic is where the future lies,' said Fergie. 'He says the city's full of middle-class wankers willing to pay through the nose for having shit spread on their tatties instead of fertiliser.'

'So what are we gonna do?' asked Alex, changing the subject diplomatically. There was an unwritten law among them that mothers and fathers were not open to criticism. Everyone else was fair game.

'We could go down the dell, have a smoke and chill out,' suggested Fergie.

'Have you got the fags like?' asked Alex.

'Certainly have,' announced Fergie, extracting a battered packet of cigarettes from his one remaining back pocket.

'My man!' said Alex.

'Count me out, guys,' said Wattie. 'I've gotta get over to Rafferty's place to tell my old man that Aunt Kate's comin' round for tea with her ugly sprog. Mum said she'll kill me and Dad if we're late. Wouldn't mind one of these weeds though, Fergie?'

'A smoke for the man,' said Fergie, extracting a cigarette and giving it to Wattie.

'A light?'

'That's a different matter,' said Fergie, backing away.

'Turd!'

Fergie laughed and pulled out a box of matches. He lit one and held it out to Wattie so that he could light his cigarette. Still sitting astride his bike, Wattie took a deep lungful and let out the smoke with a satisfied moan. 'Shit, that's one I owe you, sunshine.'

'And one you shall repay,' said Fergie in a deep, pantomime villain voice. 'Or I'll take it out of your sister's honour.'

'You leave my sister's honour out of this!'

'If only I could,' sighed Fergie. 'If I go blind, it's all her fault.'

'Get out of here!' yelled Wattie, aiming a kick in Fergie's general direction, despite the fact he was still straddling his bike, but he still had to smile at Fergie's exaggerated avoidance measures, which would not have shamed a Cordoban matador.

'Of course, if you guys were to come along with me we could maybe take a bit of a swim in the canal on the way back?' suggested Wattie, eyeing up the water as he prepared to move off.

'Count me in!' said Alex. 'I'm sweating like a pig.'

'If you're sure Rafferty has got that bloody dog safely tied up somewhere,' said Fergie.

'No problem. Khan's kept tied up in the shed all day. I think even Rafferty's afraid of him these days.'

'Then it's a done deal, my man,' said Fergie, giving a cigarette to Alex and lighting one himself.

The three of them started out along the towpath, cigarettes held in one hand, their other hands holding on to the handlebars. They weaved from side to side for no particular reason other than they were three thirteen-year-old boys in the middle of their school holidays and, as yet, without an adult care in the world.

Alex and Fergie waited at the towpath gate at the head of

4

the path leading over to Crawhill Farm while Wattie delivered the message to his father who was lying in the dust, working on a harvester in the middle of the yard.

Alex and Fergie watched as Wattie returned. 'What did he say when you told him Kate and the sprog were coming?' asked Alex.

'Begins with "s" and doesn't taste nice,' replied Wattie.

'I don't blame him. That sprog of Kate's can sure bawl,' said Fergie.

'She should stick nappies on both ends of the little bugger and give folks a break,' suggested Alex.

They moved away from the back of Crawhill Farm and returned along the towpath towards Blackbridge. When they had passed under the canal bridge separating Crawhill from Peat Ridge farm, Fergie stopped and said, 'Let's do it guys.' He put on his TV announcer's voice and said loudly, 'Ladies and gentlemen, put your hands together for . . . The Blackbridge . . . Synchronised Swim Team!'

'Fucking brilliant!' exclaimed Alex.

'Fucking magic!' added Wattie.

The three of them, filled with enthusiasm for the idea, dropped their bikes in the long grass at the side of the towpath and raced each other out of their clothes. Alex was first into the water; Fergie and Wattie jumped in on either side of him, yelling at the top of their voices.

'A slow crawl, gentlemen, if you please,' said Fergie when the splashing stopped and they'd settled down.

The three of them began an exaggerated slow crawl up the middle of the canal, the synchrony spoiled only by fits of the giggles.

'And now . . . on to our backs . . .'

They rolled over and continued with a much less successful backstroke – more akin to synchronised falling backwards out of a window – until Fergie ordered them on to their fronts again and instructed, 'And under we go . . .'

The three boys duck-dived down into the murky green waters of the canal and surfaced again with weeds all over their heads, looking, for all the world, like three aquatic Miss Havishams.

'This stuff's manky!' exclaimed Alex.

'Like your socks,' added Wattie.

'Jesus! What the . . .'

Alex and Wattie turned to see Fergie thrashing about in the water frantically.

'It's biting me!' he yelled.

'One nil to the Loch Ness monster,' grinned Alex sceptically.

'He's going down,' observed Wattie, equally coolly.

'No shit . . . something's got me . . . Jesus! It hurts.'

Alex and Wattie suddenly realised that Fergie wasn't fooling around. Any remaining doubts were dispelled when Fergie's foot broke the surface with the wriggling body of a rat firmly attached to it. Blood sprayed everywhere as Fergie waved his leg.

'Get the fucking thing off me!' he screamed.

Alex and Wattie went to his aid, Alex grabbing hold of the furry ball after two abortive attempts and causing even more pain with his efforts to pull it off Fergie's foot. But after several tugs it did come away and Alex smashed the rat down on the stone flags at the edge of the towpath until it was dead beyond all doubt. Meanwhile, Wattie helped Fergie out on to the bank where they examined his foot.

Fergie was shivering from the effects of shock and the sight of his injured foot. The animal's incisor teeth had gone clean through his foot at the base of the little toe on his left foot. It had then locked its jaws and refused to release its grip. Alex's efforts had succeeded in dislocating the animal's jaws – the reason its grip had been broken – but he had widened the wound on Fergie's foot in the process and it was now bleeding profusely.

Alex took control and insisted that Fergie lie on his back with his foot raised while he snatched his T-shirt up from the bank and tried to tear it into strips to use as bandaging. This proved more difficult than he had imagined but thanks to a weak point at a small tear in the shirt he got started and eventually finished up with four pieces of cotton. He squatted down and cradled Fergie's foot between his thighs as he wrapped the pieces of bandage round it.

'I saw them do this in the movies,' he announced. 'Guy got his arm blown off and his buddy tore up his shirt to stop the bleeding.'

'Did it work?' asked Fergie who had now calmed down a bit.

'Nope, he pegged out after the next scene, just after making his buddy promise to look after his kid.'

'Will you look after my mouse, Eck?'

'Daft bampot!'

'I'll go back and tell my old man,' said Wattie. 'I'll tell him we need an ambulance here.'

'Jammy git! You're going to get a ride in a blood cart with the lights and everything,' said Alex to Fergie.

'Maybe I can go too and avoid Kate's sprog,' yelled Wattie as he started to run back towards the farm.

Fergie was admitted to St John's Hospital, Livingston within the hour and operated on that same evening to repair damaged tendons in his foot. Alex and Wattie were to join him as patients in the same hospital by the end of the week. All three boys had contracted Weil's Disease from their swim in the stagnant water of the canal. Fergie's condition deteriorated rapidly when he also succumbed to rat-bite fever. These two infections conspired to obscure a third problem – a post-operative wound infection in his foot, which had progressed to full-blown septicaemia by the time it was recognised. There were now fears for his life.

# 1

**Glenvane**
**Dumfriesshire**
**Scotland**
**Summer 1999**

'What do sheep do, Daddy?'

Steven Dunbar thought for a moment before looking down at the little upturned face and saying, 'Not a lot really, Jenny. They just sort of . . . stand around and eat, I suppose.'

Father and daughter returned to looking at the pastoral scene before them: sheep munching contentedly in the field at the end of the village in the afternoon sunshine. Steven was leaning on a five-bar gate and Jenny watched through the bars below, one hand firmly latched on to his trousers as if afraid he might escape.

'Yes, but what do they do?' Jenny persisted. 'What's their job?'

'I don't think they actually have a job, Jenny. In fact,

they don't have much in the way of purpose in their lives at all.'

Steven Dunbar could not help but see a parallel in what he'd just said. The comment might just as well have applied to him during the last nine months since Lisa, his wife and Jenny's mother, had died. Nine months that had seemed like nine lifetimes.

They'd only been married for three years when Lisa's tumour had been diagnosed and the word 'forever' disappeared from their vocabulary to be replaced by, 'a year at most'. In the event, Lisa, the Glasgow nurse he had met during the course of one of the most nightmarish investigations of his career° had left him and their daughter after just seven months and two days. With her she seemed to take every hope and dream he'd aspired to and left behind an emotional desert, bleaker than an arctic landscape.

Steven's employer, the Sci-Med Inspectorate had been understanding about the whole thing. Apart from anything else they knew that their investigators had to have their minds on the job at all times. Anything less and they could end up by screwing up an assignment, embarrassing the government and possibly even putting lives, including their own, in danger. A man consumed by grief and hopelessness – as Steven Dunbar had been – was best left to his own devices for a while, was the official line they'd taken. He would come back when he felt ready or not at all.

The Sci-Med Inspectorate was a small body, funded by the government and run as an independent unit within the Home Office. Its function was to carry out preliminary

°See *Donor* by Ken McClure

investigations in establishing the possibility of malpractice or criminal activity in areas where the police lacked expertise. In practice, this was mainly in the hi-tech areas of science and medicine, where it was difficult for any kind of outsider to see if anything were amiss let alone know if a crime had been committed.

In practice, this often meant dealing with professional people in powerful positions and called for tact and diplomacy as well as intelligence and investigative skills. Such people often resented what they were quick to see as unwarranted outside interference in their own personal fiefdoms.

Steven had come to Sci-Med in a roundabout sort of way, as indeed had most of their investigators. He personally had studied medicine and qualified as a doctor before opting for a career in the army and seeing service with the Parachute Regiment and the SAS on assignments that had taken him all over the globe. He had, in the process, become an expert in field medicine – not something there was much call for when he finally returned to Civvy Street, but his experience had fostered in him an ability to cope and improvise in all sorts of tight and demanding situations.

Being a tall, naturally athletic man, he had relished the physical challenge of his time with the military as well as the excitement and danger of being on active service. But when he passed the age of thirty he knew that the time was fast coming when he would have to make a change. There could be no allowances made for the passing years in that line of work. You either swung with the best or you didn't swing at all, as one NCO had put it during 'Basic Wales' training with the SAS in the Welsh Mountains.

He had been unsure of what to do with his life when the time actually did come to leave the service. The army had assumed that, being a doctor, he would simply carry on with that but Steven hadn't been so sure. It had been too late for him to pursue a career in hospital medicine – with the possible exception of A&E thanks to his expertise in field medicine – and he saw life as a GP as an unattractive option after the excitement of what had gone before. That left various fringe jobs in medicine, like medical officer in the prison service or possibly a job in the private sector through an attachment to a large company as their in-house physician. The thought of feigning interest in dealing with chronic fatigue and stress management however, had not appealed.

Luckily, the job with Sci-Med had come up at exactly the right time and it suited him down to the ground. He had been taken on as one of their medical specialist investigators, his past record having shown him to be not only a good doctor but also an extremely clever and resourceful individual who responded well in the face of adversity and danger. They liked the fact that he had been put to the test in real-life situations, a far cry from the planks and oil drum problems on staff 'bonding' courses.

Steven had already successfully covered a number of assignments for Sci-Med over the past five years and liked the way the organisation worked. Investigators were given their head and allowed to handle their investigations in the way they saw fit. Administration within the Inspectorate was kept to a minimum and designed to support and help front-line people in any way it could, unlike so many government departments where administration had become an end in itself and sharp-enders were seen primarily as sources of information for the administrators to play with. 'Job Appraisal' seemed a good idea in theory. In practice it meant two people watching a third sharpen a pencil while demanding information about the process. How long does it take you? How often do you have to do it? How sharp does it have to be? Can't you use a cheaper brand of pencil? Can you supply pencil costings for the year by next Thursday?

Not all of his assignments had had a criminal element to them. In fact, the majority of them had little or no criminal involvement attached to them at all. Typical of this was his very first job, which had taken him to a hospital in Lincolnshire where the post-operative death rate had risen significantly above the figures for comparable hospitals in other parts of the country. It was a situation where people in the area might not have noticed anything amiss and, even if they had, it was not an observation that the police would be well equipped to investigate. The Sci-Med computer, however, had noticed the blip in the statistics and alerted the Inspectorate to take a closer look at the situation.

Steven had tactfully traced the problem to a consultant surgeon who had been simply getting on in years and had lost much of the skill that he'd once had. Being very senior and somewhat overbearing, other staff had been reluctant to point this out for fear of damaging their own careers. Steven had made sure that the man had been retired quietly and with as little adverse publicity as possible.

The assignment in Glasgow, however, during which he had met Lisa, had most definitely had a criminal element to it. Two separate complaints from nurses who had worked at a private hospital in the city – Lisa had been one of them – had raised fears that several transplant patients had not been given compatible organs and had died because of this. This had led to an investigation, which had eventually uncovered a plot involving millions of dollars and murder in order to steal donor organs. The whole scam had been disguised as a charitable act and even had government support.

He had narrowly escaped with his life on that occasion but, if the truth were told, it was the air of uncertainty about what he was getting into that gave his job a certain edge, which he enjoyed. He never knew what was coming next. He had received a letter the day before from John Macmillan, the director of Sci-Med. It had simply said that there was an assignment waiting for him if he felt well enough to come back. There had been no threat or cajoling involved, just a simple statement of facts. If he wanted the job he should make contact; if not, no problem, maybe next time.

Steven wasn't sure. He felt better than he had done for some time but he feared that he might still lack the motivation of old. This was why he'd come up to see Jenny the weekend before he was due to make his fortnightly visit. Jenny couldn't fill the awesome gap left by Lisa in his life but she was a pretty formidable little character in her own right and he had the responsibility of being her father. In many ways this was the one thing he had not found himself being apathetic about. Objectively, he suspected that she might be the key to his rehabilitation. She was in fact, the one thing he now had to live for.

Jenny lived with Lisa's sister, Sue, and her husband,

Richard, in the Dumfriesshire village of Glenvane, in the area where Lisa and her sister had been brought up as children. Sue and Richard had two other children – Mary, a girl of seven, and Robin, a boy of five, and they all seemed to live – to Steven's way of thinking – in glorious disarray. Richard was an easy-going solicitor, a junior partner in a firm over in Dumfries, specialising in property deals, and Sue's mission in life seemed to be to take on the troubles of all those surrounding her and sort them out. She was a much-liked and respected lady in the district – not least of all by her brother-in-law for taking on Lisa's role in Jenny's life so quickly and with hardly a second thought.

'Well?' persisted Jenny. She had learned to deal with the adult trick of looking into the distance and ignoring her questions. A good firm tug at the trousers and continual repetition of the question usually did the trick.

'They really don't do anything much, Nutkin. They just eat, sleep and . . . sort of be there.'

Jenny thought about this for a while before saying, 'Is that what you do, Daddy?'

Steven looked down at her, taken aback at what she'd said. 'What do you mean, Jenny?'

'Aunt Sue says you don't have a job at the moment . . . So do you just eat, sleep and be there?'

'I do have a job, Nutkin. I've just been on leave for a while. I'll be going back again soon.'

'Will you still come and see me?'

Steven swept her up into his arms. 'Of course I will; nothing could ever stop me doing that, Nutkin.'

Jenny looked at him without smiling. 'Something stopped Mummy,' she said.

15

'That was different, Jenny. Mummy was very ill. She didn't want to leave us. She just didn't have a choice.'

'Aunt Sue says she's in heaven but she still cares about us. Is that what you think?'

'Of course.'

'Do you think she sees everything, Daddy?'

'Shouldn't think so,' replied Steven, taking a sideways look at Jenny to see what was worrying her.

'If I were to take Robin's train without telling him and hide it, do you think she'd see that?'

'I don't think so, Nutkin.' Steven saw the relief appear on Jenny's face like the sun coming out from behind a cloud. 'But Jenny . . .'

'Yes Daddy?'

'Give Robin his train back.'

Steven paid off the cab and walked smartly into the Home Office. It had been a while since he'd had any reason to wear a suit and being 'in uniform' again seemed to help in restoring his confidence and gave an air of normality to the occasion. He was welcomed by Miss Roberts, Macmillan's secretary, and asked if he wouldn't mind waiting a few minutes as the man himself was on the phone. After declining the offer of coffee, they passed the time with pleasantries. Miss Roberts asked after Jenny and Steven enquired about her choral activities. Miss Roberts was a soprano in the South London Bach choir.

'Hectic at the moment. We're putting on a concert in two weeks' time and we're way behind with the rehearsals because of overbooking of the hall. In fact . . .'

Miss Roberts stopped speaking when the door to the

inner office opened and a tall man with silver hair stepped out. 'Dunbar, good to see you,' he exclaimed. 'Come on in.'

Steven made a face at Miss Roberts to suggest that he'd catch up with her story later and followed Macmillan into his office.

'So, how are you feeling?'

'I'm fine, thank you, sir.'

Macmillan settled himself behind his desk and rested his elbows on the arms of his chair to make a steeple with his fingers before appraising the man before him.

There was no doubt that Steven Dunbar looked well. Long rambling walks in the hills, trying to find answers to questions, although none existed, had, if nothing else, given his complexion a healthy tan and kept his weight down when otherwise his over-indulgence in alcohol over the past few months might have softened him and thickened up his middle. As it was, his lean, muscular body filled his dark-blue suit to perfection.

'Lisa's death was absolutely tragic,' said Macmillan. He had finished with the visual appraisal. It was time for the psychological one. 'You two had such a short time together. How long has it been now?'

'Nine months,' replied Steven evenly.

'You must still feel very bitter.'

'It happens to lots of people,' replied Steven. 'Slings and arrows.'

'Very philosophical,' replied Macmillan. He smiled but his eyes didn't. 'I think if it had happened to me, I'd be very angry.'

'Oh, I've been there,' replied Steven. 'But I got over it.

Mind you, you won't find me watching *Songs of Praise* for a while.'

Macmillan nodded sagely. 'Cancer, wasn't it?'

Steven nodded.

'Still a killer despite all the breakthroughs they've been making,' sighed Macmillan. The look in his eyes suggested that he'd just set Steven some kind of test.

'I think we both know that most of the "breakthroughs" aren't breakthroughs at all,' said Steven, without noticing the look. 'They're research groups trying to get their names in the papers in order to attract more grant money. When push comes to shove, the work's always "at a very early stage" and they hope "it will lead to advances in patient treatment in about five to ten years' time". It almost invariably never does and what genuine "breakthroughs" there are, are usually diagnostic rather than therapeutic. They can tell you at a much earlier stage that you're going to die but they still can't do a damn thing about it.'

'That's all a bit cynical, isn't it?' said Macmillan.

'I'd prefer, "realistic",' said Steven. 'Seeing things as they really are, is part of my job, is it not?'

Macmillan broke into a genuine smile. 'You're quite right,' he said. 'I sometimes wish they'd call the buggers to account for their supposed "breakthroughs" myself.'

'Making them repay the grant money they've flushed down the toilet might be a better idea,' said Steven.

'Research progress is always such a difficult area to appraise,' said Macmillan. 'There are so few facts to go on and that means we're left with expert opinion masquerading as the next best thing and it very often isn't. Medical research can be such a happy hunting ground for the charlatan and confidence trickster.'

'It's the loudest voice that wins through, not the brightest. The singer not the song.'

'Good,' said Macmillan. 'We are agreed on that and this may actually be relevant to your assignment,' he said. 'If you're feeling up to it, that is?'

'I'm fine, sir.'

'There's some kind of a scientific disagreement over a genetically modified crop up in Scotland. It's probably just a storm in a teacup – something to do with the paperwork in a licensing agreement – but I've got an uneasy feeling about it and it's such a touchy subject these days that I think we should take a look.'

'What sort of gene modification are we talking about?'

'The company concerned, an outfit called Agrigene, has obtained permission to grow two fields of genetically modified oilseed rape. Apparently the variety can withstand the action of powerful pesticides thanks to a couple of foreign genes their scientists have introduced to the seeds.'

'Sounds reasonable enough.'

'It probably is, if truth be told, but the government of the day made such a hash of the BSE affair that nobody believes a word officialdom says when it comes to matters of biological safety. As I recall, the relevant minister wearing a funny hat didn't seem to work too well either.'

'It was his predecessor announcing that it was quite safe to eat your words as long as they didn't contain beef that I remember best,' said Steven.

'But we're not here to question the wisdom of our masters,' said Macmillan, putting an end to that line of conversation.

This was something that Dunbar liked about Macmillan. He might look like a typical po-faced Whitehall mandarin with his regal bearing and swept-back silver hair but, underneath, he came pretty close to being one of the lads. But only up to a point and when that point was reached he was good at letting it be known without giving offence. He also had a well-deserved reputation for being fiercely loyal to his staff and was almost obsessive in his determination that Sci-Med should remain independent of direct executive control. He had come close to resigning on several occasions when bigger government bodies had tried to influence the course of his department's investigations.

'No, we just have to live with the consequences of their actions,' said Steven. 'So what exactly has this company done wrong?'

'They didn't tell anyone locally what they were doing. They did their best to keep everything quiet and persuaded the farmer involved to do likewise.'

'Can't say I blame them in the circumstances, considering what's been happening to fields of GM crops here in England.'

'Quite so, and as far as the book goes, they appear to have done nothing wrong. They went through all the right channels and are, by all accounts, properly licensed to grow their crop.'

'So what's the problem?'

'When the locals found out about it, they didn't like it one little bit and they've been kicking up one hell of a fuss ever since.'

Steven shrugged. 'I suppose I can see their point of view

too,' he sighed. 'Fear of the unknown, happily fuelled by the media, no doubt.'

'Well, it's turned into more than just a few farmers shouting the odds, I'm afraid.'

'You're now going to tell me that one of the locals is an organic farmer and he insists that his crop is going to be cross-pollinated by the big bad grass in the next field,' said Steven.

'Spot on,' smiled Macmillan, 'but there's a twist to it. The company, Agrigene, says that this chap was not licensed as an organic farmer when they sought permission for their trial. They insist that they checked the area out thoroughly beforehand for any such farms. They maintain that the paperwork for this chap must have been processed after permission for their trial had been approved.'

'But why?'

'Just so as to make trouble for them, so they say.'

'Sounds a bit bizarre, even allowing for commercial paranoia about government regulations.'

'It gets worse and this is the real worrying aspect. The opposition now maintains that the Agrigene crop in the fields is not the one that they were licensed for.'

'Now that sounds a bit more serious,' agreed Steven. 'How did they come to that conclusion?'

'They had a sample of it analysed at a ministry lab over in Ayrshire. The lab reported the presence of a third foreign gene, not declared by the company at the outset.'

'So the locals are right?'

'Agrigene deny it. They don't deny that there is a third foreign element in the genetic make-up of their crop but they say that to call it a foreign gene is a technical misunderstanding on the part of the lab that analysed their crop.'

'Sounds like the old Olympic athlete defence,' said Steven.

'Quite so. You'd think the bright thing for them to do at this juncture would be to admit to a technical oversight and apologise for it but this they stubbornly refuse to do. They maintain instead that there is some kind of conspiracy against them to discredit the company and they're determined to do battle in the courts if necessary.'

'Who do they think has conspired against them?'

'They don't know and they can't even suggest a motive.'

'Someone just doesn't like them,' said Steven.

'Paranoia or not, they're absolutely adamant that they've done nothing wrong, while the opposition in the village is calling for the crop to be destroyed. This is where you come in. I'd like you to take a look at things up there. Talk to everyone involved and try to get a feel for what's been going on.'

'Am I right in thinking that I'm going to be dealing with a lot of angry people?'

'That would be a fair summation. Brigadoon, it ain't. Tempers have been running very high and there's now talk of the GM farmer bringing in a private security firm to protect his farm and Agrigene's investment.'

Steven raised his eyebrows. 'Muscle?'

'Uniforms with dogs.'

'Not exactly designed to calm things down. Have any outsiders appeared on the scene yet?'

'Not as yet but I suspect it's only a matter of time before every civil liberties group from A to Z takes an interest.'

'What about police involvement?'

'They're aware of the situation, of course. They're keeping a low profile. I think their preference would be for a government order putting an end to the trial. That way, the Agrigene crop could be legally destroyed and everything could return to normal in the village. But the company is adamant that they will fight any such move every step of the way and we both know that once our legal friends sense a fat fee, we could be in for a very long haul indeed.'

Steven nodded and asked, 'Anything else I should know about?'

'Miss Roberts has prepared a file for you as usual. It lists all the key players and gives as much background information as we could get hold of. There is perhaps just one other thing you should be aware of; three boys from the village have been admitted to a local hospital suffering from Weil's Disease.'

'Three!' exclaimed Steven. 'From one village?'

'Apparently Weil's Disease is becoming more common these days,' said Macmillan. 'For two reasons as I understand it. One, there has been a general increase in the rat population all over the UK and two, the current fashion among the young for drinking beer out of bottles.'

'Of course,' said Steven. 'I remember now, the disease is spread through rat urine.'

Macmillan nodded and said, 'Exactly, the beer crates are stored in open warehouses. Rats crawl over them and contaminate the bottles. Jack the Lad opens his bottle of designer Krustenbufferstumpenschlotz and . . . yum, yum.'

'But presumably there's nothing to link these cases with the GM problem in the village?'

'Only that one of the boy's fathers works as a mechanic on the farm that's recently obtained organic accreditation. But no, it was a clear case of them coming into contact with rat urine. They had all been swimming in a canal that runs through their village, so it seems obvious enough where they got the disease. There was one strange feature though; a rat apparently attacked one of the boys while he was swimming. It bit his foot for no apparent reason and hung on to it for grim death.'

'Maybe the boys provoked it in some way?'

'Whatever the reason, the animal did quite a bit of damage to the boy's foot. They managed to repair the tendons with an operation at the local hospital but since then he's developed rat-bite fever.'

'Poor kid.'

'The latest now is that he now has some kind of post-operative infection on top of everything else. It's going to be touch and go.'

'And all for a swim.'

'Boys will be boys,' said Macmillan.

'The world over,' agreed Steven.

# 2

The first thing that occurred to Steven when he climbed into the cab to take him back to his flat was the fact that Jenny no longer had a father whose function it was to just, 'eat, sleep and be there'. It was a good feeling. He was back in business and the bulging file in his briefcase suggested that there was enough there to keep him fully occupied for the rest of the day and probably most of the evening.

Although it wasn't sunny, it was extremely sultry – just the way he didn't like it in London. This kind of weather shortened everyone's temper and the continual angry tooting of car horns and muttering of the cab driver only served to prove the point as they edged their way down to the river, where he had an apartment on the fifth floor of a converted warehouse building. He felt relieved to get inside and have a shower before changing into jeans and T-shirt. He poured himself a cold Stella Artois from the fridge and settled down to read through the file.

Blackbridge, he learned, was a small farming community,

lying to the west of Edinburgh, about five miles inland from the southern shores of the Firth of Forth. It had been named after a black iron bridge – now replaced by a more modern concrete one, which spanned the small river running through it from south to north, on its way down from the Pentland Hills to the sea. The village was also crossed by water, running east to west, in the shape of the Union Canal, a disused inland waterway that stretched out from the heart of Edinburgh, the capital, to Falkirk, a small town standing in the middle of Scotland's central belt.

The canal had carried horse-drawn barge traffic around the turn of the century but had been neglected now for over seventy years, allowing nature to reclaim much of its original, cobbled towpath and making progress along its banks almost impossible in places. The canal, however, was currently scheduled for dredging and restoration and was to be given new life as a major recreational feature for the population with the aid of millennium project money. Work had already started and a section of the main Glasgow–Edinburgh motorway was currently being raised to permit the rejoining of a section of the canal that had been severed during the motorway's construction many years before. There was little else to distinguish Blackbridge geographically, Steven concluded. It could have been any one of dozens of small communities lying across Scotland's most densely populated region.

The main protagonists in the current controversy appeared to be Ronald Lane, the owner of Peat Ridge Farm, who had been contracted by Agrigene to grow their experimental oilseed rape crop, and Thomas Rafferty, the owner of Crawhill Farm, which lay immediately to the east of Peat Ridge. Rafferty was officially the chief objector on the grounds that cross-pollination from Peat Ridge would ruin his credentials as an organic farmer. McGraw and Littlejohn, an Edinburgh firm of solicitors, had been retained by Rafferty and seemed to be coordinating the efforts of the other protestors – who, as far as Steven could tell, were objecting on principle to the idea of having any kind of genetically modified crop in the area.

Agrigene, in turn, had commissioned a Glasgow firm of solicitors, Macey and Elms, to represent their interests in the affair and they had adopted the position that their clients had done nothing wrong and were perfectly entitled to carry out the experimental work they had been properly licensed to do.

Rafferty's solicitors, however, had apparently come up with a trump card by producing what they claimed was a copy of a government laboratory analysis of the crop in Lane's fields, which they claimed showed that it was not the strain Agrigene was originally licensed to grow. The crop, they claimed, contained an extra foreign gene, one more than the two that had been agreed. They were demanding a halt to the whole trial on the basis of deception.

Agrigene, through Macey and Elms, were contesting this finding 'most vigorously' but adjudication in the matter was currently being impeded by the changing political scene in Scotland. The newly formed Scottish Parliament now held jurisdiction over matters agricultural through its newly formed Ministry for Rural Affairs but it had been the Ministry of Agriculture Food and Fisheries (MAFF), answering to the Westminster Parliament, that had granted the licence. There was also confusion over who held executive sway over major matters concerning health and safety.

'All I need,' sighed Steven. 'A bloody civil service squabble in the middle of a grey area.'

He examined the map of the village and surrounding area supplied by Miss Roberts and noted that the farms were indeed very close. The prevailing west wind in that part of the world might well constitute a problem, but a theoretical one, he thought. The idea of large-scale gene transfer through natural pollination was much more remote than the tabloid newspapers would have people believe. It was, however, too late for cogent argument on this subject. Public opinion had clearly perceived a danger in the genetic modification of food sources so the matter of who was right and who was wrong had become largely irrelevant. 'Don't waste your time concentrating on what *should* be,' was something he remembered from his early training, 'concentrate on what *is*.'

He gleaned very little in the way of extra information from the supplied copies of solicitors' letters. All were couched in the cold, unemotional jargon of legal prose and said no more than they absolutely had to. He looked to the background reports on the two farmers for some more colour.

Ronald Lane was a fifty-three-year-old, who had returned to Blackbridge from South Africa, where he had been an estate manager for many years. He had come home after inheriting Peat Ridge Farm from his late father. He had trained in the early sixties at Edinburgh's School of Agriculture but had apparently fallen out with his father at the time over what he saw as old-fashioned farming methods being used on Peat Ridge. The pair had never been reconciled and Lane junior had gone off to seek his fortune abroad.

He was said to be generally disliked in the village since his homecoming, being seen as 'uppity' and an outsider, despite his roots, and, as a consequence, kept himself very much to himself. He had remained unmarried and lived alone, apart from his housekeeper, a local woman named Agnes Fraser.

Thomas Rafferty of Crawhill Farm had lived all his forty-eight years in the village, having left school at sixteen to join his father and brother in working on Crawhill Farm. Although he had had to work hard when his father – a notoriously stern man – had been alive, he and his brother, Sean, had preferred to spend most of their time in the pub after the old man's demise. Consequently, the farm had been allowed to go into decline.

Sean, however, had been shrewd enough to see that there was a market for the hire of heavy farm machinery in the area. He had persuaded his brother that they should invest what remained of their capital in the purchase of agricultural machinery and set up a plant hire business. The idea blossomed into a business success and Rafferty's Plant Hire had provided both brothers with a comfortable income for many years, which they had not seen fit to augment with the bother of doing any actual farming. Crawhill had been allowed to lie fallow.

Sean had died in 1991 and Thomas had bought out his widow's share, leaving him and his wife, Trish, as the sole proprietors of the plant hire business. Without Sean's business acumen, however, the plant hire business had not being doing so well of late. Thomas had not recognised the need to invest in new machinery or keep up expensive maintenance schedules on the old stuff. He preferred to make do with what they had and keep it going on a shoestring budget, using second-hand spares and a succession of poorly paid mechanics to fit them.

It had come as a surprise to everyone when Thomas Rafferty announced that he was planning on resurrecting Crawhill as a working farm and an organic one at that. The fact that the land had not been cultivated at all for many years meant that it could be considered free of modern chemical contamination and therefore eligible for an organic accreditation, which it had now been granted.

Steven read on and noted that the licensing dates for Agrigene's trial pre-dated Rafferty's organic farm accreditation by quite some time. Some pen-pusher's mistake, he wondered. Right hands not knowing what left hands were doing? This was a fact of life in any large administration and, in this case, he could see an added complication. The setting up of the new Scottish Parliament's infrastructure had not, as far as he could tell, led to the demise of the old one, administered by the Scottish Office. He could be dealing here with permutations of *two* left hands and *two* right hands. Not a happy thought.

Steven moved on to the report from the ministry lab that had carried out the analysis on the oilseed rape crop and immediately thought it odd. It appeared that the analysis had been carried out at the instigation of the protestors. Why should a MAFF lab agree to do that? Did such labs carry out private work routinely? he wondered. He would check up on that, but even if that were the case, there must have been an original analysis carried out on the crop before the licence for the trial was granted. A comparison of the original and the latest one was surely all that was required to demonstrate whether the crops were the same or not, but the original was missing from the file. A copy of the licence itself was present and gave details of the two foreign genes that had been introduced to the grain. They had been inserted in order to enable the plant to tolerate a range of powerful herbicidal chemicals, most importantly, glyphosphate and glufosinate-ammonium weedkillers. The use of these herbicides would completely suppress weeds in the fields and permit much higher yields of the crop.

'And a bloody good idea, too,' thought Steven as he read on through the MAFF analysis. The two foreign genes were highlighted in the DNA sequence but so was a third, marked in a different colour. This apparently was the bone of contention between the two parties. The protestors, through Rafferty's solicitors, were arguing that this area represented a third, undeclared gene and therefore rendered the licence invalid. The biotech company, however, maintained that this was a misunderstanding and that the DNA sequence was not being interpreted correctly.

Steven was no molecular biologist but he did understand the principles involved in genetic engineering. In particular he appreciated the structure of DNA, the blueprint of life, and knew about the specificity of restriction enzymes that cut the molecule at particular sites. He understood the technical procedures involved in the cutting out of genes from one DNA molecule and the pasting of them into another.

This gave him an advantage over any lay investigator and,

in this instance, enabled him to wonder why the supposed third gene had not been identified and described by the analysing lab. They had just classified it as a 'foreign element' in the report.

Although one stretch of DNA sequence looked pretty much like any other to the naked eye – an apparently endless, alternating alphabet of only four letters, A,T,C and G, representing backbone of the molecule – many computerised databases had been set up to analyse these strings of letters and compare them with the DNA sequences of known genes. The lab had obviously run the sequence through a database in order to classify the suspect third section as foreign but they had not given any indication as to what it might be or where it might have come from. Steven wondered why not.

While he was thinking about this it occurred to him that this was something he could actually do for himself with the aid of his laptop. Using a modem link to the Sci-Med computer, he would type in the rogue foreign sequence and ask it to scan various DNA databases, looking for similarity. It would take a little time to key in what amounted to a meaningless string of letters and it would have to be done carefully – a bit like copy typing text in a language you didn't understand – but it was worth a try. It might well be that the MAFF lab had already tried this and failed to detect any similarity to any known gene but the fact remained that they hadn't reported doing that and, if it had been an unknown sequence, that alone would still have been worth reporting.

Steven keyed in the sequence of letters and painstakingly checked his work by reading the letters backwards, four at a time, using a postcard to cover up the others as he moved back along the screen. When he felt satisfied that his entry was accurate, he made the link with the Sci-Med computer and requested a database comparison. It didn't take long. The sequence was recognised almost immediately: it was present in the first database that the computer scanned. The sequence, it reported, was that of a DNA insertion element known in the trade as a transposon.

'Of course,' muttered Steven as it suddenly became clear to him why it was there. He now understood the biotech company's argument. This third element wasn't really a foreign gene at all. It was simply an easily detectable marker that had been used by their scientists as a convenient label in their experiments. Although foreign to the oilseed rape plant, this supposed third unlicensed 'gene' had simply been inserted to enable the Agrigene scientists to detect the presence of the two real foreign genes.

In the laboratory, it was impractical to demonstrate the presence of foreign genes by painstakingly sequencing the entire DNA blueprint of the plant so it was usual for experimenters to tag their genes with something that would be much easier to detect – usually with some kind of chemical marker. If this tag was present there was every chance that the foreign genes were too.

So why all the fuss? Steven wondered. The ministry lab must have known this when they made their report. It was common practice for scientists to use this technology. Why hadn't the reporting lab pointed this out to the protestors and their legal representatives? Or could this be a case of lawyers deliberately exploiting a misunderstanding for their own ends? Even so, he found it hard to believe that no one in the MAFF lab had pointed out that the tag could not reasonably be considered as a third foreign gene.

Once again he was forced to wonder why the original sequence had not been produced by both parties for comparison. The marker gene must have been present in the original sequence and therefore quite legal and subject to the licence whether lawyers now considered it foreign or not. There was clearly a big misunderstanding here. The big question for him now was, was it accidental or deliberate? In either case, Agrigene had the right to be annoyed and the more he thought about it, the more he could understand their frustration.

In the present climate of distrust over GM technology, however, the company might still have an uphill struggle on their hands, whatever the justness of their cause. Prosecution counsel simply asking in court, 'Were there or were there not three foreign genes present in the strain when you were licensed for two?' might carry the day. The company's reply of, 'Yes but . . .' followed by an explanation, might simply be swept away by the flow of public opinion. There were none as deaf as those who did not want to hear.

Steven moved on to the final section of the file and found the report on the three boys from the village who had gone swimming in the canal. The Sci-Med computer had been programmed to pick up on anything unusual happening in the Inspectorate's current areas of interest, whether it appeared at first glance to be relevant or not. The simple supposition was that no one really knew what was relevant and what was not at the outset of an investigation. Accordingly, the computer would collate all local newspaper reports and police incident reports emanating from the geographical area and incorporate them into the file, hence the local newspaper report on three boys who had contracted Weil's Disease.

Thirteen-year-olds going swimming in a canal seemed daft when viewed with the unfailing accuracy of adult hindsight but had probably been perfectly understandable at the time, he thought. When you were that age, you did what felt good without stopping to think. Young boys had never been noted for their foresight and vision and never would be. This was part of growing up. Learning the hard way was part of the curriculum. They'd probably never even heard of Weil's Disease or the fact you got it from contact with rat urine or that canals were one of the commonest sources of it. It was an odd thing about the rat having attacked one of them though. He hoped that the kid would be all right. The working file would be updated daily by the computer and any change transmitted to his laptop when he logged on each morning.

It was just after nine in the evening when Steven poured himself a gin and tonic and got out a fresh sheet of paper to write down a summary of his thoughts as a prelude to forming a plan of action. Some aspects of the affair seemed pretty straightforward. A farmer, growing GM crops on his land at the behest of a properly licensed biotech company, was at loggerheads with the rest of the community. Nothing unusual in that these days; it was something that had been happening all over the country. The main protestor was a would-be organic farmer shouting the odds about cross-pollination – again, par for the course – although in this case, he didn't as yet have a crop to cross-pollinate! This man was backed by most of the local community who just didn't like the idea of GM anything – again, nothing out of the ordinary in this, although it did occur to Steven that there was no indication who was paying the legal bills for the protestors. Agrigene could afford a legal battle. Could Rafferty and his fellow villagers?

A report from *a government lab* – he underlined this – gave the impression of the presence of a third, *unlicensed foreign gene* in the crop and hadn't done much by all accounts to correct what he now believed to be a false impression. This, he felt, was decidedly odd as was the fact that the original analysis had not been produced to demonstrate that the strains were (must be?) in fact identical.

It was normal practice for Sci-Med investigators to spend as much time as they felt necessary familiarising themselves with their assignment file before starting out on their investigation. Occasionally it was necessary for them to be sent on mini-courses if the subject matter should turn out to be highly specialised. This usually involved Sci-Med setting up a one to one meeting with an acknowledged expert in the relevant field to carry out a personal briefing.

Steven saw no need for any crash course in this instance; he felt quite at home with the technical elements of the investigation, but he did want to ask some questions. Firstly, he wanted to know if it were normal practice for government labs to carry out private contract work – as the MAFF lab had apparently done on this occasion. He would also ask Sci-Med if they had any information about who had paid for this work and who was footing the protestors' legal costs. Finally, he wanted to know the whereabouts of the original DNA analysis of the Agrigene crop strain. When he had the answers to these questions he would start thinking about heading north.

The response to Steven's questions arrived on his laptop at a quarter to noon next day. Yes, it was normal practice for government labs to carry out analyses on a contract basis for private companies and even individuals. This was part of a government initiative to make such labs more 'cost effective' and this kind of work was actively encouraged. No, they had no information about who had paid for the analysis of the Agrigene crop or who was paying McGraw and Littlejohn's bills, but they would try to find out. Finally, they themselves had noted that the original crop analysis had not been supplied when they had requested a copy from the ministry's licensing department. They had asked again for it and would forward it as soon as it became available – probably some time this afternoon.

Steven was a little disappointed at the response to his query about private work being carried out in government labs. He thought he had stumbled across something unusual, but he supposed that this was now the way of the world in the public sector. Everything had to make a profit these days. Colleges and universities were encouraged to cooperate with industry, form partnerships, seek sponsorship and welcome consultancies. Collaboration was the name of the game. Ivory towers and the acquisition of knowledge for the sake of it were concepts that belonged within the ivy-covered walls of the past.

He was even more disappointed that the original DNA analysis of the Agrigene crop was still not available because he saw that as the key to sorting out the whole misunderstanding. It was such an obvious thing to do – compare the original sequence to the current one – that he couldn't understand why this had not already been done. If the two sequences were identical, the crop was licensed, if not, there was a problem. It seemed so simple that he had to consider that he was missing something. He decided to phone Sci-Med to find out if there was any chance of hurrying up the access to the document.

'We've already put in an urgent request,' came the response. 'We'll send it over by courier as soon as it arrives.'

Fine, thought Steven. If he got it this afternoon and the sequence was identical he could take the overnight train up to Scotland, visit both sets of lawyers and clear up the matter of the mystery gene in a civilised manner.

At a quarter past three Macmillan phoned him in person and asked him to come in to the Home Office. He didn't give any indication why but Steven got the impression that he was less than happy about something. His ill humour had obviously transmitted itself to Miss Roberts when he arrived because she gave him a warning shrug before whispering that he should go straight in.

'Sit down,' said Macmillan, looking up from his papers momentarily.

Steven sat.

'The bastards! What do they think they're playing at?'

'Sir?'

'I've been warned off! Me! How dare they!'

Steven sat quietly until Macmillan was ready to continue.

'I understand from Miss Roberts that you put in a request for the original DNA analysis on the Agrigene crop.'

'It's the obvious key to settling the argument about whether the crop they were growing was the one they were licensed for or not,' said Steven. 'A simple comparison is all that's required. It will still leave the proximity problem to the organic farm site but at least it would get any allegation of illegality out of the way and probably put an end to our interest in the affair.'

'Well, they've "misplaced" it. Would you believe it? The licensing authority has bloody-well misplaced it.'

'Sort of weakens the case against Agrigene then,' said Steven.

'They think not,' said Macmillan. 'They maintain that the fact the original licence was for two foreign genes and the current analysis says there are three is sufficient enough to sustain the protestors' case.'

'But that's not on,' protested Steven. He told Macmillan about his identification of the third gene.

'But surely *they* must know that,' said Macmillan.

Steven shrugged his agreement. 'You would think so.'

Macmillan looked at him for a moment before saying, 'When the ministry told me the sequence was missing, it occurred to me that Agrigene might have a copy of the original analysis themselves so I called their MD and asked him. He asked me if I was, "trying to be funny". When I asked him what he was talking about he put down the phone on me.'

'What did he mean by that?'

'I called him back and when I explained what my position was and what the Sci-Med Inspectorate was all about, he calmed down a little but I don't think he fully trusted our independence. He made some remark about it being a bit like the police investigating themselves but I did get out of him what had happened. The company's copy of the licence was sent to their solicitors in Glasgow when the allegation was first made. The solicitors' premises were subject to a break-in during the next few days and guess what went missing?'

'The licence?'

'The licence,' agreed Macmillan. 'Among other things, of course.'

Steven let out a low whistle.

'I called MAFF's licensing department back and asked if their premises had been broken into too. I asked if this was the reason their copy had "been misplaced" and, if so, had the matter been reported to the police? The lackey I spoke to damn nearly perforated his backside sitting on the fence. Said he'd get back to me.'

'Did he?'

'The minister's PPS called me in person to assure me that there was nothing for Sci-Med to concern itself with in the situation in Scotland. They were on top of things and the minister would consider it a personal favour if we wouldn't "muddy the water".'

'Well, well, well. I'm beginning to think that Agrigene has a point. Someone is out to get them.'

'But why?'

'Maybe someone made a cock-up over accrediting an organic farm next to a GM crop and they're looking for excuses to pull the plug on Agrigene?' suggested Steven.

Macmillan looked at him thoughtfully as he tapped the end of his nose slowly with his index finger. 'And the minister would deem it a personal favour if we didn't muddy the water,' he intoned slowly. 'Well, I think not. Something tells me there's more to this than meets the eye.'

'So I run with it?' asked Steven.

'Your daughter still lives in Scotland?'

'Near Dumfries.'

'How far from Blackbridge?'

Steven shrugged. 'About eighty miles, I suppose.'

'Why don't you go visit her this weekend but take a quiet, unofficial look at Blackbridge while you're up there and see what you think. If you smell a rat . . . Well, to hell with the minister. We'll go ahead with the investigation anyway.'

# 3

Moira Lawson hesitated in the hallway of her bungalow, debating whether or not to put on a jacket, then decided against it. It wasn't often possible to venture out of doors in the evening in Scotland without one so she thought that, for once, she would live dangerously and enjoy the experience. 'I'm just taking Sam for his walk,' she called out to her husband in the living room. A Labrador puppy scampered round her feet, tail wagging furiously, while she listened for a reply.

She took a distant grunt as 'message received' and collected Sam's extending lead from the hall table to clip it to his collar, explaining to him, as she always did at this time, that it would be just until they got to the top of the road and then he could have his freedom. She didn't want him bounding in and out of the neighbours' gardens.

Sam strained at the lead all the way up the road, nose close to the ground, tail never still. When she stopped to speak to one of the neighbours near the top of the hill, he immediately investigated the halt to his progress by jumping up on the woman and offering his instant affection.

'You're a big soft sausage, aren't you?' laughed the neighbour, making a fuss of him. 'They're lovely at that age, aren't they?'

'Daft as a brush,' smiled Moira. 'All energy and no brains.'

'Are you taking him up by the canal?'

Moira said that she was.

'You must have heard about the three kids along in Blackbridge?'

'I certainly did, Weil's Disease; can be quite nasty apparently. Damages the liver. I was speaking to one of their mothers, coming back on the bus yesterday. She'd been in at the hospital. She was saying that they've all been through a bit of a bad time but at least her boy was getting better. Unfortunately, the same couldn't be said for the laddie who'd been bitten.'

'I heard about that. Which one of them got bitten?'

'Mrs Ferguson's son. He had to have an operation on his foot: it was torn quite badly apparently. I hear he's still very ill; some complicating factors to do with the bite becoming infected, I think.'

'Dirty things, rats, makes me shiver, just thinking about them. Mind you, who in their right mind would want to swim in the canal? It's all green slime apart from anything else.'

'What were we saying about all energy and no brains? I think it applies to young boys as well as young dogs.'

The neighbour laughed and conceded the point. Moira continued her walk. She joined the canal towpath and took

43

off Sam's lead. He was off like a rocket, but a rocket with little or no sense of direction. He gave every indication of wanting to run in all directions at the same time. Moira introduced some purpose to it all by picking up a small stick and throwing it along the towpath. As she continued with the game it occurred to her that she was enjoying herself as much as Sam. The sun was low but still warm and the wind had dwindled away to nothing. The air was full of the smells of late summer, only marred a little by the smell of the algal bloom on the surface of the canal.

Sam paused in the game to do his business and Moira took the chance to look up at the sky, thinking to herself how much nicer it would be if Scotland had more of this kind of weather. There were so few occasions when proper clothing was not a major consideration. She was very glad that she had not bothered with a jacket. The cool of the evening on her bare arms was very pleasant. The insects hovering above the surface of the still water and the drifting 'wishes' from the willow herb made her think of Peter Pan and fairies.

Sam looked up at her expectantly and she launched the stick again. 'Go on, then, you daft mutt,' she encouraged. She tried to throw the stick further this time and lost direction a little. It landed in the water. Sam bounded along to the spot but Moira did not want him plunging into the stagnant water so she called out to him to stop. Sam paused unsurely at the edge, his basic instinct being challenged by his partial training.

'Good boy,' Moira called out as Sam settled with his rear end in the air and his nose pointing down at the water.

'There's a good boy. Just you wait there,' said Moira as she walked towards him.

Suddenly Sam let out a yelp of pain and Moira saw him start to throw his head feverishly from side to side. She thought at first that he had something in his mouth – her first thought was that he had tried to pick up a hedgehog and was learning the lesson but as she got closer she could see that this was not the case at all. A small animal had attached itself to Sam's face by sinking its teeth into Sam's snout. Her blood ran cold when she saw that it was a rat.

Moira desperately wanted to help Sam – wanted to free him of the vile vermin that was causing him such pain, but she found herself unable to through her fear and loathing of rats. Her arms moved like the sails of an uncertain windmill as she tried to approach but she was forced to draw back through sheer revulsion. The nightmare moved up a gear when a second rat scampered up on to the bank and attached itself to one of Sam's front paws. Moira screamed but the sound that came out sounded totally alien, a mixture of terror and anger that she'd seldom, if ever, felt before.

She could see that Sam was starting to lose the battle. It looked as if he was beginning to tire and might fall over at any moment. When a third rat appeared on the path, Moira's concern for the puppy overcame her dread of rats. She moved in, swinging her feet at them and screaming abuse at the top of her voice as a way of neutralising her fear. When her foot connected with the third rat and sent it flying, she yelled out in pleasure and tried stamping on the one attached to Sam's paw. Frustration started to play a role when she found that just wasn't quick enough to keep up with Sam's twists and turns. 'Damn! Damn! Damn!' she screamed. 'Get off him, you filth! Leave him alone!'

45

Help appeared in the form of a cyclist coming along the towpath. He'd seen the woman ahead of him with what appeared to be a dog scampering round her feet and had rung his bell as an early warning of his approach.

'Help me!' screamed Moira. 'Please help me! Get them off him!'

The cyclist, a tall man wearing dungarees and working boots, got off his bike and snatched the tyre pump from the frame. He lashed out at the rat on Sam's paw and made good enough contact to make it release its grip. To deal with the other one he had to wrestle Sam to the ground and hold him still while he beat at the rat on his snout with the barrel of the pump. Sam was finally freed of his tormentors and whimpered pitifully as Moira examined his wounds. He was bleeding profusely.

'My poor baby,' she cooed, cradling him in her arms.

'What the hell happened?' asked the cyclist.

Moira shook her head. 'I don't know,' she gasped. 'He was looking down at the water. The next thing I knew one of these vile things was on his face.'

'He must have stumbled on their nest,' said the man. 'They can be bloody vicious when they feel threatened.' He walked over to the edge of the bank and examined the area. 'No sign of any rat holes, mind you.' He pushed down the reeds around the area with the pump he still held in his hand but didn't find anything. 'Strange,' he muttered. 'A laddie got bitten along in Blackbridge by the buggers the other week there: mind you, he was swimming in the bloody canal. Talk about shit for brains.'

Moira wasn't really interested in why it had happened. She felt weak and cold and anxious. The front of her blouse was covered in Sam's blood and she was becoming increasingly angry with this man who seemed to be ignoring her and Sam in favour of conducting some kind of forensic investigation. She had to remind herself that he had also been the one to come to their rescue and if he hadn't come along, at that particular time, God alone knew what might have happened. 'Could you possibly give me a hand?' she asked, trying to get to her feet, still cradling Sam in her arms.

'Nae hassle,' said the man. He took Sam from her and asked, 'Where are we going?'

'My house is about half a mile away.'

'If you wheel ma bike for me, I'll take care o' the dug. He needs help. What are you going to do about him?'

'There's a vet over in Blackbridge. My husband will drive us over.'

The man looked at his watch. 'It's after nine,' he said. 'If he's no there, there's a vet wi' a twenty-four hour call out in Edinburgh. You'll find it in Yellow Pages.'

'Thanks, we'll try Blackbridge first,' said Moira.

The pair of them attracted quite a bit of attention when they left the towpath and started to walk down the road to Moira's house, the man beginning to weave a bit under Sam's weight and Moira, shocked, dejected, the front of her blouse covered in Sam's blood. Several neighbours came out to ask what was wrong but Moira couldn't face telling them the story. She had to look past them. She was close to mental exhaustion. She propped up the man's bicycle on the garden wall and opened her front door to call out, 'Andrew!'

Andrew, her husband, hearing the note of anxiety in her

voice came to the door, newspaper in hand, pushing his glasses up his nose. 'Good God, what on earth's happened?'

'Sam's hurt bad. We have to get him to a vet.'

Moira's husband went to get his jacket and she turned to the man holding Sam. 'Mr? . . .'

'McDougal. Lawrie McDougal.'

'Mr McDougal, I can't begin to thank you for all you've done. I just don't know what I would have done if you hadn't come along.'

The man shuffled uncomfortably under the weight of praise and handed over the dog to her. 'Don't mention it. I just hope your dug's going to be all right, missus.'

Moira smiled and waved to him as he cycled off and her husband appeared with the car keys in his hand. Moira sat with Sam on her knee as they drove along to Blackbridge less than two miles away. 'Let's hope he hasn't gone out for the evening,' said Andrew.

'If he has, Mr McDougal said there's a vet in Edinburgh with a round the clock call-out service,' said Moira.

They drew up outside the vet's house in Blackbridge, an old sandstone building in a street running parallel to the main one. The vet, James Binnie, worked from home, his surgery being a low concrete extension tacked on to the back of the house. As most of his work was concerned with farm animals, this sufficed for the few domestic pets he had to deal with.

Andrew knocked on the front door, cradling the dog in his arms. Moira stood by his side, still wearing her blood-stained blouse. The door was opened by Binnie himself, a small man in his early forties slipping into the bespectacled, bald anonymity of middle age. He was wearing slippers and had a glass of something in his hand. 'What the dickens!—' he exclaimed at the sight that met him.

'It's my dog, Sam,' said Moira, speaking in the flat monotone that shock had induced in her. 'Rats went for him.'

'You'd better come round,' said Binnie, pausing to put his glass down on some surface behind the door and lifting his jacket from a hook there. He led the way round the back of the house, squeezing between a wall and a mud-spattered Volvo estate that was parked there. Andrew followed, lifting Sam up to clear the Volvo's door mirror. Moira brought up the rear.

The fluorescent lights of the surgery stuttered up to full illumination and Sam was laid gently down on Binnie's examination table. Moira patted his flank reassuringly while Binnie started to take a look at his injuries.

'You've certainly been in the wars, wee man,' he said, examining Sam's snout and getting a whimper of protest from the puppy. 'We're going to have to stitch these cuts, I'm afraid.' He moved on to Sam's paw, getting louder protests this time as he sought to establish any bone damage. 'Well, I think you've been lucky there, wee man. Nothing broken but we may have to send you into the vet school to have these tendons properly seen to. In the meantime we'll get you cleaned up, stitched and I'll give you a couple of jabs against infection.'

Moira breathed a sigh of relief at what the vet was saying. It all translated into a simple truth. Sam was going to be all right.

'I think you better sit down,' said Binnie to her as he noticed her wobble slightly and clutch the side of the table.

'I think maybe you're right,' agreed Moira, now smiling

for the first time. She sat down beside Andrew who was leaning forward, elbows on his knees as he watched the proceedings.

'I take it he went for the rats,' said Binnie as he cleaned Sam's wounds.

'I don't know. I'm not absolutely sure,' said Moira. 'I threw a stick for him and it went into the canal. One minute he was standing at the edge, looking at it, the next thing I knew, one of the things was biting his face.'

'The canal?' said Binnie. 'They were water rats?'

'Yes, we were walking along the towpath.'

'I didn't realise that. I sort of assumed that he must have cornered some rats in a barn. I guess he must have found their hole in the bank.'

'That's what the man who helped me thought,' said Moira. 'He had a look afterwards but he didn't see anything.'

Binnie looked at her. 'Where was this exactly?'

Moira thought for a moment before replying, 'The far side of Mossgiel, near the boundary with Peat Ridge Farm.'

Binnie looked at her again as if he was about to make some comment. Instead, he asked. 'This man who helped you, did he kill any of the rats?'

'Both,' replied Moira. 'He hit them with his bicycle pump.'

'You're sure they were dead?'

'I'm not sure about the one I kicked away but the two Mr McDougal hit with the pump looked dead enough.'

'Good,' said the vet. He offered no further explanation but went on to complete dressing Sam's injuries. 'There we are, my wee man,' he announced. 'I don't think you'll be chasing any rats for a while but you'll live to fight another day.'

Moira and Andrew thanked Binnie profusely and offered to pay there and then but Binnie said that he would send a bill. His wife dealt with the paperwork and she was over at her sister's tonight. He personally didn't know where to find anything. Andrew and Moira drove off and Binnie clicked off the lights of the surgery to return to the main house. He felt a little troubled. This was the second case of rat bite he'd had to deal with in the past week and then there was that young boy who'd been swimming in the canal and got himself bitten. He knew from recent reports that there had been a general increase in the rat population all over the country but he was beginning to find the current situation alarming. He drained his glass and decided to take a walk along the towpath.

He knew that if he walked west, along the back of Peat Ridge Farm, he must come to the place where Sam had been attacked. Unless nature had beaten him to it, he would come across the bodies of the rats that the cyclist had killed. His idea was to send one up to Vet Pathology at the university and ask them to carry out a general forensic examination of it. He left a note for his wife, saying where he'd gone in case she returned in his absence, collected a torch from a drawer in the kitchen and put on his Barbour jacket against a chill in the night air.

It took him just under fifteen minutes to reach the spot where Peat Ridge Farm ended and Mossgiel began. The sky was clear and the stars were out but the moon wasn't up yet so he had to use the torch in a slow, sweeping search for the bodies of the rats. He would have preferred to do this in the morning but the chances of the bodies still being there after a night on the towpath would be remote. He wasn't afraid of the dark – at least, he didn't think he was, but he did find himself feeling distinctly uneasy. He reminded himself that noises that would be ignored or taken for granted during daylight hours seemed to assume a greater significance after dark. The hedgerows by the side of the canal seemed to be alive with the rustling feet and claws of the night.

Binnie gasped and paused as the torch beam picked out a rat running across the towpath a few feet in front of him. It was quickly followed by another. 'What the . . .?' he exclaimed as he watched yet another join the procession. He looked to the north, the direction from which the rats were coming, and found himself looking at the gently waving silhouettes of the oilseed rape crop on Peat Ridge Farm.

A distant unearthly howl was carried to him on the night air and Binnie recognised it as Tom Rafferty's dog, Khan, over on Crawhill Farm. A shiver of apprehension rippled down his spine at the sound. Please God, the animal was securely tethered and wouldn't be roaming the banks. He'd had to deal with Khan before in his professional capacity and was therefore no stranger to the dog, but he wouldn't like his safety to depend on such a tenuous acquaintance. Khan was one bad-tempered beast by any criterion. What was it about big dogs and inadequate people? he wondered, thinking about Khan's owner, Tom Rafferty. Was it a simple mathematical relationship? The weaker the human character, the fiercer the dog? He continued further along the towpath, continuing his search for the bodies of the rats, although he no longer thought this such a good idea.

He was almost on the point of giving up when he saw them. The first one had been badly gnawed at – presumably by its fellows – but the second corpse seemed to be in better condition. He took out the plastic bag he'd brought with him for the purposes of transporting it and made to pick the animal up by the tail. He let out an involuntary yell when it suddenly turned its head and bit him on the finger. He snatched his hand away, wisely resisting – but only at the last moment – the temptation to put his finger in his mouth. Rat bite fever he could do without.

Instead, he forced the wound to bleed, allowing the blood to clean it out. At least he now understood why this rat was in better condition than the other: it was still alive!

In the torch beam he could now see that the animal's back had been broken by blows from the bicycle pump but it was still breathing, although unable to move anything save its head. He didn't want to cause any further physical damage to it, mainly because it might interfere with pathological examination he was going to request, so he resolved to put it out of its misery by asphyxiation. He unwrapped the handkerchief that he'd put round his finger and used it to cut off air to the animal's mouth and nose until it was dead. It was a very unpleasant few minutes and Binnie felt nauseous throughout. When the rat was dead, he held it up by the tail and dropped it into the plastic bag before starting back for home. By now, he was wishing that he'd never set out on this course at all. He could have been sitting at home, watching television with a whisky in his hand.

He had almost reached the clearing where he would

leave the towpath to rejoin the road when he suddenly had the unpleasant feeling that he was not alone. At first it was only a feeling, although it made the hairs on the back of his neck stand up, but then he heard rustling sounds coming from the hedgerow on the far side of the clearing. He kept moving, then he was sure he heard someone say, 'Ssh!'

In a way it was a relief to hear it. It told him that he was not the target of muggers or whoever was hiding there. They seemed to be waiting for him to pass, hoping to remain undetected. As he walked past and left the clearing to rejoin the road he caught a whiff of . . . something in the air. What was it? Something ordinary, an everyday substance that he couldn't put a name to because it was out of context, then he realised what it was. It was petrol!

In an instant he knew what was going on. The people hiding in the hedgerow were lurking at the eastern edge of Peat Ridge Farm. It was obviously their intention to set fire to the GM crop growing there. He hurried down the road to his house and called the police before he did anything else. His wife, Ann, came out into the hall and looked at him as if he were mad. 'What's going on?' she asked.

'It's been quite an evening all in all,' he replied, putting down the phone and trying to affect a smile. 'I'll have to dress this,' he said, holding up the finger with the blood-stained hankie round it. 'There's going to be an attack on Ronald Lane's place. There are some people hiding in a ditch up by the canal. They've got petrol with them.'

'Looks like you came to blows with them.'

'No, a rat did this,' said Binnie. 'This one.' He held up the plastic bag containing the dead rat. 'Pop it in the fridge, will you? There's a love.'

'My God, it was never like this on *All Creatures Great and Small*,' said his wife. 'Whatever happened to cuddly kittens and robins with broken wings?'

'Maybe I should give Ronald Lane a call as well,' said Binnie as an afterthought. 'The police might not get there in time.' As if to prove him wrong, the sound of a police siren reached them from the distance. 'I'll do it anyway,' said Binnie. 'Lane should be aware of what's going on. How was your sister, by the way?'

'Fine,' replied Binnie's bemused wife, as she watched him disappear out the door into the hall again. 'She turned green and burst into flames last Thursday.'

'Good,' came the reply from the hall as a preoccupied Binnie picked up the phone and dialled Lane's number. He had no sooner passed on the warning to Lane than he thought he'd better tell Tom Rafferty as well. He would be wondering what all the commotion was about.

The male voice that answered did not belong to Rafferty. 'Who wants him?'

'James Binnie, the vet.'

Rafferty came on the line and Binnie told him what was happening. 'I think the police are going to get there on time,' he said.

'Pity,' said Rafferty.

'It's about time you two resolved your differences,' lectured Binnie. 'The pair of you have split the village.'

'I was going to call you in the morning,' said Rafferty ignoring what Binnie had said. 'Khan's not very well. I'd like you to take a look at him.'

'What's the matter with him this time?'

'His behaviour's getting worse,' replied Rafferty. 'He's

getting really vicious, even to me, if you know what I mean. He damn nearly took my hand off when I put down his food bowl this morning.'

Binnie smiled. 'Khan has never exactly been Lassie, has he, Tom?' he said.

'I know he's always been a bit of a handful, like,' admitted Rafferty, 'but Rotweilers aren't meant to be lapdogs, are they? And it's different now. He's getting worse, I know he is.'

'He's probably getting old and crotchety like the rest of us, Tom. But no matter, I'll pop over and take a look at him tomorrow. Goodnight.'

A man's voice said something in the background that Binnie couldn't quite make out – something about having had long enough, he thought – and the phone clattered down and went dead. Binnie looked at the receiver in his hand and said, 'And good night to you, sweet prince.'

Binnie returned to the living room and was about to start explaining to his wife what had been going on when an explosion rent the air. They both rushed outside and saw an orange glow to the southwest. 'There goes the petrol,' said Binnie. 'They must be destroying the evidence: they've not had time to pour it on Lane's crop.'

'I just hope no one got hurt,' said Ann Binnie.

'Amen to that,' said Binnie.

# 4

Steven drove up to Scotland on Friday. The plan was to spend Saturday with Jenny and the others and then drive over to Blackbridge on Sunday where he would take a look around and maybe speak to a few people before travelling home again. When Saturday dawned with clear blue skies and unbroken sunshine, Steven persuaded Sue to let him take not only Jenny, but her children too, away for the day so that she and her husband could have some time to themselves – a pretty rare event these days. They could go up to Glasgow perhaps, do some shopping and have lunch somewhere nice.

Sue agreed, but only after insisting that she would prepare a picnic for them and making sure that Steven had a note of her mobile phone number just in case anything went wrong. The good weather dictated he should take the three children off down the Solway coast where they could build sand castles, dig tunnels and do the things that families did at the beach.

He listened to the excited chatter of the children in the back of the car on the way down and was pleased to hear that Jenny had been accepted by the other two as their sister – the continual fighting testified to that. He himself was always careful to bring presents for all three children when he came to visit. He didn't want to be the kind of father to Jenny who just appeared from time to time bearing gifts while opting out of all the hard parts of parenthood, but to a certain extent this was what was happening and events were being dictated by circumstances. While this was the case, he would try to be a part – a pleasant one – of all three children's lives. As for the future, he couldn't see that far ahead. In fact, he couldn't see much further than tomorrow morning when he would drive up to Blackbridge and start working again.

When evening came and the tide finally swept in to cover the sand pies and the ornate castle they had spent so long building, Steven and the three children stood in a line and watched in silence. A moment came when Jenny looked up at him and a lump came to his throat when he saw the sadness in her eyes. For a moment, just a fleeting moment, they were Lisa's eyes. 'Cheer up,' he said softly. 'There will be other days. I promise.'

Twenty minutes into the journey home and all three children fell asleep. Steven switched on the radio but kept it low. He managed to catch the news on Radio Scotland and heard the word 'Blackbridge' mentioned. It sounded loud because he was sensitised to it after reading about it in the file he'd gone through so thoroughly. It was like hearing your own name spoken in a crowded room. Turning up the volume a little, he took in a report on an abortive attempt to damage the experimental crop on Peat Ridge Farm. Although the police had got there on time to prevent the planned arson attack, and no charges had subsequently been made, feelings were running high in the village and the farm owner had now decided to go ahead with plans to call in a private security firm.

There followed an interview with Ronald Lane, who spoke with a South African accent and insisted that the rule of law must be upheld. An unfortunate accent for that kind of assertion, thought Steven. This was followed by a 'balancing' interview featuring an inarticulate ramble from a villager about 'them' not really knowing if things were safe or not. The report ended and Steven turned off the radio. He adjusted his rear-view mirror momentarily to take a look at the three in the back. They looked like sleeping cherubs, cheeks all rosy from their day in the sunshine.

Steven left at ten next morning amidst much waving and promises to be back soon but there was a last minute hitch when Robin decided that he must have left one of his toy spacemen in Steven's car. A quick search of the back uncovered the missing astronaut, trapped down the back of the rear seat squab where his ray gun had been of little use. The sky grew progressively darker as he headed north and it started raining just after eleven, turning the dual carriageway into a series of spray curtains thrown up by heavy lorries. By twelve o'clock, when he entered Blackbridge, it was coming down in torrents.

Maybe it was the darkness or maybe it was the fact that it was raining heavily but Steven took an immediate dislike to the place. It seemed to have very little in the way of redeeming features; an ugly little village full of ugly houses in the middle of nowhere, although, in reality, it wasn't that far from the capital. He felt it was the sort of place you would normally splash through in the car without even noticing. Two sweeps of the wipers and it would be gone.

Steven toured the streets slowly, taking in as much as he could and generally orientating himself with the actuality of what he'd studied on the map. He kept the said map sat on the seat beside him, referring to it from time to time to identify things. Finally he drove up the hill that separated Peat Ridge Farm from Crawhill Farm, crossing the bridge over the canal near the top where he thought about the three boys who'd had the canal adventure.

At the top of the road, he turned off into the track that would lead up to Peat Ridge Farm, just with the intention of turning his car round. Two men in yellow waterproofs stepped out in front of him. One had an Alsatian dog on a short lead, the other a mobile phone in his hand. Steven opened the car window, getting wet in the process.

'What's your business?' rasped the one with the phone.

'Just turning my car,' replied Steven.

'Don't bloody do it here in future,' snapped the man.

'Gotcha,' smiled Steven, noting the logo on the man's poncho that said he belonged to Sector One Security. He drove back down to the village. The rain was keeping everyone off the streets. He wasn't going to learn anything by walking around today. He'd have to do his snooping indoors. That gave him a choice of two places. There was a grim-looking pub at the east end of Main Street called the Castle Tavern and there was a small white-painted hotel in the middle called the Blackbridge Arms.

The hotel had a number of official looking cars parked

outside it so Steven concluded that this was where anyone from MAFF or the Scottish Executive would be. He was impressed that they were working on a Sunday, or maybe the English contingent was actually staying there. He knew that the risk of meeting anyone he knew or of seeing anyone that he recognised would be small but he decided not to take it anyway. Macmillan had said that this was to be an unofficial look around so he opted instead for the pub.

The Castle Tavern was as ugly and dirty on the inside as it was on the outside but it seemed popular: in fact, on a Sunday afternoon, it was crowded. His immediate thought on entering was that the atmosphere seemed positively aggressive but then he reminded himself that a Scots accent could make the Lord's Prayer sound aggressive. There were simply a lot of men in the room, all of them apparently talking at the same time.

As he entered, he took in the layout of the place, noting that there were tables and chairs to the left of the door, all occupied and with several domino games in progress. There were two pool tables off to the right and a bank of electronic games machines sited along the long wall behind them; they were adding electronic noise to the general cacophony.

One of the men at the pool table turned as Steven entered and said in a deliberately loud voice, 'Fuck, here's another one o' them.' It made his friends laugh. It made Steven wonder what he was supposed to be. He made his way to the bar counter and saw the barman deliberately adopt a neutral expression. He asked for a beer and was served and charged without a word being exchanged.

Steven took a sip of his beer and looked about him, observing the beer slops on the plastic bar top, the uncleared tables, the thick blue tobacco fug in the air and the ring of cigarette butts on the floor around the bar. He heard the word 'fuck' so many times in its various forms in the first few minutes that he was reminded of an assertion in some recent radio programme that swearing was so much on the increase that soon all other words in the English language would become extinct. 'Fuck' would be the only word left for communication purposes. Information and ideas would be exchanged through the use of different inflections on it. The suggestion was being given a serious try-out by Sunday lunchtime drinkers in Blackbridge.

'So, what paper are *you* with?' asked a voice at his elbow.

Steven turned to find a short man with ginger hair and a moustache standing there. 'I'm not,' he replied. 'I'm not a journalist.'

'Sorry, I thought you must be one of the English stringers,' said the man. 'I'm Alex McColl, by the way. I'm covering the attack on the GM crop story for the *Clarion*.'

'I heard there had been some kind of trouble,' said Steven. 'It was on the car radio.'

'Not much of a story. The police got there before the buggers could set fire to the crop like they'd planned.'

'You sound disappointed.'

'One man's misfortune is another's front page story,' said McColl. 'You're a stranger here; what line are you in?'

'I'm a civil servant.'

'Another one? Place is crawling with them. How come you're not drinking with your mates up at the Arms?'

'I've just arrived. I don't know my way about yet. This

was the first place I came to. How come you're not there if it's a story you're after?'

'I got seriously fed up banging my head against a brick wall. Getting the knickers off a nun would be easier than getting information out of that lot. The beer's cheaper here too.'

A newcomer arrived at the bar beside them. 'Bloody hell, it's raining cats and dogs out there,' a tall, gangling man complained, shaking the water from his thatch of dark hair and brushing it from the shoulders of his Berghaus jacket. Steven thought he spoke with an English accent but further exposure to it said it was educated Scots.

'Well, well, if it isn't young Jamie Brown of the *Scotsman*,' said McColl. 'The paper for people who need a tyre lever to open their arse in the morning. Someone else who's lost his way in the storm, I'll be bound.'

'Hello McColl,' replied Brown pleasantly. 'I suppose you're here running a competition to find out if you've any readers who can actually spell "genetically modified". Wins a trip to Disneyland, does it?'

'Ho, very droll,' replied McColl. 'That kind of joke in your column could well push your circulation up into double figures.'

'In which case I will buy some proper toilet paper and stop using copies of the *Clarion*.'

'Well, enough of this jolly banter,' said McColl, buttoning up his jacket. 'I'm off to see if I can coax a few quotes out of Thomas Rafferty, the people's champion. They tell me he's a piss artist so it shouldn't be too difficult with a bottle of malt in my pocket.'

'Good luck,' said Brown sourly. 'I've just come from

there. That's how I got soaked. I've been arguing with his minders for the last half hour.'

'Minders?' exclaimed McColl. 'What the hell does Rafferty need minders for? It's an organic farm he's supposed to be setting up, not a Swiss bank.'

Brown shrugged. 'Good question, but there were two men in suits at Crawhill insisting that, "Mr Rafferty had nothing to say to the press".'

McColl left to go try his luck, leaving Steven and Brown at the bar. 'Can I get you a drink?' Steven offered.

'Civil of you. I'll have a whisky if that's all right.'

Steven ordered the drink and watched Brown add a little water to it from a jug on the bar. The water in the jug made him think of the canal.

'You're English,' said Brown. 'Welcome to Blackbridge . . . twinned with Auschwitz,' he whispered quietly.

'It's not exactly pretty, is it?' answered Steven.

'West Lothian does these places really well,' said Brown. 'It has lots of them.'

Steven said, 'Your colleague was just bemoaning the fact that this GM business wasn't much of a story.'

'Well, it's not exactly new, is it? It's been happening all over the place down south but I suppose we have to cover it up here when it happens on our own doorstep.' Brown looked about him before saying, *sotto voce*, 'Mind you, I tend to think a few foreign elements getting into the gene pool round here might be a welcome development. Half these buggers look like they should be playing the banjo on some bridge.'

Steven hid a smile. He thought the barman might have heard but either didn't understand or was pretending not to.

An argument at one of the tables was gathering momentum. Voices were getting louder by the second. The barman tried, 'Order please, gentlemen!' but to no avail. The table was now the centre of attention.

'Ah'm tellin' you, Lane has a perfect right to protect his property, any way he chooses,' said one man loudly.

'An' ah'm tellin' you, we're all breathin' in that GM crap he's growin' up there on Peat Ridge. He can bring in a' the security guards he wants but it's still no' goin' tae stop us torchin' that shit!'

'Christ, the man's got a licence. There's nothin' wrang wi' the stuff he's growin'. He wouldn't have got the licence if there was!'

'What's the bugger doin' back here anyway? South African tosser,' interjected another loud voice.

'He was bloody born here! He's got every right to be here! It was his faither's place!'

'But it was never good enough for mister university high and mighty while his old man was alive. He pissed off and left the old guy to work the place on his own till it killed him. He should have fuckin' stayed away.'

'Gus is right,' said yet another new voice. 'Nobody seems to know what that bugger is growin' up there and lots of us have got young kids. Christ knows what a' they genes floatin' aboot are doin' tae them.'

'Jesus! It's oilseed rape, he's growin'. You can see that for yersels. The only difference is that it's resistant tae weed killers so it's easier tae get a bigger yield.'

'So the bugger says.'

'Even the government are no' convinced o' that.'

Steven and Brown watched and listened until one of the

men in the group surrounding the main protagonists nudged those on either side of him and nodded in the direction of the bar. It was obvious he was warning them of the presence of strangers.

'Whoops,' said Brown under his breath, turning away as attention swung towards him and Steven. Steven turned his shoulder a little as well and both men took a sip of their drink. The argument and threats continued but in quieter voices.

'I might get a story out of this yet,' murmured Brown. 'Sounds like Lane's dogs have arrived.'

'They have,' Steven confirmed. 'I met one on my way here. Sector One Security was holding the lead. Mean anything to you?'

'I've seen them around.'

A few minutes later, a youth, wearing a leather jacket and jeans and holding a pool cue, sidled across to them and stopped, facing them. Standing legs apart, he brought the cue to the horizontal and held it in both hands at arms' length across his thighs. He said, 'I hope you two aren't thinking of printing anything you've heard here today, are you?'

'Nope,' replied Steven quickly and truthfully and with an almost jaunty air. He did it to nullify the air of menace that the youth obviously hoped he was imparting.

'Shouldn't think so,' drawled Brown, matter of factly.

The youth betrayed a look of puzzlement for a moment. He'd got the response he wanted but was finding it strangely unsatisfying. He'd been cheated of something but couldn't think what it was. He moved off with Steven and Brown watching his back.

'Marlon Brando,' said Steven.

'In *On the Waterfront*,' added Brown.

They turned back to their drinks. 'You didn't say what you were doing here?' asked Brown.

'I'm a civil servant.'

'Is that it?'

'Matters concerning the environment,' said Steven vaguely.

'Are you one of the people who's going to decide whether Lane's crop gets the red card or not?'

'I'm not important enough to make that kind of decision. What do you think about it all?' replied Steven.

'If he's really growing a crop the company weren't licensed for then certainly I think a stop should be put to it. There's no point in having a licensing system if the company's going to get away with that sort of nonsense. But the trouble is, it's proving really hard to find out if he is or if he isn't. You can never get anyone in authority to give you a straight answer to a simple question. I got fed up asking the local suits and briefcases so I tried phoning the lab that carried out the analysis, but I hit the same wall. Getting information out of them was like drawing teeth.'

'If you say absolutely nothing to the press you can never get into trouble,' said Steven. 'It's the way people look after their pensions in the civil service.'

'Can I quote you on that?' smiled Brown.

'I'd rather you didn't.'

'As for this organic farm business at Crawhill, it's just too bizarre for words. I haven't spoken to a soul in the village who believes that Thomas Rafferty is the least bit interested in organic farming – or any kind of farming come to that. By all accounts he's a waster who's been making a living out of hiring out farm machinery. For years his only other recorded interest has been in pissing large quantities of lager against the wall, so much so that I heard his wife left him recently.'

'Maybe he's thinking of selling up,' suggested Steven. 'Maybe he's trying to turn the farm into a going concern to make it more attractive to prospective buyers?'

'That's possible, I suppose,' said Brown thoughtfully. 'In fact, I hadn't thought of that angle. So why won't he speak to the press? You'd think he'd want all the favourable publicity he could get. We've got a ready-made villain in Lane so Rafferty would seem well placed for the starring roll of organic-growing hero. And where do the minders come in?'

Steven shrugged. 'Could be the Magnificent Seven,' he said, 'come to aid the poor peasant farmer?'

'There were only two.'

Steven gave Brown a sideways glance and saw that he was preoccupied, not stupid.

'The first thing I'm going to do when I leave here is run a check to see if Crawhill has been put on the market,' said Brown. 'That was a good idea of yours. Would you like to be informed of the result?'

'If you like,' said Steven. He gave Brown his mobile telephone number.

'If this works out, I'll owe you a bottle of Scotch.'

Steven had had an even better idea but was keeping it to himself for the time being. It proposed that Rafferty had already sold the farm and was acting as some kind of front for the new owners. That might well explain the presence of the people Brown had described as minders but also begged the question as to why the new owners needed a front man at all. The obvious answer to that was that they didn't want anyone to know who they were. Steven worked the idea through to a conclusion. Why not? Because . . . it would be embarrassing for them? Why embarrassing? Because . . . the new owners were not private buyers at all. They were . . . corporate buyers. They were . . . a commercial company. They were . . . a biotech company! A rival biotech company to Agrigene!

That would make a lot of sense, Steven thought as he continued to work on the hypothesis. They move in to the area and buy the farm next door to their competitor; then they manage to get an organic farm accreditation. It would give them the perfect basis for courting public sympathy while causing trouble for Agrigene and screwing up their experimental programme.

'What kind of a civil servant are you exactly?' asked Brown.

'A thirsty one,' replied Steven.

Brown ordered two more drinks and Steven made vague noises about liaising with the new Scottish Parliament over environmental concerns. Inside, he was thinking that this theory about Crawhill might also explain where the protestors were getting the money from for lawyers and independent crop analysis. It didn't explain, however, how they had managed to get organic accreditation so easily or why the crop analysis they'd obtained was so scientifically vague.

'So you're with the MAFF people up here,' said Brown. 'Or are you with the new Scottish Parliament lot?'

'Neither really,' replied Steven. 'I'm here to assess if

anything should cause concern to the Department of the Environment but I understand that MAFF have everything under control.'

'You could have fooled me,' said Brown.

'Why d'you say that?'

'You've just heard the local mood for yourself,' said Brown with a nod to the table behind him. 'The locals are planning civil war by the sound of it and MAFF and the Scottish Executive are sitting on their arses along the road, arguing the legal niceties over who's responsible for what.'

'But they must have had meetings with the community?' said Steven.

'One of their chaps gave a talk to the locals in the village hall saying that they were currently looking into discrepancies in the licensing agreement up at Lane's place. That's the last I heard.'

'The legal wrangle's still going on,' said Steven.

'I wish to God, they'd keep people informed,' said Brown. 'There's nothing rumour likes better than a vacuum.'

Steven silently agreed.

The conversation was over but Brown was delayed in leaving by a man coming in through the doors of the pub and standing there as if about to make an announcement. As if by magic a hush fell on the place and the man in the doorway said, 'The Ferguson boy's dead. Died this morning in St John's Hospital. His mum and dad were with him, poor wee bugger.'

'I thought he was holding his own,' said one man. 'I thought the three of them were.'

'He developed a wound infection on top of everything else and it was just too much for him.'

'Christ, it could hae been Eck,' exclaimed a man at a table near Steven. 'Ah'd better get hame and tell Mary.' With that, he scraped back his chair, got to his feet and left.

'His boy was one of the swimmers,' explained one of the others. 'Makes you think when something like that happens.'

'It's about time they did something about they bloody rats up there. They're all over the bloody place.'

'It's the same all over the country, man. I saw it on breakfast TV. Somethin' to do wi' the weather getting warmer.'

'Bloody global warmin'. If it's no wan thing . . .'

'They're vicious little buggers too. I met the vet in the paper shop this morning and he was saying that he had a woman in last night from Gartside. Her Labrador puppy got himself bitten up by the canal. She was in a right state. If some guy hadn't come along on his bike, the mutt could have been in real trouble. As it was, the guy managed to kill a couple of the buggers and help her get the dog home.'

'I can remember when Meg cornered one in the barn,' said one of the other men, launching into a rat story.

'I'll have to go phone the boy's death in,' whispered Brown at Steven's elbow. 'I'll let you know about Crawhill.'

Steven nodded and found himself alone but not for long. Alex McColl returned, looking less than pleased. 'Couldn't get near Rafferty,' he complained. 'You'd think he'd be looking for all the press coverage he could get right now,' he added.

'Your colleague was just saying that,' said Steven. 'Who stopped you?'

'A couple of guys in suits. They were too polite for minders. Apart from that, they had an IQ bigger than their collar size. When I asked them who they were they told me they were, "Mr Rafferty's business advisers".'

'Everyone's got a fancy title, these days,' said Steven.

'Aye, no one shovels shit these days. It's "excrement relocation officers" we have to deal with. What's been happening here?'

Steven told him about the Ferguson boy's death.

'Well, that gives me something to file, I suppose,' said McColl, looking pleased and getting out his notebook. He missed the look on Steven's face when he said it.

'There's likely to be a pretty weepy funeral too if I'm not mistaken. I'll get a snapper along for some graveside stuff. That should keep the wolf from the door for a bit.'

Steven swallowed hard and reminded himself that he was just here as an observer. Decking a gentleman of the press would not be a good idea, however satisfying it might be in the short term. He decided to leave.

'You've not finished your drink,' pointed out McColl.

'I've had enough.'

# 5

Steven was glad to find that it had stopped raining. He was even more pleased to be out in the fresh air after suffering the thick, tobacco-filled atmosphere of the pub for more than an hour. He decided to walk for a bit to clear his head as well as his lungs, not least because he felt the imminent pressure of a decision having to be made. Macmillan had put the onus on him to decide whether or not there was anything in the Blackbridge situation that Sci-Med should concern itself with and, at this juncture, he wasn't at all sure.

Ideally, he would have liked to talk with both Lane and Rafferty but, from what he'd seen and heard so far, that wouldn't be possible without admitting who he was and openly advertising Sci-Med's interest. Macmillan had been very clear about this being an unofficial look around after being warned off by the minister's man.

Steven wondered if that might be too strong an interpretation of what had passed between Macmillan and the ministry man because Macmillan had a tendency to be hypersensitive about his department's autonomy and had clearly been very angry when he'd told him about it. The official reason given for the 'advice' had been that MAFF had the situation up here well under control so there was no need for Sci-Med to become involved. To him that had sounded perfectly reasonable – even if Macmillan had seen it as interference. But now that he was here on the spot, he could see that this was clearly not the case. As the journalist, Jamie Brown, had pointed out, no clear lead had been given at all by the authorities and anger and suspicion were obviously rife in the village.

The annoying thing from Steven's point of view as an outside observer was that it all seemed so unnecessary. An official telling the community that there might be a problem with the identity of Lane's crop was a prime example of bungling ineptitude. It had been of no help at all and had only fuelled the flames of suspicion. The man should have told them exactly what was being done about it and then told the people that he would get back to them when the matter had been investigated and resolved. Officialdom saying nothing to the press wasn't helping either. It just encouraged the papers in their eternal search for cover-ups and skeletons in cupboards.

None of this, however, meant that Sci-Med had to involve itself in the situation. Even if it should turn out that his impromptu theory about another biotech company getting involved in the purchase of Crawhill should prove to have some substance, Brown would discover this when he investigated a change of ownership. He would, no doubt, expose such a scam ruthlessly in his paper, causing maximum embarrassment to the culprits. Newspapers were good at that sort of thing – probably a lot better than Sci-Med.

It was tempting to report to Macmillan that there was nothing here for Sci-Med to concern itself with any further. Macmillan would be pleased and relieved to hear that and he personally would have a reason to see the back of Blackbridge. He thought it had all the charm of a disease.

As he neared the top of the hill between Crawhill and Peat Ridge, he left the road at the bridge and joined the towpath of the canal to start walking east, continuing to analyse the situation in his head. He had to admit that his desire to be away from this place might be skewing his judgement just a little too much. Maybe he should take some more time to consider objectively, although it was hard to see what more he could do without giving away his true identity as a Sci-Med investigator.

After some thought, he concluded that there was one more thing he could do before reaching a final decision and that was to visit the MAFF lab that had carried out the analysis on the Agrigene crop. Jamie Brown had failed to get anything out of them as a journalist. He could tackle them about their apparent vagueness in his official capacity. The lab was over in Ayrshire on the west side of the country, about seventy miles away from Blackbridge, so asking questions there was not going to ruffle any local feathers.

He felt a bit better now that he had made one firm decision. He would now stay overnight in Edinburgh and drive out to the Ayrshire lab in the morning. He could now relax and enjoy the fresh air and stretching his legs. The wind had got up a little and was helping to blow away the Castle Tavern's legacy of stale tobacco from his hair and clothes.

He could see that the canal towpath defined the southern extremity of Crawhill Farm and, as he rounded a slight bend, he got a good view of Thomas Rafferty's property. As far as he could tell, it wasn't that big: three fields lying fallow, a large barn and a compound in front of the farmhouse containing a variety of farm machinery, most of it coloured yellow. One of the machines was currently being loaded on to an articulated lorry. Steven paused to watch the procedure and admired the skill of the driver manoeuvring it up narrow ramps on to the bed of the lorry. He had no idea what the machine was or for what it would be used but he appreciated why it made sense for farms to hire such large pieces of equipment rather than buy them, particularly as there seemed such a large variety of machines available.

Some of the equipment was clearly designed for spraying so Steven wondered about a conflict of interest with Rafferty's new allegiance to the organic cause. It seemed to underline what he'd picked up in the village about Rafferty being an unlikely recruit to the organic farming crusade. Just out of interest, he would ask Sci-Med to check out the financial health or otherwise of Rafferty's plant hire business.

He was about to turn back when he became aware of there being someone else on the towpath about fifty metres ahead of him. He hadn't noticed the figure earlier because she seemed to be crouching down in the reeds with her back to him. He knew that it was a woman because of her beautiful red hair. Intrigued, he walked on a little further and gave an early indication of his presence by clearing his throat. The woman turned and looked up at him. She was pale-faced and tears were running down her cheeks.

Steven could now see that she had been arranging a small posy of flowers in the reeds and suddenly realised that this must be connected with the boy who had died after his swim in the canal.

'I'm sorry, I didn't mean to intrude,' he said quietly, feeling embarrassed about being there.

'It's all right,' replied the young woman. 'It's silly really. I just thought that I would say my own goodbye to Ian up here. The hospital seemed so strange and foreign. It was as if he wasn't really our Ian at all when he was in there, if you know what I mean? There were always so many other people around.'

Steven looked at her moist eyes. 'I know exactly what you mean,' he said with a conviction that he didn't elaborate on. 'Were you related to Ian?'

'I'm his sister, his big sister.'

'I'm sorry. It was a tragedy.'

'Thirteen years old, knew nothing about life but thought he knew it all.'

'Like all thirteen-year-old boys,' said Steven.

'Exactly,' smiled the woman, who now got to her feet and said, 'I'm Eve Ferguson.'

Steven could now see that she was an attractive woman in her early twenties, her most prominent feature being the cascade of dark red hair falling about her shoulders. From a distance he had thought it dyed. Close up, he could see it was natural. He sensed that she wanted to talk about her brother, another emotion he recognised. He encouraged her with a few gentle questions.

'Ian happened as a bit of a surprise to Mum and Dad,' said Eve. 'They must have thought their family was all finished with we two girls and then along came Ian to be the apple of my Dad's eye. I was already ten when he was born.'

'I bet you and your sister spoiled him rotten,' said Steven.

'Of course,' said Eve, smiling for the first time. 'We used to use him as a doll!'

'Your sister's not with you?'

'She got married last year. She moved away from here. Mum phoned her this morning. She'll be here for the funeral. God knows how we're all going to get through it.'

'You will,' said Steven. 'And then things can start to get better.'

Eve looked at him out of the corner of her eye and said, 'You sound as if you know all about that.'

'My wife,' said Steven. 'Nine months ago.'

'I'm sorry.'

They started to walk back along the towpath together and Steven paused again to look at the loading activity outside the barn on Crawhill.

'You'll be here about this GM crop business?' said Eve.

'Sort of,' replied Steven. 'This is the organic farm to be, isn't it?'

'So I'm told,' replied Eve. 'But it can't be Tom Rafferty that's behind that.'

'Why not?'

'He's just not the sort,' replied Eve. 'Apart from that he hasn't cared about anything that didn't come out a bottle for years. I think that's why Trish left him.'

'His wife?'

'Yes.'

'So who do *you* think is behind the organic farm idea?'

'I've no idea. It really doesn't make much sense but everyone in Blackbridge seems paranoid about something these days. People just don't know what the hell's going on. They're afraid of the day they've never seen.'

'And quite understandable if all they have to go on is rumour and fear of the unknown. I take it you're not overly impressed with the authorities right now?'

'Don't talk to me about "authorities",' said Eve with feeling. 'They're tripping over each other and the more bodies they send in the less it is that gets done. We've got people from the Department of Health, the Ministry of Agriculture, Fisheries and Food, the Ministry of Health and Community Care and the Ministry of Rural Affairs. Sometimes it seems that all that's missing is Poo-Bah and the Lord High Executioner!'

Steven smiled and asked, 'What were these last two ministries again?'

'They're new Scottish ones,' said Eve dismissively.

'You're not a big fan?'

'Of Mel Gibson, you mean?'

Steven laughed and said, 'I can see how he might have had something to do with it all.'

'I'll say! People were seduced by *Braveheart* and all that talk of freedom and self-determination. Rise up and be a nation again! Heady stuff. If Mel's speech had gone, "I will never give up my partially devolved freedom with limited tax raising powers," it might have been closer to the mark. What we've finished up with is 129 self-seeking numpties, duplicating what we already had and at much greater expense. I'm not entirely convinced that all of them can read and write. From what I've seen down at the hotel, all they can really do well is squabble.'

'I'm sorry?' said Steven, failing to pick up the last bit of what Eve had said about the hotel.

'I've been working at the Blackbridge Arms during the summer vacation,' she explained. 'I can't help but hear what's going on. The civil servants have sort of made it their unofficial headquarters.'

'So you've had a first-hand view of democracy in action and government inter-departmental cooperation?'

'Is that what they call it? Most of these bozos are about as much use as Princess Margaret. If one lot says black, the others will say white on principle so in the end nothing gets done. On top of that McKay and Smith are always at each other's throats over executive responsibility.'

'Who?' asked Steven, secretly delighted at all the information he was getting.

'McKay is from Rural Affairs, the Scottish lot; Smith is from MAFF in London. When Smith suggests something, McKay automatically insists that it should be the province of his department, then that balloon, Barclay, pops up . . .'

'Who?'

'Cyril Barclay. He's something to do with Health and Safety. He pops up and says that matters concerning health have priority over them both so any decision should be his. McKay and Smith naturally disagree about this and they start arguing all over again.'

'Meanwhile Rome burns.'

'Quite so. What exactly is your "sort of" involvement in the affair?' asked Eve.

'I'm just an observer of the situation,' replied Steven. Coming as close to the truth as he could. 'My boss asked me to get a feel for what was going on up here. You've been a tremendous help.'

'Maybe I've said too much but, then again, no one told me not to. To the briefcases I'm just a waitress.'

'And what else are you?' asked Steven.

'I'm doing a masters degree in Food Science at Heriot-Watt University.'

Steven smiled and said, 'You probably know more about GM crops than anyone else down there!'

'All they want from me is gin and tonic, so that's what they get,' replied Eve. 'Oh my God . . .'

Steven looked at her to see what had alarmed her. He followed her line of vision to a rat that was swimming across the canal. It disappeared into the undergrowth on the far bank but the look of fear and revulsion stayed on Eve's face as she obviously relived her brother's death.

'Let's go,' said Steven, putting a comforting arm around her and leading her away from the spot.

They walked back down the hill together to where Steven had left his car. 'It was nice meeting you, Eve,' he said as they stopped beside it. 'I'm sorry it wasn't under better circumstances.'

'Yes, I would probably have preferred a moonlit beach in Hawaii to the Blackbridge Canal too,' said Eve with a smile. 'But it was nice meeting you too. Take care.'

'Do you think I could contact you if I have any more questions about local matters?'

Eve looked thoughtful for a moment then she replied, 'Wait until after Ian's funeral.'

'Fair enough.'

Steven drove into Edinburgh and booked into the first large anonymous hotel he came to on the western outskirts. He was hungry; he hadn't eaten since breakfast time so he ordered chicken sandwiches from room service and a bottle of Stella Artois. He set up his laptop computer while he waited and made a modem connection to Sci-Med in London. The only incoming message said that Sci-Med had as yet failed to discover who was paying Thomas Rafferty's legal bills but they would keep working on it. Steven in turn asked them to find out what they could about the current state of Thomas Rafferty's business. He also asked them to find out if any attempt had been made to sell Crawhill Farm and finally he made a general enquiry about Sector One Security, the firm that Lane had brought in to provide protection at Peat Ridge Farm. Reputable or not?

By the time Steven had eaten his sandwiches and drank his beer, he had his reply from London. Rafferty's plant hire business was still solvent but profits had been declining over the last two years. There had been no investment in new machinery at all thanks to a reluctance in the banks to lend to Rafferty whom they saw as a bad risk because of his drinking. As a result of this, many of his machines were getting a reputation for being unreliable through age and lack of proper maintenance. He was still managing to find customers but he'd had to drop the hire price considerably in order to persuade them to take the risk and it was a considerable risk. Farmers often depended on being able to take advantage of windows in the weather. One or two days delay because of mechanical breakdown could have serious consequences.

Crawhill Farm was not currently on the market nor had it been in the recent or even distant past. Lastly, Sector One Security was a reputable firm. It employed the usual motley crew that low wages inevitably decreed but management was good and the guards were subject to competent supervision. There had been no complaints about the firm.

'Well,' thought Steven, 'Nothing to get too excited about there.' He acknowledged receipt of the message and reported that he would be visiting the MAFF lab in Ayrshire on the following day. He asked that Sci-Med warn them of his impending visit, giving an estimated time of arrival of between eleven and twelve.

Steven checked out of his hotel just after nine in the morning and began what was to be a trouble-free journey across the central belt of Scotland. The weather was grey and showery throughout West Lothian and Lanarkshire but blue skies welcomed him to Ayrshire and he pulled into the car park of the government lab at eleven fifteen, after killing some time by stopping for coffee at a hotel on the outskirts of Ayr. He didn't want to arrive early.

The lab was a two-storey concrete building, probably built in the early seventies, Steven thought, its squarish, unimaginative design being offset to a certain extent by the fact that it stood in attractive, well-maintained grounds. He parked in one of two spaces marked for visitors and noted as he got out that the director and several other staff had their own marked places in the car park. He saw this as an indication of the type of lab he was about to enter. Civil service labs were noted for their sense of order; a place for everyone and everyone in their place.

Steven called in at the general office, where he was checked against a list of expected visitors and invited to sign in. After this he was taken to the director's suite on the upper floor by a small woman, wearing a purple suit and who seemed to have some difficulty in walking. Steven guessed at a hip problem. He was introduced to Dr Robert Fildes, a red-faced man in his early fifties who looked more like his image of a jolly farmer than a scientist. The image was currently bolstered by a rather loud tweed jacket.

'How can we help?' asked Fildes. He sounded cultured and intelligent, causing Steven to lay the farmyard image to rest.

'I understand that the lab undertakes private contract work on occasion?' said Steven.

'As much as we can get these days,' smiled Fildes. 'Changed days. Sometimes I wonder if we're a government lab or a pizza parlour.'

'How does this contract business work exactly? I don't see you advertising.'

'No, we don't advertise,' agreed Fildes. 'But our expertise in certain areas is well known. Our staff are usually approached by commercial concerns on an individual basis to carry out work and the lab gets a percentage of the fee. It's all above board.'

'I'm sure,' said Steven. 'So if I want to have, say, some seeds analysed, I would approach a member of the staff here and negotiate directly with him or her?'

'If you happened to know an appropriate member of staff, that is,' agreed Fildes. 'If you didn't, you might approach me as unit director and I could tell you whether or not we had someone with the expertise you required on the staff and put you in touch.'

'I see. Perhaps you could tell me how the contract for this work was handled?' Steven took out a copy of the DNA analysis on the Agrigene crop growing in Robert Lane's field in Blackbridge and pushed it across Fildes' desk.

Fildes put on his reading glasses and read it.

'A direct contact with a member of staff, I seem to remember. Our Dr Millar was approached personally and carried out the work himself.'

'But the report would go out as being an official report from this lab? A government lab report?'

'That's right. That's the way we do things. Contract work is treated no differently to any of the other work we do here. I'm not really with you here. Is something wrong?'

'No, just a routine check,' replied Steven. 'But I'd like a word with Dr Millar, if that's all right with you?'

'I'm afraid that's not possible,' said Fildes. 'Gerald Millar is no longer with us. He took early retirement.'

Steven was taken aback. 'Must have been very recent,' he said.

'Just a few weeks ago.'

'Was this something he'd been planning to do?'

Fildes seemed a little embarrassed. 'No,' he replied. 'It rather took me by surprise as it did everyone else round here.'

'I see,' said Steven slowly. 'Then perhaps you could tell me who commissioned the analysis?'

Fildes took in a deep breath and shook his head. 'That would be a breach of confidence,' he said. 'I'm sure you understand how important that is for the people who contract for our services.'

Steven nodded. 'In normal circumstances,' he said. 'But telling an agent of the Sci-Med Inspectorate is hardly going to constitute a breach of trust. No one else need know about this.'

Fildes looked thoughtful for a moment then said, 'I suspect you have the powers to demand access if I refuse?'

Steven shrugged and said, 'I don't think it should come to that, Director, I just need the name.'

Fildes turned to the computer monitor that sat on the end of his desk and started tapping his keyboard. Steven watched a puzzled look appear on his face. Fildes adjusted his glasses and tapped some more before pursing his lips in annoyance and getting up from his chair. 'If you'll excuse me a moment,' he said, before opening his office door and asking his secretary to fetch something.

There was a wait of about three minutes during which there was a change to small talk about the pleasant nature of the lab's location and how nice it must be to live in Ayrshire.

Instead of coming right into the room, Fildes' secretary opened the door and said, 'Could I have a word please, Director?'

Fildes excused himself and went outside for a moment. Steven heard him raise his voice and say, 'But that's ridiculous,' before all went quiet again. Several minutes passed before Fildes came back into the room. 'I can't begin to tell you how embarrassed I am to have to tell you that we don't appear to have a record of the contract on file,' he said. 'The details weren't entered on the computer and the paperwork doesn't seem to be around either. I can only assume that Dr Millar must have been so preoccupied with his impending retirement that his routine must have been upset.'

Steven smiled but there was little humour in it. He said, 'In that case, I'm afraid I am going to have to ask for Dr Millar's address.'

'To my further embarrassment, I'm not going to be able to help you with that either,' said Fildes. 'Gerald's no longer in the country. He and his wife decided to go and live in South Africa for a while. They have a married son out there I believe, but that's really as much as I know.'

# 6

Steven had to wonder if he was being given the run-around. His only comfort was that Fildes seemed as uncomfortable telling him these things as he was in hearing them.

'Did Dr Millar work alone?' he asked.

'No, he had a Higher Scientific Officer and a couple of more junior people working for him. Perhaps you'd like to speak to them?'

'Maybe just the HSO.'

Fildes picked up the phone and spoke with someone named Roberta. He finished by asking, 'Will it be all right if we come along just now?'

Steven gathered that the answer had been yes when Fildes got up and said, 'If you'd care to come with me.'

Fildes led the way along the corridor outside his room and said, 'I do hope Miss Jackson can help you, otherwise you've had a bit of a journey for nothing, I'm afraid.'

This fact had not escaped Steven's notice. They entered a bright, airy laboratory where a tall, intelligent-looking woman, wearing a lab coat and with her long dark hair tied back in a pony-tail, rose from her bench stool, washed her hands in a basin, equipped with elbow-operated taps, and walked towards them, wearing a friendly smile.

'May I introduce, Miss Roberta Jackson,' said Fildes. 'She was Gerald's HSO. Roberta, this is Dr Steven Dunbar from the Sci-Med Inspectorate. He has some questions to ask you about the work you people do. I'd be grateful if you'd give him all the help you can.'

Steven shook hands with the woman and then said to Fildes, 'I'm sure I've been keeping you back, Director, please feel free to carry on with what you have to do. I'll come and see you before I go.'

Fildes accepted the implied invitation to leave and Steven and Roberta were left alone.

Steven explained to her that he had hoped to have a word with Millar about a DNA analysis he had made. 'But I hear he's no longer with you?'

'He took early retirement. He and Charlotte have gone off to Cape Town to stay with their son and his wife for a while. They had a baby a while back. This will be the first time they've seen their grandchild. It's their first.'

'That's nice,' said Steven.

'Didn't exactly do us any favours though,' said Roberta ruefully. 'Our jobs are all sort of hanging in the balance at the moment. It would have been nice to have had a bit more warning.'

'You didn't know he was planning to retire?'

Roberta shook her head. 'It came right out of the blue. He seemed to make up his mind on the spur of the moment and that was that. Now you see him, now you don't. Hi-ho, Silver, away!'

'I thought early retirement was something offered by management at a time when it was convenient for them to see the back of you,' said Steven. 'From what I've heard, it sounds as if Dr Millar's leaving seems to have turned out pretty inconvenient for all concerned?'

'It certainly is and that was my understanding too,' said Roberta, 'but apparently a member of staff can request early retirement at any time after the age of fifty, whether management likes it or not. The deal you get is not so good that way – you don't get the enhancement to years of service you get if they request it – but the bottom line is that it can be done.'

'Are there many people going to be affected by his going?'

'Three of us are in the firing line, if you'll pardon the pun. It seems likely that the other two will be taken on by other groups – they're junior SOs, so they're relatively cheap in terms of salary and easy to re-train, but I've been here ten years: I'm a bit more expensive and a bit more specialised.'

'I hope something comes along for you,' said Steven.

'Thanks. How can I help you?'

Steven brought out the lab report on the Agrigene crop and showed it to Roberta. 'Does this look familiar to you?' he asked.

Roberta shook here head. 'Not this particular one,' she said. 'I think this must be one that Gerald did himself. Hang on a minute.' She walked over to what appeared to be a very wide, metal filing cabinet and slid out the bottom drawer. She checked the reference number on the report she was still holding and then looked for a match in the drawer. 'Here we are,' she said, pulling out a large sheet of exposed photographic film, attached to a metal hanger by two crocodile clips. The film had small black ladder marks over it in regular columns.

'This is the actual DNA sequence that Dr Millar's report was based on,' said Roberta. 'Did you think there was something wrong with it?'

'No, nothing like that. The DNA comes from an experimental oilseed rape crop being grown over in a place called Blackbridge in West Lothian. Dr Millar reported the presence of three foreign genetic elements in it. The company has a licence for only two.'

'That sounds serious,' said Roberta.

'On the face of it,' said Steven.

'What does that mean?'

'I'm no expert in genetics but "genetic element" doesn't necessarily mean the same thing as gene, does it?'

'I suppose not,' agreed Roberta. 'But it usually does.'

'Exactly, it usually does, so people would read the report as saying that three foreign genes were present instead of two and conclude that it must be a different crop from the one on the licence certificate?'

'I suppose that might well be the case,' agreed Roberta, looking puzzled. 'Is that not what happened here then?'

'Take a look at the foreign elements in the sequence,' said Steven.

'I can't tell what the foreign genes are just by looking at the sequence,' protested Roberta. 'I'd have to compare it with the standard oilseed rape genome and then do a computer search for differences.'

'I've already done that,' said Steven. 'I've highlighted the three foreign sequences on this.' Steven took out his print-out copy of the sequence from his briefcase. 'What would you say about the third one?' he asked. Steven directed her to a highlighted section of the sequence.

'Oh, I recognise that all right,' said Roberta. 'That's a marker, a tetracycline transposon marker, we use it all the time.'

'Not what you would class as a foreign gene, then?'

'Hardly.'

'This is the third genetic element Dr Millar reported as being present in the Agrigene crop.'

'What on earth made him do that?' wondered Roberta.

'That's what I came here to ask him,' said Steven.

'I can see why,' said Roberta with a shrug. 'Frankly, I just can't imagine why he would do something like that and I can certainly see how it might have caused confusion. Did it?'

'It did indeed.'

'But the DNA sequence itself would be an exact match for the one associated with the licence,' said Roberta, seeing immediately what Steven himself had seen at the outset.

'If it had been possible to compare them,' he said, not really wanting to tell Roberta that both copies had gone missing under mysterious circumstances. 'Unfortunately, Dr Millar's report was all the authorities had to go on.'

'But even at that, surely someone must have pointed out that one of these "genetic elements" was just a harmless marker?'

'I'm sure they did – and they're probably still trying to,

but after hearing what the report said in simple terms, nobody wanted to listen to what they thought was a lot of scientific gobbledegook and prevarication from a big bad biotech company. Two elements good, three elements bad, was what they took from the ministry lab report and that was good enough for the opposition to start going doo-lally and demanding that the trial be stopped and the crop destroyed.'

'So what's happening now?'

'The company is putting up a fight. It's resorted to law to block any move to halt the trial or destroy the crop and is now using solicitors to argue their case instead of scientists. Luckily for them the prosecution case is not exactly coherent right now because of some Westminster–Holyrood rivalry.'

'Tell me about it,' said Roberta raising her eyes heavenwards. 'These days I think I have more MPs than I have relations! Still, if they're fighting with each other, they're not doing the rest of us much harm, that's the way I look at it.'

'But administrative paralysis can have its downside,' said Steven, thinking of the current situation in Blackbridge.

'I suppose you're right,' said Roberta. 'But I'm afraid I don't see what I can do to help?'

'No,' agreed Steven. 'This one is down to Dr Millar on his own. You wouldn't know who asked him to perform the DNA analysis on the crop in the first place, would you?' Steven asked.

'I don't think so,' said Roberta thoughtfully. 'We've not had that much contract work recently but I don't think I remember Gerald saying anything at all about this particular one . . .'

'Does the name Thomas Rafferty ring a bell?'

'No.'

'How about McGraw and Littlejohn?' Steven asked, naming Rafferty's solicitors.

Roberta shook her head. 'Afraid not.'

'Well, thanks for your help anyway,' said Steven preparing to leave, 'and I do hope things work out for you.'

'Wait a minute,' said Roberta as an idea came to her. She went back to the filing cabinet where she'd taken the sequence from and had another look at the sheet of film. 'Would you pass me that lens?' she said, indicating to the bench. Steven handed her a magnifying lens of the sort used by jewellers and she used it to examine the upper edge of the film. 'Ah, here we are,' she said. 'We usually write some ID on the film before putting it into the communal developing tank so we know which one is which.' Roberta read the marking out slowly as she deciphered it. 'Oilseed rape . . . Agrigene . . . Peat Ridge . . . Sigma 5 . . . That's it. Mean anything?'

'Some of it,' said Steven. He made a note of it all. 'I'd be grateful if you'd keep our conversation to yourself.'

Roberta smiled and said, 'Of course.'

Steven called in at Fildes' office on the way out to thank him for his help. He found him apologetic about not having been more so. 'Was Roberta able to help you at all?' he asked. Steven thought the man seemed anxious.

'Not really, but it was just a case of checking up on a few details. Nothing to worry about.'

'So we'll not be getting a roasting over the stuff that should have been on file?' asked Fildes. He said it half jokingly but Steven could see that he was genuinely worried.

94

'I can quite understand how it must have happened,' he said reassuringly. 'Dr Millar must have had a lot on his mind, not least the prospect of seeing his first grandson. Let's say, if you're prepared to forget about my visit, so am I.'

Fildes let out his breath in a controlled manner but it still came across to Steven as an indication of relief.

'That's very understanding of you,' said Fildes. 'Can I offer you some lunch?'

'I'd best be getting back.'

Just what the hell was going on? Steven wondered as he got into his car and clunked the door shut. First, both copies of the licensed sequence go missing and then a misleading (deliberately?) report is put out by a government scientist who then takes early retirement and disappears to South Africa without leaving anything on file about the contract.

Shit! This was not what he had wanted to hear at all. He had come to Ayrshire to listen to apologies from a scientist who had been a bit vague and thoughtless in the wording of his report, a scientist who would be all too keen to put the record straight and who would be offering to help in any way he could. Instead, he was left with a mess of doubts, suspicions and unanswered questions.

Steven decided that he was hungry after all. His initial plan to drive back to the east was put on hold while he pulled into the hotel he had visited earlier for coffee and opted for a smoked trout salad and a beer. The food was good, as was the beer, but neither did much to cheer him because he now recognised that he would have to report back to Macmillan that he did, in fact, think there was something suspicious going on in Blackbridge, something that Sci-Med *should* concern itself with. At this moment he did not know exactly what it was but he now believed that he should try to find out. One thing was unfortunately certain; he would not be seeing the back of Blackbridge just yet.

Millar's sudden decision to go for early retirement, and his going off to South Africa with his wife to see a first grandchild they had not seen before, suggested strongly that the man had come into some money. If they hadn't already seen their first grandchild, it was probably because they couldn't afford the trip. Now, suddenly, they could. Coincidence? Well, it could be that Millar might have won the lottery or inherited some money or an endowment policy might have matured, Steven recognised, but all the same, the possibility that he had been paid to deliberately supply a misleading report was his current personal favourite in the explanation stakes.

He then thought about the markings on the DNA sequence film – information that he'd avoided showing any reaction to in Roberta's presence. Everything was obvious with the exception of the name Sigma 5. That could be important. It could even be the name of the company that had commissioned the misleading report, knowing that it would go out on official MAFF headed paper and appear utterly convincing.

Steven wondered on the drive back from Ayrshire about how he was going to tell Macmillan of his decision. Normally, when the man on the ground decided that there was something for Sci-Med to get involved in, he would send a coded computer message, indicating that a fully-fledged investigation had now begun. This automatically triggered a number of responses at Sci-Med in London. Two credit card accounts would be activated to ensure that the investigator had access to all the funds he might need. The local police in his operating area would be informed by the Home Office that a Sci-Med inspector was in the area and they would be requested to cooperate fully with him. All further communication between the investigator and Sci-Med would be carried out using encrypted computer messaging and a special phone number, manned day and night. In addition to this, the man on the ground would have access to a wide range of back-up services and even the supply of a weapon should he deem it necessary, although Steven hardly thought this would apply in this case. In exchange for all this unquestioning support the inspector must have what Macmillan termed succinctly as, 'a bloody good reason' for calling a code red.

What Steven had to decide now was should he just call the code or should he talk to Macmillan first to discuss the 'warning off' aspect of the Blackbridge situation? On a more mundane level he also had to decide where he was going to stay because he certainly didn't want to stay in Blackbridge itself. It only had one hotel and he would be in too close proximity to officialdom because, as Eve Ferguson had already told him, the place was full of squabbling officials.

Steven decided against the hotel where he had spent the previous night simply because he didn't like it. It had been all right for one night but he had no idea at this stage how long he was going to be working on the case. He wanted something different from a concrete tower block of identical cells.

He knew where his train of thought was taking him and felt a bit apprehensive over it. He and Lisa had come to a concert at the Edinburgh Festival the year before she died and they had stayed over at a small hotel in the southwest of the city. He might be courting the ghosts of times past but he decided that he was going to go there. Seeking association with times past hadn't worked out too well in the past but he still felt that he wanted to do it.

In the immediate weeks after Lisa's death he had gone to all the places that had meant so much to them during their time together in the hope of recapturing a feeling of closeness to her, but this had failed miserably. All he had found in these places and time after time, was a mind-numbing sense of loneliness. He was acutely aware of the possibility of this happening again but then again, he reasoned, things just might be different now that more time had passed?

Steven was in Edinburgh by four thirty and had checked in to the Grange Hotel in the quiet well-heeled southwest of the city by five. He didn't have the same room as last time but the view from the window was the same. He stood there, looking out and remembering Lisa pointing out the wishing well at the foot of the garden and saying that they must visit it before they left.

So far so good, he didn't fill up with feelings of maudlin sentimentality and he wasn't as yet crushed by sadness and loneliness. He looked at the well for a few moments, remembering their laughter when they'd discovered on the morning of their departure that it wasn't a real well at all but a garden 'feature'. He smiled fondly before turning away to call Macmillan at Sci-Med.

'I feared you might phone,' said Macmillan. 'You're going to tell me that we should take it on?'

'I do think something smells bad in the Blackbridge situation,' agreed Steven.

'Are you absolutely sure?'

'I can't be a hundred per cent certain because I've had to be discreet in terms of who I've spoken to in the village, but the situation is a long way from being under control. Officials are running around like headless chickens and the opponents of GM crops are on the verge of taking matters into their own hands.'

'Even at that, it sounds like a matter for the police, not us,' said Macmillan. 'What exactly is our interest?'

'The opposition has been encouraged to believe that right is on their side. They've been told that the crop growing on Peat Ridge Farm is not the one the company was licensed for but a different one containing more foreign genes. Personally, I think it is the same crop but some trouble-making third party with an alternative agenda has commissioned a deliberately misleading report, knowing full well that "misunderstandings" would arise.' Steven told Macmillan about Millar and his sudden desire to give up work and visit South Africa.

'Hell and damnation,' said Macmillan.

'A report, coming from that particular lab, would have the official stamp of ministry approval on it. I think this is why Agrigene feel so aggrieved. You don't normally expect a government report to be deliberately misleading.'

'So you think Sci-Med should find out who this third party is?' said Macmillan.

'They've caused a lot of trouble by their actions and it

could get worse. People could get seriously hurt if this thing is not sorted out soon and it doesn't look like the relevant authorities – and there seem to be plenty of them – are making much of a fist of it. It seems to be a case of internecine strife all the way.'

'Mmm,' said Macmillan. 'I'm not sure I like the idea of Sci-Med picking up such a political hot potato. We could get our fingers badly burned.'

'Up to you,' said Steven, sensing his director's reluctance.

There was a long pause before Steven added, 'You obviously have doubts about us taking it on.'

'To be quite honest, I was thinking that *Sir* John Macmillan had rather a nice ring to it. I've recently been led to believe that this might actually become a reality in the New Year's honours list. Eleanor would be so pleased.'

'But if you should happen to rock the boat at this particular juncture . . .'

'Quite so.'

'You're calling the shots,' said Steven.

'No, you are,' said Macmillan abruptly. 'Notify in the usual way if you're quite sure.' He put the phone down.

Steven looked at the receiver, eyes wide in astonishment. Macmillan had dumped the whole thing in his lap, including his own prospects of a knighthood when all was said and done. 'Well, thank you, *Herr Direktor*,' he murmured. 'Thanks a million.'

Steven went back over to the window and looked out at the lawn. Did one biotech company playing some dirty trick on another biotech company really matter that much in the great scheme of things? he wondered. Was the possibility of a government scientist taking a backhander for being deliberately vague about a lab report such a big deal? After all, it wasn't as if the man had actually lied or falsified the report, he had just . . . nurtured a misunderstanding. Was any of it really that important?

Steven turned away from the window and opened up his laptop slowly. He connected the modem link to the phone socket, inserting the plug with an air of finality. 'Damned right is,' he muttered. He typed in the message, BLACKBRIDGE RED and hovered over the send button for a moment before adding, 'sorry'. A few minutes later he had the reply, BLACKBRIDGE GREEN, signifying that Sci-Med had understood and agreed that he was now fully operational. There was a codicil from Macmillan. It said, 'No reason to be sorry. I'd have sacked you if you'd done anything else. Good luck.'

The dye was cast. Steven took a shower, changed his clothes and went downstairs to have a drink in the bar. One of the staff thought he recognised him and asked politely if he had stayed there before. Rather than get involved in an unwanted conversation about the circumstances of his last visit, Steven said not. He had dinner in the conservatory restaurant, as he and Lisa had done before, and tried to remember as much about the details of that night as he possibly could. What Lisa had been wearing, what they had talked about, what they'd eaten, the wine they'd drank, whether they'd had one cup of coffee after or several. He remembered the mock argument over the last piece of tablet given out with their coffee. Lisa had won. Nothing was too trivial to ponder. He didn't notice any of the other diners around him and the staff scarcely registered. To them he was a man preoccupied and, happily, they respected that.

When the exorcism was over, for that's what he hoped it might be, Steven signed the bill and returned upstairs feeling much better about things. The gamble had paid off. For the first time since Lisa's death, thinking about her had brought him happy memories instead of feelings of pain and sadness. He felt much stronger because of it. He'd passed another milestone on the road to full recovery.

He shut the room door and lay down on the bed, looking up at the ceiling, thinking about what might lie ahead. The investigation was going to begin in earnest in the morning so he had to decide what he was going to do and in what order he was going to do it. He saw speaking with Ronald Lane and Thomas Rafferty as priorities. Ideally, he would have liked to have interviewed them together but he supposed that that would be out of the question, considering the current level of animosity between them. He would also have to speak to the local police at some point to find out how they viewed the situation and to find out what level of understanding they had of the scientific element of the problem. Finally he wanted to know a bit more about what officialdom was doing about all of this. He would pay a visit to the Blackbridge Arms.

As soon as Sci-Med had given him his encryption codes for the computer he would seek information about Sigma 5 and also about recent transactions into and out of Dr Gerald Millar's bank account, including details about his early retirement package. For that, Sci-Med would seek the cooperation of the Inland Revenue Service.

Steven watched the Scottish news on the television in his room. There was an item on the Scottish Parliament, which appeared to have been bedevilled with controversy since its inception, according to the reporter. Steven paid close attention. He felt he needed to know more about the Scottish Parliament. From what Eve Ferguson had told him, this kind of friction, albeit at a lower level, was proving to be a major stumbling block in Blackbridge. This requirement, he decided, was going to take care of his evening. He connected his laptop to the Internet via Netscape and sought out information on the Scottish Parliament. He was pleased to find that it had its own website and that it opened by declaring its commitment to openness and accountability.

'Just what I like to hear, chaps,' he murmured.

# 7

Steven was once more stopped by security men at the entrance to the track leading up to Peat Ridge Farm.

'I want to speak to Mr Lane,' he said to the uniformed man who had waved him down.

'No press. On your way!'

'I'm not press.' Steven showed his ID. The guard frowned and showed it to his partner who read it and then pulled out his mobile phone. Steven watched him read from his ID and wait for a response. It came with the return of his ID and a wave of the hand that he should proceed.

There was a Land Rover and a dark-green Jaguar S-type saloon parked outside the farmhouse. Steven glanced admiringly at the Jag as he walked up to the door, noting in passing that it had been bought in Norwich and had a personalised number plate.

The door was opened by a small woman in her sixties with round shoulders and wearing a floral tabard over a pink, fluffy jumper and brown skirt: she had a feather duster in her hand, which she held up in her right hand like a fairy wand. 'Yes?'

'It's all right, Mrs Fraser, let him in,' said a voice with a South African accent from somewhere behind her before Steven could say anything.

Steven entered, taking great care to wipe his feet in the presence of the person who did the cleaning and looked to Mrs Fraser for directions.

'You'll find Mr Lane in there,' she said, pointing to the left with her duster.

Steven walked towards the room and found the door ajar. He knocked quietly and got a brusque, 'Come!' in response. There were two men in the room. Neither got up when he entered.

'What d'you want?' asked the one with the South African accent whom Steven took to be Lane, unless the other one, who hadn't yet spoken, should also turn out to be South African.

'Mr Lane?' asked Steven.

'Yes, what d'you want?'

'I'd like to ask you some questions about your GM crop.'

Lane turned to his companion and said sarcastically, 'Did you hear that Phil? A man from the government wants to ask us some questions about our crop. How novel. May I suggest you ask your many colleagues who've beaten a path to my door wanting to do exactly the same thing or better still, put your questions to our solicitors,' said Lane coldly. 'Now, get out.'

'I'd rather put them to you, Mr Lane,' said Steven evenly.

'I said to get out, pally,' Lane repeated menacingly, looking over his glasses at Steven to emphasise the point.

Steven now understood why Lane wasn't exactly Mr Popular in the village. He said, 'Mr Lane, I am empowered by the Sci-Med Inspectorate to ask you anything I feel may be relevant to my investigation. Whether we do it here or at a police station or in the prison cell you will certainly end up in if you persist in obstructing me, I leave up to you. Now, shall we start again . . . pally?'

'I hope you're not bluffing, my friend,' said Lane, but a degree of uncertainty had crept into his voice.

'I'm definitely not bluffing,' Steven assured him with a level gaze.

'What exactly are you investigating?' asked the other man who obviously thought the time right to intercede. He spoke with an English accent.

'And you are?' asked Steven.

'Phillip Grimble, technical manager of Agrigene Bio-technology. It's our crop that Mr Lane is growing.'

'At the moment, I'm investigating your difficulty in convincing people that you should keep your licence, Mr Grimble.'

'You mean you're on our side?' exclaimed Lane, looking astonished.

'I didn't say that and I don't want to be on anybody's side but, from what I've learned so far, you do seem to be subject to certain misunderstandings over what you have in the fields out there.'

'Misunderstandings?' snorted Lane. 'It's a bloody set-up. Some bastard is out to fuck us up big time.'

'Why would anyone want to do that?' asked Steven.

'Christ knows. None of it makes any sense to me. The whole thing is just plain bloody crazy. We do everything by the book, jump through all the hoops, hop over all the hurdles, get all the permissions and then they turn round and say we're not really licensed because some clown in a lab coat can't tell his arse from a hole in the wall.'

'If I understand it correctly, your crop is oilseed rape that's been genetically altered to make it resistant to herbicides?'

'That's right,' agreed Grimble. 'It can withstand the action of glyphosphate and glufosinate weedkillers so these agents can be used to keep down weeds in the fields it's growing in. They're much more effective than the weed-killers that farmers are normally obliged to use so better yields can be expected in the long run.'

'From what I've read, you're not the only biotech company who's come up with this idea, are you?'

'No, of course not, but we don't pretend to be. There are quite a few companies who are going down that road. It makes a lot of sense.'

'Would these other companies have something to gain by discrediting your trial?'

'It's possible I suppose,' Grimble agreed with an un-certain shrug, 'but these guys are reputable companies, big names in the industry. They couldn't afford to get involved in anything like that. It would be a clear case of industrial sabotage. Apart from that, there's plenty of room for all of us in the market once we get our crops through the trials. As I see it, it's the media we have to worry about, not commercial opposition. They're responsible for all the scare stories surrounding our work.'

'Apart from that, pally, the "misunderstanding" started with a lab report that came from a *government* lab, not from any private source,' said Lane.

'Government labs carry out contract work for private companies and even individuals,' snapped Steven, immediately regretting that he'd said it. Lane's smugness had got his back up.

Lane's face lit up. 'Are you suggesting that someone in a government lab could have set us up at the request of a third party?' he asked.

'I'm not saying anything of the sort. I just have to consider all the possibilities,' said Steven.

'I didn't know government labs took contract work,' said Grimble.

'Neither did I,' agreed Lane who was clearly intrigued by this revelation. 'This is all beginning to make some kind of sense.'

'Don't read too much into it,' said Steven.

'Maybe the same person made sure the licence copy of the sequence went missing too?' said Lane, getting his teeth into this new line of thought. 'And maybe the same person arranged for the break-in at our solicitors when our copy went missing? Maybe you've been underestimating your competitors, Phil? Maybe they're not all as moral as you are, my friend.'

Grimble shrugged uncomfortably. 'I really can't see these guys doing something so underhand,' he said.

'Someone probably said that once about British Airways,' said Lane. 'Ask Richard Branson what he thinks.'

'Who are your main competitors in this field?' asked Steven.

'Let's see now,' said Grimble thoughtfully. He started to reel off a list of companies. Steven noted that the name Sigma was not among them.

'So where do we go from here?' asked Lane when Grimble had finished. 'What do we do now?'

'Nothing,' said Steven. 'Just sit tight.'

'Do you realise how much security is costing us?' exclaimed Lane. 'While that bunch of pen-pushers down at the Blackbridge Arms sit contemplating their navels and arguing about how many angels can balance on the head of a pin – always assuming that they can agree on whether it's a Scottish or an English pin?'

'It must be very frustrating for you,' said Steven. 'But try to look on the bright side: your crop is still in the field and it's still growing.'

'But for how much longer?' said Lane. 'These clods down in the village have already had a go at us. They've obviously been told that we're growing the crop from hell up here and there doesn't seem to be anyone in authority to disillusion them. If any of them wakes up with a headache, it's not the eight pints they had the night before at the Castle Tavern, oh no, it's down to Lane's crop and all these nasty genes in the air. We're the cause of everything from housemaid's knee to pre-menstrual tension round here!'

'I'm sure the police are aware of the situation,' said Steven. 'They'll keep an eye on things, make sure they don't get out of hand.'

'I wish I had your faith,' said Lane. 'But the police aren't going to alienate the whole community by paying us too much attention. They'll find some reason for not being around at the critical time. You mark my words, pally. Police forces work in the interest of those who pay them.'

'Where do you see Thomas Rafferty and Crawhill Farm fitting into the great scheme of things?' asked Steven.

'Rafferty?' exclaimed Lane with obvious distaste. 'The people's champion? It'll take more than a few organic carrots to save that clown's liver from an early grave. You can't tell me this organic thing is Rafferty's idea. Somebody's working him from behind.'

'Someone with influence,' added Grimble. 'My people checked the area out thoroughly before we applied for permission to grow our crop here. There was absolutely no mention of an organic farm in the offing at that time. Crawhill got its accreditation after we got our licence.'

'I suspect many of the villagers might suggest that there was no hint of a GM crop in the fields up here either,' said Steven.

'We didn't advertise it publicly for obvious reasons,' conceded Grimble. 'Do you blame us?'

'I'm just trying to keep an open mind. You don't think it possible that Rafferty, or whoever was behind the application, didn't know that the Peat Ridge crop was GM when they applied for accreditation?'

'That's not my recollection of events,' snapped Lane. 'It was some weeks after the initial hue and cry that Rafferty joined the rabble with his organic farm story and lawyers started appearing on every street corner.'

Steven nodded and said, 'Well, thank you for your help, gentlemen. I'll be in touch.'

Steven thought he would visit the police before going to see Thomas Rafferty. This involved a drive out to the town of Livingston, one of Scotland's new towns, sited between Edinburgh and Glasgow, where he drove around in a concrete maze for a while before eventually finding police headquarters, the main station for the area that included

Blackbridge. He found that the desk sergeant was apparently expecting him and took from this that Sci-Med had done their job well. He was informed that Chief Inspector Brewer was to be his contact and was shown to his office.

Brewer turned out to be a tall, thickset man in his mid to late forties, with a shock of wiry grey hair and a bulbous nose, which he was blowing when Steven entered. 'Bloody hay fever,' he complained, crumpling the used tissues and throwing them in the wicker basket by his desk. Steven noted that it was more than three-quarters full. 'What can we do for the science police?'

Steven told him that he was there to take a look at the general situation in Blackbridge and, in particular, the ongoing spat over the GM crop on Peat Ridge Farm.

'Oh aye,' said the policeman. 'It's become a case of "too many cooks", if you ask me. The civil servants and lawyers can't make up their minds over who's in the right and who's in the wrong so my lads have been left standing in the middle, dealing with the angry locals who are making up their own stories.'

'That's largely my view of the situation too,' agreed Steven. 'I heard there was an arson attempt the other night?'

Brewer nodded and said, 'Luckily, the local vet got wind of it and called us in time. We got there before the buggers could do any real damage but they had enough petrol between them to run two cars at Le Mans.'

'Local?'

'The usual suspects. They were warned in no uncertain terms that if there was any repeat of that kind of nonsense they'd be for the high jump.'

'Do any good?'

'Shouldn't think so. They think they've got a just case and that always means trouble. Believe me, there's nothing worse than a tearaway who's been given what he sees as a good reason to play Robin bloody Hood. As I see it, the only way to put an end to all this nonsense is for the men in suits to make some firm decisions and quickly. By God, there are enough of them.'

'So I hear,' said Steven. 'What about the main players on the ground, Lane and Rafferty?'

'Lane is an abrasive pain in the arse, which isn't helping the situation any but he seldom puts a foot wrong in terms of legality and he certainly knows his rights. Rafferty is generally thought of as a harmless waster, popular with the locals because he's one of them and always ready to stand his hand in the boozer where he used to spend most of his time and money. He hasn't been going there so much in the past few weeks. His wife left him a short while back so maybe he's turning over a new leaf with this organic farm thing. Trying to get her back, maybe?'

This was a new slant on things, thought Steven.

'Beats me why they can't resolve this GM situation,' said Brewer. 'If a government lab says the crop in Lane's field is not the one they were licensed for then surely that's an end to the matter. The crop should be destroyed and the company responsible punished with the full weight of the law, considering just how much hassle they've caused round here. But just because Lane and his partner start hiring a few lawyers and mouthing off about "a set-up", the suits start shitting themselves and passing the buck around like it was radioactive.'

'That's where I come in,' said Steven. 'The problem with the crop analysis is that certain key bits of evidence have gone missing, as has the scientist who performed the tests. That's what's making the legal position a bit tricky, a grey area, you might say.'

'And there's nothing lawyers like better than grey areas,' said Brewer. 'They're usually stuffed full of new BMWs and holidays in the Bahamas.'

'Spot on,' agreed Steven. 'Left to lawyers, this could run and run.'

'Does that mean we just have to grin and bear it?' asked Brewer.

'Not if I can help it,' said Steven. 'There's a third player in all of this. I don't know who as yet and I'm not at all sure why but I'm going to do my level best to find out.'

'I don't think I understand what a "third player" could hope to get out of the situation,' said Brewer.

'I'm not sure I do either,' confessed Steven. 'I thought industrial espionage might be the front runner with one of Agrigene's competitors trying to set them up in order to make life difficult but, after talking to Agrigene's technical manager, I'm not so sure any more. There's not enough to be gained.'

'But you obviously do think that the company is being set up in some way, don't you?' asked Brewer.

'I think public opinion is being orchestrated against them by people who know exactly what they are doing.'

'But what about the government report on the crop in Lane's fields? I'm told it clearly showed that it wasn't the one they were given permission to grow.'

'Out of interest, who told you that?' asked Steven.

Brewer shrugged and said, 'A bloke from the ministry talked to the residents of Blackbridge. I was in attendance. He said that there was a problem with the identity of the crop on Peat Ridge Farm and they were looking into it. One of the residents pressed him on the nature of the problem and he said that it contained three foreign genes instead of two. Simple as that.'

'That was a misunderstanding,' said Steven.

'That's what the bloke from the company said but then he would, wouldn't he?' said Brewer.

'Actually, he's quite right,' said Steven. 'But I suspect no one wanted to hear the company's side of things?'

'I suppose not,' agreed Brewer. 'You can't expect the man in the street to understand complex scientific arguments or even want to, but if a government lab said that there were three foreign genes present when there should only have been two, then that's easily understood and all he needs to know. If it wasn't for the fact that the civil servants are all at each other's throats that crop would be under a destruction order by now and we'd no longer be sitting on a powder keg.'

'And if Agrigene should turn out to be innocent of any wrongdoing, like I think they are?'

'Then that's a matter for them and the government to sort out, not the villagers or the police. A clear statement from above would be nice – any clear statement right now.'

Steven left police headquarters, having been assured by Brewer that assistance would be on hand at any time should he need it. He drove back over to Blackbridge and along the track leading to Crawhill Farm. The farmhouse was a traditional, stone-built affair without frills or features. It was pretty much what you'd see if you asked a five-year-old

114

to draw you a house. Steven knocked loudly on the front door. It was answered by a smartly dressed man, wearing a dark suit, immaculate white shirt and striped tie, who looked him up and down before saying, 'Yes?'

'I wonder if I might have a few words with Mr Rafferty?' said Steven.

'Mr Rafferty isn't giving interviews.'

Steven held out his ID, which the man examined carefully before looking at Steven thoughtfully and saying, 'Wait here a moment.' He left Steven standing on the doorstep while he disappeared inside.

Steven got tired of just standing there so he took a stroll about the yard. He found a man carrying out repairs on a combine harvester there and said, 'Nice day.'

'No' bad,' replied the man. 'What's your business then?'

'I'm here to see Mr Rafferty.'

The man looked him over before saying, 'Another civil servant. Right?'

'Sort of.'

'We'll soon have one each around here. What's your particular bag?'

'Environment,' said Steven.

'Environment? About time you buggers did something about the rat problem then. My laddie's lying in St Johns with Weil's Disease thanks to these bastards. They're all over the place.'

'I heard about that,' said Steven, now remembering Macmillan telling him that one of the boy's fathers worked on Crawhill Farm. He diplomatically didn't point out that swimming in stagnant water where rats might be present was not the brightest thing to do at any time.

'Maybe you buggers could go up the canal and start beating the bastards to death with your umbrellas and briefcases!'

Steven smiled and said, 'It's a thought and I've heard worse suggestions.'

The man broke into a smile too, approving of Steven's response. 'Nae offence like.'

'None taken.'

Steven saw the man who'd opened the door to him coming towards him. He was now accompanied by another man, also smartly dressed.

'I got tired waiting,' said Steven by way of explanation.

'Sorry about that. Mr Rafferty will see you now. Would you mind if we were present?'

'Who are you?' asked Steven as he was ushered inside the house.

'I'm Charles Childs, this is Martin Leadbetter. We're business associates of Mr Rafferty.'

Steven waited until Childs had led the way into the farmhouse kitchen and invited him to sit before asking exactly what business they were in.

'We're venture capitalists,' replied Childs.

'Venture capitalists?' exclaimed Steven. He hadn't reckoned on venture capital going into something like farming. Biotechnology, on the other hand, would be quite another matter.

Childs took his surprise as an invitation to explain unnecessarily what venture capital was. 'We're constantly on the lookout for good business opportunities to recommend to our principals. That's why we're here. We have the investment capital and Mr Rafferty has the ideal farm for investment from our point of view. The demand for organically grown produce is growing all the time.'

'And judging by the price they charge for it in supermarkets, you could well be on to a good thing,' said Steven, hoping to relax the atmosphere. People were always more inclined to let things slip out when they felt secure.

Childs was pleased at his response and smiled. 'Coffee?' he asked.

'Please,' replied Steven. 'I expected Mr Rafferty to be here?'

'He was on the telephone. I'll just go fetch him,' explained Leadbetter.

Childs had just put a large cafetière down in the middle of the table when Leadbetter returned with Rafferty. 'Sorry about that,' said Rafferty. 'I had to call the vet about my dog. He's sick again.' He stretched out his hand and said, 'Tom Rafferty, what can I do for you?'

Steven knew from the Sci-Med file that Rafferty was forty-eight. He looked younger thanks to a shock of curly red hair. He wore jeans, carpet slippers and a checked shirt, open at the collar to reveal a gold chain.

'Good of you to see me, Mr Rafferty. I'm Steven Dunbar from the Sci-Med Inspectorate in London. I'd like to ask you a few questions.'

'Fire away,' said Rafferty, helping himself to coffee. Childs had already filled the other cups on the table.

'Have you always had an interest in organic farming?'

'Can't say I have,' replied Rafferty, a bit unsurely.

'So what made you apply for accreditation?'

'A business proposition from these gentlemen.'

Steven admired Rafferty's apparent honesty. 'Does this

mean that you intend to sell the farm or at least take on business partners?' he asked.

'No, definitely not,' said Rafferty abruptly. 'I'm keeping the farm. It's mine and it stays that way. I have to keep it.'

'Have to?' asked Steven, puzzled at Rafferty's strong reaction to his question. The man suddenly looked very vulnerable.

Rafferty looked at Childs first and then directly at Steven. 'Trish, my wife, left me. She had good reason to. If I show her that I've turned over a new leaf and can make Crawhill a going concern again, I think she'll come back to me.'

Steven got the impression that Rafferty had rehearsed what he'd just said. He said, 'But you've got a plant hire business. I thought it was doing quite well?'

'Not that well. The machines are getting old. They need a lot of attention. Trish always said it was lazy money. She never liked that.'

'I see,' said Steven. 'So how exactly does your business arrangement with these gentlemen work?'

'They put up the finance for the change-over and subsidise the farm until it's up and running. When I start to make a profit they'll get their money back and a handsome return on their investment.'

'What about the plant hire business?'

'I'm not sure.'

'I see. You're taking a bit of a risk aren't you?'

'I want Trish back,' said Rafferty.

Christ, I know the feeling, thought Steven, suddenly feeling sorry for Rafferty. At least in Rafferty's case it was possible.

'I don't really think there's much risk involved,' said Childs. 'Organic produce is a winner.'

Steven nodded but inside he was thinking that this was a strange thing for a venture capitalist to say. Surely the whole point of venture capital enterprise was to deliberately seek out and invest in high-risk projects with a view to getting really big returns. When all was said and done, high street banks would be happy to invest in sure-fire winners and wouldn't demand nearly so much in return. He kept this, however, to himself. 'How far along the road have you come to getting your organic farm off the ground?' he asked Rafferty.

'Lane's GM crop is holding things up.'

'You didn't know about that when you applied for accreditation?'

'Of course not. The bastard kept it a secret from the whole village, didn't he?'

'Mr Lane says you were aware of it.'

'Bullshit.'

'The application was made in good faith,' said Childs.

'If you say so. Was it you who contracted for an analysis of the crop on Peat Ridge Farm?' Steven asked.

'Me?' exclaimed Rafferty. 'Of course not, that's an official government lab analysis.'

'So where did the report come from?'

'Our lawyers, McGraw and Littlejohn, got a copy.'

'How?'

'I've no bloody idea. I suppose someone figured out what Lane and that bloody company he's in cahoots with were up to and sent them a copy to help with our protest.'

'That's our understanding too,' said Childs.

'Does your venture capital company have a name, Mr Childs?' Steven asked.

'We're not really a company as such,' replied Childs with what he believed to be a disarming smile. 'Just a group of wealthy individuals who like a challenge.'

Steven stared at him until he felt compelled to add, 'However, if you should need to ask anything you can use any of these numbers.' He reached into his inside pocket and pulled out a business card, which he handed over.

Steven looked at it. Pentangle Venture, it said. The phone and fax numbers had a London code. 'Thank you, gentlemen. You've been most helpful.'

# 8

Steven stopped for a moment to speak to the man in the yard he'd talked to earlier. This time, he was crossing the yard carrying a can of fuel oil. 'I hope your son gets better soon,' said Steven.

'Cheers,' said the man. 'Don't forget to tell the briefcases to start swinging at these rats.'

'I'm on my way there now,' smiled Steven. 'I might just put your idea to them.'

'A hard day's work wid kill the buggers.'

At that moment an unearthly howl interrupted the conversation. 'What the hell was that?' asked Steven.

'Just Khan,' said the man. 'Tom Rafferty's dog. I think he's going to have to get him put down or maybe a part in a Hammer movie!'

'He said his dog was sick,' remembered Steven. 'What's the problem?'

'If it was human, he would have been banged up as a psychopath long ago and, if anything, he's been getting worse of late. Tom's had him for years. Christ knows what he sees in him. He scares the shit out of everyone else. Mind you, maybe that's the reason!'

'I think Mr Rafferty said something about phoning the vet,' said Steven.

'He scares the shit out of the vet too!'

The howl went up again and Steven said, 'Right, I'm off.'

He changed his mind about going directly over to the Blackbridge Arms. He felt that he needed to walk for a bit and do some thinking. He didn't want to tramp round the depressing streets of Blackbridge so he opted once more for the canal towpath, this time heading west along the southern edge of Peat Ridge Farm. He paused for a moment to look at the golden flowers of the oilseed rape crop in the fields, thinking that it looked exactly the same as any other oilseed rape he'd ever seen but then, as he reminded himself, there was no reason why it shouldn't. It made him reflect that people, including himself, tended to associate genetic alteration with physical change. In fact, they were happier when this was the case because you knew where you were with something you could see. Knowing that the genetic material of this crop had been altered in some *invisible* way put it in the same league as other things you couldn't see, like viruses or bacteria or poison. He moved on when he became aware of a patrolling security guard regarding him suspiciously and then start to move towards him.

He had now spoken to both the main parties in the current dispute. Ronald Lane was an unpleasant, abrasive individual, capable of being devious and opportunist, he had no doubt, but he was the kind who took pride in doing so within the rules of the game. There were a lot of businessmen like that. They saw it as sailing close to the wind and it gave them a buzz. Thomas Rafferty, on the other hand, was not nearly so well educated or accomplished as Lane but could probably be just as devious, given the chance. The villagers, by all accounts, saw him as a bit of a rogue, a man who drank too much and who didn't have too much liking for hard work, but this morning he had seen a man who had lost his wife and who appeared to want her back desperately. To this end, he seemed prepared to change, maybe even start out on a whole new course in life with the organic farming venture. Could this particular leopard really change his spots? he wondered or was not the road to hell paved with good intentions?

The players behind the two principals were very different characters. Phillip Grimble, the technical director of Agrigene, seemed a thoroughly decent individual who had been reluctant to even consider the company's competitors stooping to skulduggery. This could have been an act, of course. Coming across as a thoroughly decent individual was a prime requisite for any successful confidence trickster, but he didn't think that was the case. Childs and Leadbetter warranted more suspicion. Venture capitalists getting into organic farming? Backing a man like Tom Rafferty? Even for people who liked a challenge, Rafferty struck him as one hell of a risk to take on for the sake of a few fields of vegetables.

On the other hand, Pentangle had not actually put their money where their mouth was to any great extent. They had not purchased a share in Crawhill, although he conceded that that might have been down to Rafferty refusing them one. Rafferty had reacted quite strongly when asked if he had sold the farm or any part of it. At the moment, Pentangle's investment was minimal apart from the fact that they were picking up the protestors' legal bills. They had not, however, admitted to being behind the independent analysis of the Agrigene crop and that was odd. According to Rafferty, the report had been sent to McGraw and Littlejohn from person or persons unknown. Maybe that was the way it had been done but if Pentangle should turn out to have any connection with a rival biotech company, it might explain just about everything.

It was even a very clever idea to hide behind a venture capital initiative, thought Steven. The only thing it didn't explain was why they had gone to all this trouble. This was a real puzzle. According to Phillip Grimble – and he thought he believed him – there was very little to be gained from putting a halt to one GM trial on a crop that was being tested at several sites all over the UK.

Steven decided that he would ask Sci-Med to run a thorough check on Pentangle while he would pay a visit to McGraw and Littlejohn on the off chance that they might actually know the identity of the party who had commissioned the crop analysis. As he walked back along the towpath he again saw the security guard who had looked at him suspiciously earlier. He had stopped patrolling the southern edge of the field and was keeping an eye on his return.

As Steven came to a point directly opposite him he saw the man suddenly start hopping around in agitation and begin swearing loudly. 'Fucking things!' he exploded, letting fly with his boot at a rat that had run out from the crop and over his foot. He missed by a mile and the animal scampered up the bank and across the towpath into the canal.

'Bloody things are everywhere,' said the guard, regaining his composure and now obviously feeling slightly embarrassed at his impromptu dance routine when it had been his intention to come across as intimidating.

'The living's easy for them round here,' said Steven. 'Plenty to eat and a nice canal with no traffic on it.'

'Roll on harvest time and I can get my arse out of here,' said the man. 'I've heard jokes about watching grass grow. I never dreamed I'd be doing it for a living.'

Steven walked on and started thinking about the rat he'd just seen. He wondered why it had chosen to run over the guard's foot. It was a strange thing for the beast to do when it had had plenty of alternatives. It could have exited from the rape field at just about any point along the edge and yet it had chosen to come out at the exact spot where the guard had been standing. Curious, but maybe not without precedent, he thought. The boy, Ian Ferguson, had been bitten by a rat for no apparent reason, according to what he and his chums had told the authorities at the time. It had been assumed that they must have cornered the animal in some way but maybe that hadn't been the case after all? This line of thought started him thinking about the man in the pub telling the others what the local vet had said about a puppy being attacked by rats. Again, it had been assumed that the dog had come across a rat hole in the bank and got his just deserts for intimidating the creatures but this was just an assumption. Maybe he would have a word with the vet about this. There was a lot of talk about a general increase in the size of the rat population. Had anyone mooted a marked change in their behaviour? he wondered.

Steven drove over to the Blackbridge Arms and parked his car in the street outside after finding the car park full to overflowing. It was now almost two o'clock in the afternoon but he hoped he might still be able to get something to eat.

'Lunch is finished,' said a skinny girl with rounded shoulders and lank hair, who happened to be crossing the hallway carrying a tray when he entered.

'Maybe a sandwich?'

'Lunch is finished, sir,' she repeated with a smile so artificial it looked like rictus on the face of a corpse.

'Heigh-ho,' he said pleasantly. 'Maybe I'll just have a beer and a packet of crisps at the bar.'

'Please yourself.'

Steven had just looked into the door of the bar when a hand touched him on the shoulder and he turned to find Eve Ferguson standing there. 'Sorry about Mona,' she said. 'We've been run off our feet today. The place is going like a fair because of all the ministry people but the owner refuses to take on any more staff, mainly because he's a greedy git.'

'No problem,' said Steven. 'I'll just have a beer.'

'Have a seat in the back lounge,' said Eve conspiratorially. 'I'll bring you some sandwiches. Ham and cheese okay?'

'Just the job.'

Steven followed her directions to the 'back lounge' and found himself in a low-ceilinged room, furnished with a range of unmatched sofas and armchairs. It smelled of dust and axminster carpets. There were several other men there, sitting round in a circle. They seemed to be having after-lunch coffee. Steven took a seat in an old winged armchair by the window that seemed to have been left as an orphan when the neighbouring group of men had formed their circle. He sat with his back to them.

As he waited for his sandwiches, he found their conversation interesting. Their suits and briefcases said that they were ministry people; their accents said that they were Scots. After a few minutes Steven learned that they were employees of the Scottish Executive.

'For once the lawyers were quite clear,' said one. 'To proceed with a destruction order without confirmation of disparity from the licence sequence is just asking for trouble.'

'But the licence sequence still hasn't surfaced and frankly it doesn't look like it's going to. Let's face it, MAFF's licensing section haven't *misplaced* it: they've *lost* the damned thing and that's an end to it. We could be letting an illegal crop trial proceed with all the dangers that might pose, simply because we don't have a missing piece of paper. If that gets out we'll be pilloried by the press.'

'On the other hand,' said another man, 'if we do junk it, the company might well sue us and win.'

'We could always pass the buck to the Department of Health?' came the suggestion.

'McKay won't hear of it. It would be too damaging to the Scottish Parliament. Our people would be portrayed as lame-duck MPs with no real power of their own. I'm pretty sure he's been instructed to make sure this is seen as a Scottish decision, made without any interference from Westminster.'

'But if this crop really isn't the one they were licensed for it might really pose a risk to health . . .'

'Forget it. McKay's made up his mind. He won't countenance any kind of handover. I think the minister has put his job on the line over it.'

Eve Ferguson came in and disturbed Steven's eavesdropping. She was carrying a tray with a heaped plate of sandwiches and a beer on it, which she laid down on the table beside Steven's chair.

'I didn't think you'd be working today,' whispered Steven.

'I thought I would be as well working here as sitting moping at home,' said Eve. 'Mum and Dad have each other. The funeral's tomorrow.'

'How are they?'

Eve shrugged in reply.

Steven ate his sandwiches and continued to pick up snippets of information as he ate, still with his back to the talkative group and pretending to be looking out of the window. By the time the men filed out of the lounge to return to the various rooms that had been commandeered for use as committee rooms, he had a pretty good idea of the impasse. The Scottish Rural Affairs people, under their Blackbridge project leader, McKay, had marked out the problem as being very much within their jurisdiction. They had more or less said that he was under instructions from his minister to make this perfectly clear to the outside world. In fact, this appeared to be their prime objective as witnessed by an apparent reluctance to make any firm decision that went with the responsibility. They were clearly afraid of the risk of exposing themselves to litigation and probable ridicule if they lost. The Ministry of Agriculture people saw the problem as being within their province because they had actually authorised the Agrigene trial before the inception of the Scottish Parliament, which was only months old. They seemed to regard Scottish Rural Affairs as being some new hick thorn in their side, not that it sounded as if they were any keener on making decisions than the Scottish lot were. The Department of Health, on the other hand, was anxious to take charge and make a decision but weren't being allowed to because it could not clearly be established that the crop on Peat Ridge Farm was actually a health risk. Without that precondition and concession from Rural Affairs, they could not override them. Steven remembered Eve's allusion to Gilbert and Sullivan at their first meeting and saw that she'd hit the nail on the head. This lot could go round in circles for ever.

Steven decide to drive into Edinburgh and see if there was anything to be gleaned from having a word with Rafferty's solicitors about the ministry sponsored report on the Agrigene crop. Before he left, he took a look into several rooms before he found Eve Ferguson in the kitchen. 'Just thought I'd say thank you,' he said. 'I appreciate it.'

'You're very welcome,' said Eve. 'How's our environment doing these days?'

'I'm still looking into it.'

'You don't seem to have much to do with the others,' said Eve.

'We're a solitary lot, we environmental people,' smiled Steven.

Eve looked at him questioningly before saying in a child's voice, 'Who was that masked stranger, Mummy?'

'That sort of thing.'

'Well, you'd best be off or Tonto will be getting tired waiting.'

'He's an Indian. He can sit for days without moving a muscle.'

'A bit like my Tommy,' said one of the women who was washing dishes at the sink. It made the others laugh. 'I never realised he was an Indian. I just thought he was a lazy bastard.'

Eve accompanied Steven back out into the hall where she collected her coat from behind a door marked Staff Only. 'You're off too?' he asked.

'Lunchtime's over,' Eve replied. 'But I'll be back for dinners.'

'You couldn't show me where the local vet lives, could you?'

'Of course, it's not far. Has Silver gone lame?'

Steven smiled. 'No, I just need to ask him something.'

Eve showed him where James Binnie lived and then said goodbye.

'I hope tomorrow's not too awful for you,' he said.

'Thanks,' Eve replied, looking back over her shoulder.

Steven knocked on the door and waited. It was opened by Binnie's wife. He asked if he could have a word with the vet.

'I'm afraid James is out at the moment. He went over to Kirkliston to look at a lame horse. Is it an emergency?'

Steven replied that it wasn't. He just wanted to have a chat with the vet about something when he had a spare moment.

'Can you be more specific?' asked the woman.

'Everyone has been talking about an increase in the rat population. I wanted to hear a professional view of the situation.'

'And you are?'

Steven told her.

'Rats, eh? Well, I should think James would be delighted to talk to you about rats, Dr Dunbar. Perhaps you might even persuade him to remove the one he put in the fridge the other night while you're at it!'

Steven asked about this and was told about the attack on the Labrador puppy. It was the case he'd heard mentioned in the pub.

'Why the rat in the fridge?' he asked.

'James said that he wanted the vet school in Edinburgh to take a look at the creature but he just hasn't got round to taking it over yet, a familiar enough scenario,' the woman smiled.

'Do you know why he wanted it examined?'

'He didn't say. I think what worried him was the fact that he had another case of rat bite to deal with last week and then, of course, there was the tragedy of young Ian Ferguson. I think James has started to wonder just what exactly is going on.'

Steven nodded and asked when he might call back.

'It will probably be after four by the time he gets back from Kirkliston,' said Ann Binnie, 'and then he'll have to go over to Crawhill to see to Tom Rafferty's dog.'

'Better him than me,' said Steven.

'You know the dog?'

'I was at Crawhill this morning,' said Steven. 'I heard it. Made the Hound of the Baskervilles sound like a sissy.'

'Khan's a bit of a handful, I'm afraid.'

'Looking for a bit of a mouthful, by the sound of it.'

'Anyway, that's going to keep James occupied for a bit. I

think perhaps tomorrow morning might be best. He'll be going to the Ferguson boy's funeral at ten. Maybe some time when that's over?'

'Fine,' said Steven.

'I'll tell him to expect you.'

Steven walked back to his car and started out for Edinburgh and the offices of the legal firm, McGraw and Littlejohn. Finding the building was easy enough but finding a place to park near it, in the Georgian heart of Edinburgh, was another matter. He did eventually find one but it was nearly half a mile on the north side of where he wanted to be. He fed the ticket machine with enough money for an hour and started to walk back uphill to Abercromby Place.

A solid black door furnished with brass knobs and nameplate gave access to an inner glass door, which gave way in turn to a wall with a sliding glass panel in it. Steven pressed the bell below it and a young girl slid back the panel. He showed his ID and said that he'd like to speak with the partner dealing with Thomas Rafferty of Crawhill Farm.

'Just a minute,' said the girl, appearing puzzled.

It was the reply Steven expected. The first person to ask you, 'how can I help you,' in any organisation was always guaranteed to be unable to do so. He heard the girl ask someone named Mrs Logan for help. Mrs Logan, a middle-aged woman with wrinkled, parchment-yellow skin, appeared at the window and Steven made his request again. Once more he showed his ID.

'You're a doctor . . . but also some sort of policeman?' said Mrs Logan.

'Couldn't have put it better myself,' agreed Steven pleasantly.

'Just a minute.'

In all it took Steven some seven minutes more to clear the hurdles of the outer office and be shown into the inner sanctum of Hector McGraw, senior partner in the firm.

'You have me at a disadvantage, Doctor, I don't think I've ever met anyone from the Sci-Med Inspectorate before,' said McGraw, standing up to greet Steven. 'What exactly do you do?'

Steven explained briefly the function of the SMI and its powers.

'Sounds like a very good idea,' said McGraw. 'Where do we come in?'

'You're handling the action against the GM crop trial at Peat Ridge Farm in Blackbridge,' said Steven. 'You obtained a lab report on the crop from a ministry lab over in Ayrshire. I'd like to know who commissioned the report.'

'But it was a ministry report,' said McGraw.

'But commissioned privately.'

'I didn't know that,' said McGraw.

'How did you come by it?' asked Steven.

'It simply arrived on my desk.'

'Then what did you do?'

'The report clearly stated that the crop contained three foreign elements instead of the two stated in the licence, so we brought this to the attention of the relevant authorities.'

Despite the fact that McGraw had professed surprise at his visit, Steven had the distinct impression that the man's responses to his questions had been prepared in advance, as if he had been expecting someone to ask them. 'Did you check the report's authenticity?' he asked.

'Well, no,' replied McGraw, putting on a defensive grin. 'The report was on official paper. There didn't seem any need to . . .'

'So an official looking piece of paper is sent to you anonymously and you do nothing to check whether it's genuine or not. Is that what you're saying?'

McGraw appeared flustered for the first time. 'As I say, the ministry letterhead seemed to suggest that it was kosher.'

'How difficult do you think it would be to forge the letterhead?' asked Steven.

'But why would anyone want to . . .?'

'Because many thousands of pounds are tied up in this crop trial,' interrupted Steven, making it sound like that was obvious.

'Are you saying that the report was forged?' asked McGraw.

'No, it wasn't,' conceded Steven, but he suspected that McGraw already knew that. There was something about the man's smugness that suggested to him that McGraw hadn't bothered to check the report's authenticity because he had been expecting it too.

'Thank goodness for that,' said McGraw with a smirk.

'Who is paying Mr Rafferty's legal bills?'

'I think that's an improper question.'

'But one I think you should answer.'

'And if I refuse on the grounds that it would be a breach of client confidentiality?'

'I'll ask Inland Revenue to go through all the documents

on the firm's premises with a fine-tooth comb,' replied Steven.

'But they'd find nothing wrong with anything!' protested McGraw.

'I know,' replied Steven. 'But it wouldn't look very nice.'

'That is outrageous.'

Steven remained silent.

McGraw drew in breath angrily and gave him the information he already knew. 'Mr Rafferty has the backing of a venture capital company named Pentangle. They have asked for our note of fee to be submitted to them.'

'May I see the correspondence?'

McGraw got up from his desk and opened a filing cabinet. He took out a dossier and handed it to Steven without comment. Steven flicked through it and found the official letter from Pentangle giving invoice instructions. There was nothing of interest in it save for the Pentangle reference to be, 'quoted in all correspondence'. It was SigV. Steven read this as Sigma 5. He felt glad he'd come.

# 9

As he drove across town to his hotel, Steven kept thinking about the designation, Sigma 5. Although Pentangle's front men, Childs and Leadbetter, had denied having anything to do with sending samples of Agrigene's crop at Peat Ridge for independent analysis, finding the code SigV on their invoice instructions to McGraw's firm in his office was, he thought, just too much of a coincidence. Sigma 5 might not be a company name in its own right but it might well be the code name given to some project they were funding. In fact, that would probably make more sense, he thought.

But why concoct the story about the lab report being sent anonymously to Rafferty's lawyers? He supposed that it could be that they did not want to associate themselves overtly with something that wasn't entirely above board – bribing a government scientist to produce a misleading report would certainly come into that category. But whatever the reason, if Rafferty and co had seen fit to lie about it, that fact alone suggested that they were working to a different agenda.

As he drove along Melville Drive, the stretch of road running between the green park areas of The Meadows and Bruntsfield Links, Steven's phone rang and he pulled in to the side to answer it.

'Jamie Brown here,' said the voice.

'Who?'

'Jamie Brown of the *Scotsman*, we met in the pub at Blackbridge last Sunday. Remember?'

'Of course. I'm sorry.'

'I said I'd get back to you when I'd looked into whether or not Crawhill Farm was on the market.'

'Oh yes, I remember,' said Steven, feeling embarrassed that he'd gone ahead and asked for himself.

'Apparently it's not, and hasn't been in the past thirty years. Mind you, I suppose that doesn't rule out some kind of private deal going on between Rafferty and another party but as far as the normal agencies are concerned, it's no go.'

'Pity,' said Steven, 'another beautiful theory spoiled by an ugly little fact, as someone once put it.'

'It's not entirely bad news though,' said Brown. 'I did manage to establish that Rafferty does have a strong business association with an outside commercial interest.'

'You have been busy.'

'It's a venture capital outfit called Pentangle.'

'Sounds like a folk group,' said Steven.

Brown was unabashed. 'But here's the really strange thing,' he continued. 'It doesn't exist. It doesn't seem to be registered anywhere and none of our finance people on the paper have ever heard of it.'

'I don't think you can read too much into that,' said Steven, keen to discourage Brown from digging too deeply in his patch. 'Venture capitalists are often shy retiring creatures. They seldom like the glare of publicity so they may not exist as a corporate entity. They're probably just a group of very wealthy men calling themselves Pentangle for the sake of convenience.'

'Maybe,' agreed Brown. 'But here's another strange thing. Steven Dunbar isn't on the staff of any environmental department or agency in the UK. He doesn't exist either . . .'

Steven closed his eyes and cursed silently. Brown had turned out to be a better investigator than he'd thought. 'I didn't actually say that I worked for them, just that I had an interest in the environment,' he pointed out.

'So who do you "actually" work for?'

'The Sci-Med Inspectorate,' Steven admitted. 'When we last spoke we weren't officially involved. I was just having a nose around.'

'But you are now?'

'Yes.'

'That's interesting. Could we meet?'

'If you mean for interview, no.'

'Off the record?'

'Purely on that understanding.'

'Just tell me where.'

'My hotel, the Grange in Whitehouse Terrace. Eight o'clock in the bar.'

Steven pressed the 'end' button and let out his breath in a long sigh. He tried looking on the bright side. At least it was Brown and not McColl, the other scribbler he'd met in the Castle Tavern, but this was a complication he hadn't bargained for. He would have to be careful, but, still trying to look on the bright side, he reckoned that Brown, with his connections, could actually be a help.

When he got back to his room he contacted Sci-Med and asked if they had anything for him. They, like Brown, had drawn a blank on Pentangle and also on Sigma 5 but, thanks to the cooperation of Inland Revenue, they had obtained details of Gerald Millar's bank account and retirement package. Steven asked that they e-mail the figures to him so he could go through them at leisure. They said they would do this in the next half-hour. Steven stripped, had a shower and changed into casual clothes while he was waiting. The file was there when he switched his computer back on.

He found the financial details interesting. Gerald Millar had been given 'full enhancement' on his pension rights in contradiction of what he understood should happen and from what Roberta at the Ayrshire lab had told him. This simply did not fit with a member of staff having requested his own early retirement. It was the deal given to staff being retired compulsorily at the ministry's request when years of service were enhanced artificially to increase the size of their pension. Steven noted that they had also increased the associated lump sum payment. 'Nice one Gerald,' he murmured.

In addition to the retirement package, there was another recorded payment of thirty thousand pounds, paid into Millar's bank account and marked down as the proceeds from the sale of shares in two named companies. Nothing odd in that, thought Steven, but then his suspicious nature gave him second thoughts. The money might well have come from the sale of shares but had Millar actually owned these shares in the first place? he wondered. The payment could conceivably have originated from a third party who had just laundered it through an apparent share deal. He replied to the e-mail with this self same question for Sci-Med.

It was just after seven and Steven thought he'd use up the time before his meeting with Brown looking into the niggling little problem of executive responsibility out at Blackbridge. He'd been under the impression that the Scottish Executive had clear and exclusive rights to decide on matters agricultural in Scotland but from what he'd overheard at lunchtime at the hotel there seemed to be some confusion about this. The Ministry of Agriculture, Fisheries and Food still seemed to be playing a leading role. He connected his laptop to the Internet and sought out the web pages in succession of both the Scottish Executive and MAFF.

It was hard going, navigating his way through a sea of irrelevance, but in the end he came up with something called, 'The Main Concordat between the Ministry of Agriculture Fisheries and Food and the Scottish Executive'. This long document outlined an agreement between the two bodies to respect each other's territory and keep each other informed, cooperate wherever possible and generally be good pals. It struck him that the words in it had been very carefully chosen by someone doing a fair impression of tiptoeing through a minefield and reminded him of a prayer. 'Lord, help me not to stand on people's toes, particularly those that are attached to the arses I may have to kiss tomorrow.' He finally came across one telling statement that said, 'This Concordat is not intended to constitute a legally enforceable contract or to create any rights or obligations which are legally enforceable. It is intended to be binding in honour only.'

'In other words, not worth the paper it's written on,' murmured Steven, closing down the connection. Now he understood the problem.

'I thought you'd be staying at the Blackbridge Arms,' said Jamie Brown when he arrived promptly in the bar at eight.

'I never like sleeping over the shop,' replied Steven.

Brown took off his Berghaus jacket and draped it over the back of his chair. 'What are you having?'

'I'm fine just now,' replied Steven who was already nursing a gin and tonic.

Brown asked for whisky. 'So you're one of Sci-Med's people,' he said. 'A brave one too by all accounts.'

Steven raised his eyebrows.

'You were the one who exposed the transplant scam at the Medic Ecosse Hospital in Glasgow a few years back, weren't you?'

Steven agreed that he had been involved, remembering now that there had been a bit of press coverage at the time and, despite his best efforts, he had featured in some of it. Brown must have looked him up in the paper's archives. 'This is all off the record, isn't it?'

'You have my word,' replied Brown. 'I can't, however, speak for any of my colleagues over at Blackbridge should they make the connection. I should think, "Glasgow Hospital Hero called in to solve GM Riddle", might well prove irresistible to a certain little red-haired man with a Rotweiler personality. Come to think of it, you went on to marry one of the nurses caught up in that business, didn't you?'

Steven gave him a black look.

'Sorry, I didn't mean to speak out of turn,' said Brown, puzzled at Steven's reaction.

'Lisa died nine months ago. Cancer.'

'Christ, I'm sorry. I had no idea,' said Brown. After a few moments he added, 'Don't take this the wrong way but *heartbreak* Glasgow Hospital Hero might be even more irresistible.'

Steven said, 'Thanks for the warning but my picture was never in the papers at the time. There's no reason for anyone out there to make the connection, although,' he conceded, 'you did.' At this point he was actually more apprehensive that Brown might be trying to manoeuvre himself into the position of confidant in order to ensure a ready supply of information. He was not against collaboration with someone in Brown's position and certainly did not subscribe to the view that nothing should be ever said to the press on principle. He recognised that investigative journalism could be a tremendous force for good in society but it was a matter of knowing the journalist well enough to trust him. He had no reason to distrust Brown – in fact, from what he'd seen so far, he liked the man, but for the moment, he would play his hand one card at a time.

'So what's Sci-Med's interest in all of this?' asked Brown.

'Pretty much what I said at the outset. I think Agrigene may be getting a raw deal. It's only their determination to see the fight into the courts that's keeping their crop in the field; that and the executive running around like headless chickens.'

'Tell me about it,' smiled Brown. 'The MSPs are calling it teething troubles. Still, they've got their pay and holidays sorted out and right now they're off on them, thirteen weeks I hear.'

'First things first.'

'So you still think Agrigene is being set up?'

'I'm sure of it but I don't know who by or why for that matter.'

'You're no longer keen on the rival company angle?'

'I was for a while but it doesn't seem to make too much sense in terms of what's to be gained by it.'

'I suppose, as a Sci-Med Investigator, you must have already known about Crawhill Farm not being on the market? And probably about Pentangle too?'

'I didn't when we spoke in the pub,' Steven assured him, 'but I have looked into it since, when I decided to take the assignment on.'

'And Pentangle? Don't you think they're a bit suspicious?'

'Like I said, venture capitalists don't like the spotlight. They're timid creatures.'

'Not greedy bastards out to make a fast buck?'

'That too.'

'Something tells me there's more to it than that,' said Brown. 'Nobody's going to make a real killing out of selling chemical-free lettuce in Morningside. A small organic farm doesn't really sound like venture capital territory to me and there's something else that bothers me too.'

'What?' asked Steven, at once both admiring of and apprehensive of Brown's analytical skills.

'The two at the farm, there's something about them: they just don't look like venture capitalists to me.'

'You think they should be wearing smoking jackets and have fat cigars sticking out of the corner of their mouths?'

'Like I say, there's just something about them,' said Brown. 'They're something more than business associates to Rafferty, I'm sure of it. It's almost as if he's their prisoner, the way they're always hanging around the farmhouse. It's impossible to speak to Rafferty on his own and he hasn't been down to the local pub in ages when, according to the locals, he was in line for a piss artist of the millennium award.'

'Maybe he's turned over a new leaf,' said Steven. 'He told me that he wants to get his wife back so he's off the booze. That's what all this organic farm thing is about according to him; a new start.'

Brown was non-committal.

'But I do wonder what his chances are,' said Steven, thinking out loud.

'Of running an organic farm?'

'No, of getting his wife back.'

'Depends how often she's left him before,' said Brown. 'If this is the first time, she'll probably come back. If it's the second, then maybe. If it's the third, she won't. It's a bit like drowning.'

'We're both assuming that she left him because of the drink,' said Steven, 'but that may not be the case.'

'Can you think of another reason?'

'No, but I don't know either of them and I'm not a big fan of assumptions.'

'So where do we go from here?'

'We?'

'Well, I thought we might as well pool our efforts and cut down on the legwork?'

'We can give it a try,' conceded Steven after a few moments' thought. 'But no sudden moves.'

'Agreed. Will you be at the Ferguson boy's funeral tomorrow?'

'No, there's nothing for me there. I'd only be intruding. You?'

'I've been told to cover it so I'll have to, but my heart's not in it. I feel the same about being an intruder.'

'Your colleague from the *Clarion* seemed to be quite looking forward to it,' said Steven.

'McColl? Alex's not over-endowed with sensitivity at the best of times. He'll probably see it as a welcome change from seeking out the "cosy little love nests" set up by the great and good that his paper's so fond of exposing. Soft porn peddled as moral outrage is their speciality.'

'I suppose it says more about our society than it does about the paper,' said Steven.

'Regrettably true,' agreed Brown. 'Well, I think I'm going to follow my instincts and see what I can dig up about our two venture capital boys. You?'

'Maybe I'll see what I can find out from Tom Rafferty's wife. I think I'd like to talk to her.'

'Do you know where to find her?'

'Not yet but next best thing, I know how I can find out,' replied Steven, thinking of Eve Ferguson who had spoken as if she knew her well.

Brown finished his drink and left. Steven had something to eat and then went upstairs to mull over the events of the day. He had hardly sat down when the phone went. It was the man on the night desk at Sci-Med who gave him a simple instruction. He said, 'Read your e-mail.'

Steven looked at the receiver as it went dead. 'What the hell's going on?' he murmured. This sort of thing had never happened before. He made the modem connection and waited while an Internet connection was established. He downloaded an encrypted message from Sci-Med and deciphered it. It said simply, 'Be at the Edinburgh Airport Hotel at ten p.m. Ask at the desk for Mr Harvey Grimes.' Steven looked at his watch and saw that he'd better get a move on.

Fortunately the traffic proved lighter than he'd feared as he crossed town and he swung into the airport hotel car park at three minutes to ten. Asking at the desk for Mr Harvey Grimes resulted in him being directed to a room on the third floor. 'Mr Grimes is expecting you sir,' said the desk clerk.

Steven knocked and waited, glancing first to the right and then to the left to see that the corridor was empty. He had no idea why he'd done that but then he had no idea why he was here. It was a case of being caught up in a melo-drama and behaving accordingly. He thought he heard someone tell him to come in although it was a bit muffled. He entered anyway and found the room empty. 'Hello, anyone there? Mr Grimes?'

'Actually it's me,' said John Macmillan, director of Sci-Med, coming out of the bathroom, toothbrush in hand. 'Take a seat. I'll be with you in a moment. Help yourself to a drink.'

Steven poured himself a gin and sat down. What the hell was all this Harvey Grimes nonsense about? he wondered. He'd never known Macmillan to play silly games before. He was one of the most sensible and practical people he knew.

Macmillan reappeared and sat down opposite him and read his mind. 'Believe me, I hate all this cloak and dagger stuff as much as you do,' he said, 'but I'm supposed to be at a meeting in Amsterdam right now and that's what I want them to continue to believe.'

'Them?' asked Steven.

'The people who don't want you in Blackbridge.'

'I don't think I understand.'

'I told you at the outset that I thought that I was being warned off. It was being done in a gentle, diplomatic way, I'll grant you, but I was clearly being invited to read between the lines. I chose to ignore it and let the man on the ground make the decision. You called a code red and now the warnings are coming in thick and fast and the gloves are off.'

'Where's the flak coming from?'

'That's the most worrying thing,' said Macmillan. 'I can't see the source and I haven't been able to find out anything. That suggests to me that the unhappiness must be at a fairly high level.'

'I've barely scratched the surface in Blackbridge,' said Steven. 'I haven't had time to upset anyone at high level.'

'You asked for a check on something called Sigma 5,' said Macmillan. 'I'm pretty sure that's what did it. I've carried out a thorough check with our people and the guano hitting the fan coincides with them starting to ask around about Sigma 5 on your behalf.'

'Well, well, good to know I'm on the right track, I suppose, even if I don't know where it's leading, unless, of course, you've been ordered to spike the investigation?'

Macmillan shook his head. 'No, that would involve our

147

friends on high showing exactly who they are. The spear-carriers who have been relaying veiled threats don't have the authority to order me to do anything so I show them the door and the impasse remains.'

'So where does that leave me?'

'That's why I felt I had to come. I'm not at all sure where it leaves you and I'm starting to get a bad feeling about all this.'

'What could they do to me?' Steven asked sceptically.

'That's what I have the bad feeling about.'

'You can't be serious,' said Steven.

'Frankly, I just don't know but I do feel it's possible that you could be in some danger. We seem to be interfering in something that's "already under control" as I keep being told.'

'I suppose things could be said to be under control in Blackbridge,' said Steven thoughtfully. 'In which case they've obviously ordered a bunch of civil servants to run around pretending it's loonies' sports day to cover up that fact.'

'As bad as that?'

'And then some.'

'All the same, I think you should consider pulling out.'

'If I did that we'd lose our credibility,' protested Steven. 'You said when I joined the firm that Sci-Med were beholden to no one. I'd like to keep it that way.'

Macmillan said, 'I sort of hoped you'd say that. It's what I wanted to hear but I couldn't ask you. I don't have the right. You're the man on the ground.'

'So it's settled, I stay.'

'Just be bloody careful.'

'You're off to Amsterdam, then?'

'Yes. I was never here.'

Steven walked back to his car, feeling a mixture of excitement and unease. It was the sort of feeling he'd had often enough before in his time with Special Forces, usually before setting off on a mission. If serious pressure was being put on Macmillan it must mean that there was something big to hide. The fact that the pressure was coming from somewhere in government – his own employer, when all was said and done – made it all the more exciting? Intriguing? No, scary was the word he was looking for.

# 10

In his own eyes, the Reverend Robert Lindsay McNish was a failure. Worse than that, he was a fraud and a charlatan. He had lost his faith in his mid forties when his wife had run off with a car salesman, calling him in the process, 'the most boring man who'd ever walked the earth' and he'd never quite recovered. Rather than own up to an ensuing and ever-growing cynicism regarding his fellow man and especially woman, he had soldiered on, motivated solely out of personal concern about his own livelihood. He didn't feel that he could do anything else and the dog collar was a very necessary barrier between him and the rest of humanity.

For the past seven years, he had purveyed the promise of everlasting life to the rapidly dwindling band of pensioners that comprised his congregation at Blackbridge Parish Church, while no longer believing a word of it himself. He wasn't at ease with the knowledge but felt trapped by circumstance. He was rolling slowly downhill in a steep-sided rut from which there was no escape. One day, in the not too distant future, he would hit the buffers; the lights would go out and that would be that. Thank you and good night, Robert McNish.

The days when Blackbridge could sustain a church from its own population had long since gone. The building was still there but the congregation, such as it was, was now garnered from four neighbouring villages, all of which had a church building of their own. The Sunday service was therefore held in each one in rotation. It had been three weeks since the last service at Blackbridge so McNish had arranged for the local cleaner to come in a few days early to make sure it would be right for the Ferguson boy's funeral. Happily, there would be no extra cleaning bill as the service was due there on Sunday anyway.

A full house in Blackbridge Parish Church was something that McNish had not experienced at any time during his fifteen-year tenure and a full house it was going to be. This was mainly due to a large contingent of the boy's friends and classmates coming from the High School over in Livingston where he had been a pupil. Although it was still the school holidays, the boy's death and the circumstances of it had been reported widely in the local papers and on local radio and television. This had added a show business element to the death. People wanted to say that they had known Ian Ferguson, the boy on the television. Even a tenuous connection with fame was better than none.

McNish considered the prospect of a sea of faces before him with mixed emotions. He felt nervous but he also felt that he shouldn't be after so long in the job. After all, all he really had to do was convince everyone there that the boy's life had been worthwhile and that the Almighty had had a damned good reason for allowing a rat to half bite his foot off and give him a fatal disease into the bargain.

The thought sent him scurrying to the sideboard in the dining room where he took out a half-full bottle of vodka – it didn't taint your breath – and took a large swig from it. He wiped his mouth with the back of his hand and held it there for a moment, unconsciously seeking solace from the touch of his lips on skin, even if it was his own. He looked out of the manse window at the church across the street. It was a grimy, ugly, brick-built building in need of urgent attention from a competent builder, attention that it wasn't going to get, at least not until it had changed hands and become a carpet warehouse or disco or whatever churches like his became these days. McNish took another swig and put the bottle back in the sideboard. Breakfast was over.

He waddled through to the bathroom, his bare feet at 'ten to two' and turned on the hot tap in the basin, keeping his hand under it while it gurgled and splashed away the airlocks of the night and eventually started to run hot. He washed, shaved and attempted to persuade his spiky grey hair into some kind of order but, as usual, it defied his best efforts and continued to stick out at odd angles making him look as if he'd just had a bad fright. He struggled into his vestments, reflecting from the tightness across his belly that he was still gaining weight thanks to a diet dominated by takeaway food. Finally, he put on his glasses and bent over to tie his shoes – large, sturdy Doc Martin affairs, the incongruity of which he relied on his vestments to hide – and felt his diaphragm push up into his throat, bringing on an episode of heartburn. He went back to the bathroom to find the indigestion tablets.

With the taste of peppermint doing battle with regurgitated vodka, McNish left the manse and crossed to the church where he checked his watch and saw that there was still an hour to go. He acknowledged the cleaner who was polishing the edge of his pulpit and went through to the vestry to sit down and read through his crib notes. These he had made after an awkward visit to the Fergusons' house to convey his sympathy and make arrangements for the funeral. He didn't know the family at all and making conversation had been difficult, although it had emerged that he had baptised Ian some thirteen years before.

As far as he could gather, that was the last time any of them had been in church and now, today, as if by some stroke of bloody magic, they would expect him to speak knowingly about their son as if he'd been popping in and out of the manse all his life.

McNish concluded that there was very little to work with in the notes he'd made. The boy had been thirteen, not particularly bright in class, not particularly good at sports; not particularly good at anything was the real bottom line, but a joker – that at least would be useful. He had no hobbies but he liked pop music. His favourite band was . . . Damn, where was the bit of paper with the band's name on it?

McNish was foraging around for it when he was joined by the church organist for the service. She was Miss Pamela Sutton, a retired music teacher from the neighbouring village. 'Lost something, minister?' she asked cheerfully.

Miss Sutton was always cheerful and it annoyed McNish

153

intensely. He bit back the reply that sprang to his lips and edited it until it became, 'Yes, Miss Sutton. I've lost the name of a pop group.'

'Didn't know you were into pop music, Minister.'

McNish sucked in breath through his teeth for he had known that she would say that. He wanted to shake the woman until the rose-tinted spectacles fell from her eyes and she saw life as it really was.

'No, it was the name of the Ferguson boy's favourite group, Miss Sutton. Ah, here it is.' McNish removed the small piece of paper from between the pages of a prayer book and squinted at it from several angles before asking, 'Can you make out what that says?'

'T . . . Travel, I think.'

'Is there a band named Travel?'

'No idea, Minister. Not my scene, as they say.'

The church officer arrived and then the elders who were going to act as ushers today. McNish went through the seating arrangements with them and helped increase the stack of hymnbooks on the table by the door by putting back the ones he'd removed some weeks before because they were too worn and tatty. 'Needs must, Miss Sutton,' he said when he saw the organist grimace at the state of them. She held one up like it was something her cat had brought home.

The mourners started to arrive, in dribs and drabs at first but then in ever increasing numbers until downstairs was full and the upstairs galleries were opened up. McNish watched what he felt were a motley crew arrive. Very few appeared to have bothered with traditional dark clothes and black ties. Many of them looked as if they were visiting a supermarket. There was even one woman in an orange shell suit. He was acutely aware of the change to the church's acoustics that such a large number of people were making. The normal echo that gave his voice an edge of gravitas had been dampened down to nothing. He would have to speak up to make himself heard.

The hearse arrived and the coffin was brought slowly into the church on the shoulders of pallbearers, followed by the boy's family, huddling together for comfort. McNish waited until they had settled in the front pew and nodded to them self-consciously before looking up at the congregation. For the first time, he saw that they were all looking intently at him and he felt intimidated. What were they thinking? he wondered. Nothing friendly, he feared. He was looking at a sea of blank, expressionless faces.

'We are gathered here today to give thanks for the life of Ian Ferguson,' he began. 'Let us begin by singing the twenty-third Psalm, The Lord is My Shepherd, I shall not want.'

McNish felt a sense of relief when the organ music swelled and the sound of shuffling feet and throats being cleared directed attention away from him. He found it increasingly difficult to look at the congregation and recognised that he was having a panic attack. He started to suspect they all knew that he was a phoney.

In an effort to get a grip on his emotions, he concentrated his gaze on a window at the back of the church, the one that had been boarded up with chipboard after a yob had thrown a beer bottle through it a few months earlier. The music died, the congregation sat and he began again. 'Today our hearts go out to Ian's family as they struggle to come to terms with their tremendous loss. It would not be natural if they did not find themselves full of questions as they start to face up to life without him because there will be a great gap in their lives and they will miss him and his laughter and great love of joking. I would say to them that because answers are not immediately obvious, does not mean to say that there are none. It may well be that we as yet are ill-equipped to understand them. That makes them none the less valid and we must put our trust in the Lord and his decisions.'

McNish paused when he felt sure he'd heard the word 'bollocks' being murmured, followed by muted shushing. He swallowed and managed to convince himself that it had been his imagination. He continued, 'Ian, like many of his contemporaries, had a great love of pop music and was a big fan of Travel.' He glanced up from his notes when he heard a murmur of unrest and saw the family looking at each other in puzzlement. Something was dreadfully wrong and he had to pause again, feeling all at sea and embarrassed because he knew not what.

He became aware of loud whispers coming from the front pews on the other side of the aisle from the family and realised that they were being aimed at him. He concentrated on the lips of one girl who was wearing bright red lipstick and leaning forward in her seat, mouthing the word . . . T.R.A.V.I.S.

'I'm sorry, the pop group *Travis*,' he continued. 'My knowledge of pop is more than a little suspect at the best of times.'

The reaction to his joke would not have been out of place at the Cenotaph at the eleventh hour of the eleventh day of the eleventh month. The silence brought a cold sweat to his brow. The congregation were clearly against him but he steeled himself to struggle on, feeling that the next item might win them round. 'As Ian was taken from us at such an early age we are going to break with the traditional service at this time to listen to Ian's favourite recording of . . . Travis. Some of his classmates have brought along a CD player and will play the song for us.'

Two High School pupils, a boy and a girl, wearing school blazers and exuding the air of being responsible young people, moved out from the end of a pew and were escorted by an elder to a position to the right of McNish where they set up the player. They got up, folded their hands behind their backs and stood there with bowed heads as the music started.

McNish kept his eyes firmly fixed on the boarded-up window as the sound of Travis singing, 'You're driftwood, floating on the water,' filled the church. He felt his buttocks clench and his toes curl under his feet in total embarrassment as the awful irony came to him.

McNish fudged his way through to the end of the service and joined the family in the first car behind the hearse for the short trip up to Canal Field Cemetery. He could feel their disappointment at his dismal performance although they said nothing – maybe *because* they said nothing. He desperately wanted everything to be over but he knew there was a bit to go yet. There were so many following along behind on foot that there would be a considerable wait by the graveside before the actual burial could commence.

McNish found himself a clod of earth to concentrate his

gaze on while people gathered round the site of the excavated grave. The coffin sat on two rough wooden supports over the hole until such times as they would be removed and it would be lowered down into the opening by the council grave-diggers with relatives holding symbolic cords.

The fading of murmured conversation told him that everyone had now arrived and were now waiting for him to begin. He took up stance beside the coffin and began reading the burial service. 'Man that is born of woman hath but a short time to . . .' He froze in abject horror when he saw a rat jump up on to the lid of the coffin and sit there staring at him. Several mourners screamed and two women turned to flee in blind panic.

For McNish, it was the final straw. He lost the place completely and a red mist swam before his eyes and he swung out at the creature with his prayer book, shouting – almost screaming – at the top of his voice, 'Fil-thy, fuck-ing thing! Get to fuck out of it, you verminous little bastard!'

The frightened animal leapt from the coffin and ran off through a gap that opened up in front of it as if by magic as people leapt out of its way.

McNish, totally out of control, threw his prayer book after it along with another volley of abuse. Worse still, he lost his footing on the wet grass and tumbled backwards to fall down beside the maw of the waiting grave. His vestments rode up exposing his Doc Martin's to public view as he clutched desperately at one of the wooden coffin supports to prevent himself sliding into the hole. Council workers rushed to his aid and hoisted him back on to his feet where he stood, breathing deeply and staring down at the earth, his ears burning.

'Can you go on, Minister?' asked a voice at his elbow.

After a few more deep breaths, McNish nodded. Someone tentatively handed him his prayer book, as if not wanting to come too close. The book itself was badly torn and covered in mud. 'Man that is born of woman hath but a short time to live,' he continued.

McNish was acutely aware of being given lots of space as the burial came to an end and people turned to leave. The family in particular were avoiding him so he chose to walk back to the manse on his own, rather than ride in the car in deafening silence. He recognised that he was now going to be the main topic of conversation at the family gathering, which he had pointedly not been invited back to. It didn't matter. Nothing mattered. The only thing he wanted right now was a drink, several drinks, as many as it took to stop the pain inside his head.

The remains of the vodka bottle in the sideboard lasted less than a minute and was followed by a frantic search for another which he felt sure was somewhere in the house but, just for the moment, he couldn't think where. He knew that he'd put it somewhere where that damned nosy cleaner wouldn't come across it, but just where exactly that was . . .

He remembered now. He'd put it under the artificial straw in the Christmas crib, which was stored in the small back bedroom. He staggered through and retrieved it from under the baby Jesus to greedily slug from it before returning to sit down in the dining room at the table and going over in his mind all that had happened that morning. Christ! There had even been photographers there, he remembered. They had been hanging back, keeping in the background but he distinctly remembered seeing the long lenses of their cameras when the car had turned in through the cemetery gates. His nightmare was going to be all over the papers. 'A fucking rat,' he murmured. 'A dirty little fucking rat.'

McNish rose from the table unsteadily and staggered over to the fireplace where he picked up a heavy brass poker. 'Destroy me, would you? You verminous little fuckers! We'll see about that.'

Amazingly, no one noticed McNish weave his way back up the road to Canal Field Cemetery and climb up on to the canal towpath behind. Perhaps they were all staying indoors out of respect for the Ferguson family or maybe some did see him but chose not to say anything about it. The Scots were as good as anyone at not seeing what they found embarrassing.

McNish staggered along the towpath at the back of Peat Ridge Farm, waving the poker above his head and challenging rats in a loud voice to come out and get what was coming to them. He stopped when he saw one run out from the rape field and pause in the middle of the towpath. He became convinced in his own booze-addled mind that this was the one that had jumped up on the boy's coffin and brought about his nemesis. He became hell bent on revenge.

'Here, ratty watty . . . Here, ratty watty. Come to daddy . . . There's a good ratty watty.' McNish inched closer while the rat watched him.

'There's a good little . . . Bastard!' McNish launched himself at the rat and went all his length as he brought the poker down with all his might but only to make contact with a large flat stone. The pain shot up his arm and brought tears to his eyes as he lay there, close to despair. When his vision had cleared of tears he saw that the rat had not run off. It was sitting there looking at him.

'Why you filthy, fucking . . .' He paused when he saw that there were now two of them and blinked to make sure it wasn't just his eyesight. He scrabbled in the dirt with his right hand, searching for his glasses, which had come off in the fall. He made contact with them and put them back on, clumsily forcing them up his nose with the heel of his hand. There *were* two. Fear entered the equation. This just wasn't how it should be.

McNish backed away a little and tried to get up into a kneeling position. He needed to find the poker. He would feel better with the poker in his hand but it had flown off somewhere when he'd hit the stone and he couldn't see it. 'Shoo, you bastards,' he said, waving his hands at them but the rats didn't move.

Fear was having a sobering effect on him. Rats were supposed to run off when you challenged them.

These two were sitting in the middle of the path, ignoring his best efforts to scare them off. His breathing became shallow as he remained kneeling, watching the rats watching him. He backed off a little more but this time his progress came to a sudden dramatic halt when an agonising pain shot through his leg and he tried to scramble to his feet. A rat had come up behind him and sunk its teeth into the calf muscle of his right leg.

McNish clutched at the revolting creature on his leg and pushed his flabby fingers as hard as he could into its body, trying to make it release its grip. He was diverted from the task when another of the creatures started to climb up his trouser leg under his cassock. McNish cried out in terror, letting go of the first rat to try and stop the progress of the second but his vestments were making it difficult. He tried tearing at the material to get at the creature but the garment was well made – there was no great demand for cheap cassocks – and wouldn't part. Trying to protect his genitals by forcing his thighs together while jerking round in circles in an attempt to shake off the rat on his leg made McNish trip and crash to the ground. He hit his head on the path but the pain was eclipsed by that imposed by the rat bites. He started to roll over and over on the path, hoping that he might escape his tormentors by reaching the water, like a man trying to flee from a swarm of bees. This, however, did not work for water rats. Once in the water, he was theirs.

'Careful, Mac. It could be some kind of diversion,' said the yellow-jacketed security man to his colleague. They had come to the north end of the field after hearing what they thought were cries for help.

'You stay here then and I'll take Caesar up to deal with the diversion,' replied the man, reining back an eager Alsatian dog on a short lead.

'Watch yourself then. Some of these save-the-planet loonies are mad bastards.'

The guard left the edge of the field and crossed the margins to reach the fence separating it from the canal towpath. He looked left and right but saw no one. Only the dog stopped him from going back to report a false alarm. It started to bark loudly and strain at the leash.

'What do you see, boy, eh?' asked the man, cautiously

peering into the bushes between him and the canal. 'Some bugger hiding there, you think? Maybe I'll just let you flush 'im out, eh?'

The guard unclipped the dog's lead and the animal shot under the bottom wire of the fence. He went straight past the bushes and up on to the towpath where he stood, looking at the water and barking loudly. His master followed, although it took him a deal longer to get through the fence and struggle up through the undergrowth. He could now see what the dog was excited about and went slightly pale as he brought out his mobile phone to call his colleague. 'Charlie? It's Mac. You'd better get up here.'

A few minutes later the two men stood side by side looking at the body in the water.

'It's a bloke in a dress.'

'He's a minister, you arse.'

'D'you think he's dead?'

'Unless he's wearing an aqualung. He's face down.'

'Shouldn't we pull him out?'

'We'll let the police do that. They get paid for that kind of shit.'

Detective Inspector Brewer watched his men pull the body of James McNish to the side and hoist him on to the bank to turn him over on to his back.

'Christ, what a mess,' murmured one.

'The rats weren't slow getting to him,' said another. 'Look at his neck.'

'What *is* it the residents of Blackbridge have about swimming in the canal?' said the detective sergeant with Brewer. 'You just can't keep them out of it these days.'

Brewer gave a half smile and shrugged. 'Well what d'you reckon? Did he jump or was he pushed?'

'Hard to say anything right now,' replied the sergeant. 'You don't often find a Church of Scotland minister floating up the canal in full gear, so to speak. Could have been a baptism that went horribly wrong . . . or a suicide . . . He could have fallen and hit his head on the path before tumbling in or someone might have pushed him.'

'Or he could have fallen from a passing Boeing 747,' said Brewer. 'Get full statements from the guards, will you? And then we'll see what the doctor has to say.'

'Right, sir.'

'Do you know if he had any relatives?'

The sergeant shrugged. 'Wife ran off a while back. Don't know of anyone else. Seemed to be a bit of a loner by all accounts. Rumour said he drank.'

'So do I,' said Brewer.

'Jesus!' exclaimed the sergeant. 'I've just remembered.'

'Share it with us.'

'It was the Ferguson boy's funeral today in Blackbridge. McNish here must have been officiating: that'll be why he's all dolled up. Wonder if that had anything to do with it.'

# 11

Steven waited until after lunch before driving out to Blackbridge to talk to James Binnie. He left it until then because he wanted to be sure that the Ferguson boy's funeral would be well and truly over and also that the mourners would have had time to disperse. Funerals with media interest always attracted political animals who would see it as a photo opportunity, a chance to display their care and concern to the voting public. He didn't know who would be going from the ranks of the establishment but he did know that he would prefer not to be seen by them. In view of what Macmillan had said, he would be keeping as low a profile as possible from now on.

Ann Binnie smiled pleasantly when she opened the door to him and invited him in. 'James is in his study,' she said. 'He's been expecting you.'

Ann called out to her husband and showed Steven into a small, book-filled room at the back of the house where he found Binnie sitting in an arm chair, one arm dangling over the side, the other holding a glass of whisky.

'Join me?' he asked. 'I don't normally drink at this time of day but after this morning, I need it.'

Steven accepted. 'How did it go?' he asked tentatively.

'The funeral? It was a nightmare and a damned shame for the parents. They didn't need that on top of everything else.'

This was not the reply Steven had expected. 'What went wrong?' he asked.

Binnie took another sip of his whisky and paused for a moment, shaking his head as if unable to accept what he'd seen as really having happened, then he related the events at Canal Field Cemetery to Steven, who found himself horrified.

'Sounds like the man must have had a nervous break-down,' he said. 'What a time to choose.'

'I don't think choice came into it,' said Binnie, 'although I suspect booze did. McNish has been on the road to ruin for years. Well, it's all over now. They pulled him out of the canal an hour ago.'

'He killed himself?' exclaimed Steven.

'More likely he got sozzled and fell in,' said Binnie. 'I hate to speak ill of the dead but, frankly, the place is better off without that man. If you'd heard him at the cemetery this morning, he would have made a barrack-room bruiser sound like Cliff Richard. He really lost it in a big way.'

'Tell me more about the rat,' said Steven.

'What about it?'

'Did you think that was a normal thing for the animal to do in the circumstances?'

Binnie looked at him for a moment. 'Ann said you

wanted to talk about rats,' he said. 'No, I must confess that I didn't. In fact, I've been concerned about quite a few things that our long-tailed friends have been doing in recent weeks. What's your interest in them?'

'No specific interest,' said Steven. 'People keep talking about the general increase in the rat population all over the country but there's been no mention of a change in their behaviour to my knowledge. I just wondered.' Steven told him about the rat that had run out of the rape field and over the security guard's shoes. 'That's what made me think that there might also be some kind of change going on,' he said. 'I remember thinking at the time that it seemed a bit odd, out of character, you might say, as if the rats had suddenly become less timid around here.'

'I think you may well have put your finger on it,' said Binnie. 'The Ferguson boy getting bitten, a puppy being attacked and little incidents like you witnessed up at the field and, of course, what happened at the cemetery this morning. It's been adding up. It's not just that there are many more of the damned things; there *has* been a change in their behaviour as well. I'm convinced of it.'

'Any idea why?'

Binnie shrugged. 'I suppose it could be that the increase in numbers has made them a bit more aggressive. Maybe they are behaving like crowded city dwellers. This could be the first recorded incidence of rat-rage!'

Steven sipped his drink and considered for a moment. 'Your wife said you were going to ask a vet pathologist at the university to take a look at one of them?'

'She's been at you to help get it out of the fridge, right? I might have known it,' smiled Binnie.

'Something like that.'

'Well, it won't do any harm to have one dissected and get an idea of the local population's general health and state of nourishment.'

'What about toxicology?' asked Steven. He said it calmly but he knew that he was upping the stakes considerably.

'I hadn't really thought about that,' said Binnie, looking at him as if trying to read his mind. 'What exactly were you thinking of?'

'Nothing in particular,' lied Steven, for a nightmare thought had just come into his head and he was now trying to manipulate Binnie into doing something that otherwise he might have to do himself. 'I was just thinking of it as a . . . precaution.'

Binnie, however, was an intelligent man. His eyes widened as the same thought came to him. 'My God,' he said in a whisper, 'you're thinking about the GM crop aren't you?'

'Just a thought,' said Steven.

'Bloody hell,' said Binnie. 'But I suppose it's a possibility! I bet they never had this sort of thing in mind at their endless seminars about the unknown effects of GM crops on biodiversity.'

'Quite,' said Steven. 'I suspect they were thinking more about hedgerows and wild flowers and butterflies and the like. I take it they have been treating the crop up on Peat Ridge with glyphosate herbicides?'

Binnie nodded. 'And glufosinate.'

'Powerful stuff,' said Steven.

'It is,' agreed Binnie. 'Farmers haven't been able to use them freely before so no one knows much about possible side effects. I understand a couple of monitors came along from MAFF to see that they did not contaminate the perimeter ground outside acceptable margins.'

'But the rats have been running in and out of the field itself,' protested Steven. 'The margins were irrelevant in their case.'

'I can see that,' said Binnie. 'My God, if you're right and the change in animal behaviour is due to the switch to powerful weedkillers, this could spell disaster for herbicide-resistant GM crops! There must be millions tied up in them.'

'I suggest we say and do nothing until you get the report back from the vet school,' said Steven. 'If the merest suspicion of this were to get out it could wipe millions off the shares of GM companies.'

'Absolutely,' agreed Binnie. 'Apart from that, we'd have a bloody riot on our hands right here. The locals would take things into their own hands as they've been threatening to do for weeks.'

'When will you take the rat over to the vet school?'

'Right now would seem like a good time,' said Binnie, getting up from his chair.

Steven looked at the glass in his hand.

'I've just had the one,' said Binnie.

Out in the hall, Binnie put on his jacket and called out to his wife to say where he was going. Ann Binnie came downstairs and said, 'I'm impressed, Dr Dunbar. It's only taken you ten minutes to get him to do what I've been trying for days. You must let me into your secret.'

Steven walked back to his car and waved to Binnie as he passed him in his Volvo, heading off for Edinburgh. Steven drove off up the road between Crawhill and Peat Ridge, intending to do the same but slowed when he saw Eve Ferguson walking up the road ahead of him; her red hair was unmistakable. As he drew nearer he could tell from her demeanour that she was upset. Her hands were sunk deep into her coat pockets and she was hanging her head. Steven drew to a halt beside her and looked across. She walked on as if unaware that he was even there. He parked the car and got out to walk beside her. 'Penny for them,' he said.

She glanced sideways and said, 'I didn't realise it was you. I don't really want to speak to anyone right now.'

'Not even a stranger?'

'Well, maybe a stranger,' she conceded after a short pause.

They turned off the road to join the canal towpath. 'I heard what happened,' Steven said. 'James Binnie told me.'

Eve shook her head. 'It was awful,' she said. 'I can't begin to tell you how bloody awful it was. Mum and Dad should have been able to look back on today as the day their son was put to rest with respect and dignity. Instead, they'll have nightmares about it for the rest of their lives. I hope McNish rots in . . . Oh God, no I don't. What an awful thing to say. Oh my God . . .'

Eve stopped walking and broke down in tears. Steven wrapped his arm round her and drew her to him. 'It's all right,' he soothed. 'You didn't mean it.'

'Why am I having this conversation?' asked Eve through her tears. 'I don't even believe in anything. Yes I do. Oh God, I don't know what I believe any more.'

There were more tears until eventually Eve calmed down and got back her composure. Steven shushed her as she started to apologise. 'No need,' he said. 'Remember, I'm a stranger. Just say what you feel. Let it all come out.'

They walked on for a bit and then Eve said slowly and deliberately, 'When I heard that they'd taken McNish from the canal, I was so pleased.' She paused, obviously having difficulty getting the words out. 'Until today, I've never understood these people you see outside courts on the news,' she continued. 'You know, the ones leaping up and down and spraying champagne all over the place when the criminal who murdered their husband, wife, son, or whoever, goes down for life, but now I do. That's exactly how I felt when I heard about McNish. I actually felt delighted. I didn't know I could feel like that about anyone's death.'

'And now you are hating yourself for feeling that way?'

'In a word, yes.'

'Don't. Nothing you said or did or felt under the conditions you found yourself in today has any relevance to the real, rational Eve Ferguson. The phrase, "while the balance of his or her mind was temporarily disturbed" doesn't only apply to people who've committed crimes, you know. It's something that can happen to all of us under extreme pressure. The real you is the one talking now.'

Eve dried her eyes and blew her nose. 'Thank you,' she said. 'You seem to know rather a lot about these things. You're not some kind of doctor, are you?'

'Not a practising one.'

'But you *are* a doctor?'

'I work for the Sci-Med Inspectorate,' said Steven. 'I'm an investigator but I'd rather you kept that to yourself.'

'So why tell me?'

'Because you trusted me with your thoughts.'

'That simple?'

'That simple.'

'Can I ask what you are investigating?'

'The GM crop problem on Peat Ridge Farm.'

'I don't think it's an investigator that's needed,' said Eve. 'It's a couple of sheep dogs to sort out these squabbling clowns down at the hotel. I don't think they can agree on what day of the week it is.'

'The politics of the situation don't concern me directly,' said Steven. 'Just the science and what they're doing with it.'

'All right, I won't ask any more questions,' said Eve.

'I'd like to ask you one,' said Steven. 'Do you know how I could get in touch with Trish Rafferty?'

Eve looked at him out of the corner of her eye. 'Why?'

'I need to talk to her.'

'What about?'

'Life with Thomas.'

'She'd probably question you calling it a life.'

'That bad?'

'He didn't beat her up, if that's what you mean. He's just a lazy drunk. Great fun for his pals in the pub but a complete pain in the arse to be married to, I should think.'

'I gather he was pretty much always like that,' said Steven.

'So?'

'So what finally pushed her into leaving him?'

'Funny you should ask that,' said Eve. 'I remember wondering about that at the time because he didn't seem to be behaving particularly badly. In fact, he'd just bought her a new car a few weeks before she left. But she never told me why she walked out and, to this day, the subject is still off limits.'

'So you've seen her since she left him?'

'Once or twice.'

'So are you going to tell me where I can find her?'

Eve hesitated for quite a while before saying, 'Trish was the nearest thing to a friend I could get around here. She's much older than I am but she's an intelligent woman and I enjoyed her company. We could talk about things other than what was on telly last night. I'm not at all sure about your interest in her. What aspect of her life with Tom is it that you want to know about?'

'I understand how you feel,' said Steven, 'and I respect your loyalty, but Thomas Rafferty told me that everything he's doing these days he's doing in order to get his wife to come back to him. I want to know what his chances are.'

'Why? What on earth has the Raffertys' private life to do with your investigation?'

'If Trish Rafferty tells me that she's considering coming back to Rafferty when he's sorted himself out, well and good. I'll wish them both well. But if she says that there's no chance of a reconciliation, Rafferty probably knows that too and there's some other reason behind his sudden passion for organic farming.'

'Trish lives in Edinburgh. She has a flat in Dorset Place. It looks out on the canal, would you believe?'

'The same canal?'

'The very same, about fifteen miles from here.'

Steven wrote down the details and thanked Eve for her help.

'I feel like I've betrayed her,' said Eve.

'You haven't, believe me.'

Steven drove slowly into Edinburgh, wondering again about the GM crop and whether or not there was a connection between it and the change in the rats' behaviour. If there was, then he had just found the missing motive for attempting to discredit Agrigene and having their crop destroyed. The worrying drawback to this conclusion was that it implied that someone already knew about the rats' behavioural change. But who and how exactly?

Had this type of crop been tested on some other site? he wondered. Was the problem confined to the Agrigene strain or was it a more general problem connected with the weedkillers rather than the crops? The questions were coming thick and fast. Not least was the one concerning the warning off that Sci-Med had received at the outset. This suggested strongly that it was the government, or some part of it, that knew that there was a problem with the crop but, clearly, they were not willing to deal with it openly.

Could it be something so sensitive? Something so liable to attract scandal and adverse publicity that they felt forced to disrupt the trial surreptitiously and come up with an excuse to destroy it? Steven could even find support for that theory in the pension deal that Gerald Millar had received. That must have had official sanction. Millar must have been encouraged to concoct a misleading report in order to discredit Agrigene and put an end to their trial, but Fildes, his boss, had known nothing at all about it, nor had Millar's colleagues.

This suggested to Steven that it had not been sanctioned through normal channels but that it had been part of a covert operation being run from within government circles and possibly with the blessing of someone in high office. He could even put money on knowing its code name. Sigma 5. That would explain the reaction when he had asked Sci-Med to enquire about it. The whole thing had obviously gone badly wrong on the ground when the ranks of officialdom spawned by two governments had started locking horns over responsibility for what was going on in Blackbridge.

Steven tried to step back from the details and take a look at the bigger picture. He supposed that it all made some kind of chilling sense. The days when people imagined that the British government wouldn't do that sort of a thing were long gone. Too many embarrassing cover-ups and manipulations had come to light in recent years. The fact of the matter was that the public were dead set against the idea of GM crops and the government had flown in the face of public opinion by granting a plethora of licences to research companies to carry out trials on them.

It was true that many of these permissions had been agreed before public awareness had been heightened by press coverage of the subject and 'genetic' had become a scare word – Agrigene's licence was an example of this – but, once granted, the permissions lasted for several years. Agrigene's licence ran until the year 2003. Now it was all looking like a recipe for disaster.

But if the problem were a general one, concerned with the use of powerful weedkillers, there would be no point in just destroying the Agrigene crop on its own, Steven concluded. There were similar trials going on all over the UK. Herbicide-resistant oilseed rape was one of the commonest GM crops around. This tended to imply that there might be something *specifically* wrong with the crop up on Peat Ridge Farm. But what? He felt uncomfortable with this thought. From what he'd seen, the crop was exactly what its designers claimed it to be.

'Damnation,' Steven sighed. Theories were all well and good when everything fitted but when there was something that didn't fit – even if it seemed like a tiny detail – it was his experience that that usually turned out to be the hole below the waterline. He would proceed with caution and try to keep an open mind. This meant that he would have to consider other possibilities as to why a secret government initiative had been mounted in order to discredit and destroy a perfectly harmless crop.

Steven turned into Dorset Place and found visitors' car parking space outside a pleasant block of modern flats, sitting on the south bank of the Union Canal. He checked the number of Trish Rafferty's apartment on the paper in his pocket and got out to walk over to the entrance and pressed the entryphone button.

'Yes?'

'Mrs Rafferty? My name is Steven Dunbar. I'm with the Sci-Med Inspectorate. I wonder if I might speak with you?'

'The who?'

'The Sci-Med Inspectorate. It's a government body. I can show you identification.'

There was a long pause before Trish Rafferty activated the door release and Steven walked into the hall and headed for the stairs. He ran up them two at a time and knocked gently on the front door that had been left ajar.

'Come.'

Steven could see that Trish Rafferty was angry. She was

standing in the middle of her living room, arms folded and face red. She was clearly having difficulty reining in her temper. Steven, feeling distinctly uncomfortable because he had no idea why, showed her his ID.

Trish scarcely glanced at it. 'You people,' she hissed through gritted teeth. 'You people promised me that I would never see or hear from you again! Promised! Do you hear? What the hell do you think you are doing, coming here to my home?'

Steven's first thought was to say that there had obviously been some mistake and that no one from Sci-Med had contacted her before, but he stopped himself in time. It would perhaps be more useful to let the woman speak her mind.

'I'm sorry, I wasn't aware of that,' he said contritely.

'You promised me!' stormed Trish. 'That was the deal. I would tell you everything I knew. You would put a stop to it and he would not get into any serious trouble with the law. That would be an end to it. After that I was not to see you or him ever again!'

'I really am sorry about this, Mrs Rafferty. It clearly shouldn't have happened but I'm new to the job and I wonder if you wouldn't mind just filling me in on some of the details? Of the agreement, that is.'

Trish looked at Steven for a long moment then said suspiciously, 'Who the hell are you?'

'As I said, I'm from the Sci-Med Inspectorate,' said Steven evenly. He got out his ID card again but Trish waved it away.

'You're not one of them at all, are you?' she said, anger now being replaced by uncertainty in her voice. 'Get out!' she said. 'Just get the fuck out!'

Steven paused outside to look over the wall of the car park and gaze down at the canal for a few moments. Well, well, well, he thought. What was that all about? It was obvious that Trish Rafferty had had some sort of recent dealings with officialdom and she'd mistaken him for one of them, whoever 'they' were. Curiouser and curiouser . . . He hadn't imagined that Trish Rafferty had been playing any kind of active part in this affair. What was it she'd said? She'd told *them* everything she knew and that she didn't want to see *them* or *him* ever again. Could the *him* referred to be her husband? If that were the case, it seemed to answer his original question about the possibility of a reconciliation. There wasn't going to be any. The rest had been a bit of a bonus.

Steven glanced up at Trish Rafferty's window before he got in to his car. She was standing there looking down at him and she had a telephone to her ear. He would have given a lot to know at that moment who she was calling.

# 12

Steven's phone rang as he was driving back to his hotel. It was Jamie Brown.

'Where are you?' asked Brown.

'In town. Why?'

'Can we meet? I've come up with something on Childs and Leadbetter.'

Brown was calling from his paper's offices on North Bridge. They arranged to meet approximately halfway between them, in Bennett's Bar at Tollcross. Brown got there first: Steven found him standing at the bar with a whisky in front of him. The place was rapidly filling up with after-work drinkers.

'Did you hear what happened at the Ferguson boy's funeral?' asked Brown.

Steven said that he had and agreed that it must have been a nightmare for the parents.

'The paper's going to back-pedal on the theatricals as much as possible for the family's sake,' said Brown. 'We'll have to report the subsequent aquatic adventures of the minister but we're going to play down his behaviour in the cemetery, drunken sod.'

Steven nodded.

'Christ knows what the *Clarion* will do with it. Jeff, my photographer, says they had two snappers there, using big lenses. If they got a shot of the rat on the coffin, McColl will find some way of using it.'

'Surely not?'

'Want a bet?'

'No,' replied Steven, remembering what McColl was like. 'You said you had something on Childs and Leadbetter?'

'I told you I didn't think they fitted the bill as venture capitalists. I know it's the fashion to go to the gym these days but these two look as if they live in it. Come to think of it, you don't look too much like a couch potato yourself.'

Steven waved away the comment. 'Go on.'

'I had our researchers check on a possible military background for either or both of them and they came up trumps. Both were commissioned in the Royal Engineers and both served nine years. Childs from '87 until '96 and Leadbetter from '88 until '97.'

'Well done,' said Steven. He felt slightly disturbed at the news but tried to make light of it. 'So they can build bridges or maybe they were REME accountants,' he said.

Brown looked at him slyly and put on a Japanese accent borrowed from a Bond film. 'Not ordinary accountants, Bondo-San, but Ninja, *chartered* accountants!'

'There's more?'

'Both men have gaps in their service record,' said Brown. 'Childs disappears between '89 and '91, Leadbetter between '90 and '94. Mean anything?'

Steven knew damn well what it meant but he wasn't sure if Brown did and he wasn't sure that he wanted to tell him.

'It should,' continued Brown. 'There's a similar gap in yours.'

Steven looked at him with an expression set in stone.

'Nothing personal,' said Brown quickly. 'And nothing I'll ever use. I just thought as the folks were checking military records they could take a look at who was on my side.'

'So we were all seconded to Special Forces,' said Steven.

'Except me, of course,' added Brown facetiously. 'I've got flat feet and an intense dislike of anything that goes bang. Orders are something I give to Chinese takeaways so I guess I'm more suited to being . . . Oh, I suppose, something like a venture capitalist?'

Steven found it hard not to smile. Brown had done well in following up his suspicions. He said so.

'So all we have to discover now is why our peasant piss-artist, our would-be organic son of the soil, has two ex-SAS men as *business associates*.'

Steven decided that he liked Brown. He was clearly much brighter than he'd given him credit for at the outset. It was time to trust him and give a little back.

'The stakes have risen,' he said. 'This thing is much bigger than I imagined. It's not some little dirty trick by one company on another. Her Majesty's Government, or some part of it, is mixed up in it. They're definitely the ones pulling strings in the background.'

'Jesus,' said Brown. 'Why?'

'I don't know,' replied Steven truthfully.

'Christ,' said Brown. 'Does this mean that Childs and

Leadbetter are not employed as mercenaries? That they're actually still working for HM government?'

'Could be,' agreed Steven.

'Not a happy thought,' said Brown.

'The operation has the code name Sigma 5, but I wouldn't start asking too many questions about it if I were you. Apart from unpleasant things that might happen, you'll get nowhere, just like I did. It has all the hallmarks of being set up as a covert operation so that no one person will ever be held accountable. No paperwork will be kept and no one in power will ever admit to knowing anything at all about it. If anyone at the sharp end hits trouble they'll be entirely on their own.'

'But this is Tony's World,' said Brown sarcastically. 'This just cannot be. Tony wouldn't allow it.'

'Tony will know nothing about it,' said Steven. 'The "need to know basis" can work both ways. Some things never change. Politicians only think they run the country.'

'That's certainly true of the Jock parliament,' said Brown. 'Just as well, mind you. They couldn't run a raffle or even spell it in some cases. So where do we go from here?'

'As I see it, there are two weak links in the operation,' said Steven, 'and they're both called Rafferty.'

'You managed to talk to Trish Rafferty, then?'

'She's living here in Edinburgh, in a flat in Dorset Place. I was on my way back from her place when you phoned. She's definitely in on it. She let something slip when she thought I was one of the Sigma 5 lot.'

'What did she say?'

'Something about her having told them things in

exchange for them not bothering her again and *him* not getting into trouble.'

'Her husband?'

'A fair assumption.'

'Do you think she can be persuaded to talk more about it?'

Steven shook his head. 'She struck me as an intelligent, strong-willed woman who wouldn't go back on her word unless she had reason to believe that someone had crossed her.'

'So we concentrate on Tom for the moment?'

'I think so.'

'That leaves us with the problem of our two "venture capitalists",' said Brown. 'They do a fair impression of being attached at the hip to our hop-loving friend. Mind you, the mere idea of tangling with these two is going to save me a fortune on *All-Bran*. Any ideas?'

'I've an awful feeling that the next move may come from them,' said Steven. 'If Childs and Leadbetter are who you say they are, they will have reported my visit and questioning of Rafferty at Crawhill Farm.'

'So what. You had every right to be there and to question him. You're on official Sci-Med business.'

Steven told him about Sci-Med being warned off and Brown let out a low whistle. 'It's that big?' he murmured.

'I thought I was managing to keep a pretty low profile but apparently not. When I went to Crawhill and flashed my ID, I was actually knocking on the door of Sigma 5. I suspect that Trish Rafferty reported my visit too,' said Steven, thinking of her standing at the window with the telephone in her hand.

'I see what you mean by "their move",' agreed Brown. 'Any idea what it will be?'

'I can't see it at the moment,' said Steven thoughtfully.

'I'm going back to the office,' said Brown. 'I'm going to write all this down and leave it in a safe place, then I'm going to write you a letter on *Scotsman* headed paper, saying that we know all about Sigma 5 and that if you should be the subject of any "tragic accident" we are going to shake the tree until all the apples fall down. Carry it with you.'

Steven smiled, uncomfortable as always with melodrama but still seeing the sense in what Brown was saying. Publicity was to covert operations as garlic was to a vampire.

'I'll pop it in to your hotel.'

Steven had just got out the bath when his phone rang. It was Detective Chief Inspector Brewer. 'I've got something here that might interest you.'

'Where's here?'

'The City Mortuary.'

Steven wrote down the directions he was given and dressed quickly. He drove over to the old town where darkness, dirt and history conspired with a late evening mist to produce an atmosphere appropriate to the nature of his visit. He found the unprepossessing building of the City Mortuary a few minutes after leaving the car and rang the bell. It was answered by an attendant, dressed in white overalls topped by an over-large plastic apron, which came right down to the floor, almost but not quite obscuring the toes of his Wellington boots. The man sniffed loudly and scratched his stubbly chin as he examined Steven's ID before stepping back to let him come inside to bright lights and the smell of formaldehyde. There was something about mortuary attendants, thought Steven, but what it was he had no wish to pursue for the moment. He heard Brewer's voice and followed the sound.

'Ah, Dr Dunbar, I thought you'd be interested in hearing what Dr Levi here has to say about the Rev. McNish,' said Brewer. Steven had walked into the PM room where the duty pathologist had just finished work on the body of a badly mutilated male corpse. He nodded to an attendant who started threading a suture needle to begin sewing up the long primary incision that extended from throat to navel.

Levi, a small man, wearing heavy square-rimmed glasses, which seemed all wrong for his pear-shaped face, stripped off his gloves and tossed them into a pedal bin with an air of finality. The metal lid of the bin fell with a clang like a cymbal being hit by a percussionist at the end of a performance. It was obviously something he'd done many times before. It reminded Steven of a story that said Fred Astaire could walk across stage, throw down a cigarette butt and stamp it out without breaking stride.

'This man did not drown,' said Levi. 'He died from blood loss resulting from biting injuries: the tooth patterns on these injuries are consistent with rat bites. This is the one that actually did it.'

Levi waved the attendant out of the way and pointed to teeth marks on the side of McNish's neck. 'Carotid artery. I hope for his sake that this was one of the earlier bites otherwise . . .' He looked down at the horrific injuries over McNish's body. 'Well, let's say, he didn't have the easiest of passages from this life to the next.'

'So the rats got him,' said Brewer. 'What do you make of that?'

'Interesting,' murmured Steven, still looking down at the corpse as if unable to take his eyes away.

'Perhaps you know more about what's happening up at Blackbridge than I do, Doctor?' said Brewer.

'No, but somebody does.'

Brewer looked at Steven as if not knowing whether to believe him or not. 'This GM crop business wouldn't have anything to do with it, would it?'

'I don't see how,' replied Steven guardedly.

'Maybe it's like they say. There are just too many unknowns connected with something like that. They should have done more work in the lab before they started putting the stuff out into open fields.'

'Don't jump to conclusions,' said Steven, but he was wondering just how many other people were going to leap to exactly the same one.

'Of course not,' said Brewer sourly.

'Otherwise it could be a recipe for disaster,' added Steven, looking directly at Brewer so that he fully understood what he meant.

'Frankly, Doctor,' said Brewer, 'There are times when I'm tempted to torch the bloody stuff myself.'

Steven drove back to the hotel and, despite having bathed a few hours earlier, took a shower in order to free himself of the lingering smell of formaldehyde. He hated the foetid sweetness of it and the images it conjured up. The smell went but the image of McNish's body stayed with him despite the best efforts of three gin and tonics. The rats at Blackbridge had actually killed a man – maybe two people if you counted Ian Ferguson as well. That was some behavioural change. True it wasn't known just how much provocation there had been, at least not in the case of McNish. It was possible that he had fallen into the canal in his drunken state and provoked them in some way, just as it was possible that the Ferguson boy might have stood on one, but it was a worry all the same. Something would have to be done.

Just what that something would be was taken out of everyone's hands next morning when the *Clarion* story appeared, confirming Jamie Brown's worst fears about what McColl might do. The paper had used a funeral photograph on its front page. As predicted by Brown, it was the one of the rat sitting on top of Ian Ferguson's coffin with McNish looking on with eyes like a homicidal maniac in the background. The headline screamed, 'THIS SCANDAL HAS TO STOP'. The story was angled as a crusade against what the paper saw as the disgrace of an ever-increasing rat population in the Union Canal while the authorities did little or nothing at all about it. Yesterday one of these 'filthy creatures' had defiled the funeral of Blackbridge teenager, Ian Ferguson, bringing unnecessary pain and anguish to his grieving family.

'Not that your shitty little rag isn't doing exactly that,' murmured Steven as he read on.

The paper extended its heart-felt sympathy to the Fergusons and promised to keep up pressure on 'the guilty ones' until something was done and no one else would have to go through the hell they'd been through.

Steven felt like vomiting at the hypocrisy but at least the *Clarion* hadn't cottoned on to the change of behaviour angle. That was a blessing, he thought. A campaign against increasing rat numbers would probably result in a local rat cull and, right now, that sounded just fine. The paper went on to complain about the continuing strength of feeling against the GM crop trial in Blackbridge and deplored the authorities' lack of progress in sorting it out. They called for intervention at ministerial level and demanded that the relevant ministers return from their 'endless' holiday to take charge. They went on to list the ministers concerned from both the Westminster and Scottish Parliaments and gave details of their salaries and the length of their summer vacation and even where they were currently sunning themselves. 'We want organ grinders dealing with the situation, not monkeys,' demanded the *Clarion*. 'There are enough of them to start a zoo!'

Jamie Brown turned up at the hotel just as Steven was preparing to drive out to Blackbridge. He handed over the letter that he'd promised and Steven put it in his inside pocket with a nod of thanks.

'You've seen McColl's piece?'

Steven nodded.

'Makes you wonder about the human race, huh?'

'Despair would be a better word,' said Steven.

'What are your plans?'

'I think I'll have another word with Eve Ferguson. She's a friend of Trish Rafferty's. Maybe Trish said something to her or maybe just dropped a clue about what's been going on. I'll see if I can jog her memory. You?'

'I've been told to ask the authorities what they plan to do about the rat problem now that it's been highlighted by our friend McColl. Do you have any idea what they'll do?'

'They can't use poison because it would mean contaminating the entire canal and killing off everything in it. So that leaves mounting some kind of cull using firearms.'

'How successful would that be?'

'Not very,' said Steven. 'But don't quote me on that. It's the gesture that's all-important in this instance. The powers-that-be will just want to be seen doing something in order to get McColl off their backs.'

'If I didn't know you better, Doctor, I'd say you were a cynic.'

'I prefer realist,' said Steven.

'Me too but it's a lost cause. Every time I hear Barbra Streisand singing "People", I want to throw up.'

They parted company and Steven reflected on the one thing that he had not shared with Brown, the information about the change in the rats' behaviour and its possible link to the GM crop. His main reason for driving over to Blackbridge that morning was not to speak with Eve – although he intended to do that too – but to ask James Binnie if he'd heard anything back from the vet school yet about the PM examination on the rat.

'I'm afraid James is out on his rounds,' said Ann Binnie when she opened the door to him.

'I feared he might be,' Steven confessed. 'Maybe you can tell me if he's heard anything back from the university?'

Ann Binnie shook her head. 'I'm pretty sure he didn't hear anything this morning,' she said. 'If he had, I'm sure he would have said. Why don't I get him to call you as soon as he hears?'

Steven left his mobile phone number and thanked her, declining her kind offer of coffee. He walked along the street to the Blackbridge Arms and looked at his watch. It wasn't quite lunchtime. Perhaps he could snatch a word with Eve before the rush started. He went into the bar and asked for a half of lager. He sipped it slowly until Eve noticed him standing there as she was passing between the kitchen and the dining room.

'Hello,' she said. 'Staying for lunch?'

'No, I actually wanted to see you. Do you have a minute?'

Eve looked doubtful and looked up at the clock over the bar. It was five to twelve. 'Lunch starts in five minutes,' she said.

'Five minutes will be fine.'

Eve took off her apron and put on a jacket.

'I went to see Trish Rafferty,' Steven said as they started to walk.

'Was she very angry with me?'

'She doesn't know anything about your involvement,' said Steven. 'She mistook me for someone else. She thought I'd come to see her for another reason entirely.'

'I don't think I understand. What other reason?'

'Now that's something I'd really like to know,' said Steven. 'Trish Rafferty is mixed up in this GM scandal business in some way but she saw through me before she said too much.'

'Trish? Involved? You're joking.'

'I'm certain. She said enough to make me sure of that.'

'So where do I come into all this?' asked Eve.

'I'd like you to think back to your last conversation with her, just to see if you can remember her saying anything – anything at all – that you might have thought sounded odd at the time but probably dismissed as something you didn't pick up properly. Anything at all.'

'I don't think I remember anything like that,' said Eve. 'I've only seen her twice since she left.'

'And you noticed nothing strange about her at all? She wasn't worried or secretive? She didn't seem nervous?'

Eve shrugged. 'In truth, I suppose she was all of these things to a certain extent but as she had just left her husband I didn't think there was anything strange or unusual about it. It was a big step to take after all these years.'

'I suppose so.'

'I do remember thinking at one point that she might have had another man on the go. It wasn't anything she said. It was more an air of . . .' Eve searched for the right word. 'Guilt, I think. Yes, that was it. She struck me as having an air of guilt about her.'

'Could that have been about leaving her husband?'

'No, she didn't say too much about that, come to think of it, but when she did speak about Tom it was as if she seemed relieved to be away from him, not feeling guilty.'

'Good,' said Steven. 'I couldn't persuade you to visit her again, could I? This is important.'

Eve's eyes widened. She asked, 'Just what would I be getting into?'

'She just might confide in you what she was feeling guilty about whereas she wouldn't dream of telling me.'

'And then I betray her to you?'

'You tell me if it's something you think might concern me. If it turns out to be another bloke or she's fiddling her tax return or even if she turns out to be the Brighton trunk murderer, I don't want to know. Bargain?'

Eve looked anxiously at her watch. 'I must go.'

'Will you do it?'

Eve looked very uncertain. 'I really don't know,' she said. 'God, I must go.'

'Have dinner with me tonight?'

'I'm working.'

'Tomorrow?'

Eve thought for a moment before saying, 'All right. Pick me up here at seven thirty.'

Steven drove over to police headquarters in Livingston to see Brewer. He had just got out of his car when he saw Alex McColl coming out the building. He quickly ducked back in and pretended to be looking for something in the glove compartment until McColl had got into his own car and driven off.

'What did *he* want?' asked Steven of Brewer.

'The cause of death for the Rev. McNish,' Brewer replied.

'That's what I came here to talk to you about,' exclaimed Steven, suddenly alarmed. 'I hope you stalled him.'

'No, I gave him the official cause.'

'Shit.'

'Drowning.'

'What?'

Brewer pushed a piece of paper over the desk in Steven's direction. 'It's official. The PM report says so.'

Steven couldn't believe his eyes when he read through the report which concluded in 'Death by drowning'. He looked at Brewer. 'Have you spoken to Levi about this?' he asked.

'The good doctor has been hard to get hold of today. Ours is not to reason why,' said Brewer.

'Who leaned on him?' asked Steven.

Brewer just shrugged his shoulders. 'I don't know,' he said resignedly. 'I just hope to God all you buggers know what you're doing.'

# 13

Steven's first thought was to go after Levi and demand to know why he had put a different cause of death on the PM report to the one he had already given orally to Brewer and himself at the city mortuary. But when he'd calmed down he decided against it. Doing that wasn't going to solve anything and would just advertise his own involvement in the Blackbridge affair even more. He could certainly gain satisfaction from rattling Levi's cage until the man admitted that he'd been leaned on but there really wasn't any doubt about that. The real question was who had done the leaning? And he felt certain that Levi would not know the answer to that, just that the order had come down from on high.

Steven bit the bullet and accepted that he wasn't going to get any closer to Sigma 5 by pursuing that course of action so there was no point in even considering it. Instead he simply tried to analyse the motives behind such a cover-up.

Clearly, Sigma 5 did not want the press to know about

the rats' involvement in McNish's death – presumably because it did not want anyone making the connection between the GM experiment and the change in the rats' behaviour – always assuming that there was a connection. The little niggling doubt came back again, the one that said that there was nothing at all wrong with the Agrigene crop: it was perfectly ordinary oilseed rape.

The actions of the opposition in all this, however, were forcing him to consider that maybe there was something about the crop that he didn't know, something that made the Agrigene oilseed rape different from all the other GM variants. Thinking along these lines made him conclude that he should have another talk with their technical manager, Phillip Grimble.

Steven was near enough to Peat Ridge Farm to act upon that thought immediately. He turned into the track leading up to the farm and, as expected, was flagged down by security guards. He went through the ritual of showing his ID but this time he asked the one who was doing the phoning to find out if the Agrigene man was still there. He was.

'Well, Doctor, I trust you have come to tell me that the authorities have finally admitted their blunder. They've agreed to pay us large amounts of compensation and we can stop paying all these guards out there forthwith?' said Ronald Lane by way of greeting.

'Not quite,' said Steven. 'That won't be my decision, I'm afraid. I'm just here to see fair play along the way. Actually, I'd like a few words with Mr Grimble, if that's possible.'

'Words, words, words,' sneered Lane. 'We're never short of words round here. It's translating them into some kind of bloody action that seems to be the problem. You'll find him in the office along there, planning our latest defence strategy,' said Lane with a wry smile. He pointed to a door along the hallway. 'If you don't need me, Doctor, I have plenty to be getting on with.'

Steven said not and went off to find Grimble on his own. He knocked and put his head round the door. 'All right if I come in?'

Grimble looked up from the papers he was studying and said wearily, 'Please. Any excuse to stop going through endless legal jargon is welcome.'

'Problems?'

'It's the latest submission from Rafferty's lawyers. As far as I can make out, they are willing to concede that the "third genetic element" in our crop is, in fact, an antibiotic marker gene – as we've maintained all along. But now they are arguing that the insertion of such an element into the DNA of the plant has by definition altered the genetic make-up of the plant itself, thus constituting a third change, where only two were licensed. They plan to wheel out scientific experts to testify to this in court, if we ever get that far.'

'So what will you do?'

'Wheel out *our* scientific experts to point out that this is always the case with antibiotic markers and it's completely irrelevant. If we'd hit a vital gene the plant wouldn't have been able to grow. If we'd inserted it in any gene that was in any way at all important to the yield, it would have showed up in the nature of the mature plant and it hasn't. What we have here is oilseed rape that can withstand the action of glyphosphate and glufosinate weedkillers. Period.'

Grimble leaned back in his chair and stretched his arms in the air. 'That's the trouble with expert witnesses,' he said. 'If one says white, it's the easiest thing in the world to find another who'll say black. Christ, this is like trying to swim in treacle!' He rubbed the back of his head and brought his arms back down to rest on the desk. 'I'm sorry,' he said. 'How can I help you?'

'I'd like to know if Agrigene are growing the Peat Ridge oilseed rape anywhere else in the UK?' asked Steven.

'Yes, we've got four other trials running: one in Cambridge, one in Worcester and two in Leicestershire.'

'The identical crop?'

'Absolutely. All the seeds came from the same batch. We're just trying out different herbicide regimes on them to assess crop yields. No one has been able to use glyphosphates and glufosinates at will before.'

'Has any attempt been made by the authorities to stop the English trials?' asked Steven.

'Not by the authorities,' said Grimble. 'We've had a bit of bother with student protests and friends-of-the-turnip and such like but nothing like the legal shit we've been getting thrown at us up here.'

'It strikes me that you could always bring evidence that your crop here is genetically identical to your English ones,' suggested Steven.

'I did think of that,' said Grimble ruefully, 'but frankly it could go either way. The fact that the authorities seem to have it in for us up here suggests that we might end up losing our English trials as well. I've decided to fight the Scottish Executive for the Peat Ridge crop on its own merits and argue every legal step of the way. I make no bones about it; I'm stalling for time. As long as the crop's in the fields out there, our trial is proceeding.'

'I wish you luck,' said Steven. 'And I mean that.' He thanked Grimble for his help and set off for Edinburgh. It was now too late to get lunch anywhere so he picked up a sandwich at a shop in Colinton village and ate it in the nearby park, sitting on a seat by the river.

What he had learned from Grimble suggested almost conclusively that there could not be anything specifically wrong with the Peat Ridge crop. Sigma 5 would know about the other Agrigene sites and, more importantly, that the crop growing in them was identical to the one in Peat Ridge. If they were really trying to cover up a connection between the experimental crop and a worrying effect on animal behaviour, they would have to have mounted some kind of dirty tricks campaign against the English trials as well.

Steven returned to his hotel and spent what remained of the afternoon making out an interim report for Sci-Med. Although his computer had been set to encrypt the message, he still hesitated before hitting the 'send' button and decided to mark it for Macmillan's eyes only. Sci-Med was a relatively small operation and he thought he knew and trusted everyone in it, but the government involvement in this affair was making him nervous. When people couldn't tell the good guys from the bad, all sorts of pressures could come into play. Marking the message in such a way would not physically stop someone else at Sci-Med from opening it but the message would there-after be marked with the date, time and staff code of the person who had opened it. It was that knowledge that would stop a third party even thinking about it.

He sent off a full report of his progress and thoughts about the situation so far and, in a separate message, requested any information that Sci-Med could come up with on Childs and Leadbetter with respect to their military careers. He didn't expect to get back anything on their time with Special Forces – that kind of information was always notoriously difficult to obtain, if not downright impossible – but it seemed reasonable to hope for something more than the bare bones that Jamie Brown had come up with.

With work out of the way, he phoned his sister-in-law, Sue, down in Dumfries to check that it would be all right for him to come over at the weekend.

'Of course,' replied Sue. 'We all look forward to seeing you. What's it like to be back at work?'

'Challenging,' replied Steven after a moment's pause to think of the right word. 'How's my little monster behaving herself?'

'Challenging,' replied Sue and they both laughed. 'Jenny needs to know the reason for everything and she won't be fobbed off, a bit like her father I should think. I must say I'll be glad when the school holidays are over and I'll have at least two of them off my hands through the day. Actually, I think I can get Jenny a place in a new nursery school that's opened up in the village. What do you think?'

'Great idea all round,' said Steven. 'Then she can pick on someone her own size! Just let me know about fees.'

'We can talk about that when you come down. I'll put Jenny on and she can give you your orders.'

Steven had a ten-minute conversation with his daughter, which Jenny monopolised with talk of nursery school and what she was going to do and learn when she went there. She ended up by asking, 'Have you caught any bad men yet, Daddy?'

'Not yet, Nutkin, but I'm working on it.'

Steven had a drink in the hotel bar and sought advice over which restaurant to take Eve Ferguson to on the following evening. With Childs and Leadbetter constantly riding shotgun on Rafferty, he saw persuading Eve to help him get to Trish Rafferty as his best chance of making progress in that direction.

'Somewhere a bit different,' he requested, 'a bit special.'

'The Witchery,' suggested the barman. 'It's up by the castle and very atmospheric. Try their Secret Garden. She'll be very impressed, I'm sure,' he added with a wink.

'It's business,' said Steven. He phoned and made a reservation although the restaurant made a point of telling him how lucky he was to get one at such short notice.

Steven had something to eat in the bar and then went out for a walk. The area round about the hotel was affluent and pleasant: leafy lanes, large houses and walled gardens. BMW and Mercedes cars sat silently on gravel; stable conversions and lodge cottages housed aspiring professionals, while the mansions sheltered old money as they always had.

What wind there had been during the day had dropped away to nothing and the scents of late summer were heavy in the air as he walked simply for the sake of it. He found it easy to surmise that some of these homes would house people who worked for the Scottish Executive or maybe even the pillars of the establishment who ran it, people who might know just what the hell was going on out at Blackbridge.

Steven read the *Scotsman* while he had breakfast in the hotel conservatory. Jamie Brown had a piece in it about the failure of government, local or otherwise, to agree who was responsible for doing something about the increasing rat population all over the country, but particularly in the Blackbridge area which had been so recently and tragically highlighted. The local council maintained it was a district council matter; the district council thought that Rural Affairs at the Scottish Parliament should deal with it. Rural Affairs thought it was an Environmental Health matter and so on and so forth.

Brown had managed to get a couple of 'expert views' on how the matter should be tackled when responsibility had been agreed. The bottom line seemed to be that anything other than poison was going to be less than effective. The general public really had to be 'educated' about not making it easy for rats to thrive and multiply. The animals had to be denied access to all likely sources of nutrition, particularly rubbish sacks that often tended to be less than secure.

A bit late for that, thought Steven, but then he was allergic to experts who wanted to 'educate the public'. The very phrase made him want to dig his heels in. It was such a pleasant morning that he lingered in the front garden for a little while. He walked up to the wishing well at the head of the lawn and rested his hands on the brickwork for a moment, thinking of Lisa but no longer in a maudlin way. He smiled at the memory but did, however, feel a twinge of guilt over the fact that he was going to be having dinner with another woman this evening.

He walked back to the car park and got into his car. He

clipped on his belt and turned the key but nothing happened. He tried again and then once more after wiggling the steering wheel backwards and forwards to make sure that the lock was fully disengaged. To Steven's chagrin, the engine remained silent and lifeless.

The only sound, apart from the birds in the garden, was an intermittent tinkling noise, like wind chimes or distant bells.

'Shit,' sighed Steven, annoyed that a car less than thirteen months old had let him down. Surely car batteries should last longer than that these days, he thought angrily. It wasn't even winter. He tested the battery by turning the ignition back on and trying various accessories. The heater fan whirred into life, the radio worked and his headlights were reflected brightly in the windows of the hotel dining room. There was nothing wrong with the battery. He sighed and rested his hands on the wheel, wondering what to try next, when he suddenly became aware that the wind chime noise had started up again – although it was a perfectly calm morning.

During the next few seconds Steven's spine turned to ice and a cold sweat broke out on his brow as he made the connection between the tinkling sound and his turning on the ignition switch. The sound wasn't distant at all; it was coming from under the bonnet and it wasn't random noise. It was organised and musical . . . It was a tune and one he now recognised . . . Be it ever so humble, there's no place . . .

As the last line of the song neared completion he flung himself from the car and rolled down the grassy bank on to the lawn to lie face-down in the grass with his hands over his head. Nothing happened.

After fully a minute of waiting with nerve ends like broken glass, he crawled cautiously back up the bank and approached the car. The tune was still playing. He opened the driver's door gingerly and reached in under the dash to release the bonnet catch. With his nerves in their current state, he could have done without the ensuing clunk. He moved round to the front of the car and felt gently along the gap between the open bonnet and the car body. He didn't find any wires so he released the secondary catch and lifted the bonnet up.

He stared down at a small pine musical box sitting on top of the engine. The wire that normally connected the key switch to the electronic ignition system had been re-routed via a step-down transformer to a musical box that had been taped to the engine block. The tune was coming to an end again: 'There's no-o place like home . . .' It started up all over again and Steven yanked the wires from the box in an angry gesture. He pulled the musical box away from its tape anchors, feeling sick in his stomach. It could so easily have been a lump of semtex sitting there. Instead, this time it had been a warning.

A voice at his side asked, 'Everything all right?'

Steven jumped slightly then swallowed, trying to regain his composure. He turned to find the hotel manager standing there. He hadn't heard him approach.

'I saw you there with the bonnet of your car up from the lounge window,' said the man pleasantly. 'Would you like me to call the local garage?'

'No need,' said Steven. His throat was so dry that his voice came out as a croak. He cleared it and continued, 'A slight problem with the engine immobiliser. Damn thing's always playing up.'

'Security systems cause more trouble than they're worth,' said the manager sympathetically. 'The only people they really inconvenience are their owners and the neighbours. When it's windy round here it sounds like New Year's Eve in Times Square.'

Steven smiled weakly. He was in no mood for small talk.

'Anything I can do?' asked the manager.

Steven asked if he might borrow some tools. He followed the man back indoors and emerged a few seconds later with electrical pliers and a few small screwdrivers. It didn't take long to reconnect the ignition system. Luckily it was a simple job, not requiring much in the way of concentration. This was just as well because his mind was on other things.

As a scare tactic, the music box had been a big success. He had to admit that it had been a long time since he'd experienced the real paralysing fear he'd felt when he'd first realised the connection between the music and the ignition switch. The threat had been made and now he was left wondering just how serious it was. Was Sigma 5 really prepared to kill him if he didn't back out of the investigation at Blackbridge? People working for his own government?

It had been his intention to drive out to Blackbridge early and catch James Binnie before he went off on his rounds. He felt that, as he hadn't heard from Binnie yesterday, there must be a good chance of something arriving in the post for him this morning from the vet school. In view of what had just happened however, he changed his plans and returned back upstairs to contact Sci-Med. He put in a request for a firearm, the first time he'd ever done such a thing. Such a request would automatically be given priority and he had a reply within ten minutes saying that he could pick up the weapon at Livingston Police Headquarters at his convenience.

Steven drove directly out to Livingston and asked for Brewer. The chief inspector, who was already expecting him, handed over a 9 mm automatic pistol, two boxes of ammunition and a Burns Martin shoulder holster, all of which he signed for in triplicate.

'Not for our pathologist friend, I hope,' said Brewer.

'Not for anyone I hope,' said Steven. 'I dislike these things as much as you.' He told Brewer about the incident with his car.

'Christ!' exclaimed the policeman. 'Is no one ever going to tell me just what the fuck is going on in my patch?'

'I'm not keeping you in the dark,' Steven assured him. 'I'm in it myself.' He told Brewer why he had decided not to pursue Levi over the cause-of-death change on the PM report and the policeman nodded. 'Makes sense, I suppose.'

'Have you seen him?' asked Steven.

'Two weeks sick leave, I understand,' replied Brewer. 'Wonder how he'll square it with his conscience.'

'I can't see that being a problem,' said Steven. 'The pressure would have been applied along the lines of doing it for the good of the public, helping to prevent the spread of fear and alarm, giving the authorities a little time to deal with the problem, that sort of seductive crap. He'll probably end up feeling like a hero who's saved the nation. Come to think of it there might even be an MBE in it for him come New Year time. Let's watch this space.' It would be more than Macmillan was now going to get, Steven thought privately.

Brewer watched while Steven took off his jacket and

strapped on the shoulder holster, adjusting it until it felt comfortable. He loaded the gun and slipped it into place, removing and replacing it twice to get the feel of it.

'Need time on the range?' asked Brewer.

Steven shook his head. 'If I need this it'll be at close quarters and in extreme circumstances. I won't go scaring the locals. I promise.'

'But you're taking the business with your car as a serious warning?' asked Brewer.

'Let's say I'm not writing it off as a boyish prank.'

'They – whoever "they" are – obviously know your car and where you're staying,' said Brewer.

'I'll have to move,' agreed Steven. 'And keep moving every couple of days. I'll change to a rented car too. Maybe you could store mine for me?'

'I'll supply you with a pool vehicle if you like,' suggested Brewer. 'You can keep changing that too. It means you'll also have a police radio too. That might come in handy.'

Steven agreed that this was a good idea and accepted Brewer's offer to arrange it right away. He put his own car down in the police garage and took charge of a dark-grey, unmarked Ford Mondeo. He thanked Brewer for his help and offered to buy him lunch, an offer the policeman accepted and the two of them had a bar lunch in a nearby pub. Afterwards, Steven set out for Blackbridge much later than he'd planned. As he feared, James Binnie was not at home when he finally got there but Ann was able to tell him that he had still had no word back yet from the vet school.

'Maybe these things take more time than I thought,' said Steven, disappointed at the news.

'I think James was surprised too when nothing came back this morning,' said Ann. 'He'd actually asked a friend of his over there to carry out the examination and told him it was urgent. I think he expected the report back yesterday if truth be told.'

Steven said, 'Maybe I could give James a ring on his mobile?'

'Why don't you come inside and do it,' said Ann. 'I'll make some coffee.' She disappeared into the kitchen and Steven called Binnie on his mobile. It was answered after the fifth ring and Binnie sounded harassed. 'Yes? What is it?'

'James? It's Steven Dunbar. I'm sorry to bother you . . .'

'Not many people can say they had their arm halfway up a cow's arse when their phone went,' interrupted Binnie. 'I'm grateful to you for giving me the opportunity.'

Steven tried not to laugh. He asked about Binnie's friend at the vet school.

'Yes, I asked John Sweeney if he'd do it for me; we've been friends for years. We were at university together.'

'Would you mind if I went over there to the vet school and spoke to him personally?'

'I suppose not,' replied Binnie after a moment's thought. 'That's probably a good idea. I can't understand what's taking him so long.'

'Okay,' said Steven lightly. 'Just thought I'd check with you first.'

'Thanks a bundle,' replied Binnie ruefully.

'You got him then?' asked Ann Binnie, returning with two mugs of coffee and a plate of biscuits.

'At a bad moment it seems,' said Steven.

'Don't take it to heart,' laughed Ann. 'He gives everyone a hard time when he feels like it. He's not one for bottling things up, my Jim. Says what's on his mind, he does. That's why we haven't a friend left in the world.'

Steven looked at her but then saw that she was joking. 'He's a pussy cat really,' said Ann.

# 14

As Steven was driving up the hill between Peat Ridge and Crawhill farms he slowed near the canal bridge when he noticed newly erected barriers across the access steps on both sides leading down to the towpath. He stopped the car and got out. Plastic-covered notices headed 'Public Health Notice' were tied with string to the striped barriers, declaring the towpath closed to the public until further notice. They didn't say why but when he looked over the bridge parapet and saw several men dressed in white coveralls and carrying what looked to be 0.22 calibre rifles, he realised that the rat cull must have started.

The men were spaced out at intervals of fifty to a hundred metres and walking slowly eastwards with their weapons cradled in the crook of their elbows. Steven crossed to the other side of the road and looked along the towpath in the other direction. He could see another two similarly dressed men patrolling to the west before a turn in the canal obscured any further view.

As he watched, one of the men raised his weapon to his shoulder and fired at something on the opposite bank. Steven couldn't see the target or the outcome but the gesture the marksman made with his left arm suggested that he'd hit what he'd been aiming at.

He felt a sense of relief that at last someone in authority seemed to be getting something done in Blackbridge. It made him reflect on the power of the press as he got back into his car and continued his drive back to the city. But did it justify the anguish that Alex McColl must have caused the Ferguson family? Was it a case of the end justifying the means or just the lucky by-product of an opportunist tabloid crusade fuelled by hypocrisy?

Steven found a parking space in a narrow street of Victorian villas, running parallel to Melville Drive and the Meadows. He fed the nearby machine with sufficient coins for a one-hour ticket and stuck it on his windscreen before walking back the two hundred metres or so to The Royal Dick School of Veterinary Medicine, known locally as the Dick Vet. He asked at the servitor's box for Dr John Sweeney and was in turn asked his business. He wasn't surprised at the question. There were notices all around reminding staff to be vigilant in the light of continuing threats from animal rights groups. He showed his ID and the servitor picked up a phone.

'Visitor for Dr Sweeney . . . From the Sci-Med Inspectorate . . . Right, will-do.' The man replaced the receiver and turned back to Steven. He pointed to the lift and said, 'He says to go on up. Third floor, Room 308.'

John Sweeney proved to be a small man with narrow shoulders and a mop of crinkly brown hair. He wore a pristine white lab coat over a striped shirt and university tie with a large, skewed sausage knot in it. There was at least a two-inch gap between his throat and the start of his shirt collar, giving him the air of a learned tortoise emerging from his shell. He wore brown corduroy trousers and highly polished shoes of a colour somewhere between dark brown and red. 'How can I help you?' he asked.

'I understand we have a mutual friend,' said Steven. 'James Binnie, the vet over at Blackbridge?'

Instead of the smile of recognition that Steven expected to see at the mention of Binnie's name, he saw a look of caution appear on Sweeney's face, even nervousness. 'Yes, I know James. We qualified together many years ago. What is it that you want exactly?' he enquired tentatively.

'It's about the rat that James brought over to you the other day for autopsy. I was wondering if you had completed your examination on it?' asked Steven.

'The rat,' Sweeney repeated, diverting his gaze.

There was no element of question in Sweeney's voice, Steven noted. The man had simply repeated the word as if stalling for time. 'What about it?'

'We were wondering about your findings, Doctor?' Steven repeated, somewhat unnecessarily, he thought.

'It was fine,' said Sweeney.

'Fine?' queried Steven.

'I'm sorry, I should have got back to James sooner, but I've been busy with one thing and another. No, there was nothing unusual about the animal's body condition. It seemed perfectly healthy.'

'I see,' said Steven, aware that he was unnerving Sweeney by watching him intently. 'And the toxicology tests?'

'There was no trace of any glyphosphate or glufosinate compound in the animal at all.'

'So it was a perfectly normal rat in every respect?'

'Yes . . . absolutely,' said Sweeney.

Steven was convinced that the man was lying. The look on his face, the way he shuffled his feet uncomfortably and a reluctance to establish eye contact all said that he was. Steven took a deep breath before saying, 'Dr Sweeney, I know James asked you to carry out this examination unofficially, as a friend, but now I'm asking you officially, with the full weight of the law behind me, did you come across anything unusual in your examination of that rat? Anything at all?'

Sweeney's eyes opened wide like saucers. 'I can't say that I did,' he stammered.

His wordplay didn't work. 'Can't or won't?' Steven persisted.

'Can't.'

Steven let Sweeney stew in his own obvious discomfort for a few moments to see if anything else would emerge.

'Damn it, I really can't see why you people don't talk to each other,' Sweeney blurted out. 'I take it you're all on the same side?'

'What does that mean?' asked Steven calmly.

'Nothing,' said Sweeney, recovering his composure.

Steven had a thought. He remembered that many public sector employees were obliged to sign the Official Secrets Act as part of their work contract. He asked if this was the case with Sweeney.

'Yes, I've signed it,' replied Sweeney, looking relieved again.

'Then I won't bother you any more in the circumstances,' said Steven resignedly. 'It would be unfair.' He played his last card in what he saw as a losing hand. 'I would, however, add that sometimes a man has to decide what's right and what's wrong in his own mind . . . And act accordingly, regardless of what the rules might say.'

Steven left the building feeling dejected. He felt as if he were trying to run in ever-deepening soft sand. He took what was positive from the meeting with Sweeney and tried to concentrate on that. There had almost certainly been something wrong with the rat but Sweeney was under orders to keep quiet about it, maybe under the threat of breaking the Official Secrets Act. From the look of relief on Sweeney's face when he'd asked about herbicides, they had had nothing to do with it, so he supposed that that was some kind of progress.

The question that worried him now was how had the opposition known about Binnie's request to his friend? It had been a completely unofficial thing so Binnie must have mentioned it to someone other than himself and his wife, Ann. He'd ask him about that when he saw him next. In the meantime he could only hope that his appeal to Sweeney's sense of what was right in his own conscience might bear fruit and he might see fit to confide in his old friend, Binnie.

Steven saw that it was after four p.m. Time was getting on and he still had a lot to do before meeting Eve. He drove over to his hotel, got his things together and checked out, saying that he had been recalled to London at a moment's notice. This was for the benefit of anyone who subsequently tried to trace his movements through the hotel register. He drove over to an area of the city near Bruntsfield Links, where he'd noticed that every second or third house seemed to be a small hotel, and checked in to a suitably anonymous-looking one. It had the added bonus of having its own car park round the back of the building. He didn't want his car out on the street if he could help it.

When he logged on to the Sci-Med computer he found some information waiting for him on Childs and Leadbetter. Both had been trained as explosive experts during their time in the army. 'And in the occasional use of small musical boxes,' thought Steven. There were several other skills attributed to them: Childs spoke Arabic; Leadbetter was fluent in French and German and an authority in field communications; but it was the fact that *both* were explosive experts that captured Steven's attention. It suggested that this had something to do with their being in Blackbridge, although he had to admit it was hard to see what – always assuming that blowing up Blackbridge as a solution to everyone's problem was not an option, however appealing he found the notion himself. He thought he would take a leisurely bath before changing his clothes and setting off to pick up Eve.

Steven's mobile phone rang while he was in the bath. Luckily, he had propped it up on the edge. It was Jamie Brown.

'Well, we've got some action on the rat problem,' said Brown. 'I'll have to give McColl credit for that.'

'So I saw,' said Steven. 'I was out there earlier. Nice to know someone can actually get something done out there when they put their minds to it.'

'Know what you mean,' agreed Brown. 'It reminds me of a joke. How many local government administrators does it take to change a light bulb? Answer, none. They'll set up a sub-committee to investigate coping with darkness. But do you want to hear the best bit?'

'Amaze me,' said Steven.

'Nobody out there knows *who* started things moving.'

'What d'you mean?'

'No one's taking the credit for it and that's unusual in itself. But no one seems to know who sent in the rat killers.'

'But someone must,' Steven protested.

'You'd think so but it turns out not. Apparently everyone thought that someone else was responsible. When they finally got round to talking to each other, nobody claimed the credit.'

'Has no one asked the men on the banks?'

'Apparently they arrived in an unmarked truck and waved away anyone who approached them. When darkness fell they left in the same truck when it arrived to pick them up. The police had a word with them but they wouldn't tell me anything when I asked them.'

'Not even how many rats the men got?'

'One of the locals said they only had one sack with them when they left and it was about half full. Not more than a dozen or so, he reckoned.'

'That shouldn't upset the British Association for the Preservation of Rats too much,' said Steven.

'Is there one?' asked Brown, naively.

'Bound to be,' replied Steven.

When Brown rang off, Steven rang Brewer at police headquarters. 'So who's dealing with the rats?' he asked.

'Would you believe, the army?'

'You've got to be kidding,' said Steven, astonished at the reply.

'I wish I was,' said Brewer. He had an air of resignation in his voice. 'All we need now is the Berlin Philharmonic putting in an appearance and we can stage *Blackbridge, The musical.*'

'You're sure about the army's involvement?'

'Two of my lads challenged them when they were leaving this evening. They were shown army ID.'

'Well, I suppose they can at least shoot straight,' said Steven. 'It makes some kind of sense, I suppose. But who made the decision?'

'Exactly,' exclaimed Brewer. 'None of the briefcases up at the hotel knows, or no one will own up to knowing, and so the squabbling goes on.'

'Well, at least someone's shooting the rats while they set up sub-committees, request clarification, defer decisions and report upwards, downwards and sideways,' said Steven.

'I'm really surprised that there's been no involvement at ministerial level yet,' said Brewer. 'You'd think one of the buggers would have had the courage to put in an appearance.'

'This mess isn't going to do anyone's career any good,' said Steven. 'Politicians have an innate sense of that. They'll leave it to the spear carriers as long as possible.'

'Suppose you're right,' agreed Brewer.

Steven ended the call but then thought to himself that the decision to call in the army had presumably not been made by some postal clerk in the Scottish Office down in Leith or a window cleaner in Whitehall. Surely that decision must have been taken at ministerial level, so why hadn't the relevant minister – whoever he or she was – appeared on the scene to take the credit for firm, swift action in the wake of the *Clarion*'s story? Such shyness seemed well out of character. Steven found that it was difficult to work out even *where* the decision would have been made. Rural Affairs was a Scottish matter. Health was a bit of both. Defence – and therefore the army – was definitely Whitehall's province.

Steven drove out to Blackbridge and picked up Eve outside the hotel at seven-thirty as arranged. He thought she looked stunning in an emerald green dress that highlighted her beautiful red hair and said so.

'Smooth southern bastard,' said Eve with disarming frankness, but she was far from being annoyed. 'You've changed your car,' she observed.

'I'm that kind of a guy,' said Steven. 'Wild, impetuous, untamed.'

'Anchored only to this earth by your civil service super-annuation scheme,' added Eve.

'Ye gods, the night is only five minutes old and I've been shot down in flames already,' Steven complained.

'Where are we going?'

'The Witchery.'

'You must want me to talk to Trish real bad,' said Eve. 'When I go out with a bloke for a meal, it's usually a Dutch treat at Pizza Hut.'

'It's not just that,' said Steven.

'Of course not,' laughed Eve.

'How are your folks?' asked Steven, as they drove off.

'They've gone to Aunt Jean's down in North Berwick for a few days. It'll do them good to get away from here for a bit.'

Steven agreed, thinking it would do anyone good to get

away from Blackbridge for any length of time. 'How did they take the *Clarion* story?' he asked.

Eve snorted at the memory. 'Bloody rag,' she complained.

'I'm sorry. I take it they were very upset?'

'No,' said Eve quietly, sounding strangely embarrassed. 'Mum and Dad actually believed that the *Clarion* ran the story out of concern for them and their feelings.'

'I see,' said Steven. 'And what did you tell them?'

'I kept my mouth shut and let them go on thinking that.'

'Good for you. Sometimes education can be a dangerous thing.'

'Tell me about it,' said Eve. 'You know, it's so ironic that the very thing good, decent people strive to give their children is often the very thing that drives them apart. I keep seeing it.'

'Not in your case though,' said Steven.

'I've worked out what's really worth having in life and you don't find it in Harrods or the glossy pictures in the Sunday supplements.'

Steven had to seek Eve's advice when he thought they were getting near the restaurant.

'Turn left at the next junction, then left again,' Eve directed.

'What's the parking like here?' he asked.

'Go round into Castle Terrace,' said Eve. 'It should be okay at this time of night.'

They found a parking place without trouble and Steven got out to stare up at the floodlit castle, towering above them. 'Impressive,' he said. 'What's all the scaffolding for?'

'It's not really scaffolding,' Eve corrected him. 'It's the seating for the military tattoo. The Edinburgh Festival starts soon. You won't be parking here then!'

They walked the short distance to the restaurant, which was situated very near to the entrance to the castle esplanade and walked down the steps to the Secret Garden of the Witchery.

'So what do you really think Trish has got herself mixed up in?' asked Eve.

'I honestly don't know,' Steven confessed. 'She may not be directly involved in anything herself but she certainly knows something about what's going on and I think she told the authorities about it after making some kind of deal with them.'

'So if the authorities know about this, how come you don't? You're one of them, aren't you? Right hand doesn't know what the left is doing?'

'More serious than that. There's some kind of conspiracy going on, something I'm not party to.'

'A conspiracy to do what?' asked Eve.

'In the beginning, I thought it was a straightforward industrial espionage thing; one biotech company setting out to discredit another through rumour and innuendo about their experimental crop, hoping perhaps to get their licence revoked, but I was wrong. It's something much bigger although it's still tied up in some way with the crop in the fields at Peat Ridge.'

'A conspiracy involving the government and all over a couple of fields of oilseed rape?' said Eve doubtfully.

'Genetically modified oilseed rape,' Steven reminded her.

'Oh yes,' said Eve thoughtfully. 'We mustn't forget the big bad "G" word. The minute you mention that, people start running for the hills. Frankly, from what I've seen of "government" in Blackbridge, these people would be hard pushed in conspiring to cross the road safely.'

'It's got nothing to do with the people at the hotel,' said Steven. 'They're small bit-players. This is something way out of their league.'

Eve looked puzzled. 'You know, I still can't see it,' she said. 'You're going to have to do better than that if you want me to betray my friend.'

Steven topped up her glass while he pondered a decision about how to proceed, then he made it and said quietly, 'The rats' behaviour has been changing around Blackbridge.'

Eve looked at him questioningly, then her eyes widened a little as shock arrived with the realisation of what he was implying. 'The rats in the canal!' she exclaimed, then looked about her to see if anyone had overheard. She lowered her voice. 'And you think it has something to do with the genetic changes made to the crop?'

'Don't get me wrong; I don't see how that can possibly be, but the continued attempts to have it discredited and destroyed suggests that someone knows more about it than I do.'

'God, this is awful!' exclaimed Eve in a hoarse whisper. 'It never occurred to me to think . . . I mean . . . apart from anything else, this could mean that my brother died because of it! That rat might not have bitten him otherwise.'

Steven nodded and agreed. 'I'm sorry,' he said, 'but that's possible.' He now had Eve's full attention. 'McNish didn't drown,' he continued. 'The rats got him first. They severed his carotid artery. The story about him drowning was a fabrication.'

Eve grimaced and said, 'Oh my God, I don't think I know what to say. What is it that you want me to do exactly?' she asked.

'I need to know what Trish Rafferty knows about the vendetta against Peat Ridge Farm. I think it might be tied up in some way with the reason she left her husband. So try picking away at that. You might also ask her about the two men staying at Crawhill Farm, Rafferty's so-called business advisers. They're not. They're part of the plot too.'

'I'll call her in the morning,' said Eve. 'I'll suggest we meet up for a bit of a girls' night out. How much can I tell her?'

'Nothing. You must play the innocent; you're just a friend concerned for her welfare. If she suspects for a moment that you've been put up to it, she'll clam up and say nothing, I'm sure of it. Don't say anything to anyone else either,' said Steven. 'If the local yobs get wind of any connection between the Peat Ridge experiment and the rats' behaviour they'll use it as an excuse to make big trouble and someone could get badly hurt.'

'I'll do my best,' said Eve.

Steven thanked her. He picked up the sweet menu. 'What takes your fancy?' he asked.

'I think I've just lost my appetite,' said Eve.

They both settled for just coffee. Eve was now very subdued although she did her best to respond to Steven's attempts at lightening the conversation and smiled in all the right places. He, for his part, knew that she was brooding about her brother. It was inevitable but he could think of nothing reassuring to say.

It was raining quite heavily when they left the restaurant

but Eve declined Steven's offer that she should wait in the dry while he went to pick up the car and bring it round. Instead they both ran through the puddles. Steven reached out his hand and Eve took it. It was a nice moment and helped dispel the cloud that had settled over Eve. Halfway home, however, she said, 'You know, I can't see how oilseed rape, GM or otherwise, could have caused a behavioural change in the rats. A change in the weedkillers they're using on the fields would be a much better bet for something like that.'

'My thoughts too,' said Steven with a smile. 'That's always been the big worry about this kind of trial. No one really knows what effects a sudden change in the use of powerful weedkillers would have on the environment.'

'You know, it would be a good idea to check out the rats for traces of chemicals in their bodies,' said Eve.

'It's in hand,' smiled Steven.

Eve looked at him sideways and smiled. 'Of course it is,' she said. 'I'm sorry. Now I feel stupid. That was probably the first thing you did.'

'You're a very long way from being stupid, Eve,' said Steven. 'Keep thinking about it. We'd welcome your input.'

'We? I thought you worked alone.'

Steven told her about James Binnie's involvement.

'Nice man,' said Eve.

Steven pulled up outside Eve's parents' house. 'I'll need your phone number,' she said. 'I'll call you as soon as I've had a chance to talk to Trish.'

Steven wrote it down on the piece of paper that Eve tore from a small notebook in her handbag. 'Thank you for a nice evening,' she said.

'Maybe we could do it again?' suggested Steven.

Eve looked at him for a long searching moment before saying simply, 'Maybe.' Without warning she leaned over and kissed him full on the lips and ran her fingers softly down his cheek. Steven was surprised but did not draw away. Eve sat back and looked into his eyes. 'I hope that's guilt I see and not revulsion,' she said.

'Definitely not revulsion,' Steven assured her.

'Goodnight.'

# 15

It was a little after midnight when Steven got back to his new hotel but he still found room in the car park round the back. He supposed that some guests had been put off by the narrow potholed lane leading through to it so they had left their cars out in the street instead – probably hoping to be away in the morning before the traffic wardens were up and about. Steven parked his car with the front bumper hard up against the back wall of the hotel, making it well nigh impossible for anyone to open the bonnet.

Despite the rain, he still took time to look around for a number of small stones and positioned them at strategic intervals round the car so that anyone crawling underneath the vehicle would be sure to disturb the pattern he'd made. He didn't really think an attack on this car was likely; it was more a case of better safe than sorry.

On the way back round to the front of the hotel, he took a good look at the building itself, noting the position of his room window in relation to what was near it in the way of pipes and guttering – routine insurance against circumstances dictating that he might have to get out in a hurry. Once inside his room he locked the door and wedged the foot of it with a cheap ballpoint pen – insurance against the opposition gaining access with a key. He turned out the light and looked out on the rain-swept streets, pleased to see that the windows were double-glazed. It was well nigh impossible to throw anything through a double-glazed window. He closed the curtains and switched on the bedside light before taking off his jacket and removing his holster, which he hung over the single chair in the room. The gun itself, he took out and put on the bedside table. 'And you're the one who hates melodrama,' he murmured to himself.

Steven lay awake for a long time. This was due in part to the wind that had got up and the rain that now lashed against his room window but it was mainly down to the sense of unease he felt about Eve. He could still feel the sensation of her lips on his. She had been right about seeing guilt in his eyes; it had been the first thing he'd felt when she'd surprised him. He knew it didn't stand up to analysis – it just didn't make any sense, but the feeling had been real enough. Could he really still see it as cheating on Lisa? Lisa was dead and gone and nothing was going to change that. Perhaps he was more worried about what he was seeing in Eve. It hadn't escaped him that, although Eve did not look anything like Lisa, she had many things in common with her. Her Scottish directness, even her sense of humour and tendency to scythe down pretensions of any sort was pure Lisa. She was bright too, again like Lisa. Could he be sizing her up as some sort of substitute for Lisa? If he was, that would be unforgivable. Almost immediately, he rebelled against the thought. What the hell was all this about? he wondered. It had only been a goodnight kiss, for God's sake.

The rain got even louder on the window as he turned over on to his side. 'Bloody country,' he muttered before falling asleep.

Next morning, the *Clarion* trumpeted its success in provoking action over the increasing rat population at Blackbridge. 'The Pied Paper that gets things done' was how it congratulated itself. The self-styled champion of the people had done more than all the hide-bound officials put together and had got something done about the rat menace, it asserted. While 'they' all sat in the Blackbridge Arms on fat expense accounts, arguing the rights and wrongs of GM crops and deciding nothing, the *Clarion* had cut through a veritable forest of red tape and embarrassed the powers that be into taking firm action. There was a large photograph of a white-overalled man holding a rifle on the banks of the canal. 'Blow the vermin away!' the *Clarion* encouraged.

It was a typical tabloid piece, Steven thought, but there was a worrying aspect to it that captured his attention. As was usual in this kind of situation, the paper was claiming credit for having forced the authorities to do something about the rats but he suspected that the truth of the matter was somewhat different. No one on the paper would realise it, but the *Clarion* itself was being used by Sigma 5.

Sigma 5 knew about the change in the rats' behaviour and therefore must have realised that something would have to be done, but if they had just arranged for a team to be sent in, too many embarrassing questions would have been asked. The authorities would have been at each other's throats to discover who was behind it. As it was, Sigma 5 had bided its time and then used the story in the paper to make it appear as if someone high up in government had stepped in to clear up the mess in response to the paper's story of public anxiety. The local authorities would now be too reluctant or red-faced to say anything because the move had elicited such popular support and, what was more, the *Clarion* would crucify them if they did. Sigma 5 were not only powerful, they were clever too, an unfortunate combination in an opponent, thought Steven.

Jamie Brown in the *Scotsman* had covered the rat cull story too but he had concentrated on the administrative buck-passing that had been going on. He pointed out that no one in authority would say who had ordered the cull and this did not bode well for the open government that the Scottish people had been promised from their new Parliament and again highlighted the lack of clear distinction when it came to who was responsible for what in the new administration.

Today, in a recap for the readers' benefit, he reminded them which powers had been devolved and which hadn't, and concentrated on something called 'Executive Devolution'. This was a term applied to powers where Westminster retained sole law-making rights but the Scottish Parliament could make some lesser decisions within an agreed framework. Brown described this as Westminster driving the car but the Scottish Parliament being allowed to blow up the tyres.

Steven overcame a reticence about the risk of disturbing James Binnie in a compromising position with a cow and called him on his mobile number again. 'Sorry to bother you again, James, but we have to talk.'

'I'm on my way over to Letham Mains to look at a pig,' replied Binnie to Steven's relief. 'I'll be there about half an hour and then I'm free for a bit. What would you suggest?'

Steven checked his local map, which he had on the table in front of him and found Letham Mains Farm. He saw that there was a crossroads about a mile west of the farm and suggested that they meet there.

'A bit cloak and dagger, isn't it?' said Binnie.

Steven agreed but did not offer either explanation or alternative. 'Half an hour then.'

Binnie was sitting in his Land Rover, reading his newspaper when Steven arrived. Steven parked his own car about twenty metres down a farm track and went back to join him, climbing into the passenger seat and wrinkling his nose at the smell inside the Land Rover. He saw that Binnie's Wellingtons in the back were covered in what he thought just might be pig manure – the smell gave strong support to this theory. Binnie appeared not to notice.

'I had a talk with your friend Sweeney, yesterday,' said Steven. 'He hasn't called you has he?'

Binnie said not.

'Pity. He's hiding something. He said there was nothing wrong with the rat you gave him but he was lying; I'm sure of it. He had guilt written all over his face.'

'But why should he lie?'

'He was a nervous wreck. Someone must have got to him and instructed him to come up with a clean bill of health for the rat.'

'John Sweeney? Turn out a false report? I don't believe it. He's as honest as the day is long.'

'I suspect that the pressure came from within,' said Steven. 'That's always difficult. I think they invoked the Official Secrets Act and warned him of the consequences of breaking it.'

'Good God, poor chap,' said Binnie, looking over his glasses at Steven and appearing genuinely shocked. 'What the hell is going on in Blackbridge?'

'I don't know but I have to ask you if you told anyone about taking the rat over to the vet school,' said Steven. 'Ann knew; I knew; who else?'

Binnie sighed and shook his head. 'No one,' he said. 'I can't think why I would tell anyone else.'

'Someone must have known in advance or they wouldn't have had time to stop your friend issuing a genuine report,' said Steven.

'I can see that,' said Binnie. 'But I just can't think of anyone I might have told. I'd have no reason to.'

'If you do happen to remember, let me know,' said Steven.

'Why did you ask if John had been in touch?' asked Binnie.

'I tried to persuade him that he should listen to his conscience rather than just obey the strict letter of the law,' replied Steven. 'I hoped that if he felt guilty enough, he might tell you, as a friend, what was wrong with the rat.'

'Afraid not,' said Binnie. 'Want me to have a prod at him?'

'Anything's worth a try right now.'

'Like that, is it?'

'A long time ago someone told me never to go to war with the establishment because, as he said, you'll always lose. I feel like I'm confirming his belief at every turn.'

'But you work for the establishment,' said Binnie.

'I thought I did,' said Steven ruefully. He made to open the Land Rover door. 'I'd better let you get on with your work,' he said.

'I'll call you later if I get anything out of John,' said Binnie.

As he drove off, Steven doubted whether Binnie would be able to persuade Sweeney to tell him anything. Friend or not, Sweeney had clearly been scared about what he had got himself into. He would probably see keeping his mouth shut as the safe option. Steven started to wonder if breaking into Sweeney's office at the Dick Vet might be a better idea. Surely Sweeney would have written down his findings about the rat, he thought, but on the other hand it seemed equally probable that all such evidence would have been removed by the people who'd applied pressure to him. He reluctantly concluded that a break-in was probably a non-starter. The chances of success would have to be very good indeed to warrant such a risky venture and they weren't. His phone rang. It was James Binnie.

'I've just remembered,' said Binnie. 'I did tell someone else about taking the rat over to the vet school. I mentioned it to Tom Rafferty.'

'Rafferty?' exclaimed Steven.

'It was the day he called me over to see his dog, Khan. He kept insisting that Khan was genuinely ill and that was the reason he seemed to be getting meaner every day. Although I told him that, in my opinion, Khan had always been mean, I had to defer to the fact that owners always know their pets better than outsiders. I remember mentioning to him that I was going to be going over to the vet school in the next few days to have an analysis on the rat done. I offered to take over a blood sample from Khan at the same time.'

'That would make sense,' said Steven. 'If Rafferty had known about Binnie's intention then it was a safe bet that Childs and Leadbetter would also have known. It must have been them who had arranged for pressure to be put on Sweeney to kill the report.'

'Sorry about that,' said Binnie. 'I should have remembered earlier. I'm not sure if it tells you anything?'

'It does,' said Steven, without saying more. He thought about what Binnie had said as he drove on. It was always nice when things fitted and there was satisfaction to be had in understanding just how Sigma 5 had come to know about the rat autopsy.

Steven went back to wondering about the change in the rats' behaviour. Sigma 5 knew that it was specific to Blackbridge because they weren't targeting any other GM sites. But if it wasn't the crop itself and it wasn't the use of glyphosate or glufosinate herbicides, what else could it be? The crop itself had been tested . . . But the weedkillers hadn't! he concluded. Just supposing that Agrigene were using a different kind of weedkiller at Peat Ridge! Phillip Grimble, Agrigene's technical manager, had said that the same crop was being tested at different sites to try out different herbicide regimes. Could that be the source of the problem? Were they using an unlicensed herbicide? Something really toxic?

This certainly seemed to be a possibility but why on earth should a high-level, covert government operation be mounted to cover something like that up? Why wouldn't the authorities just throw the book at the company and be done with it? Steven decided that there was only one way to check on this. He would pay an unannounced visit to the storage barn at Peat Ridge Farm and check out what they were using for himself. While he was up there, near the canal, he would also try to get another rat for forensic examination. This time a Sci-Med appointed pathologist would carry out the autopsy. There was no guarantee of course that all the rats in the canal area were afflicted with whatever it was, but in view of McNish's death it certainly seemed likely that a majority were.

Steven decided that he would go to Peat Ridge Farm that very night. The idea of doing something positive appealed to him. He thought about what he would need in the way of equipment and decided not that much. He already had dark clothes and a balaclava in his bag at the hotel. He had good quality trainers for any climbing that might be involved, although he hoped that wouldn't be necessary. The only thing he needed that he didn't have at the moment was a series of small plastic bottles for taking samples from the chemical containers stored in the barn and something to carry them in. And maybe one bigger plastic container, suitable for a whole rat should he manage to get hold of one.

He decided that he would approach Peat Ridge from the canal towpath. He would go well after dark when the soldiers engaged in the rat cull would have left for the day. He would of course, have to avoid the patrolling private security men but their presence didn't worry him too much. These men were all right for dealing with amateur intruders. Being ex-Special Forces gave him a distinct edge in that department.

Going in from that side would give him access to the back of the Peat Ridge barn where, presumably, the chemicals were kept. There did not seem to be anywhere else suitable and it was certainly the only place on the farm that the rats might have access to in view of its dilapidated state. He thought it would be ideal if he could gain entrance from the rear too, rather than have to try for a front door entry where the yard lights were kept on all the time these days. He would play it by ear. He felt a slight thrill of excitement as he set off for the city to find a shop where he could buy some plastic containers and a small black rucksack.

Steven set off just after eleven thirty. It was a clear night and a half moon was shining brightly. He headed for a large lay-by he'd seen on a previous occasion, about half a mile east of Blackbridge, where he planned to leave the car before continuing on foot. It wasn't a proper lay-by and it was on a very minor road so the car shouldn't attract too much attention. He thought the site was probably used as an intermediate dump for sand and salt mixture in winter for subsequent application to the surrounding roads. It was important that he approach from the east he thought because, with a prevailing west wind, he would be down-wind of the patrolling dogs.

Steven slung his rucksack over his shoulder and locked the car before putting the keys into his right-hand jerkin pocket and zipping it up. He checked the zips on all his other pockets. He didn't want anything falling out. He climbed over the fence separating the road from the field on the south side and started out across the field towards the canal towpath.

Crossing the field presented no problem. There was a rough path round the perimeter, which he followed, but things became more difficult when he climbed over the fence at the other side and had to drop down from a low stone dyke into an area of rough ground and tall trees. The trees blocked out what light there was coming from the moon and the ground here was very soft from the rain of the previous night. There were also a great many boulders that he kept stumbling over and he guessed that the field behind him had probably been cleared of these stones at some time in the past.

He was beginning to run out of expletives when he reached the fence bordering the ground leading to the towpath. He climbed over it and up on to a more solid footing. Once up on the towpath, he pulled down his balaclava over his face. Moonlight was reflecting off the water of the canal and he didn't want his face becoming visible as he ran lightly along the path to past the southern edge of Crawhill Farm and under the canal bridge to the perimeter fence of Peat Ridge.

When he saw the lights of the farmyard over to his right, he crouched down and remained motionless for fully five minutes, just listening and watching the patrolling guards. He was pleased to see that there only seemed to be two, although both had dogs with them. When he felt confident that they were not varying their patrol pattern – it was obvious that their mere presence was meant to be a deterrent – he waited until the gap between patrols was greatest and went under the wire. He ran towards the back of the barn in a low crouching run and threw himself to the ground to remain motionless again, just listening to the sounds of the night. He was now at the southeast corner of the building so his view of the farm buildings, which lay slightly to the northwest, was obscured.

Reassured that all was still quiet, he started to search along the base of the barn, looking for somewhere that might afford him access. He had reached the centre without success when he was stopped in his tracks by the sound of one of the dogs barking. He remained rooted to the spot while the barking went on for fully half a minute, accompanied by the sound of a man's voice constantly telling the animal to shut up. Steven took off his rucksack and brought out a clasp knife from the side pocket. If push came to shove, it would be better than nothing. He slipped the knife into his jerkin pocket and redid the zip. He swung his rucksack across his back and continued his examination along the base of the wall.

He had just about given up on finding any flaw in the wall when he reached the final corner and found a series of three wooden slats had broken away from the main frame. He pulled the slats out a bit more to see if he could make the opening man size but he was rewarded with a heart-stopping moment when the panel freed itself of another rusty nail and the sound reverberated up the wall. The dog started barking again. He had certainly heard. Had anyone else?

After another minute of remaining motionless, like the statue of a cat burglar caught in the act, Steven heard the barking subside and quietness slowly returned to the farm.

Once again he had got away with it but he was living dangerously. He decided that he couldn't risk the same thing happening again so he resolved not to work any more on enlarging the opening. He would get down on the ground and squeeze through what little gap there was. It would be uncomfortable but it was just possible. He took off his rucksack and placed it on the ground, ready to be pushed through in front of him, then he got face down on the ground. The smell of wet grass and earth up close brought back memories of rugby games on winter days long ago.

Steven had a torch in his rucksack but felt he couldn't take the risk of using it until he was inside the barn so he stretched out his arm to feel what lay ahead. His fingers touched a cold plastic surface and he knew that this must be one of the chemical containers. That might be a problem, he recognised. If the containers were stacked up ceiling high at the back of the barn there would be no way for him to gain access to the interior. He changed hands and felt along to the left where he found a gap and moved into it. The jagged edge of a plank brushed his cheek as he inched forward and he cautioned himself to be more careful. It could have cut his face open had he been moving faster.

Steven reached further into the gap and let out a yell of pain as something smashed down on his hand and held it in a vice-like grip. His head filled with stars as pain shot up his arm and the dog started barking again. This time it was part of a duet; the other dog had heard as well. He snatched his hand away but the thing came with him and he now realised that it was a rat-trap. He'd unwittingly stuck his hand into it. His fear now was that bones in his left hand had been broken by the spring-loaded bar that had hammered down on them. To compound his misery, he could hear voices outside in the farmyard.

Still with the heavy metal trap fixed on his hand, Steven turned and pulled the wall panelling in towards him, drawing the slats in as far as possible in an effort to disguise where he had entered. It was also a move of self-preservation. This way he would be protected from the immediate attentions of the dogs should they be set free. The voices outside were becoming louder. He could now make out what they were saying.

'What's going on?' demanded a voice Steven recognised as Lane's.

'My dog heard something,' replied one of the guards.

'Caesar did too,' said the other.

'Did you?' asked Lane.

'Can't say as though I did.'

'Me neither,' agreed the other guard.

Steven breathed a small sigh of relief. It was only the dogs who were on his case. There was still a chance he might get away with this if he kept his nerve.

'Look, he's picked up a scent!' said one of the guards, putting an end to Steven's optimism. He could hear the animal snorting and panting on the other side of the wall. He was holding the panelling closed with his good hand but there was still a gap of a few inches at the bottom where the dog was trying to push his snout through. He failed and changed to pushing through a large paw to scratch at the earth only inches from Steven's leg. He was joined in the attempt by the other dog. Steven knew that if he were to let go of the panelling right now the dogs were going to make quite a mess of him before they were brought to heel.

Suddenly, as if to add to his nightmare, a rat came from somewhere in the darkness behind him and clambered over his thighs to drop down on the floor and escape out under the panelling. Steven nearly let out a cry of shock but managed to stop himself in time. It probably wouldn't have mattered as the dogs launched into a new frenzy of barking as the rodent had the temerity to run out right under their very noses.

'It was bloody rats they were after,' said Lane. 'Didn't you set the traps?'

Steven silently nodded.

'Let's all stop playing silly buggers and get back on patrol,' ordered Lane.

There was little or no argument from the guards, just a weak assertion from one that his animal had definitely heard something. The voices started to fade. It was the first time in his life that Steven had ever felt grateful to a rat. He let out his breath in an uneven sigh and then drew it sharply in again when he moved his trapped hand and felt a surge of pain. He let go of the panelling slowly, his fingers almost numb from the pressure on them, and started trying to free his left hand by holding it and the trap flat on the ground while he pulled back the bar with his right. The spring on the trap was so strong that it took him three attempts before he succeeded in making it move.

The blood was pounding in his temples and his teeth were gritted so hard that his cheek muscles were going into spasm before he managed to pull the bar back far enough to snatch his hand free. The bar closed with a loud snap and

Steven lay still on the ground for a moment, suffering from nervous exhaustion. He examined his left hand gingerly, feeling for any breaks and was pleasantly surprised when he didn't find any. Still not fully convinced, he stretched out his fingers and flexed them slowly. They came through the test. It really seemed as if there were no breaks, although he was in considerable pain.

He got out his torch from his rucksack and switched it on. There was a small mountain of chemical containers in front of him but along to the left he could see where they weren't piled so high. There was also just enough space between the drums and the back wall for him to squeeze along to the left and start to climb over them. His left hand wasn't much use in the climb and he could feel that it had already started to swell up. He kept it inside his jerkin as much as possible.

Steven could now see down into the barn in front of him. It was a little over half full of plastic containers. He climbed down on to the floor of the building where he started examining the labels on the drums. After a few moments he concluded that there were only three different kinds of weedkiller in the barn. He would take three random samples from each kind, making a requirement for nine plastic bottles in all. He had brought ten. He used his knife to lever up the drum caps selected at random and collected his samples.

He had just packed the containers away in his rucksack when he heard a loud crack and his stomach turned over. It took a few breathless moments before he realised that it had been one of the other traps triggering. With a bit of luck the next stage of his mission had just been accomplished for him. He climbed back over the drums at the back and dropped down into the narrow space between them and the back wall. For some reason he felt much more claustrophobic doing it this way around. He couldn't help thinking that if the drums were to tip backwards, he would be trapped there like a nun walled up in a medieval convent.

Holding the torch in front of him, he inched his way along towards the damaged panelling, doing his best to protect his injured hand from buffeting on the way. He came to a sudden halt when he felt sure that something had moved near him and then he heard a metallic scraping sound. He moved his torch beam slowly upwards in an arc. At eye level, he picked out a rat's hind legs scrabbling at the drum it was sitting on. It had been caught in a trap that had been left there but the impact of the trap had not been sufficient to kill it. Although badly injured, it was still desperately trying to free itself.

Steven squeezed himself round sideways so that he could reach into his jerkin pocket and bring out his knife. To open it, he required the help of his left hand, something that made him grimace in pain and whisper curses before the blade locked open and he inched towards the rat. Nausea at the thought was building inside him but he knew what he must do. He rested his injured hand on the rat's back and held it steady while he slipped the tip of the blade between the base of the trap and the animal's throat where it was held fast by the bar. He closed his eyes and pushed the blade sharply forwards. The warm wetness on his hand and the sudden stop to the animal's struggles told him that he'd been successful in cutting its throat.

Steven had to wait until he was outside the barn before

he could put the dead animal into the plastic container he'd brought with him for the purpose. He cleaned his hands as best he could on the wet grass, secured his rucksack and picked his moment when the guard patrol allowed him to run back up to the perimeter fence and out on to the towpath. He set off back to the car, mission accomplished.

# 16

It was almost two a.m. when Steven reached the outskirts of Edinburgh. His injured hand had made changing gear painful all the way back and he began to doubt his earlier conclusion about there being no breaks involved. Maybe having it X-rayed would be a wise precaution, he thought. When he started to wrestle with another problem – just where he was going to get some ice to preserve the rat's body until Sci-Med could get it to a pathologist – he saw how he could kill two birds with one stone. He changed his mind about returning to his hotel and started heading for the Accident and Emergency unit at Edinburgh's Royal Infirmary.

After a wait of some fifty minutes behind a woman who had scalded her foot, two drunks with facial lacerations and a variety of twists and strains, he was seen by one of the duty housemen. He was a young man in his early twenties with bad skin, sloping shoulders and a stoop, as if the stethoscope draped round his neck were proving too heavy for him. He looked Steven up and down, taking in the dishevelled appearance and dirty clothes and pursed his lips. 'What's your problem?' he asked brusquely.

'I've injured my hand. I thought I should get it X-rayed, just in case there's a break,' Steven replied.

'Well, I'm Dr Leeman and I make the decisions about what needs an X-ray and what doesn't,' snapped the houseman. He started to examine Steven's injured hand roughly, making him wince in discomfort as he separated the knuckles and flexed the fingers individually. He did it dispassionately as if he were manipulating a practice dummy. 'Now, don't tell me,' said Leeman with a sneer in his voice, 'you were quietly minding your own business when this other guy set about you for no apparent reason, right? The fight wasn't your fault in any way.'

'There was no fight; I caught my hand in a rat-trap,' replied Steven evenly.

'Oh right! Not a drunken brawl, a rat-trap,' the quiet sneer continued.

'Not a drunken brawl . . . a rat-trap,' repeated Steven in a measured, even monotone that signalled a warning. The nurse standing behind Leeman picked up on it but the houseman soldiered on in full sarcastic flow.

'And now you want us to fix you up and get you signed off work for a week so you can spend it down the boozer with your mates, right?'

'No, I'd just like my hand X-rayed to make sure there are no bones broken,' replied Steven calmly.

Leeman looked at him but broke eye contact quickly. He now realised that he was making some kind of a mistake but didn't know what exactly. He pretended to examine Steven's hand more thoroughly while the nurse in attendance put her hand to her mouth to hide a smile.

'Perhaps I *will* have it X-rayed,' announced Leeman, self-importantly. 'I don't like the swelling over the third metacarpal.' He took the admission sheet from the nurse and studied the details. He asked with feigned casualness, 'What exactly is it that you do, Mr Dunbar?'

'I'm a doctor,' replied Dunbar.

The nurse's hand went to her mouth again. Leeman was silent for a moment and he looked down at the floor. 'You don't exactly look like a doctor, if you don't mind me saying so,' he said, trying to recover lost face.

'And you don't exactly behave like one,' replied Steven, making sure he didn't get the chance. 'Perhaps a career more suited to your personality might be an idea, say lighthouse keeper in the Arctic Ocean?'

'Nurse will show you to X-ray,' said Leeman, his face reddening and anxious to end the confrontation.

'He had that coming,' confided the nurse as they walked along the corridor. 'He's an insufferable little shit at the best of times. I keep hoping we'll get Dr Ross from ER but all we seem to get are a succession of Alastairs who think they're God's gift to medicine when in reality they couldn't pick their nose without poking their eye out.'

Steven smiled but didn't add fuel to the flames. He did, however, wonder – and not for the first time – why so many people like Leeman, who clearly had so little time for the human race, should choose to become doctors.

'I bet it really was a fight,' said the nurse conspiratorially.

Steven insisted again that it had been a rat-trap but the nurse would have none of it and preferred to believe her own version. 'I suppose we can expect the other guy later?'

'Probably,' said Steven, giving up. 'Could I ask a favour of you?'

'You could try.'

'I'd like some ice, preferably in some kind of polystyrene container so it won't melt on the way back.'

'For your hand?'

'Yes, I don't have access to a freezer: I'm staying in a hotel.'

'I'll see what I can do while you're having your X-ray.'

'You're an angel.'

'That's what they keep telling us.'

The X-ray confirmed Steven's earlier finding that there were no broken bones in his hand: it was just badly bruised. He left A&E with an easier mind and a polystyrene box full of ice – just what he needed to pack the rat in before sending it off to London.

As soon as he got in, he sent off a coded message, asking that Sci-Med arrange to have a courier pick up the rat. He would leave it, suitably parcelled, in the hotel's reception. He wanted toxicology carried out on it by the best forensic analyst they could find. As for the samples of weedkiller, he wanted them analysed to the same exacting standards. He'd provided details from the labels on the drums. He wanted to know if any of the samples deviated in any way from the stated contents.

Steven took a shower and revelled in the warm soothing spray for a full five minutes before towelling himself down and putting on jeans and a sweatshirt. Although he felt exhausted, he would have to parcel up the rat before he could go to bed. There was a chance that the courier might arrive first thing in the morning and it was already close to four a.m.

The polystyrene box the nurse had given him was full to the brim with crushed ice when he opened it. This was a bonus: he could afford to use some of it on his injured hand to help reduce the swelling. He brought the tumbler from the bathroom and used it for the moment to store the ice he didn't need. He continued hollowing out the centre section of the box until the hole was big enough to accept the body of the rat, then he removed the animal from its plastic container and pressed it lightly into the ice and gently packed a further layer of ice over it.

There was no need to keep the chemicals ice cold but it wouldn't do them any harm, and it would be easier to make up just the one parcel. He pressed the nine small bottles into the ice surrounding the rat's body and secured the polystyrene lid to the box with sticky tape. He addressed the box and took it downstairs to leave with the night man, telling him that it was due for collection later that morning.

Steven slept until a little after eleven when he was woken by the sound of a vacuum cleaner out in the hall. 'The mighty Hoover speaks and I obey,' he murmured, swinging his legs round and sitting up on the edge of the bed. He was pleased to see that the swelling in his left hand had gone down overnight and it was much easier for him to flex his fingers this morning. A good start to the day, he reckoned. He checked with reception that the rat had been collected. It had.

It was too late for breakfast at the hotel so he washed, dressed and walked up to the local shops where he bought a couple of morning papers and had coffee and croissants in the Montpelier bistro while he planned his day. He had stayed two nights in his present hotel so he thought that he would check out of it and use somewhere different tonight. He would also drive over to police headquarters at Livingston at some point and change his current car for another from the pool.

Steven failed to find any mention of Blackbridge in the morning papers and took this as a good sign. The rat cull was under way and had been milked for credit and there was nothing new on the GM crop front. It was time for the vultures to move on and seek out new reservoirs of human misery. But they'd be back, he thought. This was merely a lull in the proceedings.

It was around three in the afternoon when Steven drove into Blackbridge and knocked on the door of the Binnie household. He had moved hotels and was on his way out to Livingston to change his car when he thought he would call in on the off chance that James might be there and ask if he'd had any contact with Sweeney at the vet school.

'I'm afraid James isn't back yet,' said Ann. 'Actually, I'm a bit worried about him. It's not like him not to call in. He's been away for hours.'

'Have you tried calling him on his mobile?' asked Steven.

'No reply. I keep being diverted to his answering service.'

'It could be that he's working somewhere where the signal's weak,' suggested Steven.

'I suppose. But I do wish he'd call in,' said Ann, wringing her hands. 'It really isn't like him.'

'Do you have a note of his schedule for today?' asked Steven.

'I think he had just three calls to make but I'm not sure

of the order he was doing them in,' said Ann. She brought out an A4 sized diary from the drawer of the telephone table in the hall and flicked through the pages. 'John Simpson at Mossgiel,' she read. 'Tom Rafferty at Crawhill and Angus Slater over at Hardgate.'

'Why don't you call the farms and ask?' suggested Steven.

Ann looked indecisive. 'It's probably just me being silly. I really don't like disturbing him when he's busy,' she said.

'But you wouldn't be disturbing him,' said Steven. 'You'll be phoning the farm. I'm sure they won't mind telling you if James is there or has been there, and at what time he left.'

'I suppose,' said Ann uncertainly. 'But it's like you say. He's probably out wrestling some cow in a ditch and his mobile's not picking up the signal.'

'You're obviously worried about him,' said Steven. 'I really think you should give the farms a call.'

It started to rain. Ann looked up at the sky and said, 'Come in for a minute. Maybe I will give them a call.'

Steven stood in the hall while Ann called Mossgiel Farm and asked about her husband. The only part of the conversation that he heard was, 'I see, right, thank you.' Ann put down the phone and said, 'He was there at ten thirty this morning. He left around eleven.'

Next, Ann phoned Hardgate Farm and spoke to someone called Maud. Steven guessed from their conversation that Maud was Angus Slater's wife.

'He hasn't?' exclaimed Ann. 'I wonder where he is. He left Mossgiel hours ago.'

Ann told Steven that Binnie hadn't visited Hardgate Farm yet, something he'd already gathered. 'So he must be at Crawhill,' said Steven.

Ann dialled the Crawhill number and made a face when it went on ringing without answer. 'Come on . . . come on,' she urged but still no one answered. 'Why don't I drive down there and check?' suggested Steven. 'It'll only take a few minutes.'

'Would you?' said Ann. 'I know I'm probably worrying about nothing but I'd be ever so grateful.'

Steven assured her that it was no trouble and left to drive over to Crawhill.

Unusually, the gate at the foot of the access road was open so he drove straight through into the compound in front of the house and got out to have a look around. He was reassured to see Binnie's Volvo parked at the side of the house and went up to knock on the front door. There was no answer.

He walked slowly round the compound looking for signs of life but found no one. He could see that Rafferty's mechanic, Gus Watson, had been working on a ditch-digger because an open toolbox was lying next to the partially disassembled bucket arm, but there was no sign of Gus himself.

Steven was beginning to have thoughts of the *Marie Celeste* when he heard a vehicle approaching. The high-revving, low-gear sound suggested that it was a four-wheel drive truck and so it proved to be when he saw Gus Watson swing into the yard. He drew to a halt beside Steven.

Steven said, 'I was beginning to think that Scottie had beamed you up.' He looked down at the open toolbox and the scatter of tools around the front of the digger.

'I got called away,' said Gus. 'Bloody baler we hired out to Cauldstane packed in and old Macpherson was spitting blood this morning. I had to fit a new elastic band tae the pile of shit.'

'Like that is it?' said Steven.

'It's no' a mechanic they need round here,' said Gus. 'It's a team frae *Blue Peter*. Maybe they could make spares out of squeezy bottles! Was it me you were looking for?'

Steven said that it wasn't but that he couldn't find anyone about the place. 'I was actually looking for James Binnie. I see his car's there.'

'It wasn't when I left,' said Gus. 'But there must be someone about. Have you tried the door?'

Steven assured him that he had and that he'd looked everywhere that was open. 'I didn't think anyone would be in any of the locked sheds and the big barn's locked too.'

'No,' agreed Gus, now looking as puzzled as Steven. 'Mind you . . .'

'What?'

'If the vet's here, he must have come to see Khan. Did you try looking in Khan's shed?'

'Which one's that?'

Gus led the way and Steven followed. The dog's shed was at the far end of a row of small outbuildings. Gus banged on the door and shouted, 'Anyone in there?' There was no response. 'How about you, Khan? Are you in there, you daft bugger?'

Gus looked puzzled at the silence. He said, 'That's no' like Khan. He usually goes mental when you do that.'

Gingerly, Gus turned the handle and inched the door open slowly. It jammed almost immediately on a small flat stone and Gus paused to kick it away before continuing with pained slowness. 'I don't trust the bugger an inch,' he said. He put his face to the crack to peer inside but a low growl made him close the door again quickly. It was more of a reflex action than anything else.

'Maybe we should just leave him be,' said Steven, but then he saw that Gus had gone as white as a sheet. 'What is it?' he asked. 'What's wrong?'

'There's someone lying there. I saw his legs.'

'Oh my God,' murmured Steven. 'We need something to fend the dog off. You must have spades or pitchforks round here somewhere.'

Gus went off to look and returned, still looking very pale, with a garden spade and a rusty fork. Steven took the fork and asked, 'Where's the light switch?'

'Just inside the door on the right,' Gus replied.

This time Steven eased the door open slowly, just far enough to reach his hand inside to feel up and down the wall until he found the switch. It was already down. He tried clicking it both ways but the shed stayed in darkness.

'How many bulbs in there?' Steven asked.

'Two.'

'It's unlikely they both went at the same time. Where's the fuse-board?'

'Along here. Gus led the way to the third shed along the row and pulled open a stiff cupboard door to reveal a fuse-board panel. 'Here we are,' he said. 'The fuse has come loose.' He pointed to a fuse-holder sitting at an odd angle in a row of five. 'This whole place is falling apart,' he complained. He pushed the holder back into its socket and said, 'Should be okay now.'

The two men returned to Khan's shed and Steven tried

the switch again. The lights clicked on and Khan gave a low growl but it was a subdued sound and came from somewhere at the back of the shed. The dog made no move to come towards them. Steven could now see what it was that Gus had caught a glimpse of. Only the shoes and legs up to mid calf were visible from where he stood but he knew immediately that they belonged to James Binnie. He recognised the brogues.

'We'll have to try to get him out,' he said softly to Gus.

Gus nodded and gripped his fork, holding it in two hands at the ready. 'Ready when you are,' he said, but his voice was a nervous croak.

Steven pushed the door open a little further and took a tentative step inside. He held the fork in front of him, ready to bring it into play as a barrier between him and the dog should it choose to make a rush at him. Khan was lying at the other end of the shed, watching him, his muzzle covered in blood.

'We can't risk him getting out,' whispered Steven. 'We'll have to close the door behind us.'

Gus made a grunting sound, which Steven construed as reluctant agreement. 'After three. One . . . two . . . three!'

Steven stepped inside smartly and helped pull Gus in behind him. He pushed the door to. Neither man took his eyes off Khan for a second. Holding the fork and spade at the ready they sidled cautiously across to where Binnie was lying, half hidden between two old tea chests being stored there. Gus stood guard while Steven knelt down and found Binnie's wrist. He was lying face down with his left arm trapped beneath him but his right was free. Steven felt for a pulse but didn't find one. It was no surprise. Binnie's clothes were soaked with blood. His injuries had to be horrific.

What did come as a surprise was the fact that Binnie was not the only body lying there. When Steven looked into the gap between the chests he saw to his horror that Thomas Rafferty was lying there too. He was lying curled up, like a foetus, as if he'd been hiding behind Binnie when death had come to call. Half his face was missing and his left arm had been all but torn off. The sight made Steven gasp in horror. This made Gus break eye contact with the dog and look down into the gap. 'Jesus fucking . . .' The oath did not get any further. Gus dropped his spade and vomited on the floor. Khan let out a low growl and went for him.

For such a large dog, Khan crossed the floor like lightning, teeth bared and malice shining in his eyes. He leapt into the air and hit Gus full in the chest, bowling him over like a skittle. Gus fell to the ground crying out in fear as the animal sought out his throat as he did his best to fend him off. For a moment they reached impasse as Gus managed to straighten his arms and lock his hands on Khan's throat but the dog quickly broke his grip by ducking his head underneath Gus's arm to come up and sink his teeth deeply into Gus's shoulder, tearing a lump of flesh from it.

Steven felt nauseous at the sound and then the sight of blood and tissue hanging from the corner of Khan's mouth but he knew he had to do something before the dog made his next lunge at Gus who was now paralysed with fear and shock and in no position to defend himself. He rammed the prongs of the fork he was holding into the dog's rear end and it yelped in pain and turned his attention on him instead. It kept a persistent low growl in his throat as it started to stalk him across the floor as he edged backwards, drawing Khan away from Gus. The malevolence it exuded was almost tangible.

Steven was playing a psychological game with the animal. Its muscular definition was so good that he could actually see at an early stage when it was preparing to spring at him. Every time it tensed its muscles he poked at it with the fork, interrupting it at the crucial moment and making it start all over.

Gus groaned and Steven asked, 'Gus! Can you hear me?' He didn't take his eyes off Khan for a moment.

'Jesus,' croaked Gus.

'Can you move?'

'Christ . . . it hurts.'

'Listen! You've got to get out of here. Do you understand?'

'My arm . . . Jesus my arm . . .'

'Never mind your arm; get out of here! Crawl, damn it!'

Khan snarled and made to lunge at Steven. The prongs of the fork repelled him but the sound of the animal served to concentrate Gus's attention and he started pulling himself across the floor, his progress fuelled by fear. 'Keep that bastard away from me!' he stammered.

'I'm doing my best,' muttered Steven, his eyes fixed on the slavering jaws in front of him, a piece of Gus's skin still hanging from its bloody incisors. He heard the door open behind him and a wedge of daylight entered. Khan's attention moved to the gap and Steven moved quickly to stop the animal running past him. The door closed again and Steven started to edge backwards towards it. Gus was out, now it was his turn.

He knew that the one thing he mustn't do now was fall over backwards so he was careful to check the ground behind him by feeling with his foot before committing himself to each step. The plan was to keep Khan at bay with threatening jabs of the fork until he reached the door then he would try a double lunge at the dog to force it backwards. If this was successful he would slip out of the door and slam it shut before Khan could reach him. Steven felt his heel make contact with the door. 'Gus!' he called out.

There was no reply.

'Gus, are you there?'

No reply. Steven hoped he'd made it to the house and was calling for help.

Steven steadied himself, took a deep breath and then let out a yell as he lunged at Khan, forcing him to retreat about two metres. He quickly turned and grabbed the door handle, at the same time pushing hard with his shoulder. The door jammed against the unconscious body of Gus Watson lying behind it.

Khan saw his chance and launched himself at Steven who was now half-trapped in the small space between the door jamb and Gus's body. It was the fact that the fork was almost vertical in his hand in preparation for slipping outside that saved him from death. As Khan's jaws opened and reached for his throat he brought the fork smartly up to impale the animal's lower jaw on one of the outer prongs. Khan yelped and writhed as Steven struggled to keep the fork upright and keep the dog on the end of it. If he lowered the fork – and the weight of the dog was insisting that he must – Khan would be free and his own fate would be sealed.

Still holding the dog on the end of the fork, Steven staggered back from the door so that he had more room to move inside the shed. He started to swing the dog around so that centrifugal force moved the animal outwards and upwards. With the supreme effort of an olympic athlete about to release a hammer, he accelerated the animal round in two final fast circles and then brought the fork down to the horizontal to ram it into the wall of the hut. Khan was trapped. Steven let go of the fork and picked up the shovel that Gus had dropped to begin raining down blow after rib-cracking blow at the still writhing Khan. He kept this up until all movement had ceased and the nightmare was finally over.

Steven staggered outside and fell to his knees in complete exhaustion, taking time to recover his breathing before crawling over to check on Gus who was starting to come round.

'What happened?' murmured Gus.

'You missed an episode of *Animal Magic*,' muttered Steven as he started to improvise a dressing for Gus's shoulder.

'That bloody dog was always the hound from hell,' said Gus. 'But Jesus, that was something else. People kept telling Tom to waste it but he wouldn't listen and now he's dead, poor bugger.'

'It's just a shame he had to take James Binnie with him,' said Steven bitterly.

'Right,' murmured Gus.

They heard a car come into the yard and Steven looked up to see Childs and Leadbetter get out and walk towards them. 'What's going on?' asked Childs.

'Tom Rafferty and James Binnie are dead,' said Steven. 'Khan turned on them. Call an ambulance for Gus, will you?'

'Good God almighty,' exclaimed Childs, seeing the blood on Gus's clothes. Leadbetter called for an ambulance and the police on his mobile phone and then joined Childs in going into the shed to survey the aftermath.

Steven watched the two men as he worked on Gus's shoulder. They seemed genuinely shocked and upset but in his own mind he was thinking about the small flat stone that the shed door had jammed on when Gus had first tried to open it. Gus had kicked it away without a second thought but Steven saw that that had not been an option for the two men inside. The stone could not have been there when they went in or they wouldn't have got the door open, so where had it come from? Apart from that, the two men wouldn't have gone in if the lights had not been working. This suggested that the stone had materialised and the lights had failed *after* both men had gone inside, leaving them trapped in the dark with Khan. Steven shuddered at the thought.

The police and an ambulance arrived and the process of clearing up began. The bodies of Tom Rafferty and James Binnie were loaded into the back of a small black van after cursory examination by the duty police surgeon and were taken away to the city mortuary for a more detailed post mortem. Somewhere inside the house the phone rang and Steven remembered just why he had come here in the first place. He would have to break the news to Ann Binnie that her husband was dead. He was thinking about this when Chief Inspector Brewer came up and stood beside him. 'Are you all right?' he asked.

Steven nodded. 'I'm fine.'

'You don't suppose it was rabies, do you? That would be all we need round here.'

'It wasn't rabies,' said Steven.

'Then what?'

'I guess you get psychopathic dogs just like you get psychopathic humans.'

'So the dog just went for them?'

'That's what it looks like,' said Steven.

'Poor buggers,' said Brewer. 'What a way to go.'

# 17

Steven drove back to Edinburgh feeling low after telling Ann Binnie of her husband's death and the circumstances surrounding it. It had been a harrowing experience and although Brewer had been prepared to do it – seeing it as an unpleasant but necessary part of his job – Steven had insisted, saying that he wanted to complete what he had set out to do on Ann's behalf – find her husband.

Brewer had, however, sent along a policewoman to accompany him and he had been glad of her support: he didn't know Ann well and women in general were better at offering emotional support than men, whatever the politically correct might have to say about that. Ann and James had obviously been very close but they had had no children so there was no immediate family for her to turn to. The policewoman had managed to elicit from Ann the names of a couple of women in the village that she was friendly with and they were now offering her comfort and support.

Steven reflected that one small flat stone and a loose fuse-holder were telling him that the stakes had been raised dramatically by Sigma 5 but it was hard to see why. He had the unnerving feeling that he was still missing something important in all of this. If Sigma 5 were prepared to commit murder in order to keep the secret of the rats, why weren't they doing anything effective about the problem itself? True, they had instigated the rat cull but that fell more into the public relations or grand gesture category than anything really positive.

Steven concluded reluctantly that Sigma 5 must be working to some alternative set of priorities but, right now, he couldn't see what they were. One conclusion he could reach, however, was that, if Rafferty and James Binnie had been murdered as he strongly suspected they had, then the music box in his car had been no idle threat. He might well be the next serious target. He would have to be even more careful in future. The thought made him subconsciously check on the presence of the gun under his left arm. It felt cold, hard and, although he was loath to admit it, reassuring.

But Steven could see that he wasn't the only one at risk. He had already identified the Raffertys as the weak link in the Sigma 5 operation, the one that he and Jamie Brown were planning to concentrate on. Thomas was now dead but Trish was still alive. She would currently be hearing of her husband's death from a police officer knocking on her door. Steven wondered if this would make it more or less likely that she might spill the beans about what had been going on in Blackbridge. He felt guilty even thinking it, but this might be a very good time for Eve to appear on the scene to offer sympathy and a shoulder to cry on to Trish Rafferty. It might also be a very good idea if he were to ask DCI Brewer to mount a discreet police guard on Trish, who was now the sole owner of Crawhill Farm. Considering that Childs and Leadbetter were the opposition, a discreet, *armed* guard might be even better.

Steven correctly anticipated that Eve would be at home: he remembered that she had afternoons off from the hotel – the gap between lunch and dinner. He called her to tell her what had happened but she already knew. 'It's all around the village,' she said. 'And poor James Binnie too, he was such a nice man. It's so unfair. Everyone knew that Khan should have been put down ages ago. Poor Ann, I don't know what she'll do without him. They were everything to each other.'

Steven agreed with the sentiments, then asked, 'Are you working at the hotel tonight?'

'Yes, you just caught me going out the door. Why?'

'I thought Trish might need to see a friendly face.'

'I did consider that,' said Eve. 'I actually phoned her yesterday and we arranged to meet next week for a pizza on my night off but maybe you're right. Perhaps I should go round and see her. I don't think she has anyone else.'

'Just a thought,' said Steven.

'You're all heart,' said Eve, seeing what was behind the suggestion.

'All right, I know it sounds callous,' agreed Steven. 'But I need all the help I can get right now and Trish is a potential source of information, I'm sure of it. Things are starting to heat up.'

'What makes you say that?'

'Not over the phone,' said Steven. 'Do you think you can manage to see Trish?'

'In the circumstances I can probably get one of the other girls to cover for me tonight,' said Eve.

'Meet me after you've seen her?' suggested Steven.

'All right.'

'Call me on the mobile and I'll come and collect you.'

It occurred to Steven that it had been a while since he had heard from Jamie Brown. He thought he would re-establish contact and at the same time tell him about the deaths out at Blackbridge. Brown would be grateful for the tip off and keeping on the right side of the press was always a good idea. Knowing what they were up to was an even better one.

'Sorry I haven't been in touch,' said Brown. 'I've been having a go at the Scottish Executive but I've just run into one brick wall after another. It's strange. It's not the usual case of people keeping their mouths shut because they don't want the press involved. I get the impression that they genuinely don't know what's going on. They're more embarrassed than obstructive. I can't even find out who authorised the use of the army for Christ's sake! All I've been getting is, "There's a job to be done and it's being done." End of story.'

Steven sympathised and agreed that they'd have to accept that no official channels were open to them. He pointed out that Trish Rafferty was now their only hope of getting some inside information.

'Maybe I should go see her,' suggested Brown. 'Sympathise with her over the loss of her husband and ask about her plans for Crawhill now that Thomas is dead.'

'That's in hand,' said Steven. 'Maybe you could leave it for a couple of days?'

'The *Clarion* won't,' said Brown.

'The *Clarion* doesn't know that Trish is mixed up in anything,' said Steven. 'They'll just be covering a horrific story involving a killer dog and ruing the fact that they didn't get any pictures to splash over their front page with their usual impeccable good taste. They'll see her as the estranged wife of the deceased: they'll be looking for a "My Agony" piece.

'True, but they might ask her about her future plans for Crawhill and that could be very relevant to the legal battle. It would be a bit of a blow to Pentangle and the opposition in general to the GM crop at Peat Ridge if she decided to pull out of the organic farm plan, wouldn't it?'

'Somehow, I don't think Trish will be pulling the strings at Crawhill any more than Thomas was,' said Steven.

'So you think that Childs and Leadbetter are running the show?'

'Yes. I just wish I had a clearer idea what "the show" was and what kind of hold that pair had over Thomas Rafferty.'

'So it wasn't just that he wanted his wife back that made Rafferty come up with this organic farm business?' said Brown.

'No, Childs and Leadbetter were behind it from the beginning,' admitted Steven. 'He was scared of them.'

'With their background, so am I,' said Brown.

'Maybe Gus Watson knows more than he's letting on,' said Steven. 'I hear he's out of hospital. It wasn't as bad as we all first thought. He was dead lucky to get away with no real muscle damage.'

'Want me to give him a try?'

'Nothing to lose,' said Steven. 'You'll be covering the story of Rafferty's death so it wouldn't be out of the ordinary for you to interview the man who worked for him. Find out if he knows anything about Childs and Rafferty that we don't.'

'I'll give it a go,' said Brown. 'And thanks for the tip-off.'

Eve called at eleven and said that she'd just left Trish's flat. Steven picked her up at the junction of Dorset Place with Merchiston Avenue. At that time the streets were quiet so they sat and talked for a while.

'There's a policeman on the door,' was the first thing Eve said when she got in the car.

'Good,' said Steven.

Eve looked at him sideways.

'It'll give her a bit of peace from reporters, tonight at least,' said Steven, deciding not to say anything about his fears for Trish for the moment. 'How was she?'

'Full of remorse,' said Eve. 'She feels responsible.'

'For the dog attacking them?'

'No, she had no more time for Khan than anyone else, but she seems to think that she might have been able to persuade Tom to have him put down if she'd still been with him.'

'So she's a heartbroken wife?'

'I wouldn't say that exactly,' replied Eve cautiously. 'I got the impression that she felt worse about James Binnie's death than she did about Tom's. She didn't actually say that, of course, but, reading between the lines, that's what I picked up.'

'Interesting.'

'And you were right; it was something more than Tom's

drinking that made her leave him,' said Eve. 'I got the feeling that it was that – whatever it was – rather than the fact that he was a piss artist with the brain of a ferret that was stopping her grieving too deeply for Tom.'

'But you didn't get any inkling what it was?'

'God help me, I did try winkling it out of her,' said Eve. 'See what you've turned me into?'

'You've nothing to be ashamed about,' Steven assured her.

'I thought I would say something nice about Tom, as you feel obliged to do at such times, but I really wanted to see how she'd react. I tried telling Trish that, despite all his drinking and being a bit lazy, Tom was basically a nice bloke. She looked at me strangely and said, "You don't know what the bastard did." I tried asking her what she meant but she changed the subject.'

'Now that's worth knowing,' said Steven. 'It fits in with what she said when I talked to her. She said that she had told "them" everything in exchange for some kind of agreement where she'd be left alone and "he" wouldn't get into trouble.'

'Sounds like she shopped her husband in return for some kind of assurance?'

'That's what we've been thinking all along,' agreed Steven. 'But she managed to do a deal. Jesus!'

'What does that tell you?' asked Eve, puzzled at Steven's reaction.

'If Trish Rafferty managed to do a deal with the government over whatever Tom was mixed up in, we are talking something big and we are talking embarrassing on a mega scale. It's *that* that they're trying to cover up, not a problem stemming from the GM crop itself. It was something that Tom did. But there has to be a connection with the GM crop and the rats' behaviour at Blackbridge; there just has to be. What could Rafferty have done that was so bloody awful?'

'Maybe he interfered with Ronald Lane's crop in some way? Sabotaged it?' suggested Eve.

'Now that's a good idea,' agreed Steven. 'But how would he go about doing that?'

'Maybe he sprayed some kind of poison on it and it's that that's affecting the rats in the canal?'

'Right,' said Steven. 'But he couldn't do that in any kind of systematic way. I mean, he could hardly jump in a tractor and trundle up and down Peat Ridge Farm, spraying poison over the entire crop.'

'I guess not,' said Eve.

'But maybe he interfered in some way with what Lane himself was spraying on the crop at Peat Ridge!' exclaimed Steven, excited at the thought. 'That would make much more sense. If he managed to tamper with the herbicides that they were using on Peat Ridge in some way, that might explain a lot!'

'How would you go about proving that?' asked Eve.

'I think I just have,' said Steven. He told her about his nocturnal visit to Peat Ridge Farm and of the chemical samples that he'd taken and sent off for analysis. 'You see, I thought that maybe Agrigene were using unlicensed weed-killers. It could be that Tom Rafferty interfered with them.'

'You didn't ever work for Cadbury's Milk Tray, did you?' asked Eve.

Steven came back down to earth with a bump when he

saw the one thing that didn't fit. 'But why would the government cover it up?' he exclaimed. 'That bit just doesn't make sense. They wouldn't have made a deal with Trish over something like that. They would have handed the whole thing over to the police.'

'You're right,' agreed Eve. 'It would just have been a case of one farmer doing the dirty on his neighbour . . . Unless what he did was so awful that the government just couldn't allow it to become public?'

'Now what would come in to that category?' Steven wondered out loud.

'Nerve gas? Radioactive material? Viruses? Killer bugs? Some awful carcinogenic compound that might affect the whole community?' suggested Eve.

'But where would someone like Rafferty get his hands on anything like that?'

'You're right,' conceded Eve. 'It's not as if he used any kind of chemicals on his farm. He's not grown anything for donkeys' years. Apart from that, no one in their right mind would have trusted him with a tube of Smarties on his own, let alone a dangerous substance.'

'I suppose he might have managed to get his hands on something in some kind of a behind-the-scenes black market deal,' said Steven.

'Possible I suppose,' agreed Eve. 'They say you can get your hands on anything you want if you know the right people.'

'But why would they just leave the contaminated crop in the field?' wondered Steven out loud.

'Because the law has stopped them doing anything else?' ventured Eve.

'The law wouldn't have got a look in if it had really been anything to do with any of the agents you mentioned,' said Steven. 'The whole area would have been sealed off and a massive decontamination exercise initiated. Instead, we have the GM crop standing in the field, looking as pretty as a picture and guard patrols walking slowly round it. It's almost as if Sigma 5 didn't want the GM crop destroyed. They'd rather it was slowly discredited with rumour and innuendo. And all the time it sits there in the fields, waving gently, like a red rag to a bull, angering the community, the smell of it everywhere . . .'

'It's certainly made people angry,' said Eve. 'But why do that?'

'Maybe Trish can tell us that,' said Steven. 'This may all be academic anyway. Sci-Med will tell us about the chemicals as soon as the lab comes back with a report.'

'So all we need is patience,' said Eve.

'Quite. Are you planning to see Trish again?'

'I said I'd phone her tomorrow.'

'Good. Stay in touch. You never know when she might feel like getting it off her chest.'

Steven drove Eve home to Blackbridge. They saw that the lights were on in the Binnie house as they passed. 'Poor Ann,' said Eve. 'I'll pop in and see her tomorrow.'

They drew up outside Eve's parents' house and Eve said, 'Mum and Dad are still away at Jean's. Would you like some coffee?'

Steven said that he would and followed Eve up the path leading to a grimy semi-detached council villa. While Eve searched in her handbag for her keys, he saw the curtain move at an upstairs window next door and said so to Eve.

'The McNabs,' said Eve. 'They don't miss much. I think I've just become the scarlet whore of Babylon.'

'Sorry about that.'

'Don't be. They don't matter. No one matters in this godforsaken place.'

As the door clicked shut and they stood in the darkness of the hall, Eve turned to Steven and said, 'Well, are we going to go through the ritual coffee business or go straight upstairs and do to each other what we've been wanting to do since I got in the car?'

'Sometimes I feel very old,' said Steven, but he had to admit that the nearness of Eve in the darkness excited him.

'But I suspect, my dear doctor, that you also feel very randy?' Eve came right up close to Steven, filling his senses with her perfume and brushing his cheek with her hair. He found it irresistible. He brought his mouth down hard on Eve's and hungrily explored the inside of it with his tongue.

'There now,' said Eve when they broke apart. 'Was I right or was I right?' She took his hand and led the way upstairs to her bedroom where they undressed each other as fast as was humanly possible while still trying to kiss at the same time. They fell on to Eve's bed and made love with a passion that Steven had almost forgotten. He was entirely possessed by the need to take Eve there and then and foreplay and due consideration just didn't get a look in. When he climaxed he felt as if the world had suddenly become a better place and inner peace flooded through him like a warm glow.

'Well,' gasped Eve. 'Talk about, wham, bam, thank you ma'am.'

'I'm sorry,' murmured Steven. 'Christ, I just wanted you so bad.'

'Don't be,' said Eve. 'It certainly beats the parading of inner angst I usually get and not a trace of guilt there either. Good boy!'

Steven rolled over on to his front and looked at Eve. 'I predict for you a life free from stomach ulcers and the need for psychotherapy,' he said with a smile.

'What makes you say that?'

'Your honesty. You say what you think and demand the same of others. Makes for a stress-free environment.'

'But will I be happy . . . will I be rich?'

'*Que sera, sera,*' smiled Steven.

'Maybe I'm just a shameless hussy.'

'I don't think so,' murmured Steven, nuzzling Eve's neck and moving his lips round to find her mouth and explore it at a more leisurely pace.

Eve sighed appreciatively as he moved down to suck her nipples and tease them with his teeth while his hand explored the flat of her belly and the firmness of her thighs.

'What are the neighbours going to say, Dr Dunbar?' whispered Eve as she arched her back in pleasure.

'Good morning?' suggested Steven from a distance.

'Don't you have a nation to save?' asked Eve from the bedroom doorway.

Steven blinked his eyes at the sunlight and came to his senses. 'God, what time is it?'

'It's gone nine but you looked so peaceful I thought the nation could wait for a bit.'

'My God, I feel good,' said Steven, stretching his arms in

the air and relaxing again with a stupid grin all over his face.

'What would you like for breakfast?'

'We don't make our own these days then?' smiled Steven.

'Any more shit like that and we will,' retorted Eve.

'You are incorrigible!' exclaimed Steven.

'I'm very corrigible, given the right man,' murmured Eve, coming to sit on the edge of the bed. 'Cereal, eggs or both?'

'Eggs.'

Eve turned as she got to the door and said, 'Careful with the shower. My dad installed it. It's designed to wet everything within a two-mile radius with the exception of the body standing under it. You know what dads are like.'

'I'm one myself,' said Steven.

The smile faded from Eve's face. 'You didn't say that,' she said quietly.

'I have a daughter, Jenny. She's coming up for four. Is something wrong?'

'No, of course not,' said Eve, recovering her composure. 'I just didn't realise. I suppose it never occurred to me that you might be somebody's daddy. You did say eggs, didn't you?'

Steven nodded.

Steven did battle with the shower, settled for an honourable draw, mopped up in the bathroom, got dressed and came downstairs to join Eve at the kitchen table.

'Are you working today?' he asked.

'From eleven,' replied Eve. 'You?'

'There's not much I can do until Sci-Med comes back with the results of the lab tests but I've got some shopping to do. I'm going down to see Jenny tomorrow. She lives with my sister-in-law and her family down in Dumfriesshire.'

'That'll be nice,' said Eve. 'What'll you do?'

'Go to the park or the beach if the weather's fine, eat ice cream, play games, all the things an absentee father does with his kid on fortnightly visits.'

'Is that what it feels like?'

'That's what it *is* like,' insisted Steven. 'I come in and out of her life like the phases of the moon. She knows the moon's there and it's reliable but it's not as important as the sun or the rain. It doesn't seem to affect anything.'

'And that bothers you?'

'Of course.'

'You could always give up the Milk Tray job and do something more mundane like a nice little nine till five number. You could get yourself a housekeeper and then Jenny could stay with you all the time.'

'I've thought about that,' said Steven.

'No go, huh?'

'Fraid not.'

'Well then, you can't really blame the job, can you?'

'No, I can't,' admitted Steven.

'And that's what bothers you really, isn't it?'

'You got it.'

'Ever read *The Selfish Gene*?'

'*Touché*,' said Steven.

'I wasn't trying to get at you, honest,' said Eve. 'I was just making the point that we are what we are and it's nothing to be ashamed of. More coffee?'

Steven declined and said that he'd best be on his way. Eve saw him to the door and he noticed the curtains stir next door. 'They'll tell your parents,' he said.

'Mum and Dad haven't spoken to them in fifteen years,'

replied Eve. 'Not since Mr McNab poured weedkiller on some of Dad's leeks out back. He said it was an accident but Dad never believed him. He insisted it was to stop him getting the prize at the village show. McNab's son won it with a giant turnip.'

'Life can be a bitch,' said Steven. 'I'll let you know as soon as I get the lab report and . . .'

'If you say, thank you for last night, I'll drop you where you stand,' warned Eve.

Steven shrugged his shoulders. 'See you around?' he said.

'You will if you want to.'

'I want to,' said Steven clicking shut the garden gate.

He set out for the city but slowed when he was passing the slip road to Crawhill Farm when he caught sight of DCI Brewer talking to two officers beside their patrol car. He seemed to be giving them a dressing down. Steven pulled into the side and waited until the patrol car had moved off before getting out and walking back. Brewer was about to get into his own unmarked Rover when he caught sight of Steven and waited, leaning on top of the door.

'Trouble?' Steven asked.

'We let the dog slip through our fingers,' said Brewer. 'Or should I say, I did as I'll be carrying the can.'

'You're talking about Khan?'

'I thought the dog had been taken away for forensic examination with the two bodies, but apparently not and now it's too late. The damned thing's been cremated.'

'Childs and Leadbetter?'

'Yes. Leadbetter has just told me they didn't know what to do with it when everyone had gone so they decided just to get rid of it. They didn't realise they were doing anything wrong.'

Steven looked at Brewer but didn't say anything. He suspected that Childs and Leadbetter had known perfectly well that they had been destroying evidence but he was wondering about their motives. Was there something to know about Khan that they didn't want anyone else to find out or was that just his imagination working overtime?

# 18

On the way back to the city, Steven found himself wondering about the destruction of Khan's body. Brewer had seen it as an embarrassing loss of evidence, but little more than that. It was a technical loss, not one that would affect the outcome of his report to the Procurator Fiscal in any way. There was no doubt about how James Binnie and Thomas Rafferty had met their deaths and none at all that Khan, a vicious dog with a bad reputation, had been responsible. But if Childs and Leadbetter had seen fit to burn the body, that was worth thinking through.

He saw a parallel in the fact that these two must have been responsible for pressure being put on Sweeney at the vet school to keep quiet about the rat examination. Could they, he wondered, have cremated the dog for the same reason? Had they been anxious to avoid the outcome of an autopsy on Khan's body too? Was it even conceivable that Khan had been suffering from the same problem as the rat population? Had Khan been subject to some kind of poisoning too?

The more he thought about it, the more Steven saw that it made a lot of sense. Khan had by all accounts been a mean, vicious dog that had become even more aggressive over the past few months. It seemed entirely possible that he had undergone a behavioural change just like the rats. In his book, this just strengthened the link between Thomas Rafferty and the rat problem. He was impatient for the lab report to come back.

He decided to have some coffee before going shopping for bits and pieces to take down to Dumfries in the morning and something for Jenny and Sue's kids. He thought perhaps that he might take them books this time instead of toys. He was looking forward to being away from Blackbridge, even if it was just for the weekend.

He stopped in the village of Juniper Green on the western outskirts of the city and went into the local coffee shop, asking the woman who served him for a double espresso. Almost immediately his mobile phone went off, attracting black looks and tuts from the other, exclusively female, customers. Steven smiled apologetically to the ladies of the morning and went outside to take the call.

His good humour departed as he heard a woman's voice sobbing, 'Steven?'

'Hello, who is this?'

'Steven . . . it's Sue . . . Jenny's missing.'

:Steven felt the blood drain from his face and pins and needles run up his spine. 'Calm down, Sue and tell me exactly what's happened,' he said like an automaton.

'The three of them were playing with a ball in the park this morning. Robin kicked it into the bushes at some point and Jenny went to get it . . . She just didn't come back.'

Steven had to swallow against the progressive tightening in his throat. 'I don't understand, Sue. What exactly do you mean, she didn't come back?'

'When my two went to see why she was taking so long they found the ball but there was no sign of Jenny. She'd gone, disappeared, completely vanished. They looked everywhere but there was no sign of her. They ran home and told me and I rushed up there and looked everywhere again but I couldn't find any sign of her either so I called the police.'

The woman from the coffee shop came outside and said, 'Your coffee's on the table.' Steven waved her away. 'But how could she just disappear?'

'I don't know, Steven. I just don't know,' sobbed Sue. 'The police are here and the men in the village are all out looking for her. Luckily it's Saturday and they're not all at work.'

The woman from the coffee shop appeared again and said, 'It's getting cold.'

Steven waved her away again and said to Sue, 'I'm on my way.'

He took two one-pound coins from his pocket and quickly entered the shop to throw them down on the table, attracting more shakes of the head and black looks before rushing out and getting into his car. Right now, Jenny was the only thing in the world that mattered: her safety took precedence over absolutely everything else. He started heading towards town but just as far as the nearest turn off to the outer city bypass. He then raced round the dual carriageway to the Lothianburn exit of the bypass and then joined the main road leading to the southwest.

He was thankful for the power of the police vehicle he

was driving when it enabled him to accelerate past slow-moving traffic with comparative ease on a road that was not amenable to overtaking at the best of times. Even so, he still attracted a deal of angry horn blowing when he forced the issue on a number of occasions, causing on-coming traffic to brake or take avoiding action. After thirty miles or so he was able to leave the twisting trunk road and join the main dual carriageway south. He was topping a hundred and ten miles an hour when a police patrol car latched on to his tail and turned on its lights. Steven maintained his speed and the police car dropped away as the officers got the result of their computer check on the vehicle's ownership.

Steven tried telling himself that there was no point in driving so fast. It wasn't going to make any difference whether he took two hours or three to get to Glenvane. Everything that could be done was already being done but something inside him wanted to be at the spot where Jenny was last seen and wanted him to get there as quickly as possible. He needed to feel near her. Apart from that, driving fast demanded intense concentration and helped him stop lingering on the nightmare thoughts that insisted on speculating over what might have happened to Jenny.

Some still got through however. 'Your kid didn't wander off on her own, Dunbar . . . she wouldn't do that, she's much too sensible . . . she was taken . . . she was taken by some weirdo who'd been hiding in the bushes watching the kids play, waiting his chance . . . some nutcase who likes pretty little girls under five years old . . . and you know what that means, don't you? Not many come back from that scenario, do they? In a few days time they'll find her broken little body lying in some ditch about twenty miles from where she was lifted. The guy who finds her will say he thought it was a doll lying there; they always do . . . What else do you expect? That she'll come home licking an ice cream cone and apologising for having got lost in the park? Get real, man! Face facts!'

Steven suddenly realised he wasn't going to get past the Volvo he was overtaking before an oncoming lorry reached them. He rammed on the brakes and swerved in behind the Volvo just in the nick of time. He caught a glimpse of the red-faced lorry driver mouthing obscenities at him as he passed, horn blaring out Dopplered disapproval. The Volvo driver slowly shook his head as if pitying the shortcomings of his fellow man as Steven pulled out again and roared past, this time muttering, 'Smug bastard.'

Steven took his foot off the accelerator and let the car decelerate into the village of Glenvane on the overrun. He pulled up outside the house and sat for a moment or two in silence, hands resting on the wheel, head resting on his chest, just letting the silence embrace him and calm his nerves. The metallic contraction noises coming from the cooling engine seemed soothing. After a couple of minutes he felt ready.

Sue came out to meet him as he walked up the path. She flung her arms round him and said, 'My God, you must have flown down.'

'What's happening?' he asked.

'No news yet. The menfolk are all out searching and the police are treating it as a major incident. They've set up headquarters in the village to coordinate the search.'

Steven winced inwardly at the term 'major incident'. It was a phrase he associated with murder investigations.

'Christ, Sue!' he exclaimed. 'I don't know what to say. I've never felt so helpless in my life.'

'I know,' said Sue, hugging him again. 'I feel the same.'

'Are your kids here?'

'They're upstairs.'

'Can I see them?'

Sue looked doubtful. 'Are you sure that's a good idea? They've already been questioned by us and then by the police. They're pretty upset. I think the simple truth is that they just don't know anything more than they've said. Jenny went into the bushes to get the ball and that was the last they saw of her.'

'I'll be gentle,' Steven assured her. 'I'd just like to talk with them for a few minutes. There just might be something they'll remember.'

Sue agreed reluctantly and led the way upstairs. She opened the door at the head of the stairs and said softly, 'Uncle Steven is here.'

Steven went into the room and made a heroic attempt at a smile as he saw the two of them, sitting on the floor among their toys. 'Hi kids,' he said gently as he squatted down beside them. 'What are you up to?'

'Has Jenny come back yet?' asked Robin.

'Not yet. We have to find her. I know other people have been asking you all sorts of questions but I'd like it if we could talk about what happened at the park this morning. All right?'

Robin nodded and his younger sister looked up at him with an uncertain half grin, as if unsure what her response should be.

'You were playing with a ball?'

'It went in the bushes. I didn't mean it to. I kicked it and it just did and Jenny went to get it and she didn't come back.'

'Who else was in the park at the time, Robin?'

Robin shrugged and looked doubtful.

'Anyone?'

Another shrug and another negative response.

'You don't remember?'

'Big boys.'

'Big boys were in the park? Where in the park, Robin? What were they doing?'

'On the other side, playing cricket.'

'All the big boys were playing cricket at the other side of the park, well away from where you were playing?'

Robin gave a slow, deliberate nod.

'None of them came near you and the girls?'

A shake of the head.

'You're sure? Both of you?'

'Sure,' said Robin. His sister nodded.

'Good, you're being a big help. How about adults? Were there any grown-ups in the park?'

'Maybe one . . . or two.'

'Doggies,' added Robin's sister.

'They had dogs with them?'

'Trixie and . . . Leroy,' said Robin.

Steven took the fact that the children knew the dogs' names as an indication that the adults with them were locals. After a bit more questioning, Steven accepted that the people in the park comprised some older boys playing cricket and two adults from the village out walking their dogs. No one had approached the children.

'How about cars? Were there any cars near you while you were playing with the ball?' he asked.

Robin looked down at the floor and said, 'Mummy said not to play near the road.'

'Of course not,' said Steven, but he noticed Robin's sister giving him a sideways glance.

Sue noticed it too. 'There's something you're not telling us, isn't there?' she said.

Robin looked daggers at his sister and she in turn looked unsure.

'Come on now, out with it. No one is going to get into trouble if you just tell us the truth. Mary, what happened?'

Mary looked at Robin and mumbled, 'Robin hit the car.'

Sue turned to Robin who was still hanging his head and looking down at the floor. 'You hit a car with the ball, Robin? What car? Tell me about it.'

'A blue one,' mumbled Robin.

'You were playing near the road, you kicked the ball and it hit a blue car, is that right?'

Robin nodded silently.

'What happened exactly? Did the ball bounce out into the road? Was the car moving at the time?'

'No,' said Robin, eyes wide with horror at the thought.

'So the blue car was stationary at the time? At the side of the road by the park?'

Another nod.

'Did the owner see you hit the ball off his car?'

Another nod.

'How?' asked Steven, knowing the importance of this particular nod.

'He was in the car,' said Robin.

Steven exchanged glances with Sue and swallowed hard before continuing. 'Let's just see if I've got this right, Robin,' he said. 'A man was sitting there in a blue car and you kicked the ball against it?'

Robin nodded.

'Did the man give you a row?'

A shake of the head.

'Did he say anything to you at all?'

Another shake of the head.

'You kicked the ball against his car and he didn't do or say anything at all?' said Steven, introducing a note of disbelief into his voice to prompt Robin into saying more.

'He was reading the paper.'

'And he didn't even stop reading the paper when you hit the ball against his car?'

'No, he started,' said Robin.

Steven felt an icicle run up his spine. 'He *started* reading the paper when you hit his car?'

Robin nodded.

Sue didn't see the significance of what Robin had said. She looked to Steven for an explanation. 'He didn't want the children to see his face,' said Steven flatly. 'He was hiding behind the paper.'

Sue put her hands to her face, her eyes wide with horror behind her open fingers. The children sensed that something was very wrong and became very uncertain. Steven tried to recover the situation. He managed to force a smile, hoping to reassure Robin and Mary, then he asked, 'I don't suppose you know what kind of a car this blue one was, do you, Robin?'

'One like Daddy's.'

'A Range Rover?' said Sue.

Robin nodded.

'Bingo,' whispered Steven. 'Now Robin, I want you to think very carefully. Later, when you and Mary went to the bushes to see where Jenny had got to, you found the ball but you didn't find Jenny. When you came out of the bushes . . . Can you remember if the blue car was still there?'

Robin shook his head.

'You don't know or it wasn't there?'

'Not there,' said Robin.

'I'm off to find the officer leading the search,' said Steven. 'Robin, you and your sister have been a big help. Have a think about the blue car and if there's anything else you can remember, tell Mummy.'

Steven left the car and ran down into the village on foot where he found the mobile incident room, parked outside the village hall. He brushed past the constable outside and found the officer in charge. He and two other officers were poring over a map of the district. 'I'm Jenny Dunbar's father.'

'I think it might be best if . . .'

Steven showed his ID and said, 'I'm in the business. I've just been talking to the other two kids. Jenny was taken by a man driving a blue Range Rover. Blue isn't as popular as green. Get on to all the Rover dealers in the district and get a list of the owners of blue Range Rovers. There can't be that many. Get your patrol cars to stop any blue Range Rover they come across and search them thoroughly.'

'We don't know for sure that the vehicle was purchased in the district,' said one of the other officers.

Steven was about to bite his head off when the senior officer intervened and said, 'See to it, Sergeant.' He introduced himself as Detective Chief Inspector Grant. He and Steven shook hands and Grant sympathised. He asked about the source of the Range Rover information and Steven told him. Grant gave a nod of resignation. 'Well done for getting it out of them.'

Steven came round to the other side of the table and looked at the map. It was marked out in search sectors. 'Anything?' he asked.

'Not a thing,' replied Grant.

'Will you keep on with the search?'

Grant nodded. 'I'll keep you informed of anything that happens. Right now, you're making my men nervous.'

Steven took the hint and left the incident room. He walked through the village to the park and stood there as despair welled up inside him, looking out over the green, empty sward. Some bastard was driving around in a Range Rover with Jenny in it . . . or maybe he wasn't . . . maybe he had finished with her . . . maybe . . . He let out a cry of anguish and smashed his fist into a tree trunk. The pain in his knuckles was so much sweeter than the one inside his head.

Darkness fell and the search by the men of the village and police officers on foot was called off, to be resumed again at first light. Their search of gardens, outbuildings and undergrowth in the immediate vicinity had yielded nothing but Steven did not see this as bad news. If they couldn't come up with a live little girl, he didn't want them coming up with bits of clothing or a shoe. He supposed that the blue Range Rover's entrance into the reckoning was making the local search redundant, but he appreciated that Grant would feel obliged to pursue it. It wasn't absolutely certain that the Range Rover had been used in Jenny's abduction; it just seemed bloody likely.

Steven could not sit in the house with Sue and her husband for any length of time. They were the nicest people in the world and they cared about Jenny as much as he did but he found the silence oppressive and the strained attempts at optimism even worse. He needed to be outside, moving around, because motion made him feel like he was doing something useful even though he knew that he wasn't. There was, however, little comfort to be gained from the silhouettes around him as he tramped the verges of the roads around the village. It seemed that the whole world had changed. It had become an evil, threatening place. Every tree was a centurion of the night. Every copse hid a dark secret.

At times Steven felt tears of frustration well up in his eyes. He was a doctor, trained to save lives in the most demanding of situations; he was a soldier, capable of taking on the best the opposition had to offer and winning – but here he was, absolutely useless when it came to helping his own daughter when she needed him most.

It started to rain but Steven hardly noticed. When he finally did and pulled up his collar he saw it as being welcome. Every physical discomfort the elements had to throw at him was welcome right now. Any distraction from the sheer hell going on in his head was more than welcome. He heard a car coming up behind him and stepped further across the grass verge as the road was very narrow at this point. Unfortunately, there was a narrow drainage ditch where he put his foot down and he went sprawling, face first, into the wet long grass, scratching his cheek on the hawthorn hedge as he went down. He lay there as the car swept past, its driver unaware of his presence, its headlights lighting up the hedgerows ahead and briefly restoring colour to the night. The road was black but everything else was green save for the little red object that caught his eye before darkness returned.

Jenny's bag! Steven was paralysed by the thought. Jenny had a little red plastic bag that she was very fond of. She wore it on a strap across her shoulder and carried her hankie in it. Whenever they had been out for a walk and come home, Jenny would hold the bag up in front of her and pretend that she was looking for her keys in it, just like she must have seen Sue do on many occasions. It was Jenny's bag he'd seen lying on the verge up ahead!

Steven scrambled out of the ditch, trying to run before he had fully become upright and covered the twenty metres or so to the spot in an ungainly stumbling run interspersed with continual falls. It didn't matter to him as long as the impetus was forward. He reached the spot where he felt sure he'd seen the bag and started to feel around frantically with the palms of his hands. He made contact and knew almost immediately that he'd been mistaken. It wasn't Jenny's bag: it was a potato crisp packet.

His whole body went limp and he slumped down into the wet grass to lie there with the bag scrunched up in his hand, feeling utterly exhausted and mentally numb. He had the sense to recognise that he was coming near to the end of his tether. It was time to stop tramping around aimlessly and return to the house.

Sue and her husband were drinking cocoa when Steven arrived back. He'd done his best to brush off the dirt from his clothes but the fact remained that he looked as if he had been rolling around on wet ground, as indeed he had.

'Look at the state of you,' said Sue, getting up to help him out of his wet jacket.

'I'm fine, just a bit wet, that's all,' said Steven, already starting to feel claustrophobic.

'I'm not sure if I have any clothes that'll fit you,' said Peter, who was considerably smaller than Steven. 'The police rang while you were out. They've managed to check out all the owners of blue Range Rovers who purchased their vehicles from local franchises and who are still living in the district, with the exception of two, who they think may be away on holiday at the moment. They've drawn a blank, I'm afraid.'

'Shit,' murmured Steven.

'Look, why don't you go upstairs and have a bath to warm yourself up. I'll pop your wet things in the tumble drier and you can use a bathrobe until they're ready,' suggested Sue.

Steven agreed and went upstairs to run himself a bath. While the water was running he changed into the bathrobe and put his wet clothes in the basket that Sue had left by the bathroom door. The gun and holster was a problem. For the moment, he kept it in the bathroom with him. He rested his hands on the edge of the bath and allowed the steam to condense on his cold cheeks while he thought things through. If Jenny's abductor wasn't local, did this make it more likely or less likely that she would still be alive? The thought conjured up images of Jenny as a little bundle in the back of a Range Rover speeding south . . . or north . . . or east or west. Jesus! She could be anywhere.

The wave of frustration that swept through him made him want to be out on the streets again, searching every copse and culvert, but behind the urge he recognised the hopelessness of the situation and lowered himself into the warm water to ease away his aches and pains. Somewhere out in the woods an owl hooted. There was no comfort to be found anywhere.

When he was through, Steven hid the gun under the covers of the bed he always used when he came to visit and went downstairs, wrapped in the bathrobe he'd been given.

'Feel better?' asked Sue.

'Much.'

'Your clothes are just about dry. I did all of them on "high" so God knows what sort of a state they'll be in but I thought the main thing was that they should be dry.'

'Thanks, Sue, I appreciate it.'

Peter came out from the kitchen and said, 'I've heated up some soup. You must eat something.'

Steven nodded and thanked him. He saw that it was well after midnight and said that Peter and Sue should go to bed.

'I don't think any of us are going to get much sleep tonight,' said Sue.

'You must try,' insisted Steven. 'I'll have my soup and clear up here. I'll knock on your door if there's any news. Off with you!'

Peter and Sue went reluctantly upstairs and Steven had his soup and a chunk of bread while sitting at the kitchen table. By the time he had finished, the tumble dryer had ended its cycle so he took out his clothes and found that, as

Sue had predicted, they were already dry. None of them appeared to have shrunk. Any other damage due to the high heat was irrelevant. He got out of the bathrobe and put his clothes back on, then he put the kettle on to make some coffee.

He came back into the living room and switched on the TV, channel-hopping to find a twenty-four-hour news programme. He watched it while he sipped his coffee, all the while glancing at the telephone, willing it to ring. It didn't but around a quarter past one he heard the sound of a car outside and immediately anticipated that it was going to stop at the front door. He went to the window but could see nothing although he could hear the car's engine idling. A door slammed and the engine note rose, although the car did not drive off immediately. Steven guessed from the subsequent sounds that it was doing a three-point turn. It then drove off and he was about to close the curtain when he saw a movement by the garden gate. Jenny was walking up the path.

# 19

Steven wondered if his mind was playing tricks on him. Although he rebelled against the notion that fate could be so cruel, like a man lost in the desert, wanting more than anything to find water, he acknowledged that he could be seeing what he wanted to see most in the whole world, his daughter Jenny. This possibility did not, however, stop him rushing to the door and throwing it open. It was no mirage. Jenny was walking up the path. She seemed tired, confused and frightened but, more importantly, she appeared to be unharmed.

'My Daddy!' exclaimed Jenny, using up what little energy she had in making a headlong rush for Steven.

Steven swept the little figure up into his arms, smothering her in hugs. 'Oh, my baby, my sweet, sweet baby,' he murmured, tears filling his eyes. 'Sue! Peter!' he called out. 'She's back!'

DCI Grant and his sergeant arrived within fifteen minutes. They brought with them a WPC trained in dealing with children who had been subject to trauma. The police doctor arrived shortly afterwards and it was quickly established to everyone's relief that Jenny had apparently suffered no physical harm. She was a very subdued and frightened little girl but none of Steven's worst fears had been realised and, like a successful actor on Oscar night, he was filled with an overwhelming desire to thank everyone in the entire world, such was his sense of relief. For the first half-hour or so it didn't matter who had taken Jenny away or why. The only thing of any importance was the fact that she was back safe and well. The police, however, had a different priority and wanted to question Jenny as soon as possible.

Steven sat with her on his knee, providing comfort and assurance, as Grant and the WPC talked Jenny gently through what had happened to her. Grant, with the admirable common sense he had shown throughout the enquiry, sensed quickly that Jenny was an articulate child for her age and encouraged her to tell them the series of events in her own words, rather than subject her to the demands of a question and answer session.

It transpired that Jenny had been taken away by a man who had approached her in the bushes near the road when she'd gone to collect the ball. He had told her that her daddy wanted to see her. Jenny, having been well warned about not speaking to strangers, had been suspicious and had told him that she would have to tell Robin and Mary first, whereupon the man had snatched her up and put her into his car. Jenny mimed to them how he had held his hand over her mouth. He had not struck her and the car she described was, in fact, the blue Range Rover.

She had been driven to a house 'a long way away in the country', which she thought was very 'old fashioned' because of the furniture and the smell. It smelled, 'old, like Granny's house'. She had been locked in a room but given books with pictures in them and pens to colour them in. She had been given something to eat on two occasions – 'yukky food' – and 'yukky orange juice' when she'd asked for something to drink. She hadn't been allowed to go to the bathroom but had been told to use the potty in the room. Jenny was very embarrassed about this.

'Did this man touch you at all, Jenny? asked the WPC.

'Once, when he came into the room, I tried to run away but he caught me and carried me back. He threw me on the bed and said I wasn't to try that again or it would be the worse for me.'

'Apart from that?'

'I don't think so.'

'Did he ask you to do anything for him, Jenny?'

'He said to keep quiet. I was crying a lot and he said I should be quiet. He said I was a pain in his arse and I was getting on his nerves.'

'Was there just the one man, Jenny?'

'Yes.'

'Can you tell us what he looked like, Nutkin. Was he young or old?' Steven asked.

'Old.'

'Old like Granddad or old like Daddy?' asked the WPC.

'Like Daddy.'

Jenny gave a reasonable, although childish, description of a well-built man in his thirties with dark hair who had taken her from the park, driven her to a cottage out in the country somewhere and kept her there all day. She had been fed and given colouring books to play with and, after falling asleep at some time during the evening, she had been woken up and returned unharmed.

'It's weird,' said Grant.

'Maybe he got cold feet when he thought about what he was doing,' suggested his sergeant. 'Abducting a child still gets you a lot more than a slap on the wrist, even in these "enlightened" times.'

'Possible, I suppose,' said Grant. 'But I feel there's something we're missing here.' He looked towards Steven who was also deep in thought and not liking what he was coming up with. 'Jenny,' he asked, 'did this man say anything to you when he brought you back?'

'He said, "Here we are, kid. There's no place like home. Tell your daddy that".'

Steven felt his blood run cold. Everyone was looking at him and he didn't quite know what to say. He was suffused with feelings of guilt as he realised that he'd got the whole thing completely wrong. Jenny's abduction had not been the work of some child-molesting weirdo from the darker wastelands of society, as they'd all been assuming. The whole thing had been a ploy to get at him. It had been another warning from Sigma 5 to get off the case.

'I think we should talk,' said Grant.

Steven handed Jenny over to Sue and went through into the kitchen to speak with Grant who demanded, 'What's going on?'

'They took her to get at me,' said Steven. 'It never occurred to me that they'd do anything like this.'

'Who's "they"?' asked Grant.

'I'm not sure myself,' replied Steven although he was thinking about Childs and Leadbetter. 'I'm working on a Sci-Med investigation in Blackbridge in West Lothian, a problem with GM crops. Let's say my interest is not appreciated in some quarters. They've already had a go at wiring my car. I think this was yet another way of expressing their disapproval.'

'You mean they kidnapped your daughter just to warn you off?' exclaimed Grant.

Steven nodded.

'Bloody hell, man. Whose toes have you been stepping on? The Mafia's?'

Steven felt that to reply, 'No, the government,' would sound even more ridiculous so he did not furnish an answer, instead he said, 'The family's going to need protection. I'll square it with Sci-Med and get the paperwork rushed through but I'd be grateful if you'd put your best on it. We're not dealing with amateurs here.'

'I've a couple of officers who've done a stint with the Royal Protection mob,' said Grant.

'Just as long as they're not republicans,' said Steven.

'How long are we talking about here?'

'Things will come to a head in Blackbridge quite soon,' said Steven. 'I can't guarantee it but I feel it in my bones.'

The police left and Sue put Jenny to bed. The house became quiet as befitted the early hours of the morning and Sue and Peter made some tea and toast. Amazingly, Mary and Robin had slept through all the excitement.

'God, what a relief,' said Peter, when they were all seated. 'It's just so good to have her back. I must confess now that I feared the worst.'

'I didn't dare let myself,' said Sue. 'I just couldn't bear to think about it, poor little sausage. Now, are you going to tell us what it was all about, Steven?'

Sue caught him by surprise but Steven recognised that she and Peter were entitled to an explanation. He took a sip of his tea before putting the cup back down and resting both hands on his knees. 'When you phoned me in Edinburgh and told me that Jenny had disappeared, I imagined the worst too,' he said. 'My mind was filled with nightmare thoughts about why she'd been taken and, whatever way I looked at it, I feared the most likely outcome would be that they'd find her in some field in a few days' time. It never occurred to me that Jenny's disappearance had anything to do with me and my job but that's what it looks like now. They took Jenny to get at me. They did it to warn me off the investigation I'm working on at the moment. I'm just so sorry that it has affected you and your family too.'

'I didn't realise your job could get you mixed up in anything like this,' said Peter.

'Neither did I,' said Steven.

'Can't you ask to be taken off the case in the light of what's happened?' asked Sue.

'I could but I think I'm in too deep,' said Steven, 'and it wouldn't be fair to a new investigator. I've spoken to DCI Grant and he will provide police protection for all of you from now until the investigation is resolved but I do realise that this may all be a bit more than you bargained for . . .'

Sue held up her hand to stop him. She said, 'Jenny is part of our family too, whatever daft things her father gets up to, so don't go suggesting anything silly about moving her away. We'll cope, won't we, love?' Sue took Peter's hand and he smiled his assent.

Steven felt a lump come to his throat. 'Thanks,' he said, 'I appreciate it.'

'How would it be if we were to go away for a bit?' suggested Peter to Sue's obvious surprise.

'What did you have in mind?'

'We haven't had a proper holiday this year as yet so it strikes me that this would be an excellent time. What d'you reckon, Sue?'

'Sounds good to me. Where?'

'We could all go down and stay with my parents in Norfolk without telling anyone where we're going. What do you think?'

'Knowing that all you folks were all away somewhere safe would certainly be a load off my mind,' said Steven.

Steven said that he would have to let DCI Grant know of the plan but, apart from him, no one else need know.

'Then it's settled. Let's all get some sleep.'

Jenny came out of her shell a little on the following morning under heavy questioning at the breakfast table from Sue's children about her experience. 'Did he have a gun?' Robin wanted to know. Had she been tied up and blindfolded? Was she put in a sack?

Mary asked about the cottage she'd been taken to. Was it like the witch's cottage in the story of Hansel and Gretel? Was there a black cat there? All Jenny's replies seemed disappointing to them. The whole experience had been much more prosaic than they had imagined. Steven was pleased, however. He thought that talking about it to the others would be therapeutic for Jenny. But she was still very subdued.

This was even more apparent when they all went for a walk in the village to thank the people who'd taken part in yesterday's search. Instead of scampering ahead with Sue's children, as she would normally do, she positioned herself between Steven and Sue and held on to their hands tightly. At one point, when the whole family was laughing at something Robin had said or done, Steven noticed that Jenny wasn't smiling and that her mind seemed to be on other things. He asked her gently what she was thinking about and she started to cry. 'I was frightened Daddy,' she confessed. 'I didn't like that man.'

From time to time, Steven tried to steer the conversation back to the man who'd taken her away and anything he might have said or done but he did it as casually as possible, so as not to encourage any post-event trauma. He stopped immediately when Jenny grew restless of his questions. They then talked about what children did at nursery school instead – Jenny's favourite subject in recent weeks.

There was a bad moment when the time came for Steven to return to Edinburgh and Jenny decided for the first time ever in this situation that she wanted to come with him. She clung to his sleeve in a determined fashion until he eventually managed to reassure her that she'd be safe and that no one would try to take her away again. The moment passed but Steven could see that Jenny's view of the village and her life in it had been coloured, perhaps indelibly and forever, by the events of the last two days.

As he drove back, he found himself becoming increasingly angry over what Sigma 5 had done. True, they hadn't harmed Jenny physically but the experience was going to stay with her and it would always be there in nightmares. It seemed likely that the confident little girl he'd known would never be quite so confident again.

The description of the man that Jenny had given could have fitted either Childs or Leadbetter – both were tall, athletic men with dark hair – but he recognised that such a description would fit a great many other men, simply because of the lack of distinguishing detail. Jenny was too young to give a better description. While he thought about it, Steven remembered that he had spoken to DCI Brewer on Saturday morning when the policeman was returning from a visit to Crawhill Farm where he had learned of Khan's destruction. If Childs and Leadbetter had been around to answer his questions about the fate of Rafferty's dog, then it clearly could not have been either of them who'd been involved in Jenny's abduction. But had *both* of them been around? he wondered. It was possible that Brewer had only spoken with one of them. He decided that this was something worth checking so he pulled into a lay-by and phoned him.

'No, I only spoke with Leadbetter,' replied Brewer. 'Why d'you ask?'

'You're sure you didn't see Childs at all?' asked Steven, ignoring Brewer's question.

'No, these two are usually joined at the hip but not on that occasion, or the night before for that matter.'

'What d'you mean?'

'Childs turned up at Trish Rafferty's place after you asked us to put a guard on it. He said he wanted to express his sympathy over Tom's death and find out Trish's plans for the farm. The officer on the door pointed out that it was very late and suggested he leave it until the morning. Childs agreed and left.'

'I don't suppose your man reported what kind of car Childs was driving, did he?' asked Steven.

'It wasn't on his report but I could ask him.'

Steven thanked Brewer and continued his drive. He had reached the southern outskirts of the city when Brewer called back. 'It was a blue Range Rover. Does that help?'

'It does,' replied Steven and clicked off the phone. Coincidences didn't stretch that far. It had been Childs who had taken his daughter.

Steven drove to his hotel and made contact with Sci-Med for the second time that day – he'd been in touch before he left Glenvane to make the official request for police protection for Jenny and the family. It was already there in practice – he'd noticed the dark Ford Escort with two men in it on their walk round the village, but DCI Grant would need the official paperwork. At the time of his first call, Sci-Med had not had anything back from the lab so he thought he'd ask again.

'The report's just come in,' said the duty officer. 'Do you want me to read it out?'

'Shoot.'

'All submitted samples of glyphosphate and glufosinate weed-killing chemicals contained exactly what was stated on the container labels and in the same proportions. A search for contaminating traces of other chemicals was negative in all cases.'

'Shit,' murmured Steven as his theory caught fire and turned to ashes. 'What about the rat?'

'Toxicology report on animal ref. 23567, male rat. The animal's body contained no trace of toxic chemicals.'

Steven felt utterly dejected. He was so silent that the duty man had to ask if he had heard. 'I heard,' he murmured.

'The lab want to know if they can destroy the chemical samples and ditch the rat's body or do you want them kept?'

'They can chuck them. Wait! No, tell them to hang on to the rat for the time being. They can lose the chemicals though.'

'Will do.'

Steven remembered his conversation with Sue and Peter when he had said that he couldn't give up the investigation because he was 'in too deep'. The lab had just told him that, far from being in too deep, he had actually failed to scratch the surface of the affair. The GM crop on Peat Ridge Farm had not been poisoned and neither had the rats. He had no idea what was going on.

He gazed out of the window while he tried to salvage something from the situation. The threats to his and his daughter's life had been real enough and Rafferty's and Binnie's deaths were a sad matter of fact. There was also little doubt that the rats' behaviour had changed so where did that leave him if chemical poisoning was no longer in the frame?

He thought again about Sweeney's reaction to being questioned when he'd spoken to him at the vet school and took comfort from that. Sweeney wouldn't have behaved the way he had if all he had been asked to conceal was a completely negative report. In fact, there would have been no reason to pressure him into doing so in the first place. But there had been a reason. Either the rat Sweeney had examined was in some way different from the one he had sent to Sci-Med or . . . Or what? Could it be that he had asked the lab to look for the wrong thing?

Steven reckoned that it was difficult to see what other test he could have asked for in the circumstances. Toxicology would cover the presence of all known noxious substances including those which damaged DNA and would therefore affect future generations . . . But it wouldn't have entailed a check for infection, he reminded himself. Maybe the crop or the rats or both had been infected by a bacterium or virus? Although he couldn't see how someone like Rafferty could have engineered anything like that. It was a long shot but it was worth checking out, Steven decided – if only because he couldn't think what else to do for the moment. He contacted Sci-Med again and asked for bacteriology and virology reports on the rat's body.

Eve called to say that she'd been in touch with Trish Rafferty again.

'Any progress?' asked Steven.

'She's coming home to Crawhill tomorrow,' said Trish. 'She has to sort out various things and make arrangements for Tom's funeral so I said I'd give her a hand whenever I could.'

'Well done.'

'I didn't do it for you. I did it because she's my friend.'

'Understood,' said Steven in such a way as to make Eve feel guilty that she'd said it.

'I'm sorry,' she said. 'I didn't mean to jump down your throat. It's just that I feel so guilty about all this. How was your daughter? Did you have a nice day with her?'

'I'll tell you about that when I see you,' said Steven.

'When will that be?'

'Dinner this evening?' suggested Steven.

'I can't. I'm working at the hotel.'

'Pity.'

'I'll get off about ten. Maybe we could meet then?'

'See you at ten.'

Steven returned to thinking about Childs and what he should do. This, he saw as a test of his own character. What he really wanted to do was confront Childs, put the automatic in his mouth and blow his head off for what he'd subjected Jenny to, but years of training had drummed into him the fact that letting things get personal could be the kiss of death. He must remain cold and dispassionate or at least as cold and dispassionate as he could manage. He was still human and, in this case, that meant bloody angry.

The obvious thing would be to inform the Dumfriesshire police. He felt sure that Jenny would identify Childs and the fact that he drove a blue Range Rover, which the other children had seen, would seem to be the clincher. There would be a lot of satisfaction to be gained from seeing Childs put away for what he'd done but there was a bigger picture to consider. Steven recognised, albeit reluctantly, that Childs had done what he'd done to protect his own assignment. The question he had to ask himself was, would seeing him in court bring him any closer to finding out what that business was all about or who was really behind it?

After a few minutes' thought, he could see that the only chance of that would be if Childs spoke out at his trial in order to save his own skin. The chances of that, he concluded, even in the face of a long prison sentence, were remote. Childs and Leadbetter were both ex-Special Forces, not a couple of cheap crooks on the make. If they had been selected for the assignment at Blackbridge it was because they were the best. They would keep their mouths shut. There was also the strong possibility that the establishment would find some way of not bringing Childs to court if it suited their purpose and it obviously would. The whole thing could end up with himself and a lot of policemen down in Dumfries feeling very bitter about nothing having been achieved. He would bite the bullet and do nothing for the moment.

He called Jamie Brown to see if he'd managed to speak to Gus Watson.

'I didn't get very far, I'm afraid,' said Brown. 'He's worried about his job right now so he's not inclined to rock any boats. I think he hopes that Trish Rafferty will keep on the plant hire business and do something about his working conditions, which he says are pretty bad, but, as he put it, jobs in this area are about as common as flying pigs. Mind you, if the GM people get their way, flying pigs might become a bit commoner!'

Steven felt in no mood for humour. He asked, 'What about the organic farm plan? Does he see himself fitting into that at all?'

'I don't think so. Gus didn't understand Rafferty's interest in organic farming any more than anyone else around here.'

'So what's bugging him about his work conditions?' asked Steven.

'He reckons that the condition of the machinery is much worse than it would be if it were housed properly. He's fed up repairing damage caused by exposure to the elements. Most of the storage sheds have leaking roofs.'

'Seems a reasonable complaint. Out of interest, did he ever talk to Childs and Leadbetter about the problem?'

'He did,' said Brown. 'He says they just weren't interested.'

'Surprise, surprise,' murmured Steven, pleased to get even more confirmation that Childs and Leadbetter had no real interest in the financial state of Crawhill Farm. 'Did Gus have anything to say about our "venture capitalists"?'

'Just that they're no farmers. "Wouldn't know a cow from a unicorn," was what he said, so he couldn't see where the expertise to run an organic farm was going to come from.'

'I hear Trish Rafferty's coming back to Crawhill tomorrow,' said Steven. 'We'll see what develops then.'

'That should be interesting,' agreed Brown.

Steven sat in his car about fifty metres from the Blackbridge Hotel, waiting for Eve who was late – it had already gone quarter past ten and he was beginning to wonder if anything was wrong when she finally appeared, looking harassed.

'Sorry I'm late,' she apologised. 'We've been rushed off our feet this evening. One of the girls has gone down with flu and we've been really busy.'

'No problem,' said Steven. 'What shall we do?'

'I could do with a drink,' said Eve. 'We could drive over to Livingston?'

They drove the short distance to Livingston and found a hotel bar that wasn't too crowded. 'So what's wrong?' asked Eve, reading Steven's general demeanour.

He told her what had happened to Jenny.

'Childs and the other one were in the hotel bar tonight!' said Eve. 'The bastards! Have you told the police?'

Steven told her why not.

'You must have been out of your mind with worry,' said Eve.

'I've had better days,' agreed Steven with masterly understatement.

'They really don't want you snooping around, do they?' said Eve in her attempt at matching it. 'Are you any closer to knowing why?'

'If anything, I'm further away,' Steven confessed. He told Eve about the lab report on the chemicals and the rat.

'But if it's not the weedkiller and it's not the GM crop itself, what else can it be?' exclaimed Eve.

'Trish Rafferty knows,' said Steven.

'I'll have another go at her tomorrow when she comes home,' promised Eve.

# 20

Early on Monday morning, Steven drove over to Livingston Police Headquarters to speak with Brewer. He was feeling uneasy about Trish Rafferty coming back to Crawhill and was concerned about how safe she would be in the circumstances. The bargain she'd struck with the powers-that-be had not done her husband much good in the end and he feared that she might be seen as a dangerous loose end to leave lying around, despite her role as informant in the first place. Childs' abortive visit to her flat on Saturday night had just added to his unease. With her husband now dead, his immunity from retribution was no longer an influencing factor in how she would behave.

'What would you like us to do?' asked Brewer.

'Establish a presence at Crawhill,' said Steven. 'Just let Childs and Leadbetter know that you are around. You could use their destruction of evidence as a pretext for having your forensic people go over Khan's shed again, anything you like as long as there are officers on the premises for today at least.'

'And then what?'

'Let's play it by ear.'

Steven drove over to Blackbridge, not that he had anything specific to do there this morning. He just wanted to be there and get a feel for things, as if doing so might encourage inspiration to strike. As he drove along Main Street he saw Ann Binnie coming out of the Post Office and stopped to speak to her.

'James is being cremated tomorrow,' she told him. 'Perhaps you'd care to be there?'

'Of course,' said Steven. 'I liked him a lot.'

'Ten o'clock at Mortonhall in Edinburgh. Do you know it?'

'I'll find it,' replied Steven.

'James made me promise that I'd have him cremated if he was the first to go,' said Ann. 'He said that after a life spent in agricultural Scotland, he would have seen more than enough of cold, wet earth and a bit of heat would be very welcome.' Ann smiled but her eyes didn't. Steven sensed that, like Eleanor Rigby, she was wearing the face that she kept in a jar by the door. He wanted to comfort her but didn't know how. He simply said that he'd see her tomorrow and said good morning.

He stopped a little further along the street to read a notice, tied with string to a lamppost. It was an appeal for the return of a lost dog. 'Patch' was being sorely missed by his two young owners, Alan and Ailsa, aged three and five, and a reward was being offered for information leading to the dog's return. A bad photocopy of a photograph of the two young children was incorporated. He silently wished them luck, then walked on past the hotel where highly polished cars belonging to the warring factions of Whitehall and the Scottish Executive filled the car park and spilled out on to the road. The imagery in his head was of hot air and balloons.

At the top of the hill between Crawhill and Peat Ridge, he saw that the barriers across the towpath were still in place but from the bridge he could see no sign of the white-clad marksmen he'd seen last time. He decided that he would walk out along the path anyway and ducked under the tape to start heading east with a cool wind behind him. As he passed along the southern edge of Crawhill, he saw a white Volkswagen Polo drive into the yard in front of the house and a female figure get out. The distance was too great to see her features clearly but he felt fairly sure that it was Trish Rafferty arriving home. A man who had been working on a piece of machinery and whom he suspected must be standing in for Gus Watson, got up and went to greet her. They shook hands and spoke briefly before Trish disappeared inside the house and the man returned to lying under the machine. It was starting to rain and Steven did not envy him his job.

He was about to turn back when he thought he caught sight of a movement in the undergrowth on the other side of the canal. When he stopped and looked closely at the spot he couldn't see anything, but he was sure enough to start feeling nervous. It happened again: the grass moved and Steven dropped to one knee, his hand moving to the holster under his left arm. The grass moved again and this time he heard a whimpering sound. He relaxed when he realised that no one was stalking him. The long grass was concealing an animal in trouble.

Steven went back to the bridge to gain access to the other bank. There was no towpath on that side of the canal and therefore no direct access to it from the bridge so he had to climb up on to the parapet and drop down the two metres or so into the long grass. He just had to hope that it wasn't obscuring anything nasty like a rabbit hole or broken glass. He landed safely and started to make his way cautiously through the undergrowth to where he'd heard the noise coming from.

He had barely taken five steps before stopping in his tracks when he caught the glint of metal in the grass in front of him. He knelt down cautiously and found an animal trap lying directly in front of him. It was set and had a spring in it that could have made quite a mess of his foot had he strayed into it. He noted that it was of a type deemed illegal in the UK but had hardly time to ponder this when he caught sight of another one lying off to his right . . . and yet another behind him to the left. This one had a dead rabbit in it. He was walking through a veritable minefield of animal traps and snares. There were far too many to have been set by any poacher. It had to be part of the rat-cull operation.

Steven looked around for a suitable stick to use as a probe and saw one about three metres away. He moved cautiously towards it, his eyes glued to the ground ahead, pausing to separate the long grass with his hands where necessary. He felt happier with the stick in his hand, which he continually swept in an arc in front of him before risking further progress. In the next twenty metres or so he came across four more traps. Two had dead rats in them, one another rabbit and the fourth the source of the whimpering, a small white dog.

The dog, a King Charles spaniel, had his right front paw caught in a large spring-mounted trap. From his bedraggled appearance and the damage to the surrounding area on his leg where wet fur had merged with dried, encrusted blood, Steven could see that the beast had been struggling for some time. It was no great test of deductive power to work out that his name was Patch and that he'd been there overnight.

'Well, you've got yourself into a fine mess, haven't you?' murmured Steven as he cleared an area round about the dog where he could squat down and set about freeing it. He could see that its leg had been broken by the impact of the hammer bar on the trap. 'You're going to need a vet, old son . . . and the bad news is that there isn't one locally any more . . .Easy does it . . . There we are . . .' Steven freed the dog and stopped him trying to stand up on his damaged limb. He looked around for twigs and found what he was looking for within easy reach. It wasn't often that he found his expertise in field medicine called upon but right now he was going to fashion a splint for Patch.

Whether it was the fact that he was thinking about the last time he'd had to tend to an injured colleague and the mission that they'd been on at the time or whether his nerves were strung like piano wire after the events of the last forty-eight hours, Steven reacted like lightning when a hand touched his shoulder. His assailant had barely time to utter a word before Steven had hammered his left elbow back into his stomach, spun round to bring the edge of his right hand down into the side of the man's neck and was on top of him, pinning him to the ground and holding the barrel of his automatic at the side of his head.

'Jesus,' said the man. 'Was it something I said?'

Steven took in the fact that the man beneath him was wearing camouflage fatigues and a military beret. When he had relaxed enough to look up he saw that four other soldiers had joined them. One of them, with lieutenant's pips on his shoulders, moved to the front.

'Who the hell are you?' he asked.

'I might ask you the same question,' said Steven. He realised that every eye was on the gun in his hand. He got to his feet and put it back in its holster before getting out his ID and showing it to the officer.

'*Dr* Dunbar?' exclaimed the man. 'Ye gods, if that was an example of your bedside manner, I hope you don't do house calls.' He turned to the soldier sitting on the ground, rubbing his neck and asked, 'All right Kincaid?'

'Yes, boss,' replied the soldier.

'Our job is to clear the entire area of wild animals,' said the lieutenant, who now introduced himself as Lieutenant Adrian Venture. 'I thought you would have known that,' he said with a glance at Steven's ID as he handed it back.

'I knew about the rat cull with .22 rifles. No one told me about the traps.'

'I think they wanted it kept low key, and for obvious reasons,' said Venture with a nod to the traps. 'Efficiency wins over legality. Didn't want the save-the-squirrel mob fucking up things if you know what I mean?'

Steven nodded. 'I guess young Patch here didn't know about it either,' he said, looking down at the dog, which one of the soldiers was comforting.

'Sorry about that,' said Venture. 'It's the sort of operation where you get . . .'

'Collateral damage,' completed Steven. He turned to the

soldier he'd felled and said, 'Maybe I should take a look at your neck, soldier?'

The soldier backed away.

'He is a doctor,' said Venture.

'Bet you don't get too many complaints down your surgery,' said the man and the ensuing laughter took any remaining tension out of the atmosphere. Steven examined the man and pronounced to his and everyone else's relief that no lasting damage had been done. He turned back to Venture and pointed out that it was still the time of the school holidays in the area. There was a risk of youngsters making the same mistake that Patch had made. If that happened, the shit really would hit the fan.

'I see what you mean,' agreed Venture. 'We can't put up notices advertising the traps but we could make it more difficult to reach this bank, perhaps put wire up on the parapet?'

'Good idea,' said Steven. 'Who's in charge of this operation by the way?' he asked.

'I've no idea,' replied Venture. 'Ours is not to reason why . . .'

Steven approached the soldier who was cradling the dog in his arms and asked Venture if the man might be allowed to assist him while he reset the dog's leg and applied a makeshift splint to it. It would be an easier operation with someone else holding the animal. Venture readily agreed and it was done quickly, although not without a communal wince from the onlookers. Venture asked about the dog and Steven told him about the poster in the village. The soldier looked worried but Steven assured him that the owners needn't know just how the animal had come to have its leg broken. 'I'm sure they'll just be delighted to have him back.'

Steven made his way back to the bridge, carrying the dog in his arms and with the soldiers leading the way. They helped him up and over the parapet where they parted on good terms. Steven walked down into the village and went into the Post Office where he explained that he'd found the missing dog up by the canal banks with a broken leg. It matched the description of 'Patch' on the notice outside, could the postmaster telephone the owners and look after the animal until the owners came down to pick it up?

'It's no ma problem,' said the surly man behind the counter. 'Ye canny leave it here. This is a Post Office, no' a cat and dog home.'

Steven had to swallow hard to keep his temper. This was the community the *Clarion* had described as 'the close-knit community of Blackbridge', the one that had been 'stunned' by Ian Ferguson's death.

'Will you at least make the phone call?' he asked in a calm voice.

'If you'll pay for it. That'll be ten p.'

Steven held the dog in one hand while he searched for change in his pocket with the other. He found a fifty-pence piece and tossed it at the man. 'Keep the change,' he said in an even monotone. There was a moment when the man behind the counter looked like saying something else but the look in Steven's eyes informed him correctly that he might regret it. He lifted the phone and Steven went outside to wait.

A woman, driving a Citroen estate car with two children in the back arrived at the kerb within ten minutes and was effusive in her thanks. She left to take the dog over to a vet in Livingston and Steven drove back to Edinburgh.

Eve phoned just before three in the afternoon: she sounded excited. 'I've got some news,' she announced. 'Trish has asked Childs and Leadbetter to move out of Crawhill.'

'Has she now?' said Steven thoughtfully.

'She arrived back home this morning and spoke to a deputation of village people about the protest over GM crops at Peat Ridge. They all wanted to know if she was still going to support them in "their struggle" as they called it. She told them yes but I got the impression her heart wasn't in it.'

'I think she was probably told to say that,' said Steven.

'That would make sense,' agreed Eve, 'judging by what I heard afterwards. Trish had a meeting with Childs and Leadbetter, which I managed to listen in to. I don't think they realised I was still in the house but Trish had invited me to help her make the arrangements for Thomas's funeral so I was in the next room. I heard her telling them that she would carry out her part of the bargain but when they'd done what they had to do she wanted them out of her life for ever. In the meantime she didn't want them staying in the house any more. It was different when Thomas had been there but she was a widow with a reputation to think of.'

'Good for her,' said Steven. 'Did you get any notion of what Childs and Leadbetter "had to do"?' he asked.

'No, but like you say, I think she told the villagers she was continuing Thomas's opposition to the GM crop because they had told her to. It's these two who want the trouble to continue. Talking of trouble, the police were at the farm today. They seemed to be taking Khan's shed to bits. Any idea what that was all about?'

'I asked them to put in an appearance to make sure Childs and Leadbetter behaved themselves,' said Steven. 'How did they react to Trish's request?' he asked.

'They argued and said that their job would be much easier if they were allowed to stay on at the farm but, if Trish felt strongly about it, they would move out and just turn up during the day.'

'Have you any idea what they actually do when they're there?' asked Steven, suddenly realising that he didn't know the answer to that.

'Apparently they spend most of their time out on the farm, taking measurements and testing the soil at various points. I suppose that's to do with the organic farm project.'

'Mmm,' agreed Steven but he was thinking about what Gus Watson had said about them. 'Has Gus Watson managed to speak to Trish?' he asked.

'Yes, he came in today and asked her straight about his job,' said Eve. 'Trish told him that she had every intention of keeping on the plant hire business and his job would be waiting for him when his arm was better.'

'He'd be relieved about that,' said Steven.

'He certainly was,' said Eve. 'But then he had the nerve to ask for a rise and a proper workshop before the winter came in. Working outside was all right on sunny days in summer, he said, but not for dark mornings in January with frost on the ground and his fingers sticking to the metal.'

'What did she say to that?'

'She sympathised and said that she could see the problem and that she'd have him working indoors real soon.'

'So everyone's happy at Crawhill?' said Steven.

'Like an episode of *The Waltons*.'

'But I take it we're no nearer knowing what Thomas Rafferty did that was so bad?' said Steven.

'I'm afraid not,' said Eve. 'And I don't honestly think that Trish is going to tell me.'

'You tried and I'm grateful,' said Steven.

'And I'll keep trying,' said Eve. 'We'll be together quite a bit until the funeral is out of the way. Will you be going to Tom's funeral? It's on Thursday.'

Steven said not because he hardly knew the man, but added that he would be going to James Binnie's tomorrow.

'Me too,' said Eve.

'Shall we go together?'

'Mum and Dad are coming back for it. They'll expect me to go with them,' said Eve.

'Then I'll probably see you there.'

It was raining quite heavily when Steven arrived at Mortonhall Crematorium, which was situated just off a busy main road in the southern outskirts of Edinburgh. He was ten minutes early and sat in his car in the large but almost full car park, hoping he might catch a glimpse of someone he knew among the arriving mourners. He had been warned that this was a large crematorium with more than one chapel operating at the same time. Ending up attending the wrong funeral was entirely possible. He saw two faces he recognised from the streets of Blackbridge and got out to follow them. He picked up that a large crowd had

317

been anticipated for the Binnie funeral so the main chapel had been allocated to it.

The funeral in front was not quite over and members of the family were still shaking hands with mourners at the door as they filed out so mourners for the Binnie funeral were queuing on the road outside. After a few moments Steven could see that the hearse bearing the body of James Binnie had arrived and had paused at the head of a slip road leading down to the chapel doors to await the departure of the cars currently standing there. Steven found himself thinking of aircraft circling over Heathrow and substituted hearses in his imagination, but his face remained impassive. It seemed that a world of appointments and tight schedules reached out beyond death to the very edge of the grave.

The blocking cars moved away from the chapel entrance and Binnie's hearse glided silently down to stop just past the doors. Ann Binnie was in the following limousine with three people he didn't recognise but, because of their age, he guessed at them being brothers of either Ann or James. He recognised no one at all in the following limousine – two old women and a white-haired man who walked with the aid of two sticks. The chief mourners entered the chapel and the large crowd outside filed into the chapel behind them. Binnie had obviously been a very well-regarded man, thought Steven.

Steven sat at the back, a personal decision dictated by his being only a casual acquaintance of the deceased, but it also gave him the opportunity to see who was there. He caught a glimpse of Eve with her parents near the front and of Childs and Leadbetter with Trish Rafferty standing between them: she was wearing a broad-brimmed black hat. There were several faces he remembered from the Castle Tavern whom he thought might be farm workers and a number of men wearing university ties that he took to be faculty members from the vet school.

The service seemed shorter than he'd anticipated but, again, he surmised this would be because of the busy nature of the place. People were departing the land of the living in an orderly queue, just as they had lived, a bit like waiting for buses or awaiting their turn at the dentist. A council crematorium was no place for slow marches and muffled drums.

Steven shook hands with Ann Binnie as he left the chapel and she smiled in recognition. 'Thank you for coming.'

It was still raining quite heavily and Steven had to combat an urge to break into a run as he headed back to the car park. Running would seem disrespectful in the circumstances, he thought. He had just got into his car and was brushing the rain from his hair with his hands when the passenger door opened. His hand flew inside his jacket to the gun in its holster but he stopped himself pulling the weapon when he recognised the pathologist, John Sweeney, from the vet school.

Sweeney got in and closed the door without saying a word. Steven sensed that the man was going through some kind of personal crisis.

'I telephoned James the morning of the day he died,' said Sweeney, who sat and stared straight ahead at the rain-spattered windscreen. 'I told him what I'd found out about the rat.'

'What was that?' asked Steven quietly.

Sweeney ignored the question. 'When I told him, he said,

"Now I understand what's wrong with that bloody dog." I think that's why they killed him, isn't it?'

'I don't know,' said Steven. 'What did you find out?'

'I haven't been able to face Ann,' continued Sweeney, still apparently locked up in his own personal hell of guilt and self-recrimination. 'She must know it was my fault. That's why I couldn't go to his funeral.'

'You weren't there?' asked Steven.

'I've been waiting here in the car park for you.' Sweeney turned to face Steven for the first time. 'What the fuck's going on?' he asked.

'You seem to know more about that than I do,' said Steven. 'I sent a rat's body off for analysis. They didn't find a trace of poison in it and common sense tells me that they're not going to find a trace of any virus or bacteria either.'

'No, they're not,' said Sweeney, going back to staring at the windscreen, although it was impossible to see out.

'So what's the problem with the rats?' Steven tried again.

Once again, he was ignored. 'I just didn't have the guts to stand up to them and tell the truth,' said Sweeney. 'They made it sound as if it was my civic duty to keep my mouth shut. It would be unforgivable to cause public alarm when the matter was already being dealt with, they said. Surely the public deserved a break from scaremongering about health issues and the poor farmers could do with a break. It all sounded so plausible, but then reasons for cover-ups usually do, I suppose.'

'Yes they do,' agreed Steven. 'But when you examine them closely you almost invariably find a bunch of sleazy charlatans covering their own arses.'

'That's about the size of it,' agreed Sweeney distantly. 'When I started to ask questions their attitude changed and they made it quite clear that if I didn't keep my mouth shut they'd make sure I lost my job and wouldn't get another one. And now my friend is dead because I didn't have the guts to stand up to them.'

'I don't think you should blame yourself,' said Steven gently. 'Not many people can stand up to that kind of pressure.'

People were getting into cars parked nearby and the sound of voices reached them. Steven recognised Leadbetter's voice and saw Sweeney stiffen. 'Christ! He mustn't see me here with you!' said Sweeney, making a grab for the door handle. Steven put a restraining hand on his arm. 'He will if you open that door right now,' he cautioned.

Sweeney swallowed hard and looked at Steven who could practically smell the fear on the man.

'Just sit tight,' said Steven. 'The glass is all misted up. Wait a few minutes. They'll all be gone.'

Sweeney relaxed a little but still kept his hand on the door handle. 'I'm sorry,' he said. 'But it's not just my job I'm going to lose if they find out I've crossed them, is it?'

Steven could think of nothing reassuring to say. 'What was wrong with the rat?' he asked again.

Sweeney took a few deep breaths before saying, 'What tests did you ask for?'

'Toxicology, bacteriology, virology.'

'Ask for neuropathology,' said Sweeney.

'Why won't you tell me?'

'If you find out for yourself . . . you didn't hear it from me,' said Sweeney, with the air of a man clutching at straws.

Steven decided that there would be no point in pushing him any further; Sweeney was a nervous wreck. 'As you like,' he said. He turned on the ignition and wiped the screen a couple of times. The mourners from the Binnie funeral had left and newcomers were all around. Sweeney got out and walked quickly to his car without looking back. 'Drive safely,' murmured Steven under his breath.

# 21

The murders of Thomas Rafferty and James Binnie now made more sense to Steven as he sat still in the car for another few minutes, thinking over what Sweeney had said. Binnie must have been able to work out exactly what had been going on after Sweeney's phone call that morning. He must have gone down to Crawhill to have it out with Rafferty over what he thought was wrong with his dog and, with Childs and Leadbetter being there, his fate had been sealed.

So he had been right to think that there had been a connection between the rats' change in behaviour and Khan's. It also meant that the dog's body *had* been deliberately destroyed by since Childs and Leadbetter – or rather by Leadbetter – since Childs had been down in Dumfriesshire on that day engaged on something else entirely. Steven bit his lip against the feeling of anger that welled up in him whenever he thought about it. He comforted himself with the thought that the net was now tightening around these two and whoever else was involved in this sordid business. If Sweeney was right about a request for neuropathology providing the key and the result meant as much to him as it had to Binnie, he was only one lab report away from finding out the truth. He called up Sci-Med on his mobile and made the request.

'The bacteriology report on your rat came back this morning,' said the duty officer.

'And it was negative?' ventured Steven.

'Correct. No pathogens found. Only a normal commensal flora was present in the animal.'

'Virology the same?'

'There's a serology report saying that no suspicious antibody levels were found but it's too early for direct culture analysis. Mind you, the serology result would suggest that you should put your money on a negative!'

'Agreed. All my money is now on neuropathology,' said Steven. 'Give the request A1 priority, will you?'

'Will do.'

'Is John Macmillan available?'

'Hold on.'

A few moments later Macmillan came on the line. 'I heard about what happened to Jenny,' said Macmillan. 'I didn't get in touch because I'm sure I would have ended up pulling you out of there. I let you make your own decision.'

'I came very close,' said Steven, 'but I'm going to see it through to the bitter end now and then I'm going to take up crucifixion as a hobby, starting with Childs and Leadbetter.'

'I know how you must feel,' said Macmillan. 'I've not been idle at this end but right now Sci-Med is about as popular as polio in a nursery. No one wants to know us. I don't think they even know why; the word has just got around that being seen with anyone from Sci-Med could seriously damage your career.'

'If this thing can be traced right to the top I don't think I want a career working for the bastards behind this any more.'

'Let's wait until we have the whole story,' said Macmillan.

'Everything is riding on a neuropathology report I've just asked for,' said Steven. 'Maybe you could have an expert standing by in case we need help with interpretation?'

'I'll see to it,' said Macmillan.

The minutes passed like hours as Steven waited for the report to come through. Unlike microbiology tests, where time was needed to allow bacteria and viruses to grow in artificial culture, neuropathology was more immediate. The rat's brain simply had to be examined by a histopathologist, thin sections made using a microtome and a microscopic examination carried out. The report came through at six in the evening. Steven spoke to the pathologist herself.

'I found very clear evidence of spongiform encephalopathy,' said the woman, who introduced herself as Dr Wendy Carswell.

'Spongiform encephalopathy?' exclaimed Steven. 'But that's BSE and Creutzfeld Jakob Disease and Kuru and things like that?'

'Correct,' agreed Carswell. 'For want of a better description, you've got yourself a mad rat.'

Steven's senses were reeling. 'Mad Rat Disease? How in God's name would it get something like that?' he asked.

'Sorry,' replied Carswell. 'I'm afraid I can't be of much help there. I haven't come across this sort of condition in rats before, but there again, I'm not often asked to examine rats' brains.'

Steven thanked her and contacted Macmillan at Sci-Med. 'You've heard?'

'I have. I got right on to a chap at University College London about it. He's an acknowledged expert in encephalo-pathies. He says that many animals do have their own species-specific type of this illness. He asks if there is anything to suggest that this is not the case in this instance?'

Steven thought for a moment. 'Yes, there is,' he said with some satisfaction. 'A dog was affected too at the same time. That would just be too much of a coincidence. There has to be a common factor.'

'I'll get back to you,' said Macmillan.

The phone rang ten minutes later and Steven snatched it up.

'Diet,' said Macmillan.

'Diet?'

'My man suggests that the animals have been eating foodstuffs infected with BSE. They've been getting the disease in the same way the cows did.'

'Bloody hell,' said Steven quietly.

'Now we know just how high the stakes are,' said Macmillan. 'HMG needs another BSE scandal like turkeys need Christmas. Over to you, I'm afraid.'

Steven still felt shocked at the revelation. It meant that Thomas Rafferty had been feeding BSE-infected food-stuffs to his dog and the rats must have had access to it too. How? Where had it come from? How could a man with no need for animal feedstuffs of any description get his hands on BSE-infected material and why? He had no livestock to feed apart from his dog.

He supposed that it was just possible that some infected animal feed might still be lying around somewhere, left over from the time of the BSE scandal, but that didn't seem at all likely in West Lothian. It wasn't a big cattle-farming area. Even then, there had to be more to it than that for a general rat problem to have developed. It suggested that much larger quantities had been involved, not just some old sack left in the corner of a barn.

A barn? It suddenly struck Steven that Rafferty had a large barn on his property! He supposed that he had always assumed it to be empty but what if it wasn't? He now remembered trying the door of it one day when he had been looking for someone and finding it locked. Come to think of it, why would Gus Watson spend so much time working on the plant machinery in the open yard if the barn was lying empty?

He wondered how he should approach finding out about the barn. His ill-fated night expedition to the barn on Peat Ridge, when he'd caught his hand in the rat-trap, was acting as 'aversion therapy' and making this an odyssey of fun he'd rather not repeat. But, apart from that, if the barn held the secret that Childs and Leadbetter were sitting on, they would have almost certainly taken steps to discourage intruders. He looked at his watch; it was just after seven o'clock. He wondered if Gus Watson might be in the Castle Tavern tonight.

After a moment's hesitation he phoned Jamie Brown and asked what he was doing.

'Nothing much. What's on your mind?'

'How was Gus Watson when you saw him?'

'Fine. He seemed to be recovering well.'

'Well enough to be going out to the pub in the evening?' asked Steven.

'I think so.'

Steven picked up Brown at his flat and they headed west. 'I thought if we're lucky and he's there, we might be able to "bump into" Gus in the pub,' he said. 'I need to know what's in the barn at Crawhill.'

'What do you think is in it?' asked Brown.

'BSE-infected feedstuff,' replied Steven bluntly.

'And you're telling me, a journalist, that?' exclaimed Brown.

'I've had enough of cover-ups and double-dealing, dirty tricks and all the bullshit of vested interests,' said Steven. 'All I ask is that you don't go public before we have all the facts. After that . . . you can dump on the lot of them from a great height as far as I'm concerned. Deal?'

'Deal,' agreed Brown. 'Where did this stuff come from?'

'I don't know yet. If Watson says the barn is full, as I think it is, we'll go ask Trish Rafferty that.'

'And I was thinking about a quiet night in with the telly,' said Brown.

'If Watson says the barn's empty, you can still have it.'

The Castle Tavern was less than half full on a Monday night but managed to maintain its air of general hostility and total lack of charm. Steven picked up snatches of conversation on their way through the cigarette smoke to the bar counter.

'Fuckin' telt him fuckin' straight, it's no ma fuckin' job tae dae that!'

'Fuckin' right.'

'An' another fuckin' thing . . .'

'What are you having?' asked Brown.

'Lager.'

Steven sipped his beer and Brown his whisky as they leaned on the bar and looked about them to see if Watson was in. There was no sign.

'We're out of luck,' said Brown.

'I suppose it was odds against,' said Steven. 'But worth it to savour the pleasures of the Castle, don't you think?'

'Wouldn't have missed it for the world,' said Brown. 'A warm welcome aye awaits ye at the Castle,' he added in a hushed pseudo-Scots accent.

'Haste ye back,' added Steven.

'Jesus!' exclaimed Brown. 'Look who's just walked in.'

Steven looked towards the door and saw Childs and Leadbetter come in with Alex McColl from the *Clarion*.

McColl stopped in his tracks when he saw Brown and Steven standing there and changed direction without acknowledging them. He had been heading towards the bar but now turned off to the left and sat down at a table as far away from the bar as he could get. Childs sat down beside him while Leadbetter came up to the counter to get drinks.

'Is it my deodorant?' whispered Brown. 'You would tell me, wouldn't you?'

Steven hid a smile as Leadbetter arrived at the bar and acknowledged them with a nod. He ordered three beers and took them back over to the table.

'Strange bedfellows,' said Brown.

'Maybe they've joined the same country dance class,' said Steven, but he wasn't smiling; he was wondering just what the hell they were telling McColl.

329

'Another drink?' he asked Brown.

'Might as well. I'm having such a good time.'

'I'm sorry I dragged you out here.'

'Not at all,' said Brown. 'I'd give a lot to be a fly on the wall over there though.' He nodded in the direction of McColl and Co.

Steven glanced and saw that McColl seemed to be writing furiously. 'Strikes me, we're going to read all about it,' he said.

'That's what I'm afraid of,' said Brown. 'My piece tomorrow is on the spiralling cost of building a Parliament worthy of our new MSPs.'

'Maybe he'll share the story with you.'

'Maybe the Pope will announce his engagement to Barbara Windsor.'

'Are we off?'

'I think so.'

Brown was just draining the last of his whisky when Gus Watson walked in through the door and the two men settled back down. For once, fate had been kind, thought Steven. This was the perfect "accidental" meeting that he'd hoped for. 'Hello Gus, how's the arm?' he asked.

'Hello you two,' replied Watson, tapping the white sling inside his jacket. 'It's fine thanks. The doctor reckons I'll be back at work by the end of next week.'

Steven insisted on buying Watson a pint and he and Brown started steering the conversation around to where they wanted it to be. Brown asked, 'Any chance of you getting a decent workshop now that Trish is in charge down there?'

'She's promised to do something about it,' replied

Watson. 'I'm getting too old to lie out in all weathers.'

'Beats me why you don't use the barn to work in and store the machinery,' said Steven. 'That would be much better, wouldn't it?'

'The barn's full,' replied Watson taking a long draw from his pint.

Steven exchanged a quick glance with Brown who said, 'But I thought Crawhill didn't operate as a working farm, Gus?'

'It doesn't. Tom has been storing some stuff for some guy in a suit who approached him over a year ago. You know Tom and easy money.'

'What sort of stuff?'

'Oh, nothing dodgy. I can see what you're thinking but it was nothing off the back of a lorry. Tom was no angel but this was a government deal with a proper contract and done all legal like.'

'But you don't know what it is?'

'I was there when the lorries delivered it. Sacks of granules, I think. Tom said the government had to store it until the Europeans had agreed some standard for it or something like that, so he rented out the barn to them. You know what that Brussels red tape is like.'

Brown and Steven silently nodded their agreement and Brown steered the conversation off in another direction before Watson started to suspect that he was being pumped for information. They had what they wanted to know.

Another ten minutes and McColl and his companions for the evening rose to leave. McColl was smiling all over his face. He now acknowledged Brown's presence and came over to him. 'You know,' he said gloatingly. 'Ever since I started in this business I've always wanted to ring in and say, "Hold the front page!" And tonight . . . I'm going to do it. What was it that villain in Batman used to say? Ah, I remember, so long suckers!'

With that, he turned and left, with Childs and Leadbetter holding the door open for him.

'Scoop McColl does it again,' murmured Brown. 'The journalist's journalist, the man they call . . . Alex.'

'Wee shit,' offered Watson.

Steven and Brown said goodnight to Gus Watson and left the pub. 'What now?' asked Brown.

'We can't waste any more time. We'll have to go see Trish Rafferty tonight.'

Steven felt relieved when it was Eve who opened the door at Crawhill. He felt that they now had at least a chance of getting in through the front door.

'What on earth are you doing here?' exclaimed Eve in an astonished whisper.

'I have to speak to Trish,' said Steven.

'For God's sake, Steven, the poor woman is in the middle of making funeral arrangements for her husband,' protested Eve.

'It won't wait,' said Steven. 'I know what's been going on here but I need her to fill in the blanks.'

'Who's this?' asked Eve, looking at Brown.

'Jamie Brown of the *Scotsman*. Call him insurance.'

'I know what Trish will call him,' said Eve.

'Who is it?' demanded Trish Rafferty, coming out into the hall and looking over Eve's shoulder. 'What the hell do you want?' she said when she saw Steven standing there.

'I need to ask you some questions,' said Steven.

'Sling your hook,' said Trish angrily.

'Wait!' Steven showed her his ID and said, 'I'm sorry, but under law you are obliged to answer them either here or at police headquarters if you'd prefer.'

Trish stared at Steven, her eyes flashing and then looked at Brown. 'And who's he?' she asked.

Brown introduced himself and Trish snorted. 'There's no bloody way that I'm obliged to speak to bloody reporters,' she fumed.

'No, you're not,' agreed Steven. 'We can talk on a one to one basis if you prefer.'

'You'd better come in.'

Trish said to Eve, 'Look after this one, will you? See that he doesn't pinch the silver while I talk to Sherlock here.'

Eve took Brown into the living room with an apologetic smile while Trish led Steven through to the dining room where they sat down at the table to talk.

Steven could see that Trish, arms folded across her chest, was in no mood to be cooperative so he said, 'Let me tell you what I already know. That barn out there' – he gestured with his forefinger – 'is full of BSE-infected material. The local rats have been eating it and they have developed their own form of BSE. That's why they've been going around biting everyone. Your husband is responsible for that situation in some way and you shopped him to the authorities over it. You told them everything in exchange for a promise of immunity for him and his cooperation in what they're doing here at the moment. How am I doing?'

Trish Rafferty had gone pale. She swallowed and said, 'No comment.'

'Won't do,' said Steven. 'I have to know the missing bits.

What kind of a hold do Childs and Rafferty have over you?'

'No comment.'

'For God's sake, woman, the Ferguson kid is dead; James Binnie is dead; your own husband is dead and all because of what's been going on here. Do you want to be an accessory to murder?'

'They were accidents,' insisted Trish.

'James Binnie's death was no accident and neither was your husband's,' said Steven, playing his ace. 'Someone locked them in the shed with Khan and then doused the lights. Think about it, Trish!'

'You're lying!' she stormed.

'No, I'm not,' said Steven calmly. 'James Binnie had a friend at the vet school who told him exactly what was wrong with the rats. He came here to have it out with your husband, and Childs and Leadbetter killed them both.'

Trish shook her head, unwilling to accept what she was hearing. 'No,' she said. 'They promised me nothing would happen to Tom if he just did what they told him.'

'Face facts, Trish,' said Steven kindly. 'They couldn't afford to have someone like Tom keeping their secret, could they?'

All the aggression had gone from Trish Rafferty. Her shoulders slumped forward as she saw the truth in what Steven was saying. 'The bastards,' she murmured. 'The bloody bastards. Tom was an arse but he didn't deserve that.'

Steven kept quiet and was rewarded when Trish started to talk.

'About eighteen months ago, Tom was approached by

someone who said he was from the Scottish Office about the possibility of him storing some BSE cull material. They'd been killing cows faster than they could incinerate them in that bloody stupid gesture to placate Europe. They said that they'd pay well for the use of his barn. The only condition was that he would have to bring it up to standard with regard to it being wind and watertight and secure from animal ingress. He'd need to get a licence but not for a year. The barn was empty and the money was good so Tom agreed. He pretended to the locals that he was storing animal feed there while it was waiting for a Euro-licence.'

'So it was all above board?' said Steven.

'Yes,' agreed Trish. 'It was all perfectly legal.'

Steven could see that Trish was having difficulty saying more. He tried prompting her. 'So what went wrong, Trish? What did he do that was so awful that you had to blow the whistle on him?'

Trish took out her handkerchief to hold it over her nose and mouth for a moment.

'What was it?' prompted Steven. 'He didn't bring the building up to scratch as he'd agreed, so the rats got in and started eating the stuff?'

'Not just that,' said Trish. 'The stuff looked just like animal feed so he started selling the stuff on the black market.'

'What!' said Steven, his eyes opening wide. 'But that could have started the whole BSE business all over again!'

Trish nodded. 'I tried telling him that. I argued with him until I was blue in the face and he promised he'd stop but I knew he was still doing it so I went to the authorities and told them what he was doing.'

'What happened?'

'At first they were going to lock Tom up and melt the key but then they realised what the publicity would do to them personally. They changed their minds and decided that it would be wrong to cause public panic. If Tom and I would cooperate they would put everything right and, in exchange for our help, no action would be taken against Tom. I said that I wanted no more to do with any of it, including Tom, and they agreed that I could move out. Tom could do their bidding on his own.'

'That's when Childs and Leadbetter came on the scene and the organic farm business was born.'

Trish nodded.

'So what are they actually doing here?' asked Steven.

'I don't know,' replied Trish. 'I just know that they've been taking measurements around the place and digging up samples of the soil in various places around the farm but I think that's just them keeping up the pretence of the organic business.'

Steven looked at her, trying to decide whether she knew any more or not. He decided that she'd told him all she could.

'What happens now?' asked Trish quietly.

'I'm not sure,' said Steven. 'Childs and Leadbetter have been up to something tonight and I think tomorrow's *Clarion* will tell us what it was. Maybe then I'll see what the end-game is. Don't tell them about our conversation, will you?'

Trish shook her head. As they rose to rejoin the others, she asked, 'Can you prove that they murdered Tom?'

'No,' replied Steven. 'But I know they did.'

Eve put her arm round Trish when they entered the living room and ushered her to a chair, saying that she would make some tea. She threw an accusing look at Steven who shrugged his shoulders in reply. 'We'll be going now,' he said.

'See yourselves out, won't you,' said Eve coldly.

'Well, what happened?' asked Brown as soon as the door had closed behind them.

'The barn does contain BSE-infected material but it's not feedstuffs: it's rendered cow carcasses. Trish insists that it was all quite legal but that needs checking out. I need you to find out everything you can about BSE cull material and what the government says happened to it.'

'Cull material?' said Brown. 'I thought they burned the carcasses.'

'That's what I thought too,' said Steven.

'I'll get on to that first thing in the morning,' said Brown.

'No!' said Steven. 'Tonight. Stay up all night if you have to.'

Brown looked at Steven to see that he was serious and saw that he was. 'Well, I suppose I'd just be lying awake wondering what McColl's going to come up with,' he said.

Steven drove Brown up to the *Scotsman* Offices in North Bridge, Edinburgh and dropped him there.

'I'll call you as soon as I have it,' said Brown.

Brown phoned at five a.m. 'Did I wake you? Good. I'd hate to think I was the only one having fun.'

'What did you get?' asked Steven.

'We were wrong about the carcasses being burned,' said Brown. 'That was the plan but apparently there was some kind of fuck-up over incineration capacity and the stuff has been building up ever since, all over the UK. Basically, the carcasses were either put into cold storage or sent to rendering plants where they were turned into a granular material and now it's being stockpiled in a variety of storage facilities up and down the country.'

'Any idea how much?'

'There is currently a little over seventy-two thousand tons of the stuff being stored at two official sites in Scotland. They've only managed to dispose of eighteen thousand tons in the last three years and their best estimate says they'll only manage to get rid of sixty per cent of it by the end of 2002. At the moment it's costing the tax payer over 1.3 million pounds a year to store it.'

'So why don't they burn more?' asked Steven.

'One, there aren't enough incinerators; two, they are privately owned so the owners can charge what they like; and three, the owners don't like burning that kind of stuff anyway. It makes a mess of their furnaces or something.'

'You've done well,' said Steven.

'It was dead easy,' said Brown. 'An SNP member of the Scottish Parliament started giving the Minister for Rural Affairs a hard time over this in early summer. It's all in the records.'

'Why did he do that?'

'The member claimed that there was a secret plan to start dumping a whole load of the stuff in a landfill site in the middle of his constituency and in contravention of a European agreement to burn the stuff. His constituents were up in arms and so was he. He managed to get an assurance from the minister that this would not happen and also made him cough up the figures on amounts and storage costs. I guess, with the landfill plan in ruins, the pressure is on to find cheap alternative storage.'

'But surely there must be security regulations about these storage facilities?' said Steven.

'Oh there are,' agreed Brown. 'But under the current regulations, storage facility owners are given a year's grace. They don't have to be licensed until that year has passed.'

'So Rafferty *was* operating the store legally,' said Steven.

'What's legal and what's sensible are often two very different things,' said Brown.

'And never more so than in this case,' said Steven. 'They're going to finish up with enough egg on their face to promote National Omelette Week.'

# 22

'You'd better try and get some sleep,' suggested Steven.

'No way,' replied Brown. 'The special edition of the *Clarion* will be out soon. I want to get to it before my editor does. That way, I just might have enough time to come up with an excuse before I end up covering society weddings for *Scottish Field*.'

'Call me when you hear,' said Steven.

It seemed as if he had barely closed his eyes when Brown rang back, although it was now a quarter past seven.

'It's out,' yelled Brown down the phone. 'They've gone with the banner, "LIARS! GOVERNMENT COVER-UP!" Listen to this. "The *Clarion*'s ace reporter, Alex McColl, has uncovered a government plot to deceive the public by concealing the fact that rats in the Blackbridge area have undergone a behavioural change due to the presence of a genetically modified crop growing on Peat Ridge Farm. We can exclusively reveal that the death of local minister, Reverend Thomas McNish, was not due to drowning as stated in a post-mortem report released to the press but to a rat attack, which the authorities covered up in order to prevent public panic. It is to be hoped that the *Clarion*'s timely campaign to curb the rat menace will prevent the nightmare problem of super-rats spreading to other areas of Scotland." Then they announce a new campaign and begin with "An open message to the Scottish Executive." It says, "STOP THE DITHERING AND STOP THE GM MENACE NOW!" Tell me this is a pile of crap?'

'It's a pile of crap,' said Steven quietly. 'Childs and Leadbetter set him up.'

'But why? To create a diversion?' suggested Brown.

'No,' said Steven thoughtfully. 'It's not a diversion they want to create . . . It's a full-scale riot.'

'But why?'

'I think that's been their objective all along,' said Steven, now seeing what was behind it. 'They've been poisoning public opinion in the village against the GM trial from the beginning, carefully nursing fear and suspicion at every turn so that the locals would eventually be persuaded to take matters into their own hands. This story is them lighting the fuse.'

'So what's going to happen now?'

'It's my guess that, when the local hot-heads read this, they are going to march on Peat Ridge and burn the whole lot to the ground and God help anyone who gets in their way.'

'But how will that benefit Childs and Leadbetter?' asked Brown.

Everything was becoming clear in Steven's head. He'd heard on various occasions that the two men spent their time taking measurements and sampling the soil on Crawhill. They hadn't been doing that at all! They were explosive experts. He would now bet money that they had been planting incendiary devices at specific sites on the farm so that the fire on Peat Ridge would appear to spread to Crawhill. People would assume that the fire, aided by the prevailing west wind, would have spread naturally and the barn full of BSE material would go up in flames, leaving no evidence and therefore no embarrassing problem for the government. 'The fire is going to spread to Crawhill,' he replied.

'Of course!' said Brown. 'They're going to get rid of the stuff and any residual problem with the rats will be blamed on the GM crop. You've got to admit, it has a certain beauty.'

'I'm going out there,' said Steven.

'I'll have to see my editor first,' said Brown. 'I'll stroke his fevered brow and join you as soon as I can. I'll bring a photographer. I want some shots of the stuff in Rafferty's barn. With a bit of luck we can end up screwing the lot of them, including "ace reporter" Alex McColl. That'll teach him to check his facts first. Where will you be?'

'I'm going out to police headquarters first,' said Steven. 'I want to make sure they appreciate just what's going to happen when Blackbridge reads the *Clarion* this morning. After that, I'll just play it by ear.'

Steven skipped breakfast but had some coffee before heading out to Livingston to see Brewer.

'So someone threw the good doctor to the wolves,' said Brewer, referring to Levi, the police surgeon who'd put out the wrong cause of death report on McNish. 'I think he might welcome a wee transfer to the Outer Hebrides after this morning's headlines.'

'Shame,' said Steven with total insincerity. 'I came to check that you'll be circling the wagons on Peat Ridge today?'

Brewer smiled and said, 'So you were wrong about the GM crop being harmless after all, eh?'

'No I wasn't,' said Steven flatly. 'The *Clarion* reporter was set up. He was deliberately fed a load of nonsense and he fell for it. The paper published it and now everyone is going to believe the story, not least because they want to believe anything bad about GM crops. The real motive behind this was to provoke a public attack on the farm. I hope you can handle it.'

'I'll do what I can,' said Brewer. 'But there's been a gas explosion at Fernside and there's an Orange march through Boxhall today. We're going to be pretty stretched as it is. Still, with the help of our friends in the private sector over there, we should be able to man the barricades if the natives start getting too restless.'

'I'm going over there right now,' said Steven. 'I'll keep you appraised of what's happening.'

Steven drove over to Blackbridge, hoping that Brewer was taking things more seriously than he appeared to be. He himself had pointed out that dealing with yobs who felt right was on their side was quite a different proposition from handling rowdy drunks. He sensed trouble in the air as soon as he arrived. It was not much after nine in the morning but a group of men had already gathered outside the Blackbridge Hotel and were shouting abuse at the officials they knew to be inside. He caught one shout of

'Lying bastards!' as he drove past, not slowing much in case he became a target for their anger too. He drove right up to Peat Ridge Farm and spoke to the security men who stopped him as usual. 'Have any police arrived yet?' he asked them.

'No. What would they be here for?'

'You haven't seen the *Clarion* this morning?'

Both men shook their heads.

'There's going to be trouble. Get your act together and warn the others. I'd better check if your boss has seen it.' The men got clearance from the house for Steven to approach and he roared up the drive to come to a squealing halt outside.

'Bloody hell,' said Lane when he appeared at the door. 'You've been watching too much television, my friend.'

'So you haven't seen the *Clarion* either,' said Steven.

'Comics are for children, pally,' said Lane.

'Well, some of the children are about to start playing with matches,' said Steven. 'The *Clarion* has just put you and the Agrigene crop in the frame for the deaths of Ian Ferguson and the Reverend McNish. They're blaming the problem with aggressive rats on Peat Ridge Farm.'

'But that's a bunch of crap!' protested Lane.

'Of course it is, but it's just appeared in their "comic" so who are the locals going to believe? You or the *Clarion*?'

'Jesus, I'd better phone the police.'

'I've just been to see them. I thought they'd be here by now. I've warned your security men: they didn't know either. Maybe getting in a few more might be a good idea.'

Steven got back into his car and called Brewer to ask when a police presence might be expected.

'The whole bloody world's gone crazy this morning!' complained Brewer. 'We've had calls from all over the county about incidents and accidents. I'll get some bodies over there just as soon as I can. I just don't know what the hell's going on.'

I do, thought Steven as a slight shiver of apprehension ran down his spine. The police are being diverted away from Blackbridge. He started to drive back down into the village and was alarmed to see that the crowd outside the hotel had more than doubled in size. One of the government officials was now standing on the small wall surrounding the car park, trying to reason with them but was obviously being shouted down.

Steven caught sight of Alex McColl with a young photographer in tow; they were lurking on the outer fringes like sharks circling a ship with a list. He drove on by and went round to Eve's house, hoping he might get a chance to see her and explain about last night if Trish Rafferty hadn't already filled her in on the details.

As he drew up across the road from the house, a man he took to be Eve's father opened the door and strode angrily down the path, shaking off Eve's attempts to stop him. He had what looked to Steven to be a rifle slung over his shoulder in its carrying case. Eve was distraught and in tears. Steven got out and she saw him there. She came running over to him and pleaded, 'Please, you have to stop him! He says that Ronald Lane is responsible for Ian's death. He's going to kill him!'

'Him and all the rest,' said Steven. 'It's getting very ugly round there,' he said, nodding in the direction of Main Street. 'Lane has been warned and so have the guards up there. The police should be on the scene soon.'

'God, this is awful,' sighed Eve.

'Did Trish tell you everything last night?' Steven asked.

Eve nodded. 'I'm sorry I was so rude to you,' she said. 'I see now that you had to bully her into telling you. What Tom Rafferty did was quite unforgivable.'

'The plan is to destroy all evidence of it,' said Steven. 'Childs and Leadbetter want the locals to attack Peat Ridge and then fire to break out so that they can fake its spread to Crawhill. I think they've set incendiary devices so that the barn will burn to the ground whatever the Fire Brigade might do.'

'I must warn Trish,' said Eve, alarmed at the prospect. 'She must get away from Crawhill. What are you going to do?'

'Try to stop them,' said Steven. 'But first I'll see if I can persuade your father that getting involved in any of this is a very bad idea.'

'Thanks, Steven, I appreciate it.'

'Where the hell are the police?' asked Steven, looking at his watch. 'They should be here by now. I hope Brewer isn't playing this too cool.'

'This could be them now,' said Eve. She was looking at a dark blue minibus that was just coming into Blackbridge.

Steven's spirits rose at the thought of police officers spilling out of it to disperse the crowd outside the hotel but they suddenly fell again when he failed to see any police marking on the vehicle as it passed the end of the road on its way to Main Street. 'Oh shit,' he murmured. 'It's rent-a-mob. I should have thought of that.'

Eve's mouth fell open. 'They're importing trouble-makers?' she said.

'Looks like it.'

A second minibus came into view and then a third. None of them were police vehicles. 'You go and get Trish,' said Steven. 'I'll warn Brewer and then go grab your father.'

Steven ran back to his car and called up Brewer on the radio. 'We've got big trouble,' he said. 'Three busloads of Yobs-R-Us have just arrived and there's no sign of your lot.'

'My lads are all over the place,' said Brewer. 'And do you know what?'

'They've been attending hoax calls,' said Steven, suddenly sensing what Brewer was about to say.

Brewer took it personally. 'Christ, we can't ignore it when some guy phones in to report a car accident with two dead and three children lying injured,' said Brewer. 'Any more than we can ignore a jammed level crossing or a tree lying across a main road or any of the other shit that's being phoned in.'

'Well Blackbridge is no hoax, I promise you,' said Steven with a feeling of great foreboding.

'There's one patrol car already on its way and I'll be with you shortly,' said Brewer.

'Over and out,' said Steven quietly as the sound of angry voices was carried on the air from Main Street. Eve had already set off for Crawhill; he assumed that she'd bring Trish back here for the time being. That would help him too, knowing that there were no innocent bystanders between him and Childs and Leadbetter if things got nasty – and the smart money was riding on that possibility. In the meantime, his prime objective was to find Eve's father and extract him from the mob.

Ironically, he could see that the arrival of rent-a-mob was

going to make that a bit easier than it might otherwise have been. He would no longer be the only non-local in the crowd. There would, however, be a number of men in the crowd who would know him from his visits to the Castle Tavern so he'd have to be careful all the same.

The suit he was wearing would mark him out straight away so he went to the boot of his car and brought out the sweatshirt, tracksuit bottoms, training shoes and woolly hat he'd worn on his night expedition to Peat Ridge Farm. He changed in the back of the car, put on a pair of sunglasses, then set out for Main Street, hoping to blend in with the crowd. Fortuitously, he arrived almost at the same time as a police panda car pulled up opposite the hotel. All eyes turned to look at the occupants as they got out.

Steven noticed the look of apprehension that flitted across the policemen's faces as they took in the size of the crowd and sensed its hostility, but then professionalism took over and they adopted stony expressions of authority. They made their way through to the front where two hapless officials in their shirtsleeves had been arguing with the crowd. Men in authority always imagined they could identify with the common man by taking off their jackets. One of the officers climbed up on to the wall and appealed for quiet. Steven looked around for Eve's father, but couldn't see him. What he did notice, however, was that many of the out-of-towners were carrying hold-alls. This was an added worry.

'I must ask you all to return to your homes immediately,' shouted the officer, whose appeal for quiet had fallen on deaf ears.

'Disperse and go back to your homes immed—' The

officer did not complete the sentence. A bottle smashed into his face, breaking his nose and shattering his front teeth. He fell from the wall into the arms of his partner who collapsed to the ground under the weight. A flurry of feet made sure that both officers were now out of the reckoning. The Rubicon had been crossed: there was now no going back.

The two government men were next to be attacked. One fell to the ground under a hail of blows; the other made it to the door of the hotel but only to find it locked. He too succumbed to the anger of the crowd and fell to the ground, curled up in a foetal position and squealing in pain as blows rained in on him. The anxious faces at the hotel windows disappeared as stones and bottles sailed through them to let in the sounds of the street. The panda car was bounced on its springs until its own momentum could be used to help overturn it to loud cheers. The spreading fuel puddle from its tank only acted as an invitation to a mob that was now feeding on its own evil. A match was thrown and the vehicle erupted into a ball of orange flame to the accompaniment of more loud cheers.

Throughout it all, Steven kept looking for Eve's father. He was beginning to think that perhaps he wasn't in the crowd after all when he caught sight of him with two men he recognised as regulars from the Castle. He had started to make his way through the throng towards them when one of the out-of-towners jumped up on to the bonnet of one of the civil service cars and used an electric megaphone to address the rest.

'These bastards don't give a toss for ordinary working

folk,' he yelled. 'They come to our villages, set up their experiments, kill our kids and then tell us there's fuck-all to worry about. It's all perfectly safe!' Encouraged by the cheers he continued, 'Let's show the bastards that we can look after our own. And do you know what? They're dead right. When we're finished with their GM shite, there *will* be fuck all to worry about!'

As the cheering subsided, the sound of a camera film wind-on caught the crowd's attention. Steven saw that it was the young cameraman with McColl. You son, are a few frames short of a cassette, he thought.

'No cameras!' yelled the man on the bonnet of the car as if he were Peter O'Toole in *Lawrence of Arabia*. The mob surrounded the hapless youth and his camera was taken from him, emptied, smashed and trampled underfoot. He and McColl were about to receive the same treatment when it was pointed out that the man with the photographer was from the *Clarion*. 'He's the one who broke the story!' cried a voice. 'He's on our side!' McColl and his sidekick were allowed to back away unharmed. They looked like pale, frightened rabbits, thought Steven.

The fired-up crowd started to move off up the hill leading to Peat Ridge Farm, an angry, amorphous amoeba, hell-bent on destroying anything in its path. Steven tried to keep his eye on Eve's father but, unfortunately, he was walking near the front. It wasn't going to be easy to cut him out of the herd from there.

He decided against trying to move up through the body of the mob and opted instead to fall back until there was enough room for him to move to the outside. He then ran up the flank and sidled in behind Ferguson. He sensed that it was the fact that he was carrying a gun that had put Ferguson up here in the vanguard. He didn't strike Steven as being a natural trouble-seeker. If anything he seemed out of his depth but his grief and bitterness over the death of his son was being nurtured by the others. He clearly wasn't a leader but had been adopted as a convenient figurehead.

Steven chose his moment and clipped Ferguson's heels with his right foot, tripping him and sending him tumbling to the ground. He quickly stood over him, pretending to be helping him to his feet when in actual fact he had his thumb in a pressure point behind his ear, restricting blood supply to his brain and keeping him on the ground.

'It's his ankle,' yelled Steven, without looking up. 'On you go! We'll catch up.'

Steven kept Ferguson on the ground, hiding his own face while the mob passed by on either side. When it seemed that it was all clear, he risked looking up. The two men from the Castle who had been flanking Ferguson were still standing there, waiting for him. One of them recognised Steven immediately as they approached and said, 'It's that poncey civil servant bastard! He's no wi' us!'

Steven hit him once. It was a blow from his right fist that travelled barely eighteen inches but it caught the man just to the left of the point of his chin and jerked his head sharply up, causing him to lose consciousness and go down like a bag of cement. The other man, he hit twice: once in the solar plexus and once on the back of the neck as he doubled up. Steven left both of them lying in a heap and helped Ferguson to his feet to start frog-marching him back to the village.

Ferguson started to protest loudly and Steven halted to spin him round and bring his face up close. 'Now get this,' he snarled. 'I have had just about as much of Bonnie bloody Blackbridge as I can take. Ronald Lane had nothing to do with the death of your son and neither did the crop in his fields. The man who did is now dead so there is nothing you can do about it. Your daughter cares about you enough not to want you ending up spending the rest of your life in prison for killing an innocent man and I like your daughter so I'm helping her. We can do this the easy way or the hard way. You can walk home with me in a civilised fashion or I can stick your rabbit gun up your backside and carry you in across my shoulders, but going back you most certainly are! Now, don't waste my time. You choose!'

Ferguson started walking quietly beside Steven until they reached his home without further incident or comment. Steven was dismayed to find that Eve wasn't there. He warned Ferguson to stay indoors and ran to his car to set off for Crawhill. He almost ran into Brewer's car as he turned into Main Street and both men screeched to a halt. Steven got out and ran round to talk to Brewer through his open window. 'The mob will be at Peat Ridge by now,' he said. 'There must be about a hundred of them and rent-a-mob were carrying hold-alls.'

'Two of my officers are down,' said Brewer.

'I saw it. There was nothing I could do. How many more have you got coming?'

'Five pandas.'

'Ten unarmed men?' exclaimed Steven. 'I suggest you call for several ambulances and the Fire Brigade . . . And maybe the Brigade of Gurkhas while you're at it.'

'I'll try talking to them,' said Brewer.

Steven screwed up his face and said, 'I won't tell your insurance company you said that; they'd probably invoke the suicide clause in your policy.'

'That bad, huh?'

'The only way I'd talk to that crowd would be with an AK47 in my hands.'

'I'll have a look anyway,' said Brewer. 'After all, it's my patch they're crapping on.'

'Be careful as you drive up the hill,' said Steven. 'I left a couple of them in the road. If they're still lying there you could charge them with obstructing the police in the execution of their duty.'

Brewer roared off and Steven got back into his car. As he did so, a police panda car entered Blackbridge with blue light flashing. He waited until it had passed on its way to Peat Ridge before moving off. '*Bonne chance*,' he murmured.

Steven found the yard at Crawhill deserted when he drove in through the open gates. He checked the gun in his holster and decided on a head-on approach. He went up to the door of the farmhouse and knocked hard on it. There was no response. The only sound he could hear was coming from the mob over at Peat Ridge. As he listened at the door he heard a gun shot in the distance and the sound of a small explosion. The real trouble had started.

'Eve! Trish!' he called up at the windows of the house. 'Are you in there?'

The house seemed deserted. He tried the door and found it locked. Where the hell were they? If they weren't at Eve's house and they weren't here, where else could they possibly be? The possibility that they were being held prisoner by Childs and Leadbetter presented itself. Steven went round to the back of the house and broke a pane of glass in order to release the catch on the back door. He entered and moved cautiously through the ground floor rooms with his gun held at the ready. He then moved upstairs and carried out a similar search while the sounds of explosions from Peat Ridge emphasised the silence here at Crawhill. The house was empty.

Steven clattered back downstairs and left by the front door to run quickly round the sheds, searching for signs of life. He found nothing and that just left the barn itself. Could Eve and Trish be in it? he wondered. A shiver ran up his spine as he acknowledged that Trish knew too much for Childs and Leadbetter to feel comfortable about her and so – whether they knew it or not – did Eve. It might be convenient for them to have the two women die in a tragic fire. He moved cautiously towards the tall doors, keeping an eye on the ground for any signs of trip-wires or infra-red devices, and found them – not unexpectedly – locked. He didn't want to use his gun and have the sound of the shot ring out across the farm, so he ran back to one of the sheds and returned with a hammer. Two blows and the lock parted company with the door.

As he swung back one half of the door, it was suddenly framed by a huge sheet of orange flame coming from Peat Ridge and the air was filled with the smell of petrol. The oilseed rape was on fire. Steven pushed the door to again for a moment in order to look at the sky. He was in time to see through the trees the roof of Peat Ridge farmhouse erupting in sheets of flame. 'Sweet Jesus,' he murmured as billows of black smoke from the fields started to drift in the breeze towards Crawhill.

# 23

The barn was full of unlabelled plastic sacks, stacked in rows and piled up to the roof. He opened one with his pocket-knife and took out a handful of the granular material inside to examine it in his palm. Modern industrial technology could make the most horrific of substances appear innocuous. This was slaughtered cow, reduced to dried pellets by a rendering plant. He was about to leave again when he thought he heard something and turned round. 'Eve?' he called out. 'Trish? Are you there?'

He thought he heard a muffled cry coming from he knew not where. There did not seem to be any room for anyone to hide among the tightly packed rows. He called out and got a faint response again. Puzzled, he started moving the sacks nearest him, shifting them behind him so that he could make inroads into the mountain. The muffled cries got louder so he worked harder. He could now see that a narrow tunnel had been created through the bottom rows of the sacks. He got down on the floor of the barn and started to wriggle up through it.

He found Trish and Eve, tied up and gagged and lying huddled together in fright, in a tiny confined island of space among the sacks. The lack of air and the heavy smell made Steven himself feel nauseous as he pulled off the tape stuck across their mouths and struggled to undo their bonds. Both women tried to take deep breaths and immediately started to cough as the dust got to their lungs.

'Childs and Leadbetter?' Steven asked.

Eve gasped a brief confirmation as she continued to fight for breath. She turned and tried to help Trish back out along the tunnel with Steven reversing out first. There wasn't much light coming in through the open door but Steven could see that Eve's hair was wet with sweat and she was covered in the dust from the sacks. When they finally reached the door of the barn they immediately became aware of the heat coming from the fire at Peat Ridge. The air was already thick with smoke.

'Is Dad over there?' Eve asked.

'He's at home,' said Steven.

Eve put her hand on Steven's shoulder and squeezed it. She was saying thank you when a bullet embedded itself in the barn door.

'Get down!' yelled Steven.

Two more bullets came near in quick succession and Steven and the women were forced to retreat into the barn again. Steven remained near the door, lying flat on the ground with his gun held in both hands, ready for any target that should present itself. He rolled quickly over to his right to try to get a better view and another bullet slammed into the wood, less than a foot from his head. He was well and truly pinned down.

He could now see that the shots were coming from two directions. This meant that he and the women couldn't even think about making a run for it. They would be cut down in the crossfire before they had covered ten metres. The best he could force from the situation was a stale-mate. As long as he had his gun, Childs and Leadbetter couldn't afford to rush him. He pulled out his mobile phone and punched in Brewer's number. There was no response. There was no signal in the barn. They were on their own.

Three minutes passed without a shot being fired so Steven decided it was time to check on the opposition's presence. He rolled over three times in quick succession to the other side of the door opening and a bullet thudded into the door frame, sending splinters up into the air and telling him what he wanted to know. His new vantage point, however, gave him sight of a small explosion which resulted in several trees catching fire about a hundred metres away. This was significant because the trees were on Crawhill Farm. The 'spread' of the fire had started.

Steven moved back a little: the last bullet had come dangerously close. It had missed him but he had felt it pass close to his head. He became aware of a diesel engine starting up and being revved hard. It sounded very near and his pulse rate rose as he realised that this could be a trump card for the opposition. His gun would be of little use against the bulldozer he'd noticed in the yard. It was now coming towards them. He moved back a little and signalled that the women move as far back as they could. They backed into the tunnel in the sacks because there was nowhere else to go.

The yellow monster lumbered into view, its tracks churning up the earth as Steven looked desperately for an angle to get off a shot at its driver. It was impossible. The shovel of the vehicle was being held at a height that obscured the driver from view. Steven was expecting the vehicle to come straight into the barn and for Childs and Leadbetter to alight with guns blazing but it didn't happen that way. Instead, it halted outside the front doors and a few moments later he saw the barn doors start to close. He loosed off a shot at them but it was no more than a gesture. The wood was too thick to allow a bullet from a hand gun to penetrate.

The barn doors closed completely and the bulldozer outside revved up before moving in to nudge up against them. The engine died and Steven faced the fact that he and the women were now trapped inside. Childs and Leadbetter were back to pursuing their original plan. The barn was going to go up in flames, but now with three people inside instead of just Trish Rafferty. It would all be just a tragic accident, resulting from the riot at Peat Ridge.

There was no chance of getting out through the front door so Steven searched desperately for other options. He turned to Trish and asked, 'You said that Tom didn't repair this barn as he'd agreed to do. What's wrong with it? Where are the weak spots?'

Trish looked as if she was living a nightmare, as indeed she was. 'It was rotten along the bottom of the back wall,' she said. 'But . . . they fixed it when they found out that Tom hadn't.'

Steven's hopes were dashed.

'After I told them what had been going on, the authorities inspected it and then sent men to stop the rats getting in,' said Trish. 'We're going to die, aren't we?'

Steven was reluctant to voice the affirmative that he felt. 'No we're not,' he said, not entirely convincing himself, let alone Trish. 'Did they completely renovate the barn?' he asked.

'No, they just plugged the gaps in the back wall.'

'So maybe there's a weakness higher up,' said Steven, thinking out loud. He started to fight his way up through the mountain of sacks by throwing them one at at a time behind him where he asked Trish and Eve to move them out of the way. By the time he had reached the narrow gap between the top of the sacks and the apex of the barn roof, he was finding the heat almost unbearable and the air foul but he was now committed to this course of action. There wasn't going to be time to think of another one.

He turned and shouted back to the women that he was going to try to reach the back wall by crawling along the narrow tunnel formed by the ridge of the roof.

'Be careful!' yelled Eve before he started his wriggle along the top of the sack pile. The space was so narrow that he had to keep his arms stretched out in front of him all the time: there was no room to withdraw them.

There came a point when the space between the sacks and the roof became so constricted that he had to force himself through it, grazing his stomach on the sack stitching and raking his back along the roof ridge beam. But the pain was secondary to the knowledge that it would now be impossible to turn back. There was just no room to turn round and he couldn't force himself backwards with the same strength as he could forwards. He was now committed to getting out . . . or dying in the attempt. There would be no in-between.

Steven reached the apex of the back wall where it met the roof and felt around it for any sign of weakness. It seemed depressingly solid. It took great effort, but he managed to move one sack to his left back into the space behind him so that he could move a little to the side in order to test another joint. The heat and the bad air was now joined in tormenting him by sweat running into his eyes from the effort he was expending. The beam joints still seemed secure but when he hit his fist off a roof panel in giving vent to his frustration, he felt a weakness in it. He tried again and found a definite looseness where the fixing nails had rusted away. Christ! If only he had more room to manoeuvre.

Steven fought to make more space for himself to work in but the effort of moving sacks in such a confined space was bringing him dangerously close to complete exhaustion. He managed to give himself the thickness of one more sack by gripping the sack below his belly and rolling round on to his back so that he took the place of the sack. He then forced the sack – now on top of him – back into the space he had just crawled along. After all, he would not be going back that way.

After taking a few moments to recover he brought up his knees in an agonising contortion and managed to get the soles of his feet against the suspect roof panel. He pushed with all his might and it split away from its fixing nails to move upwards, but only for about half a metre before it stopped.

Steven rested for a moment, taking pleasure in the fact that light was coming in and he could breathe in the outside air, although it was a long way from being fresh as the whole world, as far as he could see, was covered in thick smoke. He could now see that the roof panel had jammed because of a rusty metal fixing plate that was still holding fast despite its condition. There was no time for subtle strategy. The sound of one more explosion in the Blackbridge air was hardly going to matter any more. He pulled out his gun from the holster and fired twice at the plate. It flew off and the roof panel was now free to rise.

Steven replaced the gun in its holster and pulled himself up through the gap and out on to the roof of the barn where he paused to look around him although he realised that there couldn't be much time left before Childs and Leadbetter set fire to the barn. He could see that several fires had broken out on Crawhill, all looking as if they had been the result of fire spreading from Peat Ridge.

He kept himself pressed flat against the roof as he tried to see where Childs and Leadbetter might be and finally caught sight of one of them – he couldn't tell which one – about a hundred metres away and very near to the road between Peat Ridge and Crawhill.

He kept himself on the other side of the barn roof as he made his way up to the front of the building and looked down over the edge at the bulldozer, parked hard up against the front doors. For him this was now an advantage. The drop to earth would be daunting but a drop down on to the roof of the 'dozer's cab presented no real problem at all, providing that he wasn't being lined up in a gun sight as he contemplated it.

Steven could see no sign of the opposition watching the barn and committed himself to rolling off the roof to hang by his fingers for a moment before dropping down on to the roof of the cab. It was then a simple enough manoeuvre to swing his body down into the cab to begin figuring out how to start up the vehicle. The dangling ignition key was a welcome sight. He turned it to the right and hit the green button with the flat of his hand. The engine roared into life and Steven looked skywards briefly in a gesture of thanks. He knew that he might only have seconds to do what he had to do. He crunched the gear stick into reverse and almost went through the cab's screen as the vehicle lurched backwards.

There was no time to warn Eve and Trish what he planned. He was relying on them realising what the sound of the engine must mean. He pushed the stick forward into first and rammed the blade of the vehicle into the barn doors, splintering them like matches. He killed the engine and jumped down to yell to Eve and Trish that it was now safe to come out. They appeared at the door and Steven herded them quickly away from the barn in a crouching run, fearing some kind of incendiary explosion at any moment. The explosion didn't come but the sound of nearby gunfire did and a bullet whined off an empty oil drum off to their left.

It was clear to Steven that Childs and Leadbetter had decided against a quick detonation of the barn in favour of at least one of them coming back to hunt them down. Eve and Trish had found a small hillock to crouch behind. Steven signalled to Eve that he was going to move off to the right in an attempt to come up on the flank of the opposition. Eve nodded that she understood and Steven rolled off to his right then sprinted into the cover of a pile of wooden crates. He glanced back and saw that Eve was trying to attract his attention. She was pointing at something.

Steven deduced that she must have caught a glimpse of someone coming towards them but out of his line of vision. He looked in the direction she was indicating and then saw that she was holding up the flat of her hand as if telling him to hold his horses. He remained crouching low, gun at the ready, but conscious of the fact that he had already used up two shots. His eyes were fixed on Eve who still had the palm of her hand held up. Suddenly she dropped it and made a rapid pointing gesture.

Steven sprang to his feet, holding the gun in front of him in both hands, knees slightly bent. He saw Childs standing about twenty metres from him, preparing to fire at where the women were hiding. Childs managed to get one shot off before Steven fired at him, three times in quick succession. He did it coldly and without rancour but at the same time fully aware that he was settling a personal score. Jenny would never need to know what had happened here but, what was more important, she would never have to see Childs' face again, whether in a court of law or just by chance. All three bullets found their mark and Childs was dead before he even knew that Steven was anywhere near.

Steven remained on the alert, dropping again to one knee, bringing his weapon round in an arc, all the while trying to see where Leadbetter might be. There was no sign of him and no gunfire being directed at him. He concluded that Childs had come back on his own to deal with the three of them. Leadbetter must still be out on the farm somewhere.

Steven ran quickly over to where Childs was lying and prised his gun from his fingers before running back to join the women. He froze in his tracks when he saw that Eve was cradling Trish in her arms and sobbing quietly. 'The bastard hit her,' she said. 'She's dead.'

Steven could see that Trish Rafferty was indeed dead. 'God, I'm so sorry,' he said.

Eve looked up. 'Who's that coming?' she asked. Steven spun round and dropped to one knee, levelling the gun at two figures who were running towards them through the smoke. He relaxed as he recognised the gangling figure of Jamie Brown.

'Bloody hell! This place looks like Viet Nam!' gasped Brown as he and the young, scared-looking photographer with him crouched down beside them. 'Is the stuff still in the barn?' asked Brown.

'Yes, but you can't risk going in there,' insisted Steven. 'It's going to go up at any moment.'

'Just a couple of shots and a handful for the analyst,' said Brown getting to his feet and urging the cameraman – who wasn't so sure – to follow him.

'Don't do it!' yelled Steven.

'After the bollocking I got from the editor this morning, there's no way I'm going back empty handed,' Brown yelled back. The two of them disappeared from view and Steven looked anxiously after them. 'Come on! Come on!' he urged as the seconds ticked by.

The barn suddenly erupted in a sheet of yellow flame over a hundred feet high. A deafening roar filled their ears and a wall of heat hit Steven and Eve as they were blown off their feet. Steven cried out in anguish as he realised that there was no way that Jamie Brown or his companion could have survived the holocaust. He crawled away from the fire and the sickening smell of burning meat.

When they were far enough away, Eve and Steven turned to look back at the inferno. It didn't seem right to Steven to be crouching down at that particular moment, knowing that he was witnessing the cremation of Jamie Brown and his colleague. He stood up and gazed at the flames with a lump in his throat, ignoring Eve's tugging at his leg.

After a few moments, he said quietly, 'God bless you, Jamie Brown. You were one of life's nicer people.' He was still staring at the fire when Eve picked up the gun, which he'd left lying at his feet, and fired it. The noise broke the spell and he dropped to his knees in time to turn and see Leadbetter fall dead.

Leadbetter had been circling round behind them and Eve, who was sitting on the ground, had seen him appear through the bushes: he had been unaware of her presence. He had been concentrating on Steven's back, preparing to shoot him, believing him to be on his own. Eve had fired first.

'Thanks,' said Steven, feeling dazed but aware that it sounded woefully inadequate.

'Don't mention it,' said Eve. She sounded calm but Steven could see that her hands were shaking. He put his arms around her and held her close.

'Please tell me it's all over,' said Eve, a sob catching in her throat.

'It is. I promise,' said Steven, rocking her gently and kissing her hair. After a long silence while they both looked at the flames and tried to come to terms with what had happened, Steven added, 'And us? What about us?'

'I don't know,' murmured Eve. 'It would be so easy to fall in love with you. I'm halfway there already but I've got a degree to get and a career to fashion and a life to live away from here. I don't see how to fit in a serious relationship with a man who also has a daughter to consider. I'm not ready to end up pushing a shopping trolley round Tesco and wiping little noses. Does that sound awful?'

Steven smiled and shook his head. 'No, my lady,' he whispered. 'You're just telling it like it is.'

'But I don't want to be alone tonight,' said Eve.

'Then you won't be. We'll let tomorrow take care of itself.'

When the last siren had faded and darkness had descended on Blackbridge at the end of a very long day, silence returned. The only thing to remind people what had happened there that day was the smell that still hung in the air and the lingering smoke that obscured a view of the stars on an otherwise clear night. Childs and Leadbetter, the orchestrators of the whole sorry mess, were dead, but then so were Trish Rafferty, Jamie Brown and his cameraman, nineteen-year-old Kevin Miles, on only his third assignment. Ronald Lane had been blinded trying to defend his property, which had been razed to the ground. Brewer was in hospital with a broken arm and eight policemen, four security guards and ten 'protestors' had also been detained. The two senior civil servants – one from MAFF, the other from the Scottish Executive were currently in Intensive Care after the beating they'd taken and many others had been injured to a lesser degree by flying glass. The barn at Crawhill had burned with such ferocity that it and its contents were all but vaporised. Steven had never been so glad to leave any place in his entire life.

'So what happens now?' he asked John Macmillan as he sat in the offices of Sci-Med in London.

Macmillan seemed like a cat on hot bricks. Steven had sensed it as soon as he'd arrived after taking a few days off to visit Jenny and the others over in Norfolk. He watched him arrange the papers on his desk and then rearrange them.

'Not very much, I'm afraid,' said Macmillan.

'You're kidding,' said Steven.

'The official story is that these men, Childs and Leadbetter, were acting on their own initiative and went far beyond anything their brief had authorised them for.'

'Acting on their own?' exclaimed Steven. 'You can't possibly expect me to swallow that!'

'Of course not,' conceded Macmillan. 'But proving it is another matter.'

'So you're going for the knighthood after all,' said Steven angrily and then regretted it almost immediately.

'It's not that,' said Macmillan with admirable calm, 'I promise you. It's just that I cannot afford the luxury of resentment or bitterness or even bad temper. I have to be pragmatic if Sci-Med is to survive and it must. I've done all the sums and I've decided that we can't win. As I've said to you many times in the past, don't get into a fight you can't win.'

'Why can't we win?'

'Childs and Leadbetter have been disowned – as I think we always knew they would be. Apart from that, they're both dead. There will be nothing in writing that links them to any government department either in London or Edinburgh and the BSE cull material, which doesn't exist any more, was in any case being stored legally. On top of that, its connection to the rats' behaviour is now little more than conjecture.'

Steven started to protest but Macmillan held up his hand and continued, 'It could still be argued – and would be, I'm sure – that the problem was down to the GM crop, which no longer exists either.'

'But we both know the truth!' protested Steven.

'Knowing is not enough. Defending a GM crop is not a tenable position for us to adopt in the current climate of popular opinion and that is what it would amount to.'

'Christ!' said Steven, feeling helpless. 'They're going to get away with it. Isn't that what you're saying?'

'That's what usually happens, isn't it?' said Macmillan, leaning on his desk.

Steven got up to leave, shaking his head in disbelief but fearing that he might see that Macmillan was right when he'd had time to calm down. This only made it worse. As Steven reached the door, Macmillan said, 'I got the letter about the knighthood this morning.'

'And?' asked Steven without turning around.

'I declined.'

# Author's Note

## Summer 1999

There is a real village to the west of Edinburgh where 22,300 tons of BSE cull material (i.e. the rendered material from cows slaughtered under the 'thirty-month rule', instigated by the government in 1996) is currently being stored. The Union Canal, linking Edinburgh and Falkirk, runs through the Village and the barn here is one of two such facilities in Scotland, the other being at Glenrothes in Fife. In the UK as a whole, there are 41 cold storage depots, 10 dry warehouses and 2 container sites being used to store, in Gavin Strang's words in 1997 when he was Shadow Agriculture Minister, 'Mountains of carcasses and waste . . . which the government have been unable to destroy.'

The backlog has arisen because of a government miscalculation over incinerator capacity and continual disagreements with the operators. The UK simply does not have enough incinerators to deal with the sheer number of animals, slaughtered under the thirty-month rule. Apart from that, the furnaces are privately owned (as are the storage barns!) and the owners have pushed the price of their services ever upwards. This had led to embarrassing questions being asked about the sky-high cost of the whole sorry exercise. The bill for storage in Scotland alone is currently £1.3 million a year and the estimated cost of destruction is put at over £7 million.

Although the government has an agreement with the European Union that they will burn all this material, it recently investigated the possibility of using landfill sites to get rid of it. In Scotland, an SNP member of the new Scottish Parliament (Bruce Crawford, MSP for Mid Scotland and Fife) got wind of such a venture in his own constituency and asked awkward questions about it in open parliament. The relevant minister (Ross Finnie, Rural Affairs) was forced to give an assurance that landfill would not be used.

For the moment we appear to be stuck with the stuff and dependent on the security of the storage facilities. There are strict licensing regulations governing them but contractors are allowed to operate for one year before requiring such a licence. The most optimistic prediction suggests that a reduction of 60 per cent of this material might be achieved by the year 2002.